Bones of a Feather

ALSO BY CAROLYN HAINES

Bones of a Feather

CAROLYN HAINES

MINOTAUR BOOKS

NEW YORK

BONES OF A FEATHER. Copyright © 2011 by Carolyn Haines. All rights reserved. Printed in the United States of America. For information, address St. Martin's Press, 175 Fifth Avenue, New York, N.Y. 10010.

www.minotaurbooks.com

Library of Congress Cataloging-in-Publication Data

Haines, Carolyn.
    Bones of a feather : a Sarah Booth Delaney mystery / Carolyn Haines.—1st ed.
        p. cm.
    ISBN 978-0-312-59502-9
    1. Delaney, Sarah Booth (Fictitious character)—Fiction.   2. Women private investigators—Mississippi—Fiction.   3. Heiresses—Mississippi—Fiction.   4. Kidnapping—Fiction.   5. Mississippi—Fiction.   I. Title.
    PS3558.A329B655   2011
    813'.54—dc22

                                                            2011005105

First Edition: June 2011

10   9   8   7   6   5   4   3   2   1

For Priya Bhakta—a friend beyond compare,
who also happens to be smart, talented, and creative

Acknowledgments

A book is a long labor of inspiration and then just plain hard work. The St. Martin's team—Kelley Ragland, Matt Martz, Sarah Melnyk, Hiro Kimura, and the dozens of sales reps, marketers, and forces that I don't even know about that go into putting a book into the hands of the readers—has been wonderful to work with.

I also want to acknowledge the booksellers who recommend my books. The publishing world is changing, and I've never been fond of radical change in any form. But I have unshakable faith that there will always be those of us who write stories, those who sell stories, and those who can't imagine life without reading. We are bonded in a business that requires long, long hours but so much joy. So while I thank the bookstores that put my books on the shelf, I also thank the readers.

In the past year, the folks who love my characters have talked about my books and brought new readers to the Bones series. I owe these friends a lot, and I will do my best each time I sit down to write to "build" a story that fulfills my end of this bargain.

A year's worth of thanks go to Marian Young. We've been together a long time, and I couldn't have had a better agent along this road.

I've put together a real team of talented people, including Priya, who are helping me with new ideas and ventures. Rebecca Crowley at RTC Publicity, Stephanie Ryan, graphic designer, Jennifer Williamson, business brain, and Sarah Bewley, the czar of terrific workshops/fun events—I thank them all.

Suzann Ledbetter Ellingsworth provided the valuable service of reading this book. Few books are created without the input of friends and professionals. In my case, I'm lucky to have both helping me to make my story as good as it can be.

The fun continues with the next installment of Sarah Booth and her friends, which I'm busy writing now. Thank you all.

Bones of a Feather

1

Graf Milieu, my fiancé, stands in the sunlight filtering through the sheers of the bedroom window. His dark hair hangs over one eye as he drinks a cup of coffee and watches over me.

"I love you, Sarah Booth Delaney," he says, and he means every word.

"Come here." I reach for him, light winking on the diamond of my engagement ring. My hands know the contours of his body, the curve of bicep and length of thigh. Male perfection. The bed is empty without him.

"Sleep, Sarah Booth."

"No, wait," I tell him. "Don't go. Come back to bed."

"Sleep," he orders. He smiles and fades as the dream recedes and I open my eyes to a sunny morning. Graf is gone, and I'm home in the middle of the Mississippi Delta at the height of summer. Even so early in the morning, the day is already hot.

I roll out of bed and pad barefoot down the stairs toward the kitchen and coffee. The dream has left me empty and dissatisfied.

Wandering the rooms of Dahlia House, I have an inkling of what it must be like to be Jitty. This old house, my family dwelling, the repository of my roots and history, is empty without the warm energy of my significant other, Graf Milieu. That handsome hunk of man drove away at the crack of dawn this morning, headed to the Memphis airport and a flight to Hollywood. He's taken the lead in a new thriller set in Louisiana. The good news is, once the location work starts, he'll be one state away. Close enough for some "us" time.

For now, though, I'm alone in Zinnia, Mississippi, land of my birth and place where my ancestors rest. Some easy, some not. A long list of repairs on my rambling home awaits my attention. For too long, Dahlia House has been neglected.

"Follow the yellow brick road!"

The voice comes from all around me. Jitty, the resident haint of Dahlia House, has arrived to badger me. I don't have to be psychic to know she's going to tell me I should have gone to Hollywood with Graf. I should have "stood by my man," even though I would only distract him from his work. Jitty, who dates back to pre–War Between the States times, has been singing this particular song since I returned home two years ago—unwed and unbred, as she loves to point out.

"Follow the yellow brick road," she says again.

"If you show up as a Munchkin, I'm going to kick you back to Oz," I warn Jitty.

I've miscalculated her most recent incarnation. Instead of striped socks and holding a lollipop, she appears in a puff of vile orange smoke. A black taffeta dress swirls around her slender body. When she stops spinning, I realize her lovely mocha skin is now a shade of pea green and a wart mars her nose.

"Click your heels together three times, pick up that fancy cell phone, and charge yourself a plane ticket to your man," Jitty orders.

"I'm already home." While I love Graf, I don't want to abandon Dahlia House or Mississippi. The last few weeks—spending time in my childhood home with Graf, riding horses, making love, making breakfast, laughing with my business partner, Tinkie Bellcase Richmond, and our friends and helpers in crime solving, Cece and Millie—have shown me that the pull of acting isn't stronger than these things. I want to act. I want to be with Graf in Hollywood. But I also want to be here, in Zinnia, with my horses, my hound, my friends, and my private investigating.

"Dorothy didn't necessarily want to go to The Emerald City," Jitty says darkly. "It was her destiny."

"It was a dream," I remind her.

"Perhaps. Perhaps not." Jitty can aggravate the hairs off a mole.

I surveyed her with a moue of distaste. "Why the Wicked Witch of the West? I figured you're more of a bubble kind of witch. Pink frothy gown, crystal wand—a better outfit to show off that twenty-four-inch waist."

"Elphaba suits my message."

"Message? You have a communication for me?" Jitty's job was to devil me and highlight the error of my ways, but for one brief second I thought perhaps my departed mother had something to tell me. "From whom?"

"Benjamin Disraeli, actually." Jitty was smug.

"You have got to be kidding. A nineteenth-century prime minister of England has a message for me?" Things were obviously getting out of hand in the Great Beyond.

"'Sweet is the voice of a sister in the season of sorrow,'" Jitty's tone resonated, but her image began to fade before she finished.

"Hey, you can't leave like that." I hated it when she tossed out a pearl and made me feel like a trampling swine because I didn't understand it. "Jitty! Jitty!" But she was gone.

Before I could try to track her down, the phone rang.

"Delaney Detective Agency," I answered, despite the fact it was up in the air if we were still in business after Tinkie's latest brush with death. Both her husband, Oscar, and Graf wanted us to shut down the agency. The men felt we put ourselves in the line of danger too often, a point that statistically couldn't be argued.

"Ms. Sarah Booth Delaney?" a cultured woman asked. "This is Monica Levert, of Briarcliff in Natchez. I'd like to hire you."

Instinctively I glanced around to make sure Graf wasn't listening in. He'd have a hissy fit if he thought I was taking a case not three hours after he had driven away. Such is life.

"What type of case?" I asked.

"My sister, Eleanor, and I inherited a necklace. A very valuable necklace. For the past several weeks someone has tried to break into our home. Three nights ago, they succeeded. The necklace was stolen. Now the insurance company is stalling about paying the value of our policy."

An insurance claim! No dead bodies. No murders. No guns. A simple insurance claim. "What's the value of the necklace?"

"It's been passed down in the Levert family for five generations. The jewels themselves are valuable, but it's the reputation of the jeweler that makes it even more so. We're afraid a thief won't realize that and will destroy the necklace to sell the rubies individually."

"The value is . . . ?"

"Four million dollars."

I'd grown up in a society where valuable jewels were commonplace. The belles of the Delta, women of exceptional beauty and charm, felt good jewelry was a birthright. But a necklace with this appraisal was extraordinary. No wonder the insurance company was balking.

"The police have verified the theft?"

"They have, but Langley Insurance is still stonewalling. My sister and I thought bringing in reputable private investigators to reevaluate the evidence might speed things up."

"I doubt that." I had to be honest.

"Would you at least speak with Mr. Nesbitt at the insurance company? He's aware of your reputation for honesty."

Nice to hear, but in the instance of a $4 million claim, I doubted the reputation of Delaney Detective Agency would matter a whit. But what did I have to lose? "Sure, if my partner agrees."

"Eleanor and I will await your phone call," Monica said.

It took less than a minute to clear the case with Tinkie,

who not only agreed to take the Leverts' job offer but jumped in her Cadillac to head for Dahlia House. She loved Oscar, but their constant togetherness in the last weeks was driving her a little nuts.

We'd both gotten used to calling our own shots, a simpler situation for me. Tinkie had been reared in the fine tradition of a Daddy's Girl, a woman who accomplishes much through charm and the guise of acquiescence. Tinkie was about as pliable as a titanium rod, but she knew how to appear malleable. It just required a lot of effort to do so.

She roared down my drive like a bat out of hell and bounded out of her car on the heels of Chablis, her dust-mop Yorkie terrier with the heart of a lion. Sweetie Pie, my noble red tic hound, greeted them with a tenor serenade. Ah, Placido, should you ever need a hound onstage, Sweetie's voice could make an audience weep!

"Have you called the Levert sisters back?" Tinkie asked, rushing up the steps.

I held out a hand to steady her. She wore three-inch stilettos and I feared she'd topple backward and break her neck. Her sundress put me in mind of the 1960s, complete with the cutest straw sun hat. Tinkie had excellent taste and the budget to indulge it.

"I thought I'd let you do the honors." I led her toward our office on the first floor of Dahlia House in what was formerly a parlor. Our décor was taupe filing cabinets and cheap furniture. Tinkie had insisted on, and paid for, the frosted-glass door that said Delaney Detective Agency. Classic noir. The *only* classy thing about our digs.

I gave her Monica's number and she put the phone on speaker and dialed.

Monica answered on the second ring.

"We're interested in the case," Tinkie said. "Our fee is two grand up front and a grand a day, plus any unexpected expenses."

"Can you start today?" Monica asked.

"You realize we'll investigate and write the report of whatever we find." Tinkie wanted to be clear no one was buying results.

"We wouldn't dream of anything else," Monica said. "Eleanor and I are distraught over the theft. Yes, the necklace has a monetary value, but it's part of our history. I'm sure you ladies can understand what that means."

She was stroking my weak spot. "Heritage," "tradition"—two words I understood down to the bone.

"Where would you like to meet?" Tinkie asked.

"The Excelsior Tea Room. At noon?"

"We'll be there," Tinkie agreed before she punched the disconnect button.

She sat on the edge of the desk. "A new case, Sarah Booth! Isn't it exciting?"

Oh, exciting wouldn't cover it when she told Oscar and I told Graf. Unless, of course, we could make the two-hour drive to Natchez, examine the evidence, come home, and write the report without anyone being the wiser. As my aunt Loulane would say, were she alive to say it, "Discretion is the better part of valor."

If we kept our mouths shut about the case, we'd spare Oscar and Graf needless worry. It could even be interpreted as an act of love.

Out of the corner of my eye I saw a blur of black and heard the soft rustle of taffeta. A breeze kicked up outside and I could have sworn I heard, "Beware, my pretty."

"Did you hear that?" I asked Tinkie.

She shook her head. "Let's hit the road. Maybe we can get back before dark."

Great minds think alike. I called in the dogs, grabbed my purse, and settled into the passenger seat of her new Caddy.

On the drive to Natchez, I'd used Tinkie's cute new laptop computer, complete with wireless Internet, to do some research on the Levert family. Monica and Eleanor were heiresses of an estate valued at close to $10 million, not counting the necklace and other jewels. While the assets were impressive, Briarcliff, their home, was expensive to maintain. And the Levert sisters were used to globe-trotting and the luxuries of life.

They lived in Natchez part of the year and also spent time in Monaco, Vienna, Tuscany, and Rio during the carnival season. It was just the two of them, with nothing to tie them down.

Tinkie crested a steep hill and pulled into a parking space on a brick-lined street. The Excelsior Tea Room was on the second floor of a downtown Natchez building that gave a view of the Mississippi River. Tinkie and I entered and scanned the room.

"Is that them?" Tinkie whispered, pinching the fat on my upper arm.

"Stop it!" I snatched my arm away, but my gaze never left the two women seated in a corner of the tearoom. Both had shoulder-length black hair layered in a casually elegant style called a gypsy shag in the 1970s. The cut didn't look dated in the least. Nor did the women, who had to be close to fifty but looked younger. One wore red, the other black. Mirror images. Identical twins.

They rose, waving us to their table. Introductions were made as we settled into our chairs. Monica was the dominant. She did most of the talking.

"It just makes me crazy that we tried to get the police to help us, but they wouldn't do a thing," Monica said. Her chocolate eyes were hot with indignation. "We reported the intruder the first two nights. Officers drove out, looked around, then said we should get a dog or one of those expensive alarm systems. I couldn't make them understand that a historic house has certain restrictions. I mean, we've ordered new windows, but it will take weeks. They have to be handmade to fit. It isn't just like calling out Sears for an installation."

"Start at the beginning," Tinkie requested.

"Do you know anything about our family history?" Monica asked.

"No." We'd agreed to let them tell it. It's always interesting to learn what a client reveals or hides.

"The family dynasty started with Barthelme Levert," Monica said.

Eleanor leaned forward and spoke quietly. "He was a blackguard and a scoundrel. Natchez society has never forgiven us for Barthelme's brutal ways."

"Posh." Monica waved her sister to silence. "They've never forgiven us for hanging on to our fortune during the Civil War, the Depression, and this latest economic downturn. Jealousy is a cruel prod, Sister. And it's only jealousy that makes the peahens so catty."

"Tell us about the necklace," Tinkie said.

"I can do better than that." Monica reached into her designer handbag and brought out a photograph. The rubies sparkled blood red against a gold satin background. Even I gasped, and Tinkie's finger traced the delicate craftsmanship of the exquisite necklace. The design made the rubies appear to capture the light and shoot it back in a million blades of red. I couldn't help but notice the ruby ring on Monica's hand as she extended the photo—another piece of exceptional craftsmanship.

"Wow," Tinkie said. "That's some necklace."

"Barthelme was a scoundrel, but he knew jewels and good work. The necklace was created by Rodney Implace, one of—"

"The finest jewelers in the mid to late eighteen hundreds," Tinkie finished. "His creations were sought after by the monarchs of Europe as well as the Rockefellers, Carnegies, Vanderbilts, and others. That ring is his, too."

"Exactly." Monica's smile revealed perfect teeth. I checked Eleanor's dental work. Also perfection. In fact, I couldn't see a flaw in complexion, figure, or hair, which was one of the top requirements for a Daddy's Girl— bad hair might be a dominant gene and wealthy men didn't favor offspring with frizz or limpness.

"So what happened the night the necklace was stolen?" I asked.

Monica picked up the story. "As I told you, for the previous two nights, Sister and I had seen someone on the grounds of Briarcliff."

"Can you describe the person?" I asked.

"Only generically. He was tall, broad-shouldered, wore dark clothing, and moved with extreme grace." The sisters shared a look. "We have a live-in gardener, Jerome Lolly. Though he was watching out for the intruder, he never saw a thing. The thief was like a phantom. I could only catch a glimpse here, a flit of movement there."

"Footprints?" I asked.

"The lawn is thick around the house. There was no

trace to support our complaint. That's one reason the police never took us seriously."

"And Jerome Lolly saw nothing," Tinkie said.

"Not a thing." Eleanor's tone softened. "But he believed us. He's worked at Briarcliff for more than three decades and has run off a lot of curiosity seekers and treasure hunters. Briarcliff is a . . . part of the local lore."

"We don't live there year round," Monica said. "When we're absent, the mice come out to play."

They were very feline women—elegant, graceful, and nobody's fools. "Has anything ever been stolen before?" I asked.

"Statuary from the gardens, furnishings in the gazebo or porches, tack from the old stables. Nothing of real value. I think the young people have scavenger hunts that require a tiny bit of Briarcliff."

Tinkie put us back on track. "So you saw an intruder two nights before the necklace was stolen."

"Exactly." Monica squared her shoulders. "The third evening, Sister and I took something to help us relax. We were exhausted from the past two sleepless nights. I guess we finally accepted the police's opinion, that the intruder was either a prankster or a figment of our overactive imaginations."

"You both saw him?" I wasn't clear on this point.

"Only me," Monica said. "By the time I roused Sister, he was gone."

"And the night the necklace was stolen," Tinkie said, "did you see or hear anything?"

"No. I'd taken the sleeping pill. I didn't wake up. And neither did Eleanor."

"How did the thief enter your home?" I asked.

"The front-parlor window. The latch was old." Monica

bit her lip. "Briarcliff needs a complete overhaul. New windows are being built, as I mentioned. The police don't understand that these things take time."

I understood. Dahlia House needed work, too, but I wasn't loaded like the Levert gals. Old homes are a money pit, and some updates, unless carefully orchestrated, can destroy the historic integrity.

"The latch was already broken?" Tinkie pressed.

"Not exactly broken, but antique," Monica said. "It didn't take much to pressure it off."

"How would a thief know to go to that particular window?" I asked.

"These are the same questions Mr. Nesbitt at Langley Insurance asked," Monica said. "I suppose it might be one of the first windows an intruder would try. It's on the front of the house, and our bedrooms are in the back wing. And it's a walk-through window. The house was designed to capture the breezes off the river."

Most antebellum homes were built with a thought for cooling. Prior to air-conditioning houses made the most of wind and shade, to combat Mississippi's oppressive summer heat.

"Were any of the other windows even tried?" Tinkie asked.

Monica's brow furrowed, but it was Eleanor who answered. "How would we be able to tell? Chief Randall dusted, but there were no prints other than ours or Kissie's, our housekeeper. The police deduced the thief wore gloves."

"And the necklace was kept in a safe?" I asked.

"Normally, that would be the case. Old Barthelme installed an indestructible vault in the basement. It survived the Yankees and god knows how many attempts by robbers. Barthelme knew the tactics of highwaymen and pirates, and he built a safe no one could crack." Monica rolled her eyes. "He was thorough in keeping out his brethren."

I'd found a few references to Barthelme's illegal activities on the Internet. He was something of a bluebeard. His first five wives died after a few years of marriage, and none bore offspring. I was curious to hear what the Levert sisters would admit.

"Was Barthelme really a highwayman?"

"And worse," Monica said. Eleanor's disapproving look was ignored. "If he weren't our family, you know it would be delicious," she told Eleanor. "And it's such past history. What's the harm? A lot of people back then did what they had to do to survive and build a fortune. Do you think the railroad magnates were any less ruthless? Just ask the American Indians if you do."

"So he robbed people on the Natchez Trace?" Tinkie asked.

"Robbed, tortured, and murdered. I suppose old Barthelme might be termed a serial killer today. He had a very clever scheme. He'd ferry folks up and down the Mississippi River on his boat, the *Lillith*. His crewmen searched their bags for anything of value, then Barthelme would stage a robbery either along the Natchez Trace or in New Orleans, depending on whether passengers were heading north or south."

"He acquired a great deal of wealth," Eleanor said.

"And he stole slaves upriver and took them down to work the cane plantations in Louisiana," Monica threw in. "Made a very handsome profit, too. If he'd been caught, he'd surely have been lynched. He tricked the slaves into believing he was taking them to freedom. They'd run away and board the *Lillith*. Barthelme sold them in New Orleans. Pure profit."

Tinkie's face registered distaste, and I figured mine was about the same.

"He was awful." Eleanor put a hand over her eyes. "It shames me to know Briarcliff was built on blood money. Monica finds it much more entertaining than I do."

Monica didn't try to hide her amusement. "Eleanor is so straitlaced and proper. She'd like to pretend the Levert money came from something benevolent, but the truth is, great fortunes are always built on the bones of someone. Great-great-great-grandpapa Levert killed other well-off people and sold runaway slaves. It could be worse. No child pornography or prostitutes or toxic chemical production or even weapons, for that matter. He simply executed the wealthy and took what they had."

"Please, Monica." Eleanor held up her hand. "Enough. It's a fact, but I don't enjoy having my nose rubbed in it."

Monica's laughter was musical and feminine, yet I heard a note of cruelty dancing beneath it. She enjoyed tormenting her sister.

"I haven't even told them about the other ruby necklaces and the five dead wives." Monica raised her eyebrows. "Some say Barthelme quickly tired of his young brides and poisoned them. Each dead wife is buried with an exact replica of the stolen necklace."

"Get out!" Tinkie leaned back in her chair. "A necklace like that in a grave? How awful."

"That's twenty million dollars." Even I could do the math. "Locked away in coffins."

"What would you have me do, dig them up?" Monica was enjoying this way too much.

"When we were in Italy last winter, someone tried."

Eleanor paled at the memory. "It was awful. We came home unexpectedly late on a February evening. It was storming—"

Monica cut in, "And we arrived to find mounds of dirt in the family cemetery where someone had been digging. Jerome ran them off before they could remove the cement slabs, but it—"

"Was completely disgusting," Eleanor finished.

"The jewels were safe?" I asked.

Eleanor shrugged. "As far as we know. Monica wanted to look, but I wouldn't budge. The Leverts have been called everything else, but I refuse to give Natchez ammunition to call us grave robbers." Eleanor's spine was straight, and her lips a compressed line.

"Sis stood firm on that issue," Monica said, acting bored. "We could have done a two-year world tour with the money."

"We have the necklace we inherited from our mother. That's all we're entitled to, and all I want." Eleanor was visibly upset.

Monica stifled a yawn. "So now you know the family dirty laundry. Are you ready to start your investigation? The sooner you finish, the quicker we'll get our insurance check."

2

We followed the Levert sisters down the streets of Natchez, a small but bustling town that had once played a vital role in the history of the Old South. During the War Between the States, the two river towns of Vicksburg and Natchez offered control of the Mississippi River, a waterway vital to the survival of the Confederacy. Thousands of lives, both Union and Confederate, were lost in battles to take the mighty Mississippi.

Prior to the war, more millionaires lived in Natchez than any other Southern town, save New Orleans.

We left the business district and drove through a residential area, where the homes of the affluent graced huge lots. Victorian houses with gingerbread trim were tucked back on gracious lawns landscaped with huge camellias and azaleas. Time had not forgotten Natchez, but it had kissed it gently. The grace and charm of a lost era hung just out of reach.

The road curved and wound up a high bluff. At the crest was Briarcliff, a dark and brooding stone triple-decker with a widow's walk. Barthelme Levert had made his fortune on the water, so it stood to reason his home would have the architectural trappings of a sea-man's abode, yet something about Briarcliff made me think of the moors and a tragic lord.

The cliff was a sheer drop down to Natchez and the Mississippi River. Even on a hot summer day, a breeze off the river was brisk enough to cool my sweaty face as I climbed out of Tinkie's Caddy.

"Briarcliff is something else," Tinkie said. "I wonder if the ghost-hunting teams for those televisions shows have been told about it. A village of lost spirits could be here."

I agreed. A haint might comfortably take up residence. For Jitty, it would be a move to upscale digs. The thought made me smile.

The sisters pulled under a portico on the side of the house. I pictured Monica as the hunter of the pride. El-eanor . . . I wasn't sure about her. My aunt Loulane, who raised me after my parents' untimely deaths in an auto accident, might say "still waters run deep." How deep was Eleanor?

"Come in," she said. "I realize we never had tea. Let me put on a kettle."

We entered the house via a mudroom that fed into a spacious kitchen. Natural-wood cabinets gleamed from oil and care. It reminded me how I'd neglected the main-tenance at Dahlia House. How had Jitty failed to nag me about it?

"Oolong?" Eleanor asked as she turned on the gas stove.

"Perfect," Tinkie said, using her spike heel to bring me back to the present.

"Perfect," I agreed, trying not to wince from Tinkie's assault on my foot. "Where's the window the burglar used?"

"I'll show you while Eleanor makes tea." Monica led the way through a well-appointed dining room and a hallway filled with portraits of women, all beautiful, young, and smiling. "Barthelme's wives," Monica said, waving a hand dismissively. "All too delicate or too dumb, depending on which story you want to believe."

"They all died before they had children," Tinkie said carefully.

"Folks thought Barthelme was cursed," Monica said. "Some said he was sterile and blamed his wives."

"And that he murdered them?" I said. That had been broadly hinted on Internet Web sites.

"Then he met Terrant Cassio, the daughter of a Boston banker. She was his sixth and last wife. Terrant bore twin daughters within the first year of their marriage." Monica's smile was smug. "Twins run in the family."

"But the Levert name? How do you have it if the only heirs were girls?"

"In each generation, the heir of Briarcliff takes the Levert name. It's tradition."

"What happened to Terrant's children?" Tinkie asked.

"Barthelme died not long after the babies were born. He fell from the cliff, delirious with a fever." Monica pushed open the door to a parlor. She stopped in her tracks. Gauzy drapes covering the windows danced and capered on the breeze as if possessed.

Goose bumps marched along my arms, and Tinkie's eyes were huge.

Monica froze for only a few seconds. She rushed forward and slammed the windows shut. "This has to end. I closed that damn window and locked it yesterday," she said. "File your report as soon as possible. Once the insurance pays out, Eleanor and I are leaving. We'll go to Geneva or maybe Dublin. We don't have to stay here and let someone terrorize us."

"Call the police," I said. "At least now you have Tinkie and me to alibi your whereabouts and to verify your story." Though I realized she could have left the window open before she met us in town.

"And what a shame such is required," Monica said. "This is our home, the place where we grew up. Yet no one believes us. I'm sick of it." She pivoted on her heel and left the room, her footsteps echoing on the beautiful hardwood floors. In a moment I heard her say, "There's been another break-in at Briarcliff. Yes, thank you."

When she returned, she was calmer. "A squad car is on the way."

I examined the window lock, careful not to touch anything. The burglar hadn't left prints before, so it was unlikely he'd return and be sloppy. Still, I didn't want to contaminate potential evidence.

The lock was old and loose in the wood. Someone jostling the window could wiggle it enough to dislodge the latch. "When will the replacement windows arrive?"

"I'll ask Jerome," Monica said. "He handles the repairs."

Eleanor approached from the rear of the house. "Tea is read—" She broke off, staring at the window and then at us, reading the distress on her sister's face. "He came back, didn't he? He knew we were gone and came in broad daylight." A hand covered her mouth and her complexion paled. "He stole the most valuable thing we had, so what does he want now?"

That was a question neither Tinkie nor I had an answer for.

Whatever the Leverts' standing in the community, their call brought Natchez Police Chief Albert "Gunny" Randall. The nickname said it all. An ex-marine, he deployed crime-scene investigators to dust and collect evidence, but his attitude told me he knew it would all be for nothing.

At my request, Tinkie ushered the Levert sisters to the kitchen so I could have a moment alone with Gunny, the name he insisted I use.

"The Leverts have hired me and my partner to write a report for the insurance company," I told him.

He wasn't surprised. "Four million is some kind of windfall. The sisters are doing what they can to make sure the insurance company pays out."

I couldn't deny it and didn't want to. "Was there any evidence to counter the Leverts' claim?"

"Nope, but there was nothing to back up the claim, either. Not a footprint or fingerprint or pry mark on the window. Nothing else was tampered with in the house. The burglar—if there was one—went straight to the necklace."

I ignored the implication. "How did he, or she, open the safe?"

He cleared his throat. "The necklace wasn't in the safe."

"What?" The word was out before I could stop it. I

remembered Monica's earlier statement that the necklace would normally be in the vault. I hadn't followed up.

"Now you understand my skepticism," he said. "The sisters had the necklace out. For a new appraisal. Yes, I checked with Davidas's Jewelry. The necklace was due in the store the next morning for the appraisal."

"So the sisters weren't lying."

"No, but that's easy enough to set up, isn't it? Why didn't they leave the necklace in a secure vault until time to transport it? Why leave it on top of a secretary? I'm having a hard time with this, and so is Mr. Nesbitt at the insurance company. The necklace should have been secured."

"What's the point of owning something so valuable if you can't wear it and enjoy it?" I countered. I wasn't defending the sisters, but I also wasn't ready to believe they'd staged a robbery. They seemed to have plenty of ready cash. "If it were a Lamborghini parked on the street and it was stolen, you wouldn't assume they'd planned it."

He frowned. "True enough."

I couldn't believe it. Chief Gunny Randall saw my point. "What about the previous break-ins?"

"Same story. The sisters called, we came out. They say they're replacing the windows, but until they do, a middle-school kid could get into the house. Last year, someone dug around in the family cemetery. Nothing was taken. I thought, and still think, it was kids. Nothing like a spooky legend to kick up mischief."

"What about the gardener, Jerome Lolly?"

"He has a small cottage at the back of the property. He didn't see or hear anything. Not this time. Not anytime."

"Could he be behind this?" Lolly had easy access and

knowledge of the sisters' habits. He also had intimate knowledge of the layout of the house.

"He's a person of interest."

"And the housekeeper, Kissie something?"

"Kissie McClain. She's interesting. She has a record of B&E and theft. She did a stretch in the Adams County Jail. Six months. For breaking into her ex-boyfriend's place and stealing a guitar. She said it was hers but had no way to prove it. The boyfriend, also with a record, testified the guitar was his. She was convicted."

"The Leverts know about her record?"

He nodded. "They picked her up when she finished her time and gave her a job."

"Drugs?"

"The boyfriend, certainly. Kissie . . . we never saw it, but it's not improbable."

From everything I could see, Gunny was a professional lawman. "What kind of training did you have in the marines, Gunny?"

"The best." His smile told me he enjoyed a verbal one-up as much as anyone else. "My specialty was surveillance."

"I'll bet you were good at it. You'll let me know if your team finds anything here?"

"Okay. Can I get a copy of your report?"

Technically, my report belonged to my employer. "I can't see why the sisters would object. If they agree, I'm happy to make you a copy."

He nodded. "Are you staying in town?"

Tinkie and I had hoped to get back to Zinnia by nightfall, but just in case I'd asked my friend Lee to feed Reveler and Miss Scrapiron, the two horses at Dahlia House, and the dogs. "I'm not sure," I told him.

"The Eola is worth a visit. Lots of history in that old hotel. I should have this report by tomorrow." He gave a cross between a salute and a tip of his hat and returned to supervise his investigators.

If we stayed, we could write up our report on Tinkie's laptop, turn it in tomorrow when we had all of the police data, take our check, and go home. Besides, a night in the river town of Natchez held appeal. An advertisement for a "haunted Natchez" walking tour had sparked my interest. Maybe I could find some ammo to direct at Jitty. Briarcliff had put me in the mood for a good spooking.

The Eola was a grande dame nestled in the heart of Natchez. Tinkie and I took separate rooms, bought toiletries we'd failed to bring for the night, and Tinkie went on a shopping spree for new clothes. I managed with a new T-shirt that said, "I Got Down and Dirty Under-the-Hill," a reference to Natchez's riverfront district. Tinkie said it made her think of trolls.

We met in the lobby for the haunted tour. Along with a totally impractical but gorgeous cocktail dress, Tinkie purchased walking shoes, khakis, a sweater, and a jacket. Evenings along the river could be brisk, even in summer.

We fortified ourselves with a few adult beverages in the Eola bar before we met up with the tour group, an eclectic mix of tourists, locals, semiprofessional ghost hunters, and high school kids who knew the spiel by heart but enjoyed it nonetheless. Our merry company toured the town, stopping to see orbs flit by haunted houses and hear tales of gore and murder that generally accompany a haunting.

At King's Tavern, a local eatery, we had drinks and I

felt the warm spot on the upstairs bed where the ghost Madeline slept. Tinkie accused me of fibbing, but an area on the bed where a body might lie was warm to my hand.

The last stop was the bluff beneath Briarcliff, an unexpected bonus. Our tour guide gave a brief history of Barthelme Levert and his five tragic marriages. "Each bride was buried with a valuable ruby necklace. Some say it was Barthelme's attempt to assuage the guilt of murder. Wife number six survived the old pirate. She knew the art of poison and drove Barthelme mad with a potion that sent him running and screaming out of the house and over the edge of this very cliff!"

The tour concluded, and everyone began to talk and laugh as we retraced our steps to the Eola. I turned back for one last glimpse of the loess bluffs created by a long-ago earthquake that dictated the route of the Mississippi River. A large object encased in fluttering, diaphanous material sailed off the top of the cliff. I watched in soundless horror as the human-sized entity fell more than one hundred feet to smack into the water with a splash that drew everyone's attention.

"What was that?" the guide asked.

Several people laughed shakily. I clutched Tinkie's hand. "It looked like a body," I whispered.

Tinkie pushed my shoulder. "It's part of the show, Sarah Booth. We got our money's worth on this tour."

Her comment drew agreement from the others. Even the guide chuckled.

As we meandered back to the Eola, Tinkie chatted with an older couple from St. Francisville, Louisiana. I couldn't shake the sense of tragedy that flooded me at the sight of the lace-clad missile dropping into the swift current of the Mississippi River. There had been no scream, nothing to indicate the object was alive. Still, I couldn't let it go. The menacing gloom that hung over Briarcliff had slithered into my bones.

A. J. and Carlie Wells, the older couple from down river, were also staying at the Eola, so we pushed through the revolving door one after the other, Tinkie's bright laughter leading the way. I loved her laugh, and I determined to shake off my glum mood.

Tinkie suggested a drink at the bar, so we followed her, until she stopped abruptly in the doorway. Like a line of ducks, we tumbled into one another. "What the—" And then I saw what had brought my partner to a dead halt— *El Hombre Siniestro.*

He wore a tuxedo and sat, one foot cocked on the bar rail in a *GQ* pose. His dark hair was pulled in a queue at the nape of his neck and an ill-tempered scowl claimed his face. He glowered as if we'd intruded on his most private moment.

Ignoring him, we settled at a table in the corner. We had a round of drinks and chatted pleasantly for half an hour.

"I think we'll head upstairs," A. J. said. "It's been a long day." He and Carlie slipped out of the bar, leaving me and Tinkie with the Thunder God. The tuxedoed man tapped the bar with his thumb as he scowled.

"Who the heck is he?" Tinkie whispered.

"An ass." I liked brooding well enough, but I didn't like it forced down my throat. When the waitress came to take our order, I buttonholed her. "Who is that guy?"

"He just arrived. From out of town."

"Transylvania?" I asked. My wit was lost on her.

"No, I think New Orleans. His name is Don Cipriano. He's the most handsome man I've ever seen." She sashayed past him, her hips swaying just a little more than normal.

Cipriano had the bad-boy appeal down to a science. I didn't need Madame Tomeeka, Zinnia's talented psychic, to tell me he was arrogant, overbearing, boorish, tormented, and aware of the figure he cut. In my younger days, he would have been like mainlining heroin. Now, though, I had Graf and a better understanding of the joys of a real relationship.

"We'd better check the harbor and see if he came with a coffin filled with dirt," I murmured to Tinkie.

"He's dangerous, all right." Tinkie, too, had a weakness for handsome men, though her marriage to Oscar was solid.

"As Aunt Loulane would say, 'Look, look, but looking and getting are two different things.' We can look all we want as long as we don't touch."

"Righto," she agreed. "But he is a perfect . . . specimen."

How correct she was. Broad shoulders, balanced features, big feet clad in polished boots. The tuxedo looked custom-tailored.

With a mere tip of his head, he acknowledged us and stood. To my surprise, he approached our table. "Ladies, may I buy you a drink?"

"We've ordered." My protective shields were on full alert. This man was a force to be reckoned with, and he knew it.

"May I join you?"

"Please do." Tinkie indicated a chair. "What brings you to Natchez, Mr. Cipriano?"

"So, you know my name. I haven't had the pleasure."

Tinkie made the introductions. "Natchez is a small

town. I'm sure eighty percent of the population knows who you are."

"Should I be flattered or concerned?"

"Depends on your intentions." Tinkie was so much better at banter than I was. While I might be a better horsewoman, she had mastered the opposite-gender verbal-parry.

"I have no intentions." Don Cipriano signaled the waitress for another drink. There was something decidedly Old World in his manners. Old world and old money. I'd had my brush with both in the body of Hamilton Garrett V, a man I'd ultimately done wrong. Maybe it was a guilty conscience that made me try harder with Cipriano.

"So you're vacationing in Natchez?" I asked.

"A smart man combines business and pleasure whenever possible." His dark gaze drilled into me.

"I grasp the pleasures of a visit to Natchez. I'm just curious about your business." My deflector shields were taking a beating, but I could still fire back.

"I'm a collector."

"Don't tell me. Rare books?"

His laughter was rich, espresso-strength. "Hardly. So you're a reader?"

His amusement didn't totally mask the darkness that flitted in the depths of his eyes. "When I have time," I said. "So what do you collect? Butterflies? Art?"

"Nothing so exotic. Antiques. I have a store in New Orleans." He patted his chest. "I normally carry a card, but the tuxedo . . ."

"We love New Orleans." Tinkie interjected a lighter tone into the conversation. "Sarah Booth and I had a case—"

"A case?" He took the drink from the waitress's tray before she could put it down. "Are you doctors?"

"Private investigators," Tinkie said.

"Is that why you're in Natchez?" If his interest was feigned, he was a good actor.

"Yes."

"Cheating husband? Missing wife? Murder?" he asked, and I thought I heard excitement in his tone.

"Nothing so deadly." Tinkie ate the last olive in her martini. "Just an insurance case. And we have much to do tomorrow, Sarah Booth. We should get some rest."

She was right. Tomorrow would be busy. We stood together. "Have a nice evening," I said.

"Ladies." He executed a courtly little bow. "I hope our paths cross again."

3

Tinkie retired to her room—and a long phone chat with Oscar. She was good at smoothing things over with her husband. I didn't have that particular talent, so I decided against calling Graf. In all likelihood, he was still jammed in traffic on the road to the apartment he'd rented in Los Angeles. By a stroke of good fortune, he'd found a chic place within a reasonable drive from the studio. Due on the set early in the morning, he'd probably hit the hay as soon as he arrived home.

Behind me, the soft rustle of fabric was followed by a distinctive British accent. "M' lady, perhaps if you birthed a male heir, you could rest easy as Queen. As Loulane would say, 'The proof is in the pudding.' And no ruler can resist Delaney pudding."

"Jitty!" I whirled to find her bedecked, begowned, and bejeweled. She was stunning, even if the cut of the dress imprisoned her usually bodacious breasts. A scarf wound cunningly around her neck was anachronistic. "First the Wicked Witch of the West with a message from Disraeli. Now—"

"My king threw me over because I didn't conceive a son. Don't let that be your fate." Her elegant hands chopped the air and she made a gruesome noise.

I wasn't in the mood to banter historical trivia with Jitty, but it was pointless to argue. "So now you're Anne of the Thousand Days. One of two Boleyn sisters given to King Henry in an effort to woo control of his power through sex."

"Anne lost her head." Jitty touched the scarf at her throat.

"And Mary lost her chance at true love." Both sisters were tragic, in my book. Bred and bartered for the purpose of gaining money and power.

"And all because they failed to do the bed boogie and get themselves with a male heir to the throne." Jitty's pretentious British accent was fading.

"Doesn't the male sperm determine the child's gender?" I should have paid more attention in family planning class. "At any rate, I don't have to worry about being the king's consort." I couldn't imagine a parent willingly using me as a bargaining chip in a deadly game for a king's fickle favor. People did amazing things for political clout. "So what's shaking in the royal regions of the Great Beyond? Costume party?"

"Guess again," she said.

Jitty seldom left Dahlia House. I'd learned she could travel wherever she chose, but she liked to be close to home, which in her case was the Delaney family cemetery on the grounds of my ancestral home. Jitty was there, along with Aunt Loulane, my parents, and a number of other deceased relatives.

"Dahlia House was boring without me? You had no one to torment?"

"What's the story with the stolen necklace?" Jitty was good at answering a question with a question on a totally different topic.

"Looks like the Levert sisters were careless and someone who knows the layout of the house and their habits broke in and swiped the jewelry." I didn't tell her I was puzzled by the fact that someone broke in again today, in broad daylight—and apparently took nothing.

She glanced around the room. "Nice digs. I can see why you decided on a vacation night."

"We're going home tomorrow." The most recent burglary was not in our purview. We'd do our report, maybe a nice lunch in town, then book it back to Zinnia.

"Good." Jitty strolled across the room. I couldn't help but admire her posture and carriage. Either her dress came with a corset that could make a limp noodle stand tall or Jitty was playing the role of Queen to the hilt. "Graf won't like it when he figures out—"

"Stop!" I put up a hand. "Stop now. Graf doesn't own me nor does he tell me what to do."

"Can you say pigheaded?" Jitty reverted to a Delta drawl. "Girl, you are determined to ruin this, aren't you?"

"I've learned one thing, Jitty. I have to set my boundaries early. If I concede and go along with Graf's whims, that's tantamount to lying."

"Lyin' might be the best mode here. If he ever sees how hardheaded you truly are, he's gone run for the hills."

"Better sooner than later."

"Sarah Booth, haven't you ever heard of a honeymoon period? Even the president of the United States gets cut a little slack when he first goes into office. You need to ease Graf into your personality. Hide the thorns, prickles, and warts until you got that golden band on your finger. Every Delta girl worth her salt knows this."

"My mother wouldn't agree."

Jitty sighed. "Your daddy was a man in a million. James Franklin took pride in your mama's spunk. Most men don't want a woman with a personality like a cactus. He could handle your mama and her ways, but that bond doesn't come along every day."

"I don't deserve less. I think you're selling Graf short."

Jitty peered through the window at the quiet Natchez street. It was a weekday, and with the shops closed, the town had settled into a late-summer snooze. "Consider his fears and concerns, Sarah Booth. That ain't sellin' out your personality, it's showing regard for someone who loves you."

I couldn't argue that. "Okay."

"Then get your butt home tomorrow."

I could see the downtown lights through her. She was fading, but she wasn't pulling one of her famous quick-draw disappearances. She wavered and blinked and finally dissolved on a low, sweet laugh.

"See you at Dahlia House," I said to the empty room.

My sleep was troubled by dreams of a darkly handsome man. He stayed in the shadows, watching me, gliding in and out of a thick fog that weighed down my arms and legs like quicksand. I struggled, and he made no offer to help me.

I awoke sweating and breathing hard to the ringing of the telephone on the nightstand. I answered automatically, still confused by my surroundings and oppressed by the sense of danger and helplessness from the dream.

"Ms. Delaney, it's Eleanor Levert." Her voice was breathy with panic.

The bedside clock showed nearly three a.m. "What's wrong?"

"Monica is missing. Has been for hours. The police won't do anything." She started to cry.

"I'm sure she's fine." The words were rote, merely what someone says in such a situation. "Maybe she had a date." The Levert sisters were extremely handsome women. I had no doubt suitors paid court in droves.

"We don't date anymore," Eleanor said. "We both decided at fifty we'd had enough. We're not man-haters or anything. It's just that we have so many other interests to pursue. And we do everything together."

I'd pegged them for early forties. My, my, money and a life of luxury might not buy youth, but it sure kept the wrinkles and sags away. "When was the last time you saw Monica?"

"She said she was going into the gardens to think," Eleanor said. "That was just as dusk was falling."

"She never came back inside?" That was eight hours ago.

"I went to my room. Monica insisted we pack for Geneva. She decided we had to escape Natchez before we were hurt. I got the suitcases from the attic, put hers in her room, and took mine. I got involved selecting my wardrobe for the trip. She wanted to head for New Orleans as soon as the insurance check came through. From there, we were going to Europe." She fought to control the tremor in her voice but was only partially successful. "What's happened to her? What if she's hurt?"

"When did the police arrive?" I held the phone with one hand and grabbed my jeans with the other.

"I finally called them about midnight. They said she wasn't missing until twenty-four hours had passed."

"They refused to check it out?" Monica wasn't a teenager likely to strike off after a spat with parents or boyfriend.

"They think we're insurance scammers and crooks." Eleanor sounded defeated. "They aren't interested in hunting for my sister."

"I'll wake Tinkie and we'll be there as soon as possible." Monica might be perfectly safe at a hotel or apartment playing the cougar to some buff young man, but Eleanor was worried. Extremely worried.

"Thank you," she said before she hung up, and I thought there was just a tiny amount of relief in her voice.

I pulled on my shoes and a sweater and knocked at Tinkie's door. She appeared, hair tousled and a frown on her face. "Sarah Booth, what in heaven's name are you doing up at this hour?"

"Monica Levert has disappeared from Briarcliff. Eleanor is distraught, and the police won't do anything until tomorrow."

Traces of sleep evaporated. "Let me get dressed." I hunted for her practical shoes while she found the clothes she'd left in a trail on the carpet. Tinkie wasn't a slob by any stretch, but her family, the Bellcases, had always had domestic help. Why hang up clothes when someone else would do it?

To her credit, she was dressed in under two minutes, and we left the Eola and got in her car. As we approached Briarcliff, Tinkie slowed, using the Caddy's high-beams to search the dense bushes. I'd never thought of camellias and azaleas as sinister, but these huge heritage shrubs were twenty feet tall. An army of invading Huns could hide in them.

The car's headlights threw moving shadows that gave me hope and then the creeps. Anyone or anything could be lurking in the towering vegetation.

As we drew closer to the house, I caught a glimpse of it in the light of a gibbous moon that peeked through a scudding cloud cover. The dark gray stones glittered with a silvery cast, a place of half and full shadows. Not a single window held a light.

"This stone heap is scary," Tinkie said, voicing my thoughts.

"Monica is probably somewhere on the grounds, but it's possible she turned an ankle or something." I opted for the most logical and least tragic explanation. I didn't believe Monica would willingly worry her sister. They were very close.

"I hope Eleanor has some high-beam flashlights." Ever the practical one, Tinkie stopped the Caddy in the circular drive by the front door.

A light came on, giving the façade of the house a more inviting look. We crunched along the gravel drive to the front door. Earlier, we'd gone in under the portico, but Eleanor greeted us at the front entrance. She came out on the small entrance alcove, a breeze catching the folds of her robe and sending it billowing behind her like a vision from a 1940s Hitchcock film.

"I've searched the entire house. Monica isn't here," she said, her voice breaking halfway through.

"We'll check the grounds," I said. "Do you have any good lights?"

"In the pantry. We keep them for storms." Eleanor led the way, and Tinkie and I were soon outfitted with hefty flashlights that cut an arc through the blackness of the night. Without further ado, we started in the gardens where Monica was last seen.

"At the back of the property is Jerome's cottage," Eleanor said. She'd opted to stay in the house in case Monica returned. If that happened, she'd call us.

"Can the gardener help us look?" Tinkie asked.

"He could if he were home," Eleanor said. "I've called repeatedly, but there's no answer."

The hair on the nape of my neck tingled. Jerome *and* Monica were absent. A tête-à-tête or an abduction? It could be either, or neither. But it was at least a good place to start. Tinkie had come to the same conclusion, and we set off through the maze of the garden, our flashlights allowing us a narrow path in the dense darkness.

When we were out of earshot of Eleanor, Tinkie pulled me to a stop. "Do you think Monica is boinking the gardener?"

"Maybe."

"I don't buy that business of giving up on men," Tinkie said. "Women who are doing exactly what they want say stuff like that. I mean, I expect you to say it any minute."

"What are you talking about?" I wondered if Jitty were somehow influencing Tinkie.

"You're so determined to be upfront and honest and

put everything out there. Men don't like that. They want to be deceived and coddled and catered to. They need the *illusion* of control. Surely by now you've learned that, Sarah Booth."

We were standing in the middle of a garden at an estate that looked like the setting for a Frankenstein movie with one half of our client team missing and Tinkie was lecturing me on appropriate behavior with men. "Let's find Monica, then you can sort my love life."

"Point taken." She aimed her flashlight and set off to the north.

The stiff breeze blew strands of my hair into my eyes, and slender oak and dogwood branches slapped at my face. By the time we made it to the gardener's cottage, I was exasperated. A bottle tree clanked and jangled in the wind. The multicolored bottles that had been stuck on bare limbs would be beautiful in sunlight. Now, though, the noise was unsettling.

The beam of our flashlights showed a modest, Creole-style cottage set on six-foot pilings with an inviting front porch. A single light burned in the front window.

We headed up the steps. Tinkie knocked loudly on the front door. "Mr. Lolly! Mr. Lolly!"

No answer.

"Do you think he's inside?" Tinkie asked.

Emptiness seeped from the house. "No." I didn't think anything alive was in residence at that moment. While the structure of the house was symmetrical and handsome, something was off. I felt as if someone watched me, excited by our presence. If Jerome Lolly was as creepy as his house, I didn't want to meet him in the dark.

"Listen!" Tinkie's fingers dug into my arm.

A muffled sound drifted from the east. I couldn't be

certain what it was. There was a rhythm, a familiar cadence, but I couldn't put my finger on it until I heard the wild whinny of a horse.

"Holy Christmas." Tinkie's grip tightened until I winced. "If the Headless Horseman comes crashing out of the tree line, I'm breaking into the cottage."

I wasn't certain inside was any safer than out, but I respected Tinkie's decision. I had the thought we'd been dropped down into a really bad fairy tale. All sorts of evil spirits and ghoulies might roam the grounds of Briarcliff. "See if the door's unlocked."

She gave the knob a twist, and the door swung wide without a sound. "We don't have permission to enter," she reminded me.

"Lolly is Eleanor's employee. She sent us to find Monica. I think we're within our rights." I stepped over the threshold and fumbled for a light switch. When I found it, I prayed as I flipped it up. Warm, wonderful light filled the room. Glancing around, I could say two things about Jerome Lolly. He was a neat man and he loved horticulture. Books on plants and gardening filled one wall, but my eye was drawn to a meticulous miniature re-creation of a schooner.

Tinkie and I approached it together. *Lillith* was the boat's name.

"Wasn't that Barthelme's ship's name?" Tinkie whispered, though there was no one in the cottage to hear her.

"Yes." My skin rippled with goose bumps. The replica of the *Lillith* could have any number of interpretations. Maybe it was as simple as the fact that Jerome liked boats, but I didn't think so.

"There's no obvious sign of Monica," Tinkie said.

"We might as well search the whole place." We were there. We'd already entered. It only seemed logical to make the most of our current situation. Besides, Jerome Lolly had begun to interest me. He didn't fit the picture in my head of "the average gardener."

To prove the point we found a half-empty bottle of expensive red wine and the remnants of a meal on the oak counter in the kitchen. Two plates and two glasses implied Jerome hadn't dined alone.

Tinkie held a glass up to the light. "There's a lipstick stain. Could be Monica's shade." If anyone could match a color, it was Tinkie, or our journalist friend, Cece Dee Falcon, formerly known as Cecil. They took matters of appearance seriously.

"A kidnapping victim doesn't generally swill wine and eat cheese and expensive crackers." Tinkie put the glass down.

"Jerome had company, but it doesn't mean it was Monica."

A voice boomed from the doorway. "You're right about that. Such clever lasses."

We whirled to find a fifty-something-year-old giant of a man planted at the threshold. He filled the frame with his large shoulders, long legs, and big hands.

"Care to tell me what you're doing here in my wee cottage?" A beard hid his expression.

"Looking for Monica Levert." Jerome looked and sounded like he'd been carved from highland rock. He was a manly man, and the idea of an affair between him and Monica no longer seemed unlikely. "She's gone missing, and her sister asked us to find her. Eleanor said there was a gardener's cottage back here. We thought maybe she'd gotten ill and—"

"Cut the bullshit. You thought I'd abducted the woman." He took a step. "Holding the lovely employer hostage, for . . ." He shrugged. "Her favors? Money? What?"

Tinkie lifted her chin a fraction of an inch, a warning to anyone who knew her well. "You're right, Mr. Lolly. We thought you might be involved. Eleanor has tried to call you all evening, but you haven't answered."

"I had a date. And then I heard something in the gardens, so I went to look." He closed the door. I heard a funny *click,* and I wondered if he'd locked it. The possibility was unsettling, to say the least.

"Have you seen Monica?" Tinkie asked.

"About five o'clock. She came by to talk about the rose garden. She has plans for the space." Jerome didn't look particularly pleased.

"Where did you meet her?" I asked

"It wasn't an arranged meeting. We happened upon each other and came here to look at some options. Chance meetings occur outside the storybooks you ladies love to read, you know." His mockery was tainted with humor. "We talked, she told me what she wanted, and she left. Then I went to buy the necessary supplies to fulfill her demands."

The Scottish burr of his speech was pleasing, even when his words were sharp. "How long have you worked here?" Abrupt subject changes sometimes rattle a suspect.

"I started when I was a young man. Hired by Mr. and Mrs. Levert when I came over from Skye."

"The twins' parents hired you?"

"Indeed. The two Miss Leverts were finishing high school. I've known them that long, you see."

I pointed to the dishes in the kitchen. "Who was here?" I asked.

"Monica." He focused on me when he spoke. The only hint of discomfort was a mild flush to his cheeks.

"You and Monica shared a bottle of wine."

His smile was slow. "We each had a glass. While we talked about plans for the rose garden. As I mentioned, she's a lass with a strong will. She has her ideas, and sometimes she won't listen to reason."

"So you talked, shared some wine, and then she left?" Tinkie asked.

"Exactly. At five thirty she walked back to the main house. She said she had to pack. They were leaving for Europe again."

Eleanor had seen Monica around seven thirty, so if Jerome was being truthful, he wasn't the last one to see the missing sister.

"Did she say anything about her evening's schedule?" Tinkie asked.

"She talked only of packing. Monica doesn't confide in me." Lolly relaxed a little. "She tells me what she wants, and I mostly do it. Unless it's the wrong plants. Then I do what needs doing. No point wasting money on something that won't flourish here."

"What were her instructions for the rose garden?" I asked.

"Buy the materials to put in a fountain this fall and beef up the color around the front and the drive. Monica wanted Bermuda Mystery Roses that bloom most of the summer. Wanted an archway with the Seven Sisters." His tone reflected his approval. "She's a sensible woman, more often than not, when it comes to plants. I could say otherwise when it comes to . . . other things."

"And what might those other things be?" I pressed.

"Men and friends. Not much luck on either count." He crossed his arms. "Now I've spoken out of school." There was regret in his tone. "Please, I have a lot to do."

"Did Monica seem troubled to you?" I asked.

"No, she . . ." His brow furrowed. "Hold a minute. She was a mite troubled. Someone tore up my vegetable patch the last week, and she took it personally. I told her not to make so much of it, but she did."

This was the first we'd heard of a vegetable patch assault. "How do you mean tore it up?" I asked.

"I shouldn't say 'someone.' It was a horse. Stomped all over my baby turnips and my melons. Horses like melons, you know."

I did know. I often gave Reveler and Miss Scrapiron watermelon. "I heard a horse earlier."

"I hear it, but I never *see* it," he said. "It's a big devil. Hoof the size of a platter."

Reveler was a hefty horse, but not that big. "You think someone deliberately rode the horse into your garden?"

He shrugged. "Hard to say if the rider put the horse to it, or if the horse is running loose around the grounds. Briarcliff is close to three hundred acres. These are hard times. Could be someone turned the horse out here, thinking there was forage or maybe the creature would be fed. Folks know the Levert sisters have a lot of money."

"You've checked the stables on the grounds?"

He nodded. "Hasn't been a horse in there for decades." He turned slightly away. "People in town say it's the ghost of Barthelme's horse, a right fierce devil. Solid black and swift. Barthelme rode him on the Natchez Trace when he was robbing travelers. That foolish writer man who did the book on Natchez has stirred up talk of ghosts."

Lovely, a highwayman's ghost horse. If Jitty was eavesdropping she might take a notion to dress up as a jockey. "What writer?"

The gardener's lips pressed into a thin line. "You'd best ask the sisters. I've spoken out of turn for the second time. In Scottish legend, the third time will turn me to stone. So be off with the two of you."

"We need to *find* Monica before we can ask her anything." Tinkie brought us back to the immediate matter. "Will you help us hunt for her?"

"Is she truly missing, or is this one of her games?"

"If it's a game, she's worried her sister. And us," I said. "Is Monica in the habit of disappearing?"

Jerome drew in a long breath. "She's headstrong. When she doesn't get her way, she makes people suffer, but I don't think she'd deliberately make Eleanor think she was hurt or in trouble. Now let me fetch a light."

He was back in a moment, and we left the well-lit cottage for the darkness of the night.

4

Jerome strode under a canopy of trees so dense it blocked the night sky. I squeezed Tinkie's arm, slowing her down so I could whisper, "Should we trust him? He could have kilts and a broadsword hidden in the woods with the idea of whacking off our heads."

"Fine time to bring that up. But the kilt sounds mighty interesting. What do Highlanders wear under them?" She urged me forward as his light disappeared around a sharp bend in the trail. "We don't really have a choice. Jerome knows the grounds."

"And he could be leading us to the cliff. We'd never know until—"

Before I finished speaking, the moon broke free of the clouds. The woods released us to a sweep of manicured carpet grass. Two hundred yards ahead was the cliff's edge. Jerome waited, his flashlight beam playing across our faces. "Did anyone check at the bottom of the cliff?" he asked.

"Holy shit." I remembered the object in the sheer material falling into the river.

"I'll call the police." Tinkie reached into her pocket for her cell phone.

"Wait." I restrained her. "We don't have any more evidence than when Eleanor called them." Out on the open lawn, the wind was constant and strong. I had to lean close to Tinkie and speak loudly.

"Are you coming?" Jerome yelled.

We walked reluctantly to the bluff. There were no railings or markers or even steps down to the water. The cliff had been cut out of the land by the passage of the river, the wind, and time. We pointed our flashlights down, but the beam failed to reach the bottom. Moonlight revealed a section of the cliff dropped straight to the water. We stood above a rocky jut of land. Downriver the Natchez-Vidalia Bridge connected Mississippi to Louisiana. The twin, cantilevered spans were, technically, the tallest bridge in the state.

Moored upriver from the bridge was a riverboat casino. The wide Mississippi seemed tame and slow moving, but I knew better.

"No sign of her down there." Jerome's stronger flashlight beam swept the land and the river. "If she's on the grounds, we'll find her."

He turned toward the house. Tinkie and I lingered a moment before we followed him. A gust of wind from the north carried an out-of-season chill, and Tinkie gasped. It caught me unprepared, too. It was summer in Mississippi. Jack Frost had long been run out of the territory, but this wind had plenty of nip in it. I thought of Edgar Allan Poe's poem "Annabel Lee." The wind moaned low and plaintive through the trees.

In many ways, Briarcliff brought Poe's work to mind. The house was menacing with the moonlight striking silver in the damp stone edifice. The gothic overtones of the architecture and setting couldn't be denied.

A pale, fluttering object scuttered across the lawn. I rushed to pin it with my foot. When I picked it up, I realized it was part of a gossamer gown, a strip of lace that likely adorned the hem. Holding it triggered a gut-dropping twist of anxiety.

"The thing I saw fall in the river could have been wearing something like this," I told Tinkie. It could have been a woman.

"We have to show this to Eleanor." Tinkie spoke with determination but didn't move.

"And Jerome." I, too, hesitated. The gardener was now far ahead of us, headed to the back lawn. I forced myself to call out to him.

"Come on, if you're comin'," he grumbled.

When we caught up with him, I showed him the lace. He shook his head. "Could have blown in from anywhere. Never felt a wind like this, this time of year." Earlier he'd kept his face blank, but now I clearly saw distress. It struck me that he recognized the fabric, and I wondered again if Monica and Jerome had more than an employer-employee relationship.

"We must show this to Eleanor," I told him. His reluctance to be a part of that scene was clear.

"I'll keep searching the gardens. She has to be around here."

In all probability she was safe, but if someone had

been able to break into Briarcliff and steal a four-million-dollar necklace, who was to say they hadn't returned to harm the sisters.

"If you find anything, let us know," Tinkie told him.

"Do you think you have to tell me that? I'm not daft, lass." He strode around the side of the house, leaving us to face Eleanor and show her the scrap of material we'd found and which might shed the worst light possible on Monica's strange disappearance.

Eleanor's hands trembled as she clutched the lace. "It's hers. It's Monica's. She has a gown . . . she bought it in Geneva. She called it her Gloria Swanson gown. When she wore it, she was ready for her close-up." Her fingers stroked the airy fabric. "She loves beautiful things." Her head dropped to her chest and she sobbed. "Where *is* she?"

Tinkie and I exchanged a look. We wouldn't tell her about the object falling into the river. We had no proof it was Monica—or anyone else. There was no point putting that kind of fear in Eleanor's mind until we found evidence. But I had every intention of telling the Natchez police chief.

While I comforted Eleanor with a glass of sherry, Tinkie stepped outside to call the chief. When authority figures need to be motivated, Tinkie is the gal for the job. When they need to be pissed off, that's my terrain. The job of consoling Eleanor fell to me.

I touched her shoulder gently. "Eleanor, we found out that Monica went to talk with Jerome about the rose garden earlier in the evening. She came back here and you spoke with her before dusk, so that would have been around eight. When she went to the garden, what was she wearing?"

The first inkling of hope showed in Eleanor's face. "She was wearing a dark gray slack suit by her favorite designer. It fit her perfectly. I remember because she was silhouetted against the sunset and I thought how it was cut exactly for her." She gripped the fabric scrap. "She wasn't wearing her nightgown."

"Can we check to see if the gown is in her room?"

"I should have thought of that." She sprang to her feet and motioned for me to follow her through several lavishly decorated rooms and up a curving staircase so beautifully crafted it looked as if it floated on air.

Thick carpet covered the upstairs hall and absorbed the sound of our footsteps. An intruder could easily have slipped in and moved around the house without being detected.

Eleanor passed several doors before she pushed one open. "I never go in her room," she said. "Because we were twins, we became very territorial. People think twins share everything, but it isn't true. Sometimes we have to fight harder for an individual identity. Monica loves her privacy, and I've always honored that. This makes me feel like I'm violating her."

"She'd do the same for you," I told her.

She flipped on the light. Monica's room was awash in shades of lavender and periwinkle blue. I was surprised by the colors.

"She loves the beach," Eleanor said. "My room is green and rust. I love the mountains. Though we're identical, we do have our differences."

We decided that I would go through Monica's spacious walk-in closet and lingerie lowboy while Eleanor searched her dresser.

Tinkie joined us. "The police are on the way. Gunny is coming personally. He apologized for not acting on your initial call, Eleanor."

"It's hurtful when the people in your hometown don't believe you." She closed the bottom drawer of the dresser. "The gown isn't here. You didn't find it, either, did you?" Her voice broke and she cleared her throat. "What's happened to my sister?"

"We'll find her," Tinkie said.

I noticed that she made no promises about finding her alive and safe.

Monica's gown wasn't in her room, the bathroom, or the laundry hamper, a fact none of us could ignore.

We returned downstairs, and Tinkie put on coffee while I sat with Eleanor. Gunny arrived as Tinkie brought in a tray with the fresh coffee and cups. When I answered the door, I noticed dawn was lighting the eastern sky. I wanted a good look at the base of the cliffs, but I would wait until I could tell Gunny about what I'd witnessed during the haunted tour without Eleanor overhearing. I figured Gunny would be as interested in the bluff—and what went over the edge of it—as I was.

Gunny went through a list of questions very similar to those Tinkie and I had already asked Eleanor. Her answers were consistent. Weariness touched the corners of her eyes. For the first time, I saw her true age in the puffiness and dark circles. Her posture was perfect, but her voice was rough with grief and worry she tightly controlled.

"Why don't you try to rest?" Gunny said when he'd finished. "My men are scouring the grounds. If there's any evidence of foul play, we'll find it."

"Jerome can help," Eleanor said. "He knows Briarcliff better than anyone except a Levert."

Gunny nodded. "He already is. These ladies"—he indicated Tinkie and me—"have some questions to answer before I send them home."

"Lie down," Tinkie told Eleanor, leading her to the stairs. "We'll stay here. I promise. Any news at all, and I'll get you."

"But you haven't had any rest, either," Eleanor said.

"It's okay. We're fine." Tinkie almost pushed her up the stairs.

When the door to her room clicked shut, I turned to Gunny and relayed what I'd seen during the haunted tour.

"Someone was on that cliff top? You're sure?" he asked.

"I didn't see a person, but something as large as a human body doesn't just hurtle off a cliff by itself."

"Let's take a look." He strode out the door.

At the edge of the bluff the wind was still kicking up, a contrast to the perfect summer sunrise. Golden peach light pushed against the blue of night. The river glinted like molten silver.

"Whatever it was came from there." I pointed to the south, where the bluff protruded over the water. I wasn't great with geometry, but the object had struck the water, not land.

We started that way, but Gunny waved us back. "Let me check for footprints."

It wasn't likely he'd find anything in the thick Saint Augustine grass, but Tinkie and I held back. He knelt down and brushed at the grass. "Take a look at this," he called.

A slash in the ground looked as if someone had struck it with a golf club or some type of mallet. "A horse did that," I said. "A horse that's been shod." I pointed to a trail of marks that gouged the grass.

Gunny looked up at me. "Are you certain?"

"Yes."

"The Levert sisters said it had been years since horses were kept on the property, but the gardener said one is running loose," Tinkie volunteered. "He thinks someone couldn't feed it, so they turned it out in the woods."

"And it just gallops around Briarcliff?" Gunny was skeptical.

"Until someone catches it, or it bolts out in front of a vehicle on the road, or gets injured and bleeds to death." I knew I had to do something about the horse before I left Natchez. While horses are large, imposing creatures, they are incredibly fragile. And they have no ability to fend for themselves if they're dumped out.

"Do you think it's possible the horse threw its rider over the bluff?" Gunny asked.

I hadn't thought of that scenario. I calculated the distance from the hoofprints to the cliff. "It's possible. But who would be riding a horse in a peignoir?"

"Excellent question." Gunny rose to his feet. "I suppose I have to call out the search and rescue and see if we can find a body in the river."

"I'm not going to tell Eleanor that," I said. "I don't believe Monica would be out here riding a horse in her nightgown, so I don't think Eleanor needs to know about the flotilla. If you find something, would you contact me or Tinkie?"

"I will." He shifted his gaze from Tinkie to me. "What do you think happened to Ms. Levert?"

"I don't have a theory yet. We don't really know the sisters."

"Monica has a . . . reputation in town. When Eleanor called, I didn't come out because Monica's been known to . . . spend the night elsewhere. And then rub the wronged wife's nose in it."

Gunny was doing his best to be circumspect. I thought to follow up that statement, but Tinkie spoke first. "Do you think the person who took the necklace abducted Monica?"

"To what purpose?" Gunny asked.

"Ransom?" She frowned. "Except there's been no ransom request."

"Yeah, get back with me when one comes in." Gunny was almost condescending.

"It's the only thing that makes sense." Tinkie put her hands on her hips. "People don't just disappear, and Monica is waiting for half of a four-million-dollar payday. She wouldn't just leave two million behind. Even if it weren't for the money, she wouldn't disappear and leave her sister to worry."

Tinkie's logic, when it involved money, was infallible. Perhaps it came from having a banker husband and a bank owner for a father. "She's right," I said.

"But there's been no ransom demand." Gunny wasn't buying a kidnapping. "And she's been gone, what? Twelve hours? My bet is she found a guy and decided to have her fun. Look, we'll check the river and keep an eye out. I'll speak with the cab company in town and see if a driver came out here last evening to pick her up."

The standard rule of thumb is a kidnap victim's best

chance of being recovered unharmed is within the first twenty-four hours. The more time that passes, the less likely the victim's survival.

"If she was taken for money, maybe the kidnapper is waiting for daybreak," I said.

"Anyone foolish enough to take Monica would have a real-life 'Ransom of Red Chief.' He'd pay Eleanor to take her back." He called over his shoulder as he left, "I'll call if I find anything in the river."

Tinkie and I went into the house, moving quietly in the hope Eleanor was asleep. From the front window we watched Gunny deploy his men. Half a dozen continued to comb the grounds of Briarcliff with the help of Jerome Lolly. Another six got into their vehicles and followed Gunny back to town.

I sank into a chair and stifled a yawn. Tinkie tested the coffeepot to see if it was still warm, then poured us each a cup. "What do you think happened to Monica?" she asked, handing me the java.

"From what the chief says, it sounds like some angry wife might have hauled her off."

Tinkie fanned her face. "She must be hot stuff. Maybe she is rolled up in bed with a lover."

"Maybe." I couldn't believe she'd up and leave without a word to her sister. They appeared to be totally devoted to each other. They vacationed together, played together, shared houses and . . . insurance money. "Do you think Eleanor might have pushed her . . ." I couldn't finish.

"No-o-o!" Tinkie was scandalized I'd suggest such a thing. "They're identical twins. Eleanor is too genteel. Besides, she loves Monica."

"Two million dollars is a lot of reason to bump someone off."

"That doesn't explain the hoofprints," Tinkie said. "I don't believe for a minute a strange horse is running around, showing up at a potential crime scene. A human trespasser was here at Briarcliff last night. Someone up to no good."

That's why I valued Tinkie. She had a no-nonsense streak of practicality that put things in perspective.

"You're so right."

The words came from behind us. Eleanor Levert stood in the parlor doorway, her face as pale as the starched white curtains in the kitchen window. One hand gripped the door frame. She teetered, as if she were about to collapse.

"What is it?" I was on my feet and at her side in seconds. A good thing, too, because she slumped into my arms. Tinkie helped me maneuver her to the sofa.

"Call a doctor," I urged Tinkie.

"No." Eleanor's hand batted the air. "No doctor. Don't call anyone."

"You're ill," Tinkie said gently. "This has been a terrible shock. It might be best to have your blood pressure checked."

Eleanor pushed free of us. She rocked back and forth on the sofa, her features drawn in pain, but it wasn't physical, it was emotional.

"Tell us what's wrong," I said.

"I can't."

"You can trust us." Tinkie rubbed her back. "What is it?"

Eleanor stopped rocking. She looked into Tinkie's blue eyes for a long moment. "I don't know what to do. I'm afraid."

"You heard from the kidnappers." I made a statement, not a question.

She looked down at her lap. "He said if I told anyone, he'd kill her."

"What do they want?" I pressed.

"The insurance money." She spoke softly.

"The entire four million?" Tinkie asked.

"Yes."

"How did they know the amount?" I asked.

"Natchez is a small town. Mr. Nesbitt at Langley Insurance would have had to clear the settlement with the main office in Chicago. There could have been a leak anywhere. I think the man I spoke with was Southern. He spoke so harshly, it was difficult to tell, but I believe he had a drawl. I just don't know. I was upset."

"What did he say? Exactly."

She took a breath and looked up at us. "He said, 'We have your sister. We haven't hurt her, but we will. Collect the insurance from the necklace tomorrow. We'll contact you with further instructions. If you call the police, your sister will die slowly and painfully.' And then he hung up."

I knew Tinkie was traveling the same mental road I was. The ransom demand sounded professional and well thought out. It was reasonable to assume there was more than one kidnapper. One to guard the hostage while the other picked up the money.

"We should contact the police chief," Tinkie said.

"Absolutely not." Eleanor jolted up like someone had hit her with a hotshot.

"We're not equipped to handle a ransom situation." Tinkie rose slowly. "Gunny will bring in the FBI."

"No!" Emotion mottled her pale face. "I will not risk my sister's life by calling in the police, the FBI, or anyone else. If you won't help me, I'll take care of this myself."

"Be reasonable," Tinkie said. "Your sister's life is at stake. Let the professionals handle it."

"That man threatened to kill Monica slowly and painfully if I didn't do exactly what he said. I believe him."

Tinkie waited for my response, but I couldn't support her. If someone snatched her or Cece or Millie, I wouldn't call the FBI. I would handle it myself.

"Do you think the insurance company will pay out tomorrow?" I asked. Tinkie shot me a look that would curdle milk.

"If you and Tinkie turn in your report, I might be able to push it through."

"The FBI can get marked bills," I said. "You'll stand a better chance of recovering the money and putting the kidnappers behind bars."

"I don't care about the money. I want Monica home safely. I'm sure once she's back, I'll want to punish these lowlife thieves, but now, the only thing I care about is my sister." She grasped each of our shoulders. "Please, will you help me?"

5

"Give us a minute." Tinkie motioned me out of the room.

When we were in the hallway, she whispered, "We can't do this. We don't know a thing about handling a ransom. Monica's life is on the line, Sarah Booth."

"I agree."

"You can't be hardheaded . . ." She stopped. "You agree?"

"I do. Eleanor should call the FBI."

Tinkie blew out her breath. "Thank goodness. I thought you were going to want to sign on to handle this."

"She *needs* to call the FBI, but she isn't going to." Tinkie was right, but so was I. If we didn't help Eleanor, she'd take matters into her own hands. As unprepared as we were to deal with this kind of situation, Eleanor was worse.

"Look, we came here to do a report for an insurance claim. Finding a thief is one thing, but dealing with a hostage situation is another. This is way out of our league." Tinkie tapped her toe on the hardwood floor. Normally, she'd be wearing high-fashion shoes, and the *tap-tap-tap* would be very effective. The walking shoes she wore diluted the effect. "I don't like this."

I put my arm around her shoulders. "I don't, either, but you know I'm right."

She stepped away from me. "If we can't convince her to call the police when it's time to make the drop, then we walk out. I won't be part of a ransom gone wrong."

Anything other than trying to advise Eleanor was way out of our depth. "Let's try to move her toward calling Gunny." The Natchez PD might not have the manpower or training to handle a sophisticated kidnapping, but I felt certain Gunny was the kind of officer who would recognize his limitations and call in the feds.

We returned to the parlor, where Eleanor sat on the sofa staring out the front window at the glorious vista of a perfect morning. A robin's egg sky capped the lush green foliage of a Southern summer. I sat down beside Eleanor.

"Tell me everyone who has access to the house and your personal business," I said. "Everyone."

Her shoulders visibly relaxed. "Then you'll help me."

"To a point." Tinkie perched on a wing chair. "You should call the authorities, Eleanor. They have experts who handle these situations. Our best advice is for you to put this in their hands."

"They mess up as often as not." She dared Tinkie to deny the statistics. "Monica is all I have in the world. We're the last of the true Leverts. I have to get her back, no matter the cost."

"Which brings us to another list we need to make," I said. "Who inherits Briarcliff after you and Monica die?"

A frosty smile touched Eleanor's lips. "Your assumption is that the kidnapper will kill Monica and then come for me."

There wasn't time for games or finessing. "It's a possibility we can't ignore. Who stands to gain?"

"If Barthelme Levert were alive, I fear he'd take strong action. He wasn't a man who liked to be pushed into a corner." A hint of color stained her cheeks. "The closest heir, the only heir other than me and my sister, is a cousin. Millicent Gentry."

She spoke the name with such disdain I hardly had to ask. "You aren't close to this Millicent?"

Eleanor's nose tilted upward slightly. "There's a vulgar Southern expression that perfectly describes Millicent. She's as crazy as a shit-house rat."

Tinkie turned away to hide her smile, and I struggled not to laugh. "I gather you don't get along."

"Millicent is a lazy lout. She's gone through her parents' inheritance. She *sold* the family property to a *subdivision developer*. That was Levert land. It had been in the family for generations. Barthelme even plowed it with a mule when he first came to Adams County. Now there are tract houses with tiny, treeless lawns and overweight women in polyester shorts living on it." She'd worked herself into a real righteous anger.

A cousin would know the family history. She'd have local connections. She'd know the house and the comings and goings of the sisters. And the only thing that stood between her and the Levert money was the sisters. She was a very good suspect. "Is Millicent capable of putting together something like this kidnapping scheme?"

"Millicent is greedy enough to try it." Eleanor's eyes flashed with fury. "And if she is behind this, I promise I'll squeeze every last drop of Levert blood from her silicone-enhanced body."

Tinkie gave me a wide-eyed look. Eleanor was a refined lady, but when she was pissed, she was well and truly pissed. "Where can we find Millicent?"

"She inherited one of Barthelme's homes on Wonderland Drive. It's a beautiful pink Victorian she's managed to ruin with a lawn full of lighted, animated gnomes." She grimaced. "Incredible. She turns them on every night. Her neighbors have gone before the city council to try to stop her. Oh, and while you're there, ask to see her doll room." A hint of humor had returned to Eleanor's face.

"Doll room?"

"Every Halloween Millicent dresses up like a doll. You know, Shopping Barbie, Convertible Midge, Chatty Cathy—whatever is hot and popular and by all means attractive. She has a life-sized model of the doll made, with her features, and dresses it in her costume. Then the doll is placed in her doll room. It's like a window display at a freak show. "

Visions of a wax museum jumped into my mind. I would have used the word "macabre," but Eleanor had indeed proven her point about the shit-house rat.

"How are you related to Millicent?" Tinkie asked.

"She's my great-grandfather's sister's great-grandchild."

I wasn't certain how to calculate that degree of kinship. Maybe a cousin fourth removed? "She's your closest kin?"

"She is. As you can tell, the Levert bloodline didn't produce a lot of breeders. Mother had only Monica and me. Our father, Middler Levert, was an only child." She shrugged. "No one in the family was overly fond of children. Monica and I never wanted any, but when I think about Millicent getting her hands on Briarcliff, I think I may adopt."

"Since there aren't any other relatives, who else has access to Briarcliff, other than Jerome Lolly?" I had to get a list and get busy. The kidnappers could call back at any moment. If Tinkie and I were to be prepared, we needed to make tracks.

"Kissie, who cleans for us, has a key. She comes and goes as she pleases, but she's a delightful young woman. She'd never do a thing to harm Monica."

I raised my eyebrows. Tinkie and I would have to investigate everyone, no matter how slim the chances, and Kissie had an arrest record.

"Who else?" I asked.

"That historian fellow has been hanging around." A strange expression crossed her face. "In fact, shortly after he showed up we had the first robbery attempt in the family cemetery. And the mysterious horse and rider was seen on the bluffs."

"Tell us about the attempted grave desecration."

Eleanor leaned forward. "We returned home unexpectedly late one night. Bitter cold, as I recall. When Monica drove up to the house, someone was silhouetted running across the lawn. They disappeared into the woods, and then that horse came out of nowhere running wild without a rider. It was like a nightmare. Monica and I rushed into the house and locked the doors. The next morning we found where the grave had been disturbed. The thief left his shovel. I'm sure he meant to have the ruby necklace, but those graves are sealed with heavy cement slabs."

"How did a historian know about this?" I asked.

"I'm afraid we'd told him the old stories about Barthelme and his black horse. He used to terrorize the slaves by riding around on Diablo late at night, or so the family legend goes. Ask the kids in town—they'll all claim to have seen old Barthelme riding the cliffs by the river. John, the historian, was all over the story. He practically salivated when Monica told him about the millions of dollars' worth of rubies in the graveyard."

"But this John person—"

"His name is John Hightower. He's from England. Lovely accent that hides a roachlike intellect. He's writing a book about the first Mississippi Levert. Claims he traced Barthelme from England."

"And he's been here, in your home?" Tinkie asked.

"Monica and I met with him. He sounded like an interesting man, and of course we were eager to discover what he'd learned about Barthelme. Unfortunately, it was just more of the same."

"Meaning what?" I checked my watch. It was nearly nine o'clock. Tinkie and I needed to shake a leg.

"He had an alleged proclamation signed by a magistrate showing Barthelme was supposed to be hanged in Liverpool for horse theft, adultery, and sinking a competitor's ship. I'm not certain any of it was true. Turns out Hightower is a descendant of the man whose ship Barthelme supposedly sank. That put a new light on his findings, and one Eleanor and I didn't care to participate in. The man's family has carried a grudge for nearly two hundred years. Like I said, he has the cockroach's ability to survive the passage of time."

I was glad I was sitting. The problem with digging up bones under the family tree is that some of them are bound to be stinky and crooked. "Is this Hightower fellow still in Natchez?"

"My dear, he's taken the garage apartment of Helena Banks Gorenflo, one of my archenemies."

I wondered what kind of archenemies a heritage Southern belle acquired. "And who is Helena Banks Gorenflo?" I asked.

Tinkie's face showed astonishment. Apparently I'd committed a Daddy's Girl faux pas with my failure to recognize the name of a dame of society.

"She's president of the Confederate Belles for Justice," Tinkie said quietly. "A society of women descended from females who fought to preserve the spirit of the Confederacy."

"Helena refused membership to Monica and me. She said Barthelme's wife, Terrant Cassio, was not a loyal Confederate. She said Terrant was the daughter of a Yankee banker who flimflammed the people of Natchez by offering loans through her father's bank and then cheating the property owners with pernicious interest rates."

"Is it true?" I asked. Between Barthelme and Terrant, it's a wonder the town didn't tar and feather the duo and send them packing.

"Helena can't prove a thing." Eleanor sniffed. "She's just being awful. Monica challenged her at the last meeting to show proof or allow us to join. We have documentation that Terrant Cassio Levert was responsible for building the orphanage for children of the war. Terrant did a lot of good things for Natchez. Helena only wants to focus on the negative."

"Does everything to do with your family go back to the War and beyond?" I couldn't help myself. Something to say in favor of the Delaney family—we didn't inherit enemies or hand-me-down grudges from one generation to the next. We were quite capable of making plenty within our own generation.

"History is important in Natchez," Eleanor said.

"So Mr. Hightower is in town, and he knows about the necklace?" I made a note.

"He is and he does. He was here the day it was stolen. Monica may have mentioned the reappraisal to him."

"Why would she do that?" Tinkie asked.

Eleanor's lips thinned. "To goad him. She shouldn't have done it, but he was so eager to see the necklace. She had it out of the safe for the reappraisal and she showed it to him. I thought he'd swallow his tongue with lust."

"That was stupid." The words flew out of my mouth.

"He's such a spineless little man, hiding behind his notebook and pen." Eleanor twisted her hands in her lap. "Monica enjoyed getting him worked up. It's one of her least pleasant characteristics, but some people just get under your skin. It was hard not to torment him."

I couldn't hurl another stone or my glass house might shatter.

"Is it possible Hightower might have figured out a plan to abduct Monica for the insurance money?" Tinkie asked. Her body language told me she'd found a potential suspect she liked the look of.

"He's a brilliant man. And devious. But he's a coward."

"Kidnapping is rather a cowardly act," Tinkie pointed out. "He knew about the necklace, the money, Monica's habits. He has a score to settle with the Levert family. Motive, means, and opportunity."

Eleanor started. "Do you really think . . ." She stood.

"It's a theory," I said. "He's a good suspect, but so is Cousin Millicent. Is there anyone else?"

Eleanor resumed her seat. "We've had tiffs with people in town, but I can't imagine any of them would abduct Monica. She's fierce. I'm more the milquetoast sister. It seems they would have taken me instead."

To the contrary, a kidnap/ransom plot would target the stronger twin, hoping the weaker sister would obey and fork over the cash without calling the cops. Which is exactly what was happening.

"What about the housekeeper?"

"Kissie?" Eleanor was shocked. "No! Kissie wouldn't be involved."

"She has a key, right?" Tinkie asked.

"She does. And knows the house and grounds inside and out."

"Was she aware of the necklace?" I asked.

Eleanor thought a moment. "My sister and I didn't behave wisely, I see that now. Monica and I have operated with a sense of . . . privilege, I suppose you could say. It didn't occur to us that anyone might try to harm us. Here at Briarcliff, we've always felt so safe and . . . untouchable. That's very arrogant, isn't it?"

Tinkie cut in before I could respond. "Tell us about Kissie. How long has she worked for you?"

"Two years. She keeps the house when we're traveling. She's a remarkable young woman, actually. Very talented."

"How so?" I asked.

"She sings with a local band. She's a songwriter and a vocalist."

"Not much of a music scene in Natchez," I said.

"Why hasn't she gone to Nashville?" If a singer-songwriter wanted a career in the music business, Nashville was the closest town to peddle her wares.

"She did. Monica and I helped her. But it didn't work out." Eleanor was clearly uncomfortable talking about this.

"What happened?" Gunny had revealed a little about Kissie McClain's life. I wanted to see how much Eleanor actually knew.

"She got involved with the wrong sort."

"Drugs?"

"Yes, she met a man involved in methamphetamines. Kissie never used, but she got caught up in his troubles. She was arrested here in Natchez. He accused her of stealing his guitar, of all things. Only it wasn't his guitar. It was hers, and I know that for a fact because Monica and I bought it for her. We tried to intervene in her behalf, but she asked us to let it go. Anyway, she did some time in jail for breaking and entering and theft. When she got out, we helped her and gave her a job."

I didn't have to look at Tinkie to know what she was thinking. Kissie was another wonderful suspect. The best place to determine her possible involvement in Monica's abduction was by talking to her personally, and we might be able to make more headway than a lawman.

"Tinkie, we should file that report with the insurance company and speak with Kissie, Millicent, and John Hightower."

Eleanor rose and grasped Tinkie's hands. "So you'll help me? You won't turn this over to the authorities?"

"We'll ask a few questions. Maybe we'll help," I said.

Eleanor's relief turned to worry. "What if the kidnappers find out you're asking questions?"

"No one will find out," Tinkie said. "We'll be the souls of discretion. I promise."

That was going to be a hard promise to keep. We headed out the door just as the sun burst over the tops of the huge oak trees. It was going to be a long and arduous day.

We booked our rooms at the Eola for another night. Before we wrote the insurance report we showered and changed. Tinkie was subdued, and I knew she'd spoken with Oscar. How much she'd told him, I couldn't ascertain. Whatever it was, Oscar couldn't be pleased. Whatever he'd said to Tinkie had taken the wind out of her sails.

When the report was finished, we delivered it to the Langley Insurance Agency and personally handed it to Mr. Nesbitt.

"You're certain the necklace was stolen?" he said, doubt evident in his voice and expression. "Did you find any reason to believe the Levert women may be responsible for the disappearance of the necklace?"

"Yes and then no," Tinkie said. "The necklace is missing. The sisters are distraught."

We'd decided against mentioning Monica's disappearance. We didn't need the entire town talking. If the kidnappers were local, gossip could cost Monica her life.

"This is a huge settlement," Mr. Nesbitt said. "The necklace was supposed to be kept in a secret vault in the house."

I didn't respond. Sometimes it was smart to say nothing.

"And you determined the necklace was there before it was stolen?" he asked.

I pointed at the report. "It's all in there. The necklace was removed from the vault in preparation for a new appraisal." We had to tell the truth. Whether the policy paid out or not, Tinkie and I couldn't fib about the circumstances of the theft.

"Who removed it?" He held the report in his hand, but he hadn't bothered to read it.

"Monica did."

"Was anyone else in the house?"

"Mr. Nesbitt, we've included everything in the report. You can corroborate most of it with the Natchez Police Department's report. The Levert sisters had control of the necklace. It's up to you to determine whether the policy will pay out or not, but I believe the necklace was stolen," Tinkie said. "That's all we can tell you."

"Thank you, ladies," he said. "And have a good day."

He had no intention of confirming whether the claim would be paid or not. The truth was, our report would have no impact one way or the other. Our report was an extra fillip, a supporting opinion.

Mr. Nesbitt dismissed us with a curt good-bye, and we drove to Wonderland Drive and a beautiful pink Victorian laced with gingerbread and green shutters. A wraparound porch was as inviting as a glass of lemonade on a hot summer day. The sun climbed the sky, sending the temperature and humidity way up. It was summer; the cotton was high, and the living steamy.

The sidewalk to Millicent Gentry's home was lined with five-foot shrubs interspaced with gnomes hammering, sawing, and building. Frozen in the act of work under oaks and in flower beds, they waited for someone to flip a switch and crank them into mechanical life—like figures out of a Tim Burton film.

Tinkie skirted around them as we made our way to the house. When we rang the bell, a beautiful blonde with spangled blue eyes answered. If she was related to the Levert sisters, it wasn't evident in her appearance.

"How do you ladies do?" she asked, as friendly as if we were longtime neighbors. "Can I help you?"

"Millicent Gentry?" I'd sort of expected a gorgon with rubbery, doll-like flesh and bad plastic hair.

"That's me," she said, still smiling. "Who are you?"

We introduced ourselves and explained we were working on the insurance claim for Monica and Eleanor.

Millicent put her hand to her mouth and gasped. "The Levert ruby necklace has been stolen!"

"I'm afraid that's true."

"Poor Eleanor and Monica. They must be awful upset. I guess they'll just have to dig up one of the old wives for a replacement." Her grin was irreverent, but her eyes narrowed. "So what are you doing here?" The lovely blond hair hid a facile brain. She'd quickly put the facts together and come up with the sum of suspect. "Did the sisters accuse me of taking the necklace?"

"Absolutely not," Tinkie said. "They thought you might be able to help us. As a member of the Levert family, they knew you'd want to figure out who did this terrible thing."

Tinkie's lie smoothed over the moment. Millicent opened the door for us to enter. "Come on to the back porch," she said. "I was just fixing myself a Bloody Mary. Would you girls care for one?"

"Yes." We spoke in unison. It was nearly eleven, which was brunch time by anyone's standards. We hadn't had much sleep or any breakfast, and a spicy drink would hit the spot. We followed her through the house, and sure enough, I caught a glimpse of a large room filled with mirrors and life-sized replicas of our host in various costumes. There must have been two dozen—Candy Candystriper, Polly Pole Dancer, Bitsy School Girl—all tricked out and dressed to perfection.

While we settled into white wicker porch furniture cushioned in a bright floral print, Millicent made the drinks. She returned with a tray laden with our beverages, cheese straws—a fine Southern delicacy for a ladies' brunch—cucumber sandwiches, cherry tomatoes, and lemon squares.

"Were you expecting company?" I asked. How in the hell had she whipped up a tray of delicious food so fast?

"Honey, around Natchez it's a good thing to always be prepared for a visitor. Sometimes neighbors come over to fuss about my paint job or my dog. Ol' Roscoe tends to paw through their garbage or dig up their flower beds. Once he stole Miss Bigelo's gigolo's underpants and took them all over town. Had I not had fresh Gulf shrimp and Mama's famous comeback sauce, Miss Bigelo would have killed Roscoe." Her laughter was infectious.

"Your dog really stole someone's underwear?" Tinkie was appalled.

"Roscoe has a nose for trouble." Millicent opened the screened door and called for the dog. "Miss Bigelo is principal at the private Catholic school. As you can see, it was awkward for her. Especially since her lover was pastor at the Final Harvest True Church of the Pentecost— a married man, I might add."

"A conflict of apocalyptic proportions," Tinkie said.

Millicent tipped her glass at Tinkie in a toast. "You are the cat's meow," she said. "Anyway, I served them the shrimp and patched over the whole episode."

"How did everyone in town recognize the preacher's underwear?" I asked.

"Because the organist at the Presbyterian church had given them to him as a gift. She was in the post office on a Saturday morning when Roscoe trotted by with them in his mouth. She knew instantly the pastor had dropped them somewhere he shouldn't. She came to my house to accuse me of having an affair with him. She knew Roscoe was my dog. Everyone in town knows Roscoe. Now where is that darn hound?"

"I gather the underwear was distinctive?" I almost hesitated to ask.

"Oh, dear, they were . . . one of a kind." She laughed heartily. "They had a Moses-like figure on them and the saying 'When God calls, Peter rises to the challenge every time.' "

Tinkie choked on her Bloody Mary and almost spewed. I made no effort to control my laughter. "That's a most amusing story."

"Honey, spend an afternoon with Roscoe and you'll have enough material for a book. That dog finds trouble. I try to keep him home because I know folks who'd gladly kill him. But Roscoe is Roscoe. If I kept him behind a fence he'd just pine away and die."

"How did you patch this over?" Tinkie asked.

"By saying the underwear accidentally got into my clothes at the dry cleaner's. I said I'd put them in the trash and Roscoe got them out. Since everyone knows Roscoe's crazy for digging in the trash, everyone believed it."

"A clever fabrication," I said. Millicent was all devilish charm and entertainment—she was also capable of cunning. She might exude magnolia charisma, but there was a clever brain at work.

"So what was it Monica and Eleanor thought I could do about the necklace?" she asked. "They hate my guts. Did they send you to search the house?"

"Well, actually, they didn't send us." Tinkie crunched the celery from her Bloody Mary. "We came on our own initiative."

"To what purpose?" Millicent's eyes twinkled merrily, but I wasn't fooled.

"We need your help," Tinkie said. "The insurance company is stalling. As the only legal heir of the Briarcliff Estate, aside from the sisters, I thought it might be in your best interest to help."

I had to hand it to Tinkie. She was a genius.

"What can I do?" Millicent asked.

"The insurance company wants the whereabouts of every heir accounted for. Where were you on Monday?"

"That's easy enough," she said. "I was on a shopping spree in Jackson. You can verify it at Belinda's Costume Emporium. It's time to get ready for my next Halloween getup. I'm thinking Elvira Mistress of the Dark."

"An excellent choice."

She retrieved her purse and brought out a sales slip with the time and date. "Any more questions?"

6

We left the pink Victorian without a tour of the doll room. By this time we stopped for lunch at a unique restaurant tucked under the skirts of a giant Aunt Jemima. Perhaps not the most politically correct structure, but the food was homemade and delicious. I was tempted to order a second slice of lemon meringue pie. Only Tinkie's appraising eye roving over the waist of my tight jeans made me resist.

Tinkie pushed back her plate. Far be it from me to comment on her fried chicken gnawed down to the bone. There wasn't even a breaded crumb of crispy skin lurking on her plate.

She must have read my mind. "To hell with moderation. Let's split a piece of chocolate pie," she said, waving at the waitress.

When we left, I thought I might roll out to the car, but managed to bend into the front seat. Tinkie drove to Helena Banks Gorenflo's mansion, a Tara replica out Highway 61. The house centered a four-hundred-acre estate. The "garage" apartment was a converted carriage house measuring close to four thousand square feet. Behind the apartment was a swimming pool and tennis courts. John Hightower, British biographer-slash-grudge-holder, had fallen into the lap of luxury.

We'd deliberately failed to warn him of our imminent arrival, so when we climbed the stairs to knock on his door, he opened it with a mildly puzzled expression. "Can I help you?" he asked, very proper.

"We're private investigators," Tinkie said. "We'd like to speak with you."

"Oh, dear." He paled. "And what, may I ask, are you investigating?" Guilt was writ large on his face.

Tinkie's smile revealed perfect, glistening white teeth. "You, Mr. Hightower. You. May we come in?"

Had he been a smarter little piggy, he'd have said "not by the hair of my chinny chin chin." As it was, Tinkie merely pushed at the door and he fell back, giving us entrance to his beautifully furnished abode.

John Hightower was an oddity amidst the dark paneling, leather sofas, weight machines, and fitness equipment that spoke of a man deeply involved with physical image. He was slender, pasty, balding, and had the musculature of a cooked egg noodle. His belt was notched at the first hole. I had a terrible suspicion his waist was smaller than mine.

My first thought was John Hightower couldn't pull off a practical joke, much less a kidnapping. Especially not the abduction of a woman as fierce as Monica.

Tinkie and I seated ourselves in matching wingback chairs.

"I don't think you should be here." He rested his slender hands on the back of a sofa.

"Did we ask for your thoughts?" Tinkie was a powerhouse. She'd sensed that he would yield to a forceful woman and she was dead on.

"Well, no, but—"

"We ask the questions and you answer." Tinkie leaned forward. Even though he was ten feet away, he flinched. "You were at Briarcliff five days ago, is that correct?"

"Briarcliff?" He acted as if he'd never heard the word. "Five days ago?"

Tinkie's left eyebrow shot almost to her hairline. "Are you on drugs, Mr. Hightower? Do you need medical attention?"

"I'm fine." He mustered his grit. "I was at Briarcliff. It was my final interview with the Levert sisters."

"I'll bet," I said. "You revealed a personal bone to pick with their family and they tossed you off the property."

To my surprise, color flooded Hightower's face. "I do have an issue with the Leverts. The course of my family's personal history might have been very different had it not been for that blackguard, Barthelme Levert."

"That was two hundred years ago." I couldn't help it. "You want what? Revenge? Reparation? For an event that happened four or five generations back? In another country? You want the wrongs of history redressed? Well, get in line."

Beneath the pudding was steel, and I caught a glimpse of something ugly lurking behind his mild exterior. Hightower's eyes sparkled dangerously. "Barthelme sank my ancestor's ship. That act pushed the Hightower family

into poverty. Brewster Hightower was taken to the work-
house because he couldn't pay his bills. Creditors pounced
on his Liverpool home, and his family was put out on the
streets to starve. He died a broken man."

"Boo-hoo." His mealymouthed whining grated on my
last nerve. How much did he hate the Levert family?

"I think you ladies, and I use that term loosely, should
leave," he said, all huffy. The dangerous anger was cloaked
again, but I knew it was there—and easily provoked.

"We're not going anywhere." Tinkie probably didn't
approve of my tart remarks, but I could tell Hightower
pissed her off, too.

"I'm writing my book, and it will be published," Hightower said. "The Levert sisters can send as many strong-
armed henchmen as they want. I'm not backing down.
Barthelme's evil deeds will be publicized and available
for all to read."

"The Levert sisters don't give a damn what you write
and publish." I moved to confront him. "They want their
necklace back."

"What?" He looked from me to Tinkie.

"Return it and they won't press charges."

"I hardly think they're in a position to press charges of
any kind against me," he said. "I've done nothing wrong.
I heard the necklace was stolen, but I had nothing to do
with that."

"When was the last time you saw Monica?" Tinkie
pressed.

"At Briarcliff. Several days ago. But that won't be the
last they see of me, I assure you. Once my book is published, I intend to run them out of town. It's biblical. The
sins of the father shall fall upon the son. Generations of
Leverts have profited from the blood money Barthelme

accrued. I am the avenging angel of the Lord. I shall bring them down and smite them with the truth of their family heritage."

"What is it you feel the Leverts owe you?" I asked.

"Money. A lot of money. Barthelme ruined my family. We never recovered. He came to this country and built a fortune while my ancestor rotted in debtor's prison. I want what would have rightly been Brewster's."

"Did it ever occur to you that maybe you should work at a career and earn the things you want?" I asked.

"You're just another child of privilege," he sneered. "Let me guess—you live in the family home. You trade on your family name. You were educated by your parents."

He was three for three, but not in the way he assumed. My parents left me something far better than money. They'd left me a good name.

"Mr. Hightower, where were you last night?" I hardly thought he had the physicality to drag Monica out of Briarcliff even if he'd managed to knock her out. My bets were on him having Monica abducted, then being unable to resist goading her, rubbing her nose in his superiority.

"I had dinner with Helena Banks Gorenflo, my hostess."

"And when did you leave?" I asked.

"At half past nine. We had Cornish hens stuffed with cranberries and pecans. Delicious. She has the best chef in the Southeast." He'd regained his composure *and* British accent, which had begun to slip. I wondered if anything about John Hightower was genuine.

"Delightful, I'm sure," I said. "And after that?"

"I was here, reading." He pointed to a book on the table beside my chair. "Sir Kingsley Amis."

"You were alone for the remainder of the evening," Tinkie said.

"I don't require someone to read to me. In England, our schools believe in literacy, not social promotion."

"Oh, for heaven's sake." I was up to my ears in his Continental insults. "Can anyone verify you were here?"

"Why?" It took him long enough to ask. Was that because he knew the reason behind the questions?

"There's a method to our madness," Tinkie said. "Just bear with us and answer."

"I'm an adult. I don't need a tender."

"So no one can vouch for your whereabouts. Did you ever ask Monica or Eleanor for financial restitution for what you view as past wrongs?"

"I gave them a chance to do the right thing. They refused to listen to me." He drew himself to his full height. "I've researched this impeccably. The stories are true. Barthelme was a blackguard, a thief, and a murderer. He has much to answer for. As does Monica, the deceptive bitch. Eleanor is a scorpion of a woman." "Smug" was the only word to describe him. "Those two women will suffer."

"How?" My heart beat faster. There was something in his face, some satisfaction in the idea of others' suffering that made me wary.

"The things they value most will be taken from them. Like the necklace. Do you think it's coincidental that Barthelme's prize necklace is missing? The Lord works in mysterious ways. Barthelme harmed many people to get the money to commission that necklace. Now it's gone. The hand of Providence at work."

"Sounds like the hand of a common thief." I'd had more than I could stomach. John Hightower contorted and twisted facts, history, and religious doctrine to suit his own needs.

Tinkie sensed my need to decamp. "We'll leave, but we aren't finished with you, Mr. Hightower."

"That's where you're wrong, ladies. I have nothing further to say to you. Not now, not ever."

"Hey, John, just remember, you can run, but you can't hide." I was determined to have the parting shot as Tink and I glided out the door.

From the car, we saw him peep through the curtains, watching us.

"That wasn't a waste of effort," Tinkie said. "Hightower is despicable, greedy, lazy, and motivated by revenge. He would feel justified in abducting Monica. I seriously think he views himself as God's instrument of revenge."

"He isn't religious *or* British."

"When we get back to the hotel, we'll check him out."

"While we're here, we might as well call on Mrs. Gorenflo," I said.

"We should have called ahead," Tinkie said. "She may not see us on such short notice. There is etiquette to consider."

"Not a problem." I pulled out my cell phone and dialed info. The operator connected me for no extra charge.

I could see the big house through the trees. Someone was walking around a pool, but it looked like a young girl instead of a middle-aged woman. Then again, liposuction, Botox—the tools of perpetual youth—were at the disposal of Mrs. Gorenflo.

Her phone rang four times before a soft voice answered. I told Mrs. Gorenflo we were calling at the behest of the Levert sisters. Simply curiosity won out over formal manners. She invited us up for a glass of tea.

Tinkie parked at the front door, and the maid showed us into a house that looked like an upper-crust mansion, circa 1920. I was smitten with the huge mirrors, the black and white tile of the foyer, the heavy drapes in a shade of peach that perfectly complemented the dark maroon walls.

The *tap-tap* of high heels alerted us to Helena Banks Gorenflo's arrival. She came forward, hand extended. While she wasn't a beauty, she was a handsome woman of the Joan Crawford variety. She shook our hands and ushered us into a parlor.

"So you're here at the behest of Monica and Eleanor," she said. "I should tell you up front, it's a waste of your time. The Levert sisters lack the pedigree to join the Confederate Belles for Justice. There's nothing I can do about it. Facts are facts. Besides, we can't include Briarcliff on the tour of homes, our annual fund-raiser. Every member must have a home fit for the tour."

"Why can't you tour Briarcliff?" Tinkie asked.

"People are terrified of the place. It's haunted, you know. Headless horsemen, family members screaming as they run off the cliff." When she saw our expression, she laughed. "Surely you've heard tales of old Barthelme haunting the house and grounds. He rides his black devil horse along the bluff, sparks flying from the horse's hooves. The story goes that if you look into Barthelme's eyes, you'll be driven insane and jump from the bluff. Folks in town won't go near Briarcliff after dark."

"Surely you don't really believe in ghosts and hauntings," Tinkie said.

"I do, and I'm not alone. Strange things happen at Briarcliff. And before you waste your breath pleading Monica's case, I assure you the entire board of the Confederate Belles for Justice stands behind this decision. There was not one dissenting vote."

"Monica will be disappointed to hear that," Tinkie said.

Helena laughed. "She's already heard it. A number of times."

"When did you last speak with her?" Tinkie asked.

"A week ago. She was very angry with me." Helena smiled. "Are you by chance related to Oscar Richmond of Zinnia?" she asked Tinkie.

"He's my husband. Avery Bellcase is my father." Tinkie laid out the cards of her own pedigree.

Helena looked at me. "And you are . . ."

"I was found floating in a rush basket on the Mississippi River wearing a coat of many colors. I have prophetic dreams and I sense I was a prince in a past life. That's all I know."

Tinkie reached back and pinched me so hard on my ass that I yelped and jumped forward, almost knocking into Helena.

"Prince, my eye," Helena said severely. "It's clear you have no breeding whatsoever."

Ouch, what a smack down. I barely managed to hide my grin. Hightower was a dangerous, whacked-out religious hypocrite. Helena Gorenflo was an elitist society snob. Did I sniff romance in the air?

"We're not here about family pedigrees," I said. "We're private investigators with questions about the theft of a ruby necklace."

"Oh, yes, I heard the vulgar thing was stolen." Satisfaction ruled her features. "Who would want it? Every woman who clasped a Levert necklace around her neck died within the year."

"Except for the one Levert to whom you object so strenuously. Terrant Cassio Levert. She had twins and lived a long life."

"After she murdered Barthelme." She mimed surprise. "Don't look so shocked. The whole town knew she killed him, and not a single person lifted a finger to accuse her. That's how much Bartheleme was hated. They let his murderer go scot-free."

I glanced at Tinkie. She shrugged. It seemed pretty clear that five young women—not to mention numerous travelers, river workers, and slaves—died at Barthelme's hands. So the sixth wife got the drop on him. Perhaps it wasn't legal, but it was a type of justice.

"Have you ever seen the necklace?" Tinkie asked.

"One of the twins wears it on occasion. They're overly proud of it, you know. The thing was tacky beyond belief. And gaudy to boot. I can't recall the jeweler who designed it, but he was far overrated."

"When was the last time you saw it?"

Helena had obviously given up offering us tea or inviting us farther into her home. We stood in the foyer, opulence visible in all directions. Beautiful décor. Old money, antiques, quiet good taste.

"The Fourth of July fête. I think Monica wore it then. And little else, I might add. Her red minidress was a scandal. She's too old for that kind of exhibition. At least Eleanor dresses appropriate to her age."

"Why would Monica wear the necklace to a Fourth of July event?" In my experience, Independence Day was generally a picnic and fireworks, not a ball gown and jewels.

"Because she's uncouth. Which is another reason she'll never be a part of the Confederate Belles for Justice. We can tolerate a lot of things, but not her conduct."

It wasn't worth asking if the prejudice against the Leverts was the family history or the fact that Monica looked fifteen years younger than her true age. The old green-eyed monster was likely at work here.

"Do you know anyone who might want to harm the Levert sisters?" I asked.

This brought her up sharp. Speculation glinted in her eyes. "Has someone harmed them?"

"Please answer the question," Tinkie said.

"Everyone in town with breathe in his body might have reason, but I don't know who would actually act against them."

"Not even Mr. Hightower?"

"Oh, please. He'd love to hang them in a public exhibition, but he isn't a violent man. He needs them hale and hearty to wage his literary battle."

"Sounds like so much fun," I threw in.

"I'm sure you'd rather settle your disagreements in a parking lot brawl behind a juke joint. John is a civilized man. And he has the makings of a bestselling book. Murder, scandal, ghosts, unpleasant heirs. He'll be the darling of the literary world, and all on the backs of the Levert sisters. And just let me add, Monica has spent an inordinate amount of time on her back."

"She must have slept with someone you cared about," I said, before I thought.

"Get out of my house." Helena pointed out the door. "Go now before I have to resort to legal recourse."

"Right." I couldn't hide my sarcasm. "Thanks for your time, Helena." I knew my lack of formality would get under her skin.

"Good day, Mrs. Richmond." Helena ignored me as she closed the door.

In the Caddy headed back to the Eola, Tinkie spoke. "Monica and Eleanor have made a lot of enemies. "

"Do they have *any* friends in Natchez?"

"We haven't met anyone who likes the sisters. That would be awful, wouldn't it? To live in a place where everyone hates you."

"Speaking of friends, we need to let Cece know what we're up to." Cece Dee Falcon was the society editor at the *Zinnia Dispatch*, and her journalistic instincts had served us well more than once.

Tinkie pulled off the road. "I have to go home, Sarah Booth. Oscar is pitching a fit. We're obligated to attend the Sunflower County Economic Development dinner at The Club."

The Bellcases did have certain social requirements that came with owning/managing the bank. While Tinkie was a fine private investigator, she was also Oscar's wife. Duties attached to the title. "It's okay." I put a hand on her shoulder. "I can manage here for a day or so. Really."

She stared out the front windshield. "It's a tough balancing act, to be a wife and a P.I."

"I know, but you do it so well." I rumpled her hair. "Don't ever apologize for being a good partner to Oscar."

She pulled back onto the road and in a few moments we were clearing the Natchez city limits. "Are you really going to stay?" she asked.

"I feel I have to."

"But you won't have a car."

"Not a problem in Natchez." The town was compressed. "Eleanor might loan me one. Or I'll rent one. In fact, it may work to my advantage."

John Hightower, Helena, and Millicent had seen the Caddy—a distinctive tomato red with white leather interior. A different car could give me an advantage if I had to tail someone. My personal car, an older model Mercedes Roadster that had belonged to my mother, was as eye-catching as Tinkie's Cadillac.

"Are you going to talk to Kissie McClain?" she asked.

"I am. But I may invite her to the Eola."

"And you'll call me if you need anything?"

Her guilt was unnecessary. "You're two hours away, Tink. I'm only asking a few questions."

"I'll be back as soon as I can."

"Just placate Oscar. The one thing we don't want is for him to feel you've put this job ahead of him."

Tinkie's smile was tentative. "Sounds to me like you've learned the first lesson of being a Daddy's Girl."

"Heaven forbid." I made the sign of the cross.

Laughter was the best note for us to part on. She dropped me off at the Eola and I watched as she drove away. She wouldn't be far, and I had no gut feeling that anything dangerous waited in the wings.

7

I was crossing the lobby of the Eola, headed for the elevator and my room, when a baritone voice called my name. My skin responded to the masculine tone with a delicious shiver before I saw Don Cipriano.

"Miss Delaney, would you have a moment?" he asked as he strode toward me.

I was taken with his attire—black from his jeans and boots to his open-throated poet's shirt—a perfect accoutrement to his darkly handsome features.

"Of course." I ignored my gut's loud clamor to cut and run. Don Cipriano worked on me. He was one of the most sexual men I'd ever met, and though my heart belonged to Graf, my body wasn't dead to the heat this strange man generated.

He tucked my hand through his arm and escorted me toward the bar. "It's a little early for a drink." I had much to do and never drank with a dangerous man while I was working. Too many Delaneys had fallen off that horse for me not to take notice.

"They serve coffee," he said, flashing a dimple in his right cheek I'd missed before.

When we were seated at a table in a dark corner, he sighed. "Why are you working for the Levert sisters?"

I was taken aback by his question. "Why would you care?"

He shrugged. "Natchez thrives on gossip. I understand Monica and Eleanor Levert are not to be trusted."

"Again, I have to ask why it concerns you if I work for them, trustworthy or not."

He stared deeply into my eyes, and for a split second, I was drawn into the brown depths. "Because they're liars and cheats."

The harshness in his voice shook me out of the trance. "You seem to know more about the Levert sisters than you should. Would you care to explain yourself?"

His hand reached across the table and found mine. Warm, strong fingers turned my hand over, and I found myself knowing I should stop him but unwilling to do so. He stroked my skin, a tiny smile playing at the corners of his mouth. "You have a number of stars in your palm, Miss Delaney."

"And that signifies what?"

"Adventure, excitement, affairs of magnitude. Starred events can be good luck or crisis. There's no way to tell. But you've recently had several . . . adventures. This past spring, there was heartache."

I tried to pull my hand away, but he held it. He leaned closer, his warm breath teasing my skin. "Let me look further." He studied the etched lines. "A plump mound of Venus signifies a woman who enjoys sensual pleasures." His finger traced the base of my thumb with such delicious delicacy I had to grit my teeth.

"But here"—he touched the top line—"I see heartache. Romance has not been a smooth ride for you."

"You can say that to almost any woman and she'll agree." I had to put some perspective on this. Once again I attempted to withdraw my hand, but he held it firmly, his thumb moving sensuously in the cup of my palm. My heart thudded, and I ignored the impulse to run.

"What are you afraid of?" he asked.

"I'm not afraid," I lied.

"You are. I can feel your blood pounding." His pointer slipped to my wrist, where he pressed a pulse point. "The blood never lies, Miss Delaney. I know these things. It's a gift, a part of my heritage. I'm able to sense things about people, to know more than they wish to share."

The need to flee grew stronger by the second, but I couldn't allow him to know he was getting to me. "Are you part Gypsy, Don Cipriano?"

"I am," he said. "Romanian Gypsy. My mother was an aristocrat, dazzlingly beautiful but of questionable character. My parents met in a small port city. Her sailboat docked to resupply and she met my father one evening in a bar. She seduced him, a simple man with the gift of prophecy. Their consuming passion overcame their different backgrounds. For a brief time they were happy, but one morning she was gone, vanished without a trace. I was an infant, too much of a burden for her to take. "

"Sounds like a fairy tale or the plot for a romantic

novel," I said. He was making this up out of whole cloth, but I couldn't deny he projected sadness.

"Or a tragedy." He brought my hand to his lips and pressed a kiss into the palm. Despite my best intentions, my body reacted.

When he released me, I put my hand under the table, fingers curled in a tight fist. "What did you wish to speak to me about?"

"To warn you."

"About the Levert sisters?" I squeezed every ounce of skepticism I could into those four words.

"Perhaps it isn't them. But there is danger around you."

"How much will it cost me to have it removed?"

His eyes locked with mine. "I wish I could. If a fee would affect such a thing, any cost would be worth it. You're in danger. You and your friend. But mostly you. If it is the Levert sisters who pose this threat, stay away from them."

"Surely you can see whether they're the threat or not." He was scaring me, but I refused to show it.

"No, I can't. I can only see darkness hovering over you. The source isn't evident. But I had to warn you, Miss Delaney. Take care." He stood, bowed slightly, and then walked away.

I sank back into the chair as though someone had sucked my spine from my body. Don Cipriano might be a crank, a kook, or a manipulator, but he had presence and personal power, and he had succeeded in frightening me. I had no desire for another injury, physical or emotional.

My room had been cleaned and the bed made. I shed my clothes and stepped under the shower's stinging hot spray.

Weariness made my shoulders droop, but I wanted to interview Kissie McClain before the afternoon got away from me.

And I didn't want to think about Don Cipriano.

I let the water sluice over my head, hoping to wash away the thoughts of him.

When I turned off the shower, I thought I heard someone in my room. Grabbing a towel, I opened the bathroom door. Someone wrapped in a white sheet held a bow and arrow. The figure stood perfectly still at the foot of my bed.

"Who are you?" I blinked water from my eyes.

"The hunt is on. Beware the prey doesn't turn into the huntress."

"Jitty?" What in heaven's name was she up to now? I blotted my face to clear my vision. The sheet was actually a toga that draped gracefully over her athletic figure. She wore a crown of laurel leaves.

"I am the daughter of Zeus and Leto, conceived in passion and born on Delos, a floating island, because jealous Hera refused my mother a haven on earth." She came toward me. "There are times when virtue is the only path."

I'd been a theater major in college, and Greek mythology had been one of my favorite studies. I reviewed the hierarchy of the gods and demigods. "Artemis! She was the daughter of Zeus and Leto." I tried not to smirk at my knowledge.

"No sun shines on those who betray true love." Jitty was the voice of gloom.

"Are you talking about Don Cipriano?" Had Jitty buzzed from Dahlia House to the Eola to warn me to steer clear of the Gypsy? If so, it was wasted effort. I had no intention of falling under Don Cipriano's mesmerizing spell.

"You're drawn to him." Jitty sat on the foot of the bed. When she crossed her leg at the ankle, the entire goddess effect was totally ruined. "Stay away from that man, Sarah Booth. He's trouble. A mistake like him can't be hidden or undone."

"But he looks so virile, Jitty. And I'm ovulating right now. I hate to miss this chance to snare a sperm." Oh, this was delicious. Jitty, who'd preached bed and bred for the past two years, was now hoisted on her own petard.

"You got the very devil in you, Sarah Booth Delaney."

"Artemis. Goddess of the hunt and wild things." A rare opportunity to torment Jitty presented itself. "And I sure am feeling wild for one tall, dark, and handsome stranger. Fact is, now that I'm all cleaned up, maybe I should ring his room and invite him for a game of ride the bronco."

I don't think I'd ever seen Jitty at a loss for words, but she was momentarily stunned. "I don't know what's come over you, Sarah Booth, but I'm gonna find Tinkie. Either that or them men in white jackets. You're talkin' crazy."

I dug underwear and a pair of jeans out of my suitcase and pulled them on. "There's no call to rile Tinkie or anyone else. I'm finished having fun with you."

She circled me. "The Gypsy man didn't get his hooks into you?"

"He's compelling, but I've made a commitment to Graf. Disloyalty isn't one of my many vices."

"Lord almighty, Sarah Booth, you 'bout sent me into cardiac arrest."

"Impossible. You're already dead. So what's with the Artemis getup?"

"I considered Athena."

"The Goddess of War?" Thank goodness for Professor Brent and his love of all things Olympic. Athena sprang fully formed from the head of Zeus, her father. Grossly enough, he'd eaten her in an attempt to destroy her. The gods and goddesses of Greek mythology were a bloodthirsty lot, their lineage a tortured mess. Which may have been Jitty's point when she thought I was going to jump in the sack with Don Cipriano.

"Goddess of War, pregnant women, the hunt. One's as good as the other." A smile lifted the corners of her mouth. " 'Cept both of them goddesses were virgins, and I sure can't say the same for you."

I'd had her at my mercy for less than five minutes and she'd already turned the tables. "Go back to Dahlia House. I'm not about to do anything stupid. And I'll be home tomorrow."

"How you gone get home? You don't have a car."

Excellent point. "I'll call Cece."

"Done and done." She was gone without a trace as the phone began to ring.

Cece was on the other end, and I wondered for the thousandth time exactly how far Jitty's powers might reach.

"I've just gotten off the horn with Tinkie," Cece said. "She thinks I should drive to Natchez to keep you company."

"Keep me out of trouble, you mean." I was on to my friends, but I could only be grateful that they cared about me.

"Natchez-Under-the-Hill has been known to lure more than a few damsels into unsavory circumstances. Drinking. Dancing. Fornicating."

"In other words, you want to go juking and use me as an excuse." An evening with Cece was always fun, and Natchez was a town where we could play.

Her laughter was warm and bright. "Tinkie told me about Don Cipriano. All I can say is, 'yum-yum.' "

Cece was a tough gal, but I wasn't certain I'd throw her in front of that train. "I get the sense there's more to him than he's letting on."

"I think you're right. Don Cipriano is the name of a character in a D. H. Lawrence novel. A Heathcliff figure. He's using an alias, and an obvious one for any student of literature."

"I knew that. Sort of." I was only a little indignant. "But who would think to reference that character in a novel? He could have picked Heathcliff—the name suits him perfectly. Dark and brooding." I rummaged through my suitcase for a blouse. "He's just too clever for his own good." And too interested in the Levert sisters. Had he warned me about them because he was involved in the scheme to rob them and abduct Monica? I wouldn't put it past him. Thank goodness I hadn't revealed any of my business to him.

"I thought it might be fun to figure out who he really is," Cece said.

"Excellent plan."

"I'll be there as soon as I can sneak out of the newspaper office."

Knowing Cece, that wouldn't take long. While I waited for her, I decided to track down Kissie McClain and see what she might know about Monica's disappearance.

A guitar's plaintive twang drifted from the beautiful old home where Kissie McClain rented an apartment. By looking at the mailboxes and reading the names of the occupants, I deduced that the house had been broken up into five different residences. Kissie rented 3-C in the back.

A female voice, low and resonant, accompanied the guitar. The song led me down a winding gravel drive that ended in a small car park at the rear of the house. The singing originated from a second-floor gallery.

"Miss McClain," I called.

The music stopped.

"Kissie McClain," I called again.

"Who wants to know?"

I identified myself, and she invited me up without hesitation. The back door opened onto a narrow hallway that cut through the center of the house. A broad staircase took me upstairs, and I found 3-C without difficulty.

Kissie McClain wasn't what I expected. She could have been a throwback to the 70s with her tie-dyed T-shirt, long chestnut hair, and tight hip-hugger jeans. My first thought was that I hoped Jitty would not see the outfit. Jitty had a serious love affair with the fashions of the 70s and was prone to showing up as a hippie-child.

"What do you want?" Kissie asked, but there wasn't aggression in her tone.

"To ask some questions about the Levert sisters."

Her dark eyebrows, angled to begin with, arched even

more. "I don't talk about my employers." She started to shut the door.

Using my foot and my hand, I blocked her. "Please, they need your help."

That gave her pause. "They've been really good to me. I'll do whatever I can to help them, but I won't discuss their private business. There are enough vultures in town hoping to pick their carcasses clean."

I instantly liked Kissie. She was loyal and straightforward. She signaled for me to enter. Beads, à la 1971, hung in a doorway that probably led to her bedroom. The sofa in her sitting area was covered in a multihued throw, and plants jammed every windowsill. Candles burned in saucers on the kitchen counter. Incense lingered in the air, though none was burning. She was definitely living in a time decades past.

"How long have you worked for the Leverts?" I asked.

"Long enough to know they're good people. Everyone in town is jealous because they have money and an estate and they can do what they want and tell the busybodies to kiss their asses."

"And they do that regularly, I'll bet."

Kissie gave me an appreciative look. "You can respect that, can't you?"

"Indeed I can. Sucking up to those who consider themselves high society has never been one of my favorite pastimes."

She indicated a rattan chair that had seen better days. "Want some green tea?"

Tinkie enjoyed the tea leaf, but I was coffee 100 percent of the way. "I just have a few questions and then I'll be out of your hair."

"Shoot." She dropped onto the sofa. "I've got a gig tonight at King's Tavern, and I need to practice a few of my songs."

"Do you write your own material?"

"Most of the time. I cover a few artists I like. Rosanne Cash. Lucinda Williams. They have some fine songs. Mostly I write my own, though."

"That's a tough business."

"It's not for sissies, but nothing worth having ever comes easy."

Words to live by. "You know the Levert necklace is missing," I said. She nodded and I continued. "Monica and Eleanor hired me and my partner to report to the insurance company on the theft of the necklace. We've done our report and found no cause for Langley Insurance not to honor the policy."

Kissie clapped. "That's good news. I was afraid they'd try to stiff Monica and Eleanor."

"Mr. Nesbitt was justifiably concerned the theft was . . . staged."

"Yeah, any excuse not to pay up. Ask the folks down on the coast what happened after Katrina. Like they *staged* a hurricane."

I didn't want to debate the pros and cons of insurance companies. "The good news is, we believe Langley Insurance will cut a check very soon."

"I'll bet Monica and Eleanor are chilling champagne right now. Hey, maybe they'll come to my gig tonight. Sometimes they do, to show support for me. They're really cool."

It was clear Kissie had no clue Monica was missing and being held for ransom. That answered my most pressing concern. I didn't believe Kissie was responsible, but her past history had proven she sometimes hung out with unsavory characters.

"Kissie, have you noticed strangers around Briarcliff, or anyone asking questions about the estate or the Levert sisters?"

She took a deep breath. "You think my boyfriend is involved in the theft of the necklace, don't you?"

"I wasn't accusing anyone."

She picked at a string on her jeans. "I don't have much taste in men. I'll admit that. But I'd never do anything to hurt Eleanor or Monica. They've been like family to me."

Sometimes family committed the most grievous of sins, but I didn't go there. "Do you think your boyfriend could be involved?"

"No way. I'd kill him myself, and he knows it. Marty's selfish and full of himself, but he's not a thief. Music is his thing. He'd step on someone to get ahead, but he wouldn't steal from them."

"Does Marty have a last name?"

"Marty Herman." She rolled her eyes. "He goes by Marty Diamond. Herman doesn't sound like much of a country music name."

"Do you perform solo?" I asked.

She hesitated, and in that split second I saw a young woman who was not as self-assured as she pretended to be. "Most of the time I do, though sometimes I like to play with Marty."

"Does he write, too?"

"No. He sings my stuff. He's got a more commercial voice. He's going up to Nashville this fall and take my songs with him."

"You aren't going?"

She pushed up from the sofa. "Naw. I tried that once and it didn't work out so well for me. Marty can go and try his hand. He's a real ambitious man, and he knows how to talk with the star-makers. I'd just be a hindrance if he had to worry about me. What matters is that he takes my songs. He says I have a couple that some of the big stars might want to cover. Besides, I got responsibilities at Briarcliff."

If looks weren't deceiving, Kissie was an honest young woman with integrity. She also had somewhere to be. She'd checked her watch at least twice.

"Can you think of anyone who might want to harm the Levert sisters?"

"They piss off everyone, but it's all social stuff. Nothing big." She picked up her guitar. "Listen, I have to practice. Marty said there might be a record producer in the audience tonight."

I stood. "Thanks, Kissie. I have a friend coming into town tonight. Maybe we'll catch your act."

She brightened. "Great. I go on at nine. Just for a couple of sets."

"Country?"

"Kind of folksy blues and country all mixed together," she said.

"My friend is a journalist. If she likes what she hears, maybe she'll do a story."

I thought her face would split with a wide smile. "Thank you so much, Ms. Delaney. Good press is hard to come by, and every little bit helps. I'll call Monica and Eleanor and see if they want to come, too."

I didn't dissuade her. Eleanor would handle the invitation, and tonight, when Cece was there to ask interview questions, I hoped to learn more about Marty and possibly catch a glimpse of him. Kissie wasn't aware of Monica's disappearance, but that didn't mean that someone she knew, like the star-hungry Marty Diamond, wasn't involved.

8

The pleasures of shopping have always been lost on me, but I cowboyed up and went to a lovely little shop only a few blocks from the hotel to buy a blouse for my night out with Cece.

Juking requires a physical look as well as a pair of rotating hips. Months had passed since my friends and I ventured to Sunflower County's hot blues club, Playin' the Bones, but I hadn't forgotten how to dress for good times.

Cece and I were due for a bit of mischief, and while I was engaged to Graf and had the rock to prove it, Cece was footloose and fancy free. It would be fun to find her a man to date. Let me add that when Cece's fancy gets to shaking, anything can happen.

When she arrived a little after six, I was dressed in a

black, curve-hugging top with several interesting cutouts on the chest and back. I'd never really understood buying clothes with holes in them, but the blouse was half-price and it hugged all the right places.

"Graf would have you arrested in that, dahling," Cece said as she air-kissed both my cheeks.

"You're just jealous." She looked stunning herself in cowboy boots with red and turquoise insets, black jeans, and a red silk shirt that caught each movement in a soft shimmer of fabric.

Cece had once been Cecil Falcon, heir to the vast Falcon estate of land and a lineage dating back to the 1700s and the *Mayflower*. She'd thrown it all over to follow her biological destiny and surgically altered herself to conform to the female trapped inside. Her decision had cost her plenty—her inheritance, her family, and a cushy life. There's something to be said, though, for being your own person. Cece was that—and one of the best friends in the universe.

"I am jealous," I countered. "Your hips." I put a hand on either side of her waist. "No matter how thin I get, my hips will never look like yours in a pair of jeans."

"But you have other assets, dahling." Cece gave me a knowing look. "Graf has agreed to write a tell-all book describing those attributes in great detail as soon as he's famous."

I ignored the threat, because I knew Graf wasn't the kiss-and-tell kind of guy. When she was done teasing me, I told her about Kissie McClain. Cece agreed King's Tavern, though it was in the heart of downtown Natchez and not Under-the-Hill, was a good destination for dinner and entertainment. But first, we headed down the steep slope that was the bank of the Mississippi to a cluster of bars and eateries at the edge of the river. This was the current incarnation of Natchez-Under-the-Hill, a place with a reputation for wild fun. We parked and walked along the main street.

"This is pretty tame compared to what it used to be," Cece said as we passed bars, cafés, and restaurants lit with neon. Loud music poured out onto the summer evening. "Before the War of Northern Aggression, this was a hotbed of river pirates, thieves, conmen, and prostitutes. It's a bit upscale now."

She was right. Laughter rang out as a group of young people jostled out of a bar and onto the street. They linked arms and moved toward another nightspot. If there was danger about, they were oblivious to it.

"Not much criminal activity here," I agreed.

"It depends on what you consider criminal." Don Cipriano stepped out of the darkness. Once again he wore only black, making his figure hard to distinguish from the dense shadows cast by the building he stood beside.

"Oh, my," Cece said, faking a timid spirit, "it's the dark lord himself. I must say, sir, you've captured the essence of the tormented Byronic hero perfectly." She gave a genteel opera clap.

"A woman of literary pursuits." He stepped forward, grasped her hand, and brought it to his lips. Even Cece, who was well prepared for his gothic charm, was momentarily flustered.

"Give it up, Don. We're onto your game." I kept a safe distance. Even knowing he was a lying fake, I was still affected by his presence. The man had sex appeal oozing from his pores.

"Don Cipriano Viedma," Cece said. She'd regained her composure. "Character in *The Plumed Serpent*. A general in the Mexican army but not Spanish, as most officers were. He was of Indian extraction. A man doomed by his own beliefs, yet one with the sexual powers to subdue even the strongest woman. Willing surrender, I believe, is what Lawrence was writing about."

"Astute as well as beautiful," he said, completely un-ruffled by the fact we'd blown his cover. In fact, he was amused.

"So if you aren't Don Cipriano, who are you?" I asked. "Not a New Orleans antique shop owner."

"No, that was a fabrication. I'm Barclay Levert."

He was full of surprises. And lies. "Eleanor told me there's only one Levert here. Millicent Gentry, a cousin."

"Eleanor doesn't know about me."

"So you're a big secret? A wild branch on the Levert family tree." I didn't believe it for a moment. He looked like the Gypsy he claimed to be, not a Levert. "You were born to play that role."

"Other than my name and the tiny fabrication about an antique shop in New Orleans, I've told you the truth."

"If you truly were a Levert, I daresay Eleanor and Monica would know about you."

"Perhaps not Eleanor." He walked slowly around us. "But I'm a Levert. My mother gave me nothing, not even her family name, before she abandoned me. But my fa-ther knew who she was. He told me before he died."

I remembered the story he'd spun to me. "Your mother, an aristocrat, no doubt, abandoned you in the arms of your noble, Gypsy father who raised you single-handedly and against all odds. Right?" I hadn't believed it the first time and I certainly didn't believe him now. Cece looked at me as if I'd lost my mind, but Don Cipriano, aka Bar-clay Levert, only arched an eyebrow.

"All true," he said. "Monica could tell you the truth, if she would. But she won't. She never will. I'd bet she's never even told her sister about me."

"Wait a minute." I studied him in the dim light. There was the same smooth forehead, the widely spaced dark eyes, the full lips and straight nose. His skin tone was olive where the Levert sisters were pale as English roses. If he favored his father's Gypsy heritage, it was possible. "Who is your mother?"

"Monica."

"Impossible."

"Not at all. Monica was sailing along the Florida coast. I believe the boat belonged to one of her Palm Beach conquests. At twenty, she had many, many wealthy lovers. Anyway, she docked in a small inlet near Tarpon Springs. My father was a sponge diver. With this olive skin and black hair, he could pass for Greek. They met, Monica stayed for nearly a year with him. Then she left, without ever telling him her true name."

He cocked his head in a careless gesture. "Lucky for me, my father checked the boat registration, tracked it back to the man Monica *borrowed* it from, and figured out who the mother of his son was. But she wanted nothing to do with either of us. When she left, she desired no reminder of the year she'd spent with my father and her son. Not a pretty story, but true."

"I don't believe it," I said so hotly Cece put a hand on my arm to restrain me. "You're a liar."

"That I am." His open enjoyment of my outrage made me want to slap him. "But I'm not lying about this. Monica Levert is my mother. I'd say ask her, but she'll lie. You're left with only my word—and my total willingness to submit to a DNA test."

Monica couldn't answer his accusation, and I wondered if he knew this. "Eleanor has no idea you exist?"

"I doubt Monica shared that particular bit of history. At the time, I believe Eleanor was in Italy with her own sexual pursuits. They're both narcissistic women, but of the two, I prefer Eleanor. She has more human qualities. My mother would probably have eaten me for breakfast had my father not intervened."

"Very interesting that you turn up now, just when a valuable necklace has been stolen." Cece joined the fray. "How long have you been in town?"

"Three weeks."

"But you—" I started.

"I checked into the Eola yesterday. Before that . . ." His eyes sparked with devilment. "I had other accommodations." He'd applied his many sexual talents and earned a place in someone's bed. Even a fool could see that Barclay Levert, or whoever he might be, worked on women. Cece might label him a Byronic hero, but I knew him for exactly what he was—a bad boy. He exuded the charm, the heartache, the promise of "I can be fixed if only you'll love me enough." Total hogwash.

"Why are you here, in Natchez?" I asked.

"To claim my birthright."

"By means fair or foul?" Cece asked.

I wanted to stomp her foot. Her phrasing was archaic, as though we lived in the nineteenth century. She was still caught up in the Heathcliff thing.

"By whatever means necessary." His chuckle was as soft as a touch, and as intimate. "You would do the same. Both of you. The facts of my birth were beyond my control. My father would have married Monica. He loved her. When she disappeared one day without even a note, he ultimately honored her desire to be rid of us. He sought her out once and was rebuffed, and after that he never tried to involve her in our lives, never asked for help for my clothes or food or education. He was an honorable man."

"But you are not," I said.

"No. I am not." He moved toward me so swiftly I didn't have time to react. He grasped my arms and pulled me so that my face was only an inch from his lips. His very sensual lips. "I am not honorable, I am angry. Furious. My father died in pain, without medical care, because we couldn't afford it. Monica has all the money in the world, and my father couldn't afford good doctors." He held me tightly and leaned so close I could feel the pressure of his words on my face. "I am angry, and I have every right to be." He let me go so suddenly I almost fell. It was as if he'd melted my bones.

Cece's arm wrapped around my waist to support me. "I'm sorry for all you've lost," she said, "but that isn't Monica's responsibility. You're a little old for child support now."

"I'm her son. I didn't ask to be born. What does she owe me?"

Cece sighed. "First you have to prove you're related. DNA can do that. Have you had a test?"

The streetlight shimmered in his wavy hair as he nodded. "I don't have any of Monica's DNA and I don't know how to get any."

"A court can order a test," Cece said.

"I hoped Monica would give it willingly. I've been waiting for the opportunity to ask."

"That's convenient," I said as endless possibilities

came to mind. Barclay's revelations had thrown the case into a totally new light. What if he'd abducted Monica for a DNA sample and was holding her until the results came back?

"I'd hoped once she met me, she'd want to know me." He paused a beat. "Or perhaps you could get a DNA sample for me. Hair from a brush, a toothbrush. You have access to the house and everything in it."

"I don't steal from my clients," I said hotly.

"Not even for the sake of justice?"

His question stopped me. In my heart of hearts, I did believe Monica owed him something—if she was truly his mother. People shouldn't run around dropping babies like sacks of laundry and leaving them behind. There was a duty to a child, an obligation that went something to the effect that if a life was brought into the world, the people responsible for creating the baby also had responsibility for caring for him or her. If Barclay was telling the truth, Monica had violated him in a way many people never recover from.

"And why should I believe you?" I countered.

"It's easy enough to determine the truth," he said. "I'd be a fool to lie about it and then come here in search of DNA evidence."

"He has a point." Cece's gaze moved from his dimple to his broad shoulders. It wasn't hard to guess what thoughts were flying around in her head; I could almost hear the "boom, chicka, boom" sound track for a bad 70s porn flick. I used my hip to nudge her back to reality.

"He *does* have a point," she insisted, irritated that I'd interrupted her fantasy.

"Following the family tradition of legally changing

my name, I am indeed a Levert. I have a right to my inheritance." The anger was building again. Barclay Levert had a lot of issues and a short fuse. Was he capable of violence? I couldn't say for certain.

My theories on how inherited wealth ruined most kids would be of no interest to Barclay. He wanted what was his, and he had yet to come to the realization that what he most desired—his mother's love—could never be demanded or legally awarded in a court of law. Monica had cheated him greatly, and it could never be redressed. For that, I could find pity for him. Cece, who'd undergone a similar emotional battering by her unaccepting family, would relate even more.

"Monica and Eleanor don't have to give you anything," I pointed out.

He considered what I said. "I know that. But I believe the Levert name means much to them. I am Monica's son, a true Levert, whether she wants to acknowledge me or not."

"Have you spoken to her?" Cece asked.

"I was hoping for the DNA proof first. That's why I approached Miss Delaney and Mrs. Richmond in the Eola bar. I heard they were working for the sisters on the missing necklace. Gossip in Natchez is like the wind. My intent was to ask them to help me."

"But you didn't. You said you were some strange fictional character," I pointed out.

"I didn't sense a willingness to hear me out."

"Sarah Booth and Tinkie can be pretty pigheaded at times," Cece cut in.

"So Monica has no idea you're in town?" I asked.

"She doesn't. I've followed the sisters—from a distance. I admit it. I saw them in the tearoom the other day waiting for you and your partner. I watched them for a long time, but I didn't approach."

"And what do you know of Briarcliff?" I asked.

"I know the stories." He offered the crook of an arm to each of us. "Shall we stroll? Let's find a quiet place to sit and talk. I'd like to buy you a drink. I need your help, and I'm not too proud to ask for it."

Cece attached herself without a qualm. Her hand caressed his biceps and she gave me a look that said, "Watch out, this bad boy has met his match."

I almost felt sorry for Barclay. Almost. Reluctantly I tucked my hand through his other arm and we set off for the far end of the street.

"Bennator's is quiet. We can finish this conversation without interruption," he said as he escorted us to the quaint little restaurant. The place was dark, quiet, and perfect for conversation. This wasn't a hangout for the young or tourists. This was a place where locals could drink quietly and hold a discussion.

We found a table in the back. Barclay settled into a chair and then glanced from me to Cece. "I'm going to tell you the truth," he said. "It isn't pretty, but it's all I have."

An hour later, I'd learned more about the tortured Levert lineage than I ever wanted to know. No one has more interest in family history than a member who's been shut out. Barclay had devoted endless hours researching Barthelme Levert and his offspring. He was determined to claim his place in the family and demand acceptance, with or without the money. He longed to be part of something from which he'd been denied. Even my cold, hard heart was dented by the cards he'd been dealt.

"The enjoyable thing about Barthelme is that no matter how bad I am, he will always be worse," Barclay said.

"Now that's inspirational." I hoped Cece would heed the warning, but it was clear to see Barclay had captivated her. They shared many of the same wounds—always a dangerous link of compatibility.

What I'd learned in our conversation was that Barclay wasn't aware Monica was missing. No one in town seemed to be. Based on what I knew of small towns, that wasn't normal. If word got out that a wealthy heiress—especially one as controversial as Monica, was missing—the talk should be flying.

"I'm going to Briarcliff tomorrow and demand DNA," Barclay said. "I wanted to wait, hoping to meet my mother and her sister and win them over. But that isn't happening. I'll have to force the issue, so I might as well get it done."

That was a bad idea. The sight of Barclay might unsettle Eleanor to the point she'd reveal too much. Before I could dissuade him, Cece piped up.

"I like a man who knows what he wants and goes after it." She wasn't exactly slurring her words, but she was tipsy. She leaned toward Barclay's shoulder, and he shifted to give her support.

It was time for fresh air, food, and a date with Kissie McClain. Cece wasn't normally the kind of drinker who let a few rounds lay waste to her. "Let's go, party girl." I slipped an arm around her.

Barclay came to my assistance. I was about to tell him I could manage when Cece poked my ribs. I yelped and jumped backward, and she fell completely into his embrace.

"Are you going to faint?" Barclay asked. If he was aware of her ruse, he was too much the gentleman to call her out on it.

"I think I may." She flung her head back, exposing her long, bare throat.

"Perhaps I can revive you." Barclay kissed the pulse point in her neck. Cece's eyes flew wide open. Behind his back, she waved me away.

"I'll meet you at King's Tavern," I said. Far be it from me to stand in the way of true lust. Both Barclay and Cece knew the rules of the game they'd engaged in.

I eased around the table and was walking to the door when it opened on a lanky man in jeans, a Western shirt, boots, and a cowboy hat. Barclay saw him and forgot all about the woman in his arms. He assisted Cece to her feet, but his total focus was on the man. He deposited Cece on a chair and moved toward the cowboy with intent. He stopped when he was almost in the man's face.

"Who the hell is that?" Cece asked, completely sober. Her arms akimbo, she looked aggravated.

"Hush!" I wanted to hear whatever exchange passed between the men.

"I know what you're up to," Barclay said as he squared off, blocking the cowboy's path. "You are a bastard."

"I'm gonna send you straight to hell," the stranger said before he whipped around and left the bar.

"Excuse me, ladies." Barclay took off in pursuit.

"Who was that?" Cece delicately dabbed at a sheen of perspiration on her forehead.

"I don't know, but we definitely need to find out."

We rushed out the door of the bar, but when we got to the street, it was completely empty. Music pulsed in the distance. The slot machines on the riverboat casino docked below us *dinged* faintly on the humid night. Barclay and the stranger had vanished like spirits on the wind.

9

If the barkeep in Bennator's knew the strange man, he wasn't telling, not even when Cece flashed cash in front of him. Barclay never returned, so we drove to King's Tavern. It was almost time for Kissie's first set.

Tinkie and I had visited King's Tavern on the haunted tour of Natchez. One of the city's oldest structures, dating back to the late 1700s, the building had served not only as a restaurant and inn, but also a post office.

After we took our seats, I filled Cece in on the ghost of Madeline, a young woman and mistress of the tavern owner, Richard King. Madeline was a beautiful girl, and local legend said she was murdered by King's wife and bricked into the fireplace. A female skeleton, along with two males, had been found there along with a jeweled dagger. The identity of the two male skeletons was never resolved.

"I'm sure Madeline is still around." Cece waved a hand, mocking the story. "She's probably lurking in some creepy corner, waiting to give you a whispery touch."

"The bed upstairs does have a warm place where it's said she slept. And some staffers have seen footprints appear on a freshly mopped floor." I laid out the evidence, but I didn't try to convince Cece of ghosts. Some lessons can only be learned, not taught.

Cece put her napkin on her lap and sighed. "I know you're trying to divert me from the fact Barclay is very attractive."

The possibility of spirits couldn't compete with a big hunk of manly corporeal flesh. "He is. He's also a liar with anger issues."

Cece heard me; she just wasn't interested in my observations. "He didn't appear to know about Monica's abduction."

"Like I said, he's a liar. And he's not stupid. One thing I failed to ask is how he makes a living. But I think we both know. He sponges off women."

"A gigolo." Cece straightened the flatware on the table, though it was perfectly aligned.

"That would be my guess."

"Gigolos can be a lot of fun." Her focus stayed riveted on the table.

"As long as you accept what he is and don't expect more. I just don't want to see you hurt." Cece was smitten. I'd known Barclay would intrigue her, but I never thought she'd fall so hard and so fast. I felt responsible.

"What would you be like, Sarah Booth, if your parents hadn't loved you? If your mother had run away and disappeared? If your family made it clear they had no use for you?"

"I can't answer that. I agree Barclay has a right to be angry but not to steal or kidnap."

"Do you have proof he's responsible for either act?"

Her defensiveness told me how deep she was already in. Cece had embarked on a kamikaze mission of love. "I don't. And I hope I don't find evidence he's involved. Believe it or not, Cece, I like Barclay. He is . . . charismatic, to say the least. But if he's a criminal, he'll have to pay the price."

She nodded. "And if he isn't, then he deserves to be acknowledged as a legitimate Levert heir."

"And that's something neither of us can guarantee."

A hush fell over the restaurant. Kissie walked onstage with a stool and an acoustic guitar. She perched on the stool and adjusted a microphone.

"Welcome to King's Tavern," she said. "My name is Kissie McClain, and I'm performing some songs I wrote. Tonight, I'm happy to say I'll have some help. Please welcome Marty Diamond."

Polite applause spread around the restaurant. I shifted my chair for a better view and then nearly fell out of it when the stranger from Bennator's sauntered on the stage with a microphone.

Kissie strummed her guitar and they started a duet about the Mississippi River and a star-crossed love. The song was beautiful, but my attention was fixed on Marty Diamond. He was a handsome man, though a bit sullen for my taste.

His dark hair was professionally cut to look untended. His piercing gray eyes and a chiseled jawline said if his singing career failed, he could model. Not much worry there, the man had a lovely voice, a perfect accompaniment to Kissie and the love ballad she'd composed.

Cece leaned close. "Do you think Barclay has been sleeping with Kissie?"

And I knew then where Barclay had spent his first three weeks in Natchez. Cece hit the nail on the head. A lot of things clicked in my brain. Kissie knew Briarcliff in and out. The house, the grounds, the sisters' routine. Where the necklace was kept. Yet Kissie hadn't known Monica was missing—which made me wonder if Barclay had duped her into complicity.

"Sarah Booth, is Barclay sleeping with that singer?" Cece thumped my leg with her foot.

"My best guess would be yes." As much as I wanted to spare Cece any hurt, I had to be honest. If Barclay and Kissie were working together, they were a dangerous duo—in more ways than one.

"I don't believe it." Cece's chin lifted, a sure sign a good case of the stubborns had set in.

"You don't have to believe it, until I find proof. Just use caution around Barclay. If he's in this with Kissie, he's smart." I remembered what Coleman Peters, the sheriff of Sunflower County and a former beau, had once said about the low intellect of most common criminals. They were caught because they weren't very bright and couldn't keep their mouths shut about their crimes. Many, many criminals were turned in by jilted lovers or betrayed spouses.

The flip side of Coleman's observations was that smart criminals were difficult to catch. They seldom talked, trusting no one with their secrets.

"How will you find proof?" Cece had come to help me, but I'd have to drag her kicking and screaming to the conclusion of Barclay's guilt.

"I'll ask Marty Diamond." If Barclay had seduced Kissie into helping him rip off the Leverts, Marty might have plenty to say about the would-be dark lord of Briarcliff.

"I want to hear this," Cece said.

Why not? She was a journalist with great interview skills and a knack for asking tough questions. "Let's waylay him after this set."

"Your wish is my command."

For the moment she was diverted from Barclay, and that could only be a good thing.

We ate our dinner and listened to the performance. Kissie had some great songs, and Marty Diamond had the voice and stage presence to render them effective. Kissie's voice was good, but Marty brought magic to the music. He could sell a song. With a couple of stanzas and a few smiles and winks, he won the audience.

"Why isn't he in Nashville?" Cece asked.

Something told me the answer had everything to do with Kissie McClain.

The first set went without incident. The musicians took a fifteen-minute break and came back to conclude to a packed house. As they took their last bows, Cece and I paid up and went outside to wait. After twenty minutes, I left Cece guarding the parking lot while I went back inside to look for Marty.

The waitress pointed me upstairs where I'd visited the bedroom with the warm spots on the bed. To be honest, it was slightly creepy upstairs, and I braced for Jitty to pop out just for a laugh. I didn't hear anything until I got to the top of the steps.

A man and a woman raged at each other in an emotional argument. I couldn't understand what they were saying, so I did the only logical thing—moved closer to the shut door.

"You're being played for a fool." I would bet a small fortune the speaker was Marty Diamond.

"That's a damn lie," a female said. "I know what I'm doing. This is for us. We can go to Nashville with a cushion."

"I wouldn't bet on it. You have a felony conviction. If this goes south, no judge or jury will believe a word you say."

Heavy footsteps approached the door and I jumped back. Marty pulled the door open and halted, staring at me. "What do you want?" His face was flushed with anger.

"I need to speak with you."

"People in hell need ice water." He pushed me aside and clattered down the stairs.

Kissie came to the doorway, fright and desperation still on her face. "I saw you in the audience."

"I have questions for you—"

Her expression betrayed nothing. "Leave me alone." She picked up her guitar and brushed past me. "I don't have time for this."

The night was balmy for summer, and Cece wasn't ready for bed. Though it wasn't yet midnight, Natchez had basically shut down. The nightspots Under-the-Hill were still in full swing, but a drowsy quiet had settled over the rest of the town. Cece went to the Eola bar for a final nightcap, but I was done in. I went straight to my room and called Graf. It wasn't late in Tinseltown, and I needed to hear his voice.

"How are things in Zinnia?" he asked. Billie Holiday sang in the background. Graf loved her music, and whenever he was lonely, he put Billie on.

Guilt hit me like a sledgehammer. My fiancé was in a city where beautiful young women were a dime a dozen, yet he was alone. Not to mention I'd conveniently forgotten Graf was completely unaware I was on a case. The truth had to be told.

"I'm in Natchez. Cece is here, too, but she's down in the Eola bar."

"And you're safely in your room," he said, teasing me gently.

"Absolutely. Cece is a free agent, but my heart is taken." Even as I said the words I felt like a cad. I wouldn't betray Graf with another man, but was taking a case deception enough?

"Is Cece working on a story in Natchez?" Graf jumped to the best possible reason for my presence in the river city.

"She's keeping me company. Tinkie and I took an insurance case. Stolen necklace." Well, maybe not the whole truth.

Billie wailed about her lover man, and time ticked by in silence.

"This is what I do, Graf."

"I know," he said. "I do understand. It's just that I want you to be safe."

"And I love that. " We weren't on different pages, we just had different needs. "This won't be dangerous." The skin on the back of my neck prickled. I turned around, expecting to see Jitty behind me, but no one was there. Aunt Loulane would say someone had walked over my grave. It was a disturbing thought.

"I've given this a lot of thought," he said, "and it isn't right for me to ask you to give up what you love, but I can't promise I can endure a lot more. When you put yourself in the line of fire, you take my heart along with you. If you keep getting hurt and scaring me . . . if I feel I'm going to lose you to some crazed individual, I'm afraid I'll make myself stop caring, Sarah Booth. Not because I want to, but because I have to protect myself."

"I don't want to be hurt, and I don't want to hurt you. I love you, but I have to feel free to live. I promise I'll be careful."

"Keep yourself safe. If it looks dangerous, promise me you'll walk away."

My relief was immense. Graf wasn't going to issue an ultimatum or ask me to change my life. He would try to accept it, and it was up to me to safeguard his heart. Even though I was tired, I wanted to dance around the room. "You have my word. Now, want to hear about the Levert sisters and their blackguard ancestor, Barthelme Levert?"

"Tell me a story," Graf said.

And I did. We talked for nearly an hour. I filled him in on Natchez history and the things I'd learned in my short stay there. I hung up happy.

When my cell phone rang again, I thought it was Graf with another good-night kiss. "Forget something, baby?"

"It's Eleanor. I got another call from the kidnappers." She rushed on. "I heard Monica crying in the background. The man said they would hurt her if I didn't get the insurance money."

My good mood evaporated. "Was the voice familiar?"

"It sounded like the same person who called before."

"Eleanor, please reconsider calling the police. They

can tap your phone and trace these calls. They might be able to locate Monica."

"No!" Her will was iron. "I will not endanger my sister over mere money. I'll collect the insurance money tomorrow. I'll give it to him. Every cent of it."

"Will Langley Insurance pay out that fast?" I'd never actually worked an insurance case, but I'd assumed it would take months to get a company to fork over so much money.

"They will, or they will suffer the consequences. My sister's life hangs in the balance. I can cash out some stocks, but I can't raise enough to free Monica without the insurance settlement. Monica and I . . . aren't liquid."

So without the insurance money, she couldn't ransom her sister. The kidnapper was someone who knew the sisters' business far too well. Not a coincidence, I was willing to bet. "What else did he say?"

"He'll call tomorrow with instructions for the drop. Have you and Mrs. Richmond found anything useful?"

I should have informed her about Barclay, but I wasn't certain he was truly related. "Did Monica ever live in West Palm Beach and sail?"

"Why are you asking this now?"

"It may relate. Just work with me."

"When she was very young she met an architect. He was an avid sailor, and he taught her. She sailed around the tip of Florida and into the Gulf, where she stayed for a while."

So far, Barclay's story jibed. "What do you know about her time in Tarpon Springs?"

"What's this about?" she asked.

I took a deep breath. "There's a man in town claiming to be her son." I didn't want to tell her over the phone, but she would hear it sooner rather than later. Gossip could, and often did, travel faster than the speed of light. Barclay was not a presence anyone could ignore.

"That's the most ridiculous thing I've ever heard. Monica never had a child."

"Is it possible? This man claims she lived near Tampa for nearly a year. Once she gave birth, she left—or that's the story he's telling."

"I would certainly know if my sister had a child. This man is a liar. And you say he's in Natchez? Now? Is he behind Monica's abduction?"

"I intend to find out. I promise you." My grip on the phone made my knuckles white. I relaxed my hand. "He wants a DNA test. He's asked me to gather a sample of Monica's from you. A hair from her brush. Her toothbrush. Something that can be tested."

"Are you working for him or for us?" Eleanor snapped.

"For you," I said quietly. I understood her fury. "It's the simplest way to disprove his claim, if it isn't true."

"Monica can give him a sample when we get her back. It's her choice. Not mine."

"Eleanor, I'm not saying this is the case, but it's very strange that all at the same time, someone has been breaking into Briarcliff for the past several weeks. A necklace is stolen. Your sister is taken, *and* a man claiming to be an heir shows up in town."

There was a pause. "Do you think these events are connected?"

"I honestly don't know. But we can't discount they may be. We really need to validate or disprove Barclay's claim. Besides, if he is Monica's son, it in no way obligates you to view him as an heir."

"I'll think about it."

I didn't push it. There was no point. Eleanor was upset. Maybe by morning she'd come to her senses and see the best way to deal with Barclay was head on.

"Did you record your phone conversation with the kidnapper?" This whole business made me nutty. Monica had been missing for twenty-four hours. The kidnapper seemed in no hurry, as if he knew obtaining the insurance money would take a bit of time even with the pressure the Leverts could apply. I hoped Eleanor might recognize the voice.

"He caught me unprepared. I didn't get the equipment yet."

I closed my eyes against the frustration. Eleanor had promised she'd buy a recording device for her phone. I would pick one up in the morning and deliver it, but it wouldn't recapture the last call.

"Is there anything about the voice you recognize? Think hard."

"Definitely Southern. Almost as if his drawl was exaggerated. Like he was mocking the way we talk here." Her voice grew excited. "Does that help?"

"Delta accent? North Mississippi? Coastal?" There are distinctions between the regions that someone attuned to nuances can detect. Eleanor would definitely recognize the faintest whiff of commonness.

"He could be from Natchez. I can't be certain."

"Would you know his voice if you heard it again?"

"Oh, yes. Absolutely."

If we ever got him in custody, Eleanor might be able to put him behind bars for a long, long time. But that was a mighty big if.

"Write down everything he said, exactly as he said it. I'll pick it up tomorrow morning."

"I hate the thought of Monica held captive another night." Eleanor sounded weepy.

"I don't have the experience to advise you on this. If we mess this up, Monica could be seriously hurt." She would likely be killed, but stating the obvious wasn't necessary. Eleanor was hanging on to her composure by a thread.

"He said if I called the police, he'd gut Monica and throw her in the river for the gar to eat."

This guy was definitely local. The Mississippi River alligator gar, a species of fish with numerous teeth and a body armored with tough scales, were legendary in appetite and bite. "What time did he call?"

"About ten minutes ago. I called you as soon as I hung up."

So he'd waited until he reasoned Eleanor would be asleep, hoping for the advantage startling her would give him. So far, it was working.

"I'll check with the insurance company tomorrow," I said.

"The police chief came by this afternoon. He wanted to know if Monica had come home and I fed him a story about how she'd gone to New York City and forgot to tell me. I got rid of him as quickly as I could."

She was obviously worried the kidnappers would think she'd gone against orders. "Was he satisfied with that?"

"For the moment. Have you made any progress determining who might have taken my sister?"

"Some, but nothing definite. I interviewed Millicent, John Hightower, Helena Banks Gorenflo, and Kissie. They each have something to gain, but I can't point the finger of blame at any of them. Not yet."

"You can find her, Ms. Delaney. I know you can. I'm counting on you."

And that was the problem.

10

The next morning, I spent more time than usual applying makeup in an effort to cover the damage of a tormented night. In a vivid dream, I'd been a helpless bystander while Monica was held in chains in a dungeon—a good, old-fashioned Sheriff of Nottingham dungeon with a torturer in a black mask, red-hot pokers to jab into her eyes, thumbscrews, and all the other trappings. Things were damn dire for her, and Robin Hood wasn't around to save the day. The nightmare had been so vivid, my need to save Monica so pressing, I'd awakened trying to run in bed. The sheets looked as if I'd deliberately tied them in knots.

Showered and with a thick coat of foundation hiding some of the dark bags, I was happy to leave the scene of my delusions.

Cece was waiting for me when I called her room, and she was eager to relay her nocturnal activities—ones far different from my own. We met in the hallway. She rolled her eyes. "Dahling, the only movie part you'll get today is as the reanimated dead. What's wrong?"

At our table in the hotel restaurant, I told her about Eleanor's call and her unwillingness to involve experts to save her sister.

"This whole kidnapping thing is playing out in slow motion, and it doesn't make sense," she said. "Eleanor acts like she's in a trance. Maybe she doesn't watch television, but she should know the longer this drags out, the less likely Monica will survive." She threw up her hands. "Even the kidnapper isn't in a hurry. There's absolutely no sense of urgency."

"I get the feeling the Levert fortune has slowed everything down. In their world, it's rude to rush. Even a kidnapping." It sounded ridiculous, but Cece understood what I meant. The extremely rich had a different relationship with time. Things happened at a speed that suited them, and the kidnapper had demanded a huge ransom. The only good news was that Eleanor had heard Monica in the background, which meant she was still alive. Of course, her voice could have been tape-recorded and played back.

"I'm in over my head," I confided to Cece. "This isn't following any playbook I know. It seems to me the kidnapper has to be someone close to Eleanor or Monica." I pushed my toast around the saucer. "Lots of people can't accept their friends will hurt them. Then again, the Levert sisters don't appear to have a tremendous number of friends."

"True. I had no idea how deeply the sisters are loathed

until last night." Her lively expression told me she'd come across something good.

"What did you get up to after I went to bed?"

She signaled the waitress for more coffee. "I thought Barclay might show up in the hotel bar. He didn't, so I entertained myself with someone else."

Cece had her ways, and the idea she'd replaced Barclay in her affections made me heave a sigh of relief. "And?"

"Monica Levert wasn't particular about trespassing."

"Meaning she stomped around on someone's fenced property or she tampered with someone's husband?"

"She seems to relish rustling other people's bulls. It's habitual conduct. She's built a career of pilfering the men attached to her social peers." Cece sipped the fresh, hot coffee and sighed with pleasure. "I met a man last night. Wayne Griffin. From Nashville. He's still suffering from his moment of bliss with Monica and still coming back to Natchez in the hope he'll see her out somewhere. Luckily he has a weakness for good Scotch and a sympathetic ear."

"In other words, you plied him with liquor and pumped him."

"I haven't forgotten the tactics of being a man, dahling." Cece arched her eyebrows. "He wasn't a cheap date, let me say, but it was worth it. I solicited great info. Monica tied him in knots and then dropped him. His wife got the house, the kids, and six grand a month in alimony."

"Six grand? He must print money. Doctor or lawyer?"

"Insurance. He writes policies for the country music stars."

"I hope the affair was worth it." Talk about a lifetime of pain for momentary pleasure.

"He said it was well worth it. Believe it or not, he had no regrets."

The surprise must have shown on my face. Most men enjoyed a good romp, but when it impacted their pocketbooks, remorse was generally intense.

"He said Monica turned him inside out. He would have given up everything for her." Cece sipped a mimosa. "Still would. He said if she gave him another chance, he'd walk away from everything. She made him feel incredible, like he was the best lover in the world."

"Did he say what she did?" If Monica had a secret move that could make a man throw over his money, I wanted to know what it was. The waitress brought our shrimp grits and biscuits. My mouth watered to the point I almost embarrassed myself.

"He said she had no boundaries." Cece daintily tasted her grits. "These are heavenly. There's just enough spice in the shrimp to complement the sharp cheese. Excellent."

"What does that mean? No boundaries."

She took a bite of biscuit. "He wouldn't say."

"What a freaking tease." I dug into my food.

"He promised to show me. Tonight."

"What about Barclay?" My spirits rose. She'd thrown over the idea of romancing the bad boy, even if it meant having a fling with an adulterer who bled green every time he paid his alimony.

"I haven't given up on Barclay. Once I learn what Wayne has to show me, I'm going to turn Barclay inside out. He'll tell me every secret he ever thought of having, and I'll have my way with him."

I wisely kept silent and sipped my orange juice. Cece, like all my friends, was impossible to dissuade once she'd set a course. The best plan was to put Barclay behind bars for burglary and kidnapping—if he was guilty—and safely out of her reach. "So what did Mr. Griffin say about Monica other than she was hot in bed?"

"That she was the most selfish person he'd ever met." She put her fork down. "According to him, all the women in town hate her. His words, 'There are dozens of society ladies who might pay to have her abducted. Permanently.'" She made sure no one was eavesdropping on us before she continued. "Is it possible the ransom is just a ruse to cover up a murder?"

My gut twisted at her words. "I hadn't considered that, but I will now." Cece had just put another boiling kettle on the back burner of my brain. "Is Eleanor held in the same low regard?"

"She's managed to keep her paws off the husbands of her friends, so she isn't despised like Monica, but there's no love lost for her, either. The Levert sisters are viewed as arrogant and entitled. The redeeming grace, at least from the male perspective, is Monica's . . . shall we say, sexual talent."

"If Aunt Loulane were around, she'd tell Monica a smart woman doesn't shit in her own nest."

"I don't think Aunt Loulane would tell her anything. Your aunt had too much class to associate with Monica." Cece popped the last bite of biscuit in her mouth. "So what's on the agenda for today?"

"Don't you have to show up at the newspaper?" Cece had a lax work situation because the publisher knew she'd bird-dog a story until she brought it home no matter how many hours overtime she worked. Nonetheless, Cece normally appeared at the office at some point during the day.

"I promised Tinkie I'd keep an eye on you. I took a vacation leave."

Cece's holidays were valuable. Giving one up was a supreme sacrifice for friendship. "Thanks. Let's make the day count, then. We need to track down Marty Diamond, but first we have to stop by Langley Insurance and see when Eleanor can expect her settlement."

Cece pushed back from the table. Her gaze swept the room, and I wondered if she scanned for Barclay. He was nowhere in evidence. Which made me relieved but also worried. He could be up to anything nefarious.

I'd signed the check when my phone rang. It was a number I didn't know. I answered as Cece and I walked through the wonderful old lobby toward the parking lot. I instantly recognized the soft burr of the Leverts' gardener's voice and I touched Cece's arm to halt her.

"Miss Delaney, it's Jerome Lolly. We had an intruder out here at Briarcliff last night."

"Did you call the police?"

"I haven't told anyone. Miss Eleanor is so . . . agitated already, what with the necklace stolen and Miss Monica taking off without a word to anyone. I spooked the intruder and he left, so I waited until morning to call you."

"Can you identify the intruder?" I felt a shiver of apprehension. Had the kidnapper come back? Was he after Eleanor, too, or was he merely trying to intimidate her?

Jerome cleared his throat. "I don't want to sound like a kook, but it was a man wearing some kind of goggles, hiding in the bushes, watching the house."

"Did you recognize him?" The kidnapper knew every step Eleanor took, so it was logical he was watching

Briarcliff—and her. But to do so on the property was bold. No wonder he knew when the house was empty and vulnerable. Jerome had given me the best lead.

"I couldn't get close enough. I caught a glimpse of his face, with the goggles, in the moonlight. I tried to sneak up on him, but he must have heard me coming. Or seen me. He was gone by the time I got there."

"Night-vision goggles," I said.

"Very likely. This is a rogue at work. The police should be called in."

I had to stall him until Eleanor agreed. "I'll meet you at Briarcliff and you can show me where the intruder was." I put my phone away. "Time to get hopping. Jerome found an intruder spying on the house last night."

"Oh, goody," Cece said, pretending to clap her hands. "This case has everything, Sarah Booth. Stolen jewelry, a family of thieves and killers, a secret baby, a kidnapping, sexual misconduct, and now a spy. It just doesn't get any better than this."

While I drove to Briarcliff, Cece rode shotgun and chatted on her cell phone with a colleague at the Natchez newspaper. I'd left a message for Mr. Nesbitt at Langley Insurance to get back with me. He wouldn't be in until eleven.

Cece closed her phone and high fived me. "I got Marty Diamond's address. Folks who want to be singing stars give up a lot of their privacy. My friend at the Natchez paper knew all about him."

"Did she say anything interesting?" Reporters often knew more than they ever printed.

"He got in some trouble when he was a teenager, fist fighting, that kind of thing. Jassine said it was normal kid stuff. When he found he could sing, he left the fighting behind. His one goal has been to hit it big as a country star. Jassine said he was 'walking ambition.' "

"Did she say anything about Kissie?"

"Jassine likes Kissie and Marty. She says they're going places in the music world, but they need each other. Her take is Marty could never find better, more original material than what Kissie writes. And Kissie won't find a singer who delivers better than Marty."

"A match made in heaven. Or hell."

"Marty has a cabin on the edge of the national forest." She tapped her notebook. "Directions."

A perfect place to hold a hostage. "Great. Let's tend to the goggle-eyed snooper first and then head out to talk with Marty."

We pulled up in front of Briarcliff. Cece studied the house. A storm was building to the west, and with the morning sun coming up behind the mansion, the whole place was cast in a peculiar, disconcerting light.

"Was the monster's name Frankenstein, or was that his creator?" she asked.

"Both," I said.

"This is one creepy place." She walked along the driveway parallel to the house. "There must be fifty rooms."

At least, but I didn't say anything.

"Have you searched the house to make sure Monica isn't here?"

The thought had never occurred to me. "Like she wasn't abducted? Like she's hiding in there?"

Cece laughed. "No, like she was taken hostage but never removed from the property. Think about it. How hard would it be to snatch her, knock her out with a little chloroform, and hide her in one of the rooms?"

She had a point. "I'll make sure Eleanor checked the house thoroughly."

"A lot of these old plantation houses had cisterns, too. You might be sure someone explored the grounds."

"Jerome Lolly, whom you'll meet in a moment, is in charge of the grounds, and I think he's very capable."

"Except when it comes to spies hiding in bushes." Cece was teasing, but on a certain level she was hammering a point.

Jerome rounded the corner of the house looking as sleepless as I felt. We followed him to the front lawn, where a disturbance in the shrubs was clearly evident. In a fine old noir movie, there would be a cigarette butt, coffee cup, or sandwich wrapper—some evidence of a watcher passing time. At Briarcliff, nothing was that simple. Only a few snapped twigs indicated someone had worked their way into the dense branches of the shrubbery.

"Tell me what you saw last night," I said.

"The man was crouched down. It was the moonlight glinting off the goggles he wore that caught my eye."

"Night-vision gear," Cece said. "He was serious about watching the house."

"Damn pervert," Jerome said, "spying on helpless women."

The Levert sisters were far from helpless. In the town's perception, they were dangerous. "Have you spoken to Eleanor this morning?"

"No. She can't take much more of this. Aren't you being paid to take care of these things?"

"In a word, no!" Cece stepped in front of me. "Sarah Booth was hired to handle an insurance investigation, not a—"

I signaled her to hush. Jerome knew Monica was missing, but he wasn't aware it was a kidnapping and that a ransom had been demanded.

"Hey!" She coughed and caught her breath, and her reasoning. "Anyway, Sarah Booth is doing everything she can."

Jerome rubbed his face. "Sorry, ladies. I was out of line." His gaze shifted to the house. "The sisters act like they're invincible, but they aren't. They've behaved badly in Natchez, but the town brought it on itself. Folks were cruel to both sisters, because they were beautiful and had money. Jealousy and envy. That's what's at the root of all this."

"We've heard some harsh things about the sisters. Monica in particular," I said.

Color rushed into his face. "Monica hurts people. At first, she did it to strike back at those who'd hurt her. Now she does it because she can. She never wanted those men. She wanted to show everyone in town she could have them—that she can have whatever she sets her cap for. And she can. She's powerful when she makes up her mind. But there's another side to it. Monica is getting older. Beauty, like roses, fades. She's more than aware her power is diminishing. It's a sad thing to witness, like the ruin of a monarch."

Thunder rumbled overhead, as ominous as the house itself. "Are you in love with Monica?" I asked.

"Monica . . . I understand her." The color in his face deepened. "The sisters are two halves of a whole. Monica is the strength. Eleanor is the softer side. They're a pair." His hand slashed the air. "There's no separating them. Neither man nor God can accomplish that."

Yet someone had.

Jerome grasped my shoulder with firm, strong fingers. "Please don't upset Eleanor anymore."

"A four-million-dollar necklace has been stolen. Eleanor—the sisters—have to deal with this." I felt dishonest not telling Jerome about Monica's kidnapping. He clearly cared for both women, and he would be a great asset.

"I'm on the alert now. If that man shows up again, I'll catch him. No need to worry Eleanor about this anymore. Just tell her it's been resolved. I don't want either of them afraid to walk out the door."

"I don't know." I was torn. Would this information make Eleanor more careful or more terrified?

Lightning split the sky, and rain pelted down. Jerome motioned toward the house. "Best get inside before you drown."

Before I could say anything else, he jogged down the garden path, disappearing in the heavy wall of rain.

Cece and I dashed for the front porch. The door opened, and Eleanor called us into the house. "Have you found something?" she asked.

"Nothing definite." I wiped the water from my face on my sleeve. "We should search the property and the grounds. Are there any cisterns at Briarcliff?"

"There's one behind the rose garden. It hasn't been used in years, though."

"Why don't I stay here and help Eleanor search the house?" Cece offered.

"That would be a huge help." I would be free to seek out Marty Diamond and his cabin in the woods.

"Tinkie should be here soon," Cece said. "I'll give her a call and ask her to hurry."

"You're a genius." I gave her a hug and whispered in her ear, "Keep an eye on Eleanor. She doesn't look good." Worry and anxiety were eating her alive.

"Got it." Cece hugged me. "Be careful."

11

The minute I entered the Homochitto National Forest, I felt as if I'd stepped into a scene from Tolkien's great works. The rain had abated, but thunderheads were massing in the west. The gray skies contrasted with the summer green of the trees, giving the landscape a fantastical feel. The flat vistas of the Delta have their own charm, but the forest's rolling hills held a haunting beauty and tantalizing possibility of a world where nymphs and sprites ruled. I had to hand it to the state of Mississippi for preserving vast stretches of wilderness.

Cece had written copious directions. I had no trouble finding the isolated cabin where Marty Diamond supposedly hung his Stetson. It was picturesque, the kind of place a soulful singer would occupy. It would also make a terrific hostage hideaway.

The cabin was out of sight at the end of what would be termed in the pine barrens a "logging road." In other words, two ruts with minimal clearance on either side. It was tight, even for Cece's little hybrid. I doubted another human being was within a five-mile radius.

No vehicles were visible. I exited the car to examine the road. No fresh tracks. Maybe Marty had spent the night in town.

Easing onto the front porch, I peered through a curtainless window. The interior was neat, spartan. There was no sign of Marty or anyone else. The door opened at my lightest touch, which indicated no one was being held there against her will.

Breaking and entering isn't a charge a private investigator can afford on her record, but I'd driven nearly an hour, and I wasn't leaving empty handed.

Just to be on the safe side, first I circled the cabin, peeping in every window available. Empty. If someone was inside, he was moving around to avoid me. The back of my neck tingled at the thought. Hide-and-seek had been a favorite childhood game. My friends and I had loved to play at dusk, just as the shadows gathered and the balance shifted from light to dark.

Too many times I'd crept around the woods and fields of Dahlia House, hoping to find a hidden playmate—only for my friend to jump out and startle me. The game produced a delicious chill that was also a little unpleasant. I felt the same way as I moved around Marty Diamond's woodland home.

Back at the porch, I called his name loudly. No answer. Time to fish or cut bait. I stepped across the threshold and entered. The room was simple but cozy. Hand-woven tapestries—instead of the redneck's normal décor of dead-animal heads—adorned the walls. In the far corner were several beautiful guitars and what appeared to be recording equipment. If ever a place existed for creative energy, this was the spot.

In the kitchen a plate, a bowl, and a cup waited in a drain board. Marty Diamond used earth-friendly detergent and cloth towels. On some level, the guy had green tendencies.

The bathroom was clean. No prescription drugs in the medicine cabinet. The bedroom finally yielded results. A pair of thong underwear lay beneath the edge of the bed. In the search of Monica's room, I'd seen her underwear drawer. Though I couldn't prove the panties on Marty's floor belonged to Monica, they matched several pairs in her drawer. My conclusion was that Monica had been in the cabin. Voluntarily or by force, I couldn't say. Had she merely cougared Marty? Or was the explanation much darker?

I slipped the undies in my pocket. If Monica was a prisoner, there was no evidence of restraints. Yet again, I'd uncovered a tidbit of evidence that followed no particular direction, just a revolving finger of blame, pointed at first one suspect, then another. The harder I looked, the more confused I became.

On the trip back to Briarcliff, I called Tinkie. Cell phone reception was sketchy, but I gathered the party she'd attended had been a huge success and Oscar was back on track supporting her private investigation career. She was only a few miles from Natchez—with Sweetie Pie and Chablis in tow. She'd head straight for Briarcliff.

I needed to put video cameras in Tinkie's house to record how she managed her husband. She had some secret weapon to bend Oscar to her will.

I phoned Cece, who'd just finished a search of the grounds with Jerome.

"We found the cistern." There was an edge to her voice I couldn't fathom.

"And?"

"I don't think anyone's been near it for the last hundred years."

Again, her tone was all wrong. "Is Jerome with you?"

"That's exactly right."

"I'll be there in fifteen minutes. Meet me at the house."

Pressing on the accelerator, I risked a speeding ticket to get back to Briarcliff. I arrived just as Tinkie opened the back door of her Caddy and my beautiful red-spotted hound jumped from the backseat followed by the dainty Chablis. They were an odd duo, but despite the difference in size, both had enormous courage and heart.

"Oscar has a banking convention in Memphis. It was bring the dogs or kennel them, and you know how Chablis hates to be away from us." Whatever her rationalization might be, Tinkie's wide grin held no remorse for bringing the canines.

Sweetie almost knocked me down with the delight of our reunion. Chablis gnawed my shoelaces and flung her head wildly, growling with mock fierceness. "It's good to see them."

"The Eola doesn't allow dogs," Tinkie said matter-of-factly. "You'll have to distract the staff while I sneak them in."

Rules were meant to be broken, at least where Chablis and Sweetie were concerned. Tinkie normally was by-the-book with social conventions, but anti-dog policies were on her hit list. If she ever ran for office, her platform would be equal opportunities for pups.

Eleanor, who'd witnessed the arrival of the dogs, shook her head. "You can stay here. This old house could stand the joy of a hound and a . . . a . . . a little fluffy creature."

I hid a smile. My first reaction to Chablis had been contempt. She was so glitzed, pampered, and fragile—she appeared to be more toy than dog. Appearances can be deceiving, and in Chablis's case, they were. I loved her every bit as much as Tinkie and Oscar did. And they loved Sweetie with equal fervor.

"We couldn't intrude on your privacy," I said to Eleanor. "It's a kind and generous offer, but—"

"Of course we can." Tinkie's face was alight. "It's the perfect solution, and when the kidnapper calls again, we'll be here. When an excellent offer."

Eleanor faced me. "Your partner is right. Having you in the house is the smartest solution. We found no sign of Monica, but someone has been inside the north wing. The problem is, I can't say when. It could have been weeks ago or yesterday."

"The north wing?" Cece's tone said it all. "How many wings are there?"

"Two. North and south. We use the central part of the house, especially in the summer. The air-conditioning and all. Costs a fortune to cool the whole place, and there's only the two of us. So we shut off the other wings."

I didn't need the tour. I needed facts. "What did you find?"

"The blue room bed was disturbed. Kissie cleans the rooms once a season. I called her and she said she worked there a month ago and left it in mint condition."

As if on cue, an old model Honda pulled down the drive. Kissie climbed out from behind the wheel. "What's going on? I could tell by your voice, Eleanor, something's wrong." She looked from one to the other. "What the hell is it?"

"When was the last time you were in the north wing?" I avoided her question with one of my own.

"About a month ago, I oiled the furniture and changed the bed linens. I left the rooms ready for a guest."

Eleanor's eyelids fluttered briefly as though she might faint. "The sheets were twisted, like someone had tossed all night."

Or had sex. I read the same thought on Cece's and Tinkie's faces. Monica could have met assignations there.

"Any idea who might have been in the room?" Tinkie asked.

"No clothes or personal items had been left behind," Eleanor said.

"I'd like to have a look." It wasn't that I doubted Eleanor, but there was always the chance a clue had escaped her attention—like the thong in my pocket.

"And I need to hook this up." Tinkie brought a recorder to attach to the phone. The next time the kidnapper called, we could at least record the man's voice to analyze it. Phrasing or an accent could be a big help.

I pulled Eleanor behind Tinkie's Caddy. Kissie didn't need to hear what I was about to ask. "Was Monica sleeping with Marty Diamond?"

Eleanor blanched. "Kissie's beau?"

I pulled the panties from my pocket. "I believe these are hers."

She examined the label. "Yes, they probably are. She has her lingerie imported from France and this is the brand she likes. My sister is very particular about such things."

I took them from her and returned them to my pocket. "Monica has made a lot of enemies in town. She went out of her way to hurt people and ruin relationships. Why?" It was obvious that Eleanor was fond of Kissie. Monica had spoken of her with affection. I didn't understand why Monica acted in a way so reckless of others' feelings.

Eleanor's face sagged. "I don't know what motivates Monica. I tried to tell her not to sleep with men who were attached. She could have had her pick of European royalty or highly successful entrepreneurs. Her conduct appalled me, but she is my sister. Even when she was wrong in her behavior, I defended her."

Cece and Tinkie kept Kissie occupied, while I continued to talk with Eleanor. "This gives Kissie motive to hurt Monica. I get the sense Kissie really cares for Marty. If she knew about his betrayal—and with Monica, of all people—she'd be hurt and furious. To quote my aunt Loulane, 'Hell hath no fury like a woman scorned.'"

"Even so, Kissie wouldn't—"

"Don't discount her. We can't discount anyone. And I want a DNA sample. Barclay deserves an answer to his parentage. If Monica did have him and then abandon him, he has a right to know it."

Eleanor drew a hairbrush from her pocket. "I came to the same conclusion. Monica will never acknowledge him as a true son—she just isn't capable. But he deserves the truth. Maybe it'll give him some peace." Longing flooded her face. "I wanted a child, back when I was younger. Monica loathed the idea of a baby, but I wanted one."

I took the brush with relief. "Don't let us hold you up from going to see Mr. Nesbitt. We'll take care of things here." Eleanor was exhausted. I patted her shoulder. "Good luck with the insurance money."

"I fear I'm going to need a great deal of luck," she said as she got in her car and drove away.

I decided on a bold move. "Kissie, do you recognize these?" I brought the panties from my pocket.

The songwriter stepped back as if I'd pulled a snake out. "Where did you find those?"

"At your boyfriend's cabin. Now why would he have a pair of sixty-dollar underwear?"

"I left them." Chagrin gave way to suspicion. "What were you doing at Marty's cabin?"

"That doesn't matter. How did Monica's underwear get there? Was Monica sleeping with Marty?"

Cece and Tinkie followed the conversation like a tennis match. They focused on Kissie, who went white with anger. "How dare you say such a thing? Marty wasn't interested in Monica. I left the panties. Monica gave them to me. As a gift."

She pointed to the house. "Ask her if you don't believe me." She put her words to action and started toward the door.

"Monica isn't home." Yet again, I was convinced Kissie was telling the truth.

"Where is she?" Kissie slowed down long enough to evaluate each of us. She must have read our worry and distress. "What's going on? Everyone acts like . . . Where is Monica?"

We couldn't keep it from her any longer. "She's been kidnapped."

"By who?"

"We thought Marty might be involved." I said it clearly.

Instead of anger, her reaction was disbelief. "Marty? Take Monica? Why would he do such a thing?"

"For four million dollars in ransom," I said.

Kissie put the whole business together. "The insurance money from the necklace. You think I told Marty about the money and *he* took Monica? But everyone in town knows about the four million. It's all people are gossiping about."

"Four million would go a long way toward buying a singing career."

"But Marty was furious with me when I helped . . ." The sentence faded to a halt.

"When you did what?" Tinkie asked gently.

Kissie pushed her long hair back from her face. "I might as well tell you. I let Barclay spend a few nights in the north wing. Please don't tell the sisters. I was trying to help. Really." She spoke faster and faster. "He's Monica's son. I know it. And the sisters are all alone. They don't act lonely, but they are. The only person left in the family is that terrible Millicent. I thought if Monica and Eleanor could just meet Barclay, they'd see he's one of them. A Levert." Tears glimmered in her eyes, but she blinked them back. "I didn't mean to do anything harmful. I was really trying to do something good."

I didn't know what to say. Barclay had stayed on the grounds of Briarcliff. Had the fox been in the henhouse all along? He could have obtained everything he needed to abduct Monica without any problem.

"Are you going to call the police?" Kissie asked. She was afraid.

"No." Tinkie took the underwear from me and gave them to Kissie. "No, we're not. Eleanor doesn't want to involve the police."

"Is Monica okay?" Kissie couldn't hold the tears back any longer. "Barclay wouldn't hurt her. She's his mother.

He's angry she abandoned him, but deep down he wants to win her love."

"You must tell Eleanor what you've done," Tinkie said.

"If Monica is hurt because of something I did, Eleanor will never forgive me." Kissie wiped her face with the back of her hand. "And I don't blame her."

"Let's not get the cart before the horse," Cece said. "Why don't you track Eleanor down and talk with her, Kissie?"

Still wiping her face, Kissie nodded. "I have to make her understand."

I didn't envy her that job, but Cece was right. The sooner the better.

Once Kissie had driven away, I signaled Tinkie and Cece to a huddle. "Let's poke around the old stables. There's a horse on these grounds, and someone is riding it. This is no ghostly apparition but flesh and blood. And I suspect it's Barclay. He's been here, on the property."

"Jerome and I went over this place thoroughly," Cece said, slightly wounded at my implication her search hadn't been thorough.

"Jerome may not have shown you the stables," I pointed out. Everyone had secrets and a motive to want to harm or help Monica.

"Just a minute." Tinkie fetched paper from her car. "Let's draw out the grounds and figure the most logical place for the stables. Remember, back when they were built, water would have been important."

For someone who would rather have a bikini wax than ride a horse, Tinkie occasionally had lightning bolts of livestock brilliance.

We gathered around the hood of her car as she drew out the estate, finally settling on the far northern corner, which dipped toward what might be a branch or creek. The foliage was almost impenetrable, but we'd fight our way through.

We slipped around the far side of the house, hoping to avoid Jerome. I didn't want the gardener involved in this search. Our luck held as we fought through honeysuckle vines and into dense underbrush growing over what must have once been incredible bridle paths. Riding Reveler or Miss Scraprion through the wide-open cotton fields was one of the delights of my Zinnia life. The grounds of Briarcliff offered another type of ride, one of hushed forests, the fluttering of birds above us, the sense of slipping into a secret world.

As we pushed our way toward the back of the property, we tried to piece together the information we had.

"This whole case is off-kilter." My attention distracted, a limb whacked me across the bridge of my nose. "Crap!" Tears filled my eyes and I stumbled. Only Cece's quick reach kept me from falling.

Sweetie Pie, who'd stayed at my side, hit a scent and tore off to the south, baying like she was on the trail of the most bloodthirsty pirate since Bluebeard. Chablis was hot on her heels. Tinkie tried to call them back, but they ignored her. One thing about Sweetie, she had the keenest nose in the Southeast, and she'd find us when she tired of tracking her prey.

We trudged on, doing our best to calculate directions from the sun—when we could see it through the thick canopy of trees. The grounds of Briarcliff covered close to four hundred acres, a square bigger than half a mile on all sides. We couldn't hope to bulldoze through that much wilderness. Once we found the small creek or branch or spring or whatever water source should be in a low area, we'd call it quits if we didn't find the old stables.

Since I was in the lead, I stopped at an impenetrable wall of underbrush and vines. "I don't think we can go any farther unless we come back with machetes."

"Wait a minute." Cece grasped a limb of the underbrush. "This is dying." She shook it. "I don't think it's attached."

We all grabbed limbs and pulled, and the whole mass gave.

"This was put here deliberately to hide something," Tinkie said.

We cleared a narrow lane and hurried into an open area where all underbrush had been removed. Straight ahead were the old stables. The bare ground was covered in fresh hoofprints.

"Well, well," Cece said. "We begin to unravel the mystery of the Briarcliff horseman."

She was answered with a soft whinny from inside the stables. Cece and Tinkie turned to me. "Aren't you going to check it out, Sarah Booth?" Cece asked. "If it's filled with old horse poop, I'll ruin my shoes."

"Sure." I stepped forward slowly. The stables were as dark and foreboding as the house, and I was reluctant to investigate, even though I knew I'd find only a horse. It wouldn't make sense for the rider to remain in the vicinity if he hoped to keep his identity secret. He could easily have heard us a mile away.

Tinkie cleared her throat when I didn't move.

"Okay." I signaled her to desist. "I'm going." I marched

to the door that looked like a black maw. The whinny came again, soft and curious. I stepped into the darkness and moved toward the sound of rustling. There had to be a light, but I didn't know where to begin groping for it, and I would have to feel for it because I couldn't see a thing. Something big shifted to my left, but I couldn't see what. I was operating on sound alone.

"Sarah Booth?" Tinkie called from outside. She sounded concerned. "Have you found something?"

I considered hiding and waiting for them to come searching. It would serve them right for sending me into the barn alone. I grinned in the darkness at the scenario that played out in my head.

Something brushed my cheek, the softest of touches. Gossamer against my skin. My grin vanished, as did thoughts of pranking my friends. Someone was in the barn with me. Someone I couldn't see, but who could obviously see me.

"Sarah Booth?" Tinkie sounded almost frantic.

"Hush." The voice was soft, seductive, confident.

"Sarah Booth?" Tinkie was closer.

"Stay quiet," the voice whispered. "I insist."

"Sarah Booth, this isn't funny. We're coming in!"

I opened my mouth to call out to her. A hand covered my face, shutting off the sound.

"Be still," the voice ordered, but there was no sense of rush or urgency in his tone. I heard the sound of a latch opening and the creak of a rusty hinge. The horse grew excited, whirling in his stall.

I couldn't breathe, and I struggled, but he held me tight against a strong chest.

To my relief, I heard Sweetie's frantic baying, and this time she was coming straight for me. I began to fight against my captor's grip. Sweetie was coming. Surely Tinkie and Cece would realize I was in danger.

My lungs screamed for oxygen. The last things I heard were the wild whinny of a horse and the deep-throated growl of my hound.

12

A kaleidoscope of green spun above my head when I gained consciousness. A concerned Tinkie shifted into view. She hovered over me, shaking my shoulder and lightly slapping my face.

"Hit me again and I'm going to hurt you." I pushed her back and propped up on my elbows. I was lying on the ground outside the stables. Sweetie Pie rushed to cover my face in doggie kisses, an expression of anxiety on her noble countenance.

"Dahling, we thought you'd been killed." Cece knelt beside Sweetie, who'd pressed herself against me.

My memory was fuzzy. I'd walked into the stables, and then someone had grabbed me. He'd shut off my air and whispered into my ear, a murmur that still sent a chill through me. "His hand was big, calloused. He clamped it over my mouth and . . ." And I'd fallen like a sack of potatoes.

I struggled to a sitting position against the protests of my friends. "Where is he? Did he come out?"

"He who? Did you find someone? All we saw was a horse running out of the stables lickety-split. It was huge and black. An enormous animal. It galloped right by us and disappeared in the woods." Tinkie pointed vaguely south. "We thought you'd been trampled."

"A man grabbed me. He told me not to call out to you." I began to tremble. "He nearly suffocated me." And I could only say for certain he had a strong chest and rough hands. I hadn't gotten a look at him. "Surely you saw him?"

"We didn't see a man," Tinkie admitted. She glanced toward the barn. "I'll get a big stick and we'll take a look. If he's still in there, Sarah Booth, I'll beat him till he begs for his mama."

I restrained her. "Don't go in there. Let me gather my wits and we'll all go together."

Tinkie put her hands on her hips. "We have to buy guns, Sarah Booth. We just have to. We can't chase after felons armed with sticks and rocks."

Instead of answering, I gathered myself to stand.

"Not so fast. Let's check you over," Cece said.

A careful examination of my skull showed no injury or wound. My attacker hadn't harmed me, but he'd used the Vulcan sleeper hold. And that whisper. Every time I thought of his warm breath against my ear, his hand covering my mouth yet also caressing . . . it infuriated me.

Almost as bitter was the fact he'd sneaked up on me

and caught me off guard. I could still hear his voice, confident and taunting. I'd have to be more careful in the future. This was a smart and bold man.

Tinkie pulled me to my feet. "No police. Eleanor will kill us if uniforms show up at Briarcliff for any reason."

"Then you two should say *adios* to her and this case and head home." Cece got snappy when she was worried. "It isn't reasonable for her to ask you to risk your lives."

Cece was right. Clearly. Yet I had never walked away from a case. And while the man in the barn could have twisted my head off with ease, he hadn't really harmed me.

"Let's see what's in that barn." I didn't want to get into an argument with Cece about the danger. I'd been foolish to enter the stables alone, and she was feeling guilty for letting me.

Lined up like the Mod Squad, we walked in together. I was in the middle, and this time a dangling cord tickled my face. I grabbed it and pulled. Light flooded the barn. Which meant there was electricity to the building. The Levert sisters had enough assets to light most of Natchez, if they chose to, but normal people would shut off the power supply to an unused building. To prevent fire, if nothing else.

"Well, well," Cece said as she surveyed the interior. "This tells a story."

"That horse isn't a stray," Tinkie said. "Someone is caring for it."

"And very well." Two barrels full of fresh rolled oats and sweet feed stood against one wall. Three hay bales had been stacked in a corner, and a bucket of fresh water was in the stall. I wished I'd caught a glimpse of the horse. The breed and condition of the animal would tell me a lot about the owner. Big and black, while accurate, were far from specific.

At the end of the stables we found the tack room, where a beautiful English saddle rested on a stand and a bridle hung from a peg. I ran the stirrups down the leathers. Judging by the length, the rider was tall. Stashed in a corner were old football pads and a helmet. I picked it up and examined it. "We've solved the mystery of the horse and rider on Briarcliff property. It's a high school jock from the nineteen seventies," I said. "At least we know he isn't a phantom and we know how he gets the horse to the estate."

"And I found how he escaped," Cece called. We joined her at a back door that stood slightly ajar.

"We still don't know why he's doing it, or where he came from." Tinkie peered anxiously at the gray square of outdoors visible through the barn door. She was ready to get back outside. "The problem with owning four hundred acres is you can't watch it all the time."

Thunder rumbled in the distance, a warning of bad weather to come. "Predictions are for another line of thunderstorms to come through, maybe tornadoes," Tinkie said. "Let's get out of here. There's nothing else we can do right now. The horse knows his way around the estate. He's been running free for a couple of weeks now. He'll come back here as soon as we leave."

She was right, but it didn't sit well to leave with the matter unresolved. "We have to find the rider. I think it's Barclay, but we have to know for sure."

Cece had had enough. "I mean it, Sarah Booth. You

need to walk away from this. We should get our asses out of this creepy place and head for the Eola bar for a cocktail."

Tinkie linked arms with both of us. "If it is Barclay, then we need to confront him."

Jerome was digging weeds in the Briarcliff herb garden. He did his best to ignore us, working without looking up even as we called his name. When Tinkie persisted, he finally put aside his shovel.

He reluctantly agreed to keep the dogs for a couple of hours. He seemed to approve of my hound and tolerate Chablis. Like most people, he judged Chablis on appearance, but if he was around her long enough he'd recognize she had courage and heart.

We kept the secret of the horseman to ourselves. Cece thought we should question Jerome about the stables, but Tinkie and I decided not to corner the gardener until Eleanor was present. He might lie to us, but he seemed to genuinely care for the sisters.

On the way to the Eola, Tinkie drove by Langley Insurance. Eleanor's luxury car wasn't there, but we spotted it at the bank. Obviously she'd received the insurance money and was putting the check into her account so she could pay the ransom. Which meant the kidnappers' demand might come as early as today. Clearly they knew Eleanor's every step.

Now it was a waiting game. When would the kidnappers call?

Anxiety is an appetite stimulate for me, and apparently for my friends. We were starving and opted to go Under-the-Hill for a late lunch and adult beverage. Once we had our Bloody Marys, we rehashed the elements of the case.

"Be smart and let the professionals handle this. Monica could be killed and you two can easily get injured."

"It's okay," I assured her. "Tinkie and I will be safe, I promise."

"If you get hurt again, Sarah Booth—or you, either, Tinkie—you'll end up losing the men in your life. You can't expect a person to risk his heart over and over again," Cece said.

"I know." I didn't need to have my nose rubbed in the truth. Whenever I risked my physical safety, I put Graf's emotional well-being, as well as my friends', on the line.

We ate our lunch and moved away from discussing the case as Tinkie filled us in on her activities in Zinnia. The gala had been a smashing success, and Tinkie's abilities as a hostess put Oscar squarely in the limelight. As wife of the president and daughter of the owner of the bank, this was part of Tinkie's job description, and I admired the way she handled it with grace and charm.

"But along with partying, I did have time to make a few phone calls." Tinkie grinned. "John Hightower does have a book contract. With a major publisher."

"How did you find that out?" I never underestimated Tinkie, but sometimes she surprised even me.

"Harold's cousin is a respected literary agent. She checked into it for him. She didn't divulge the details, but apparently John Hightower will deliver a book that blazes a trail through the South more devastating than Sherman's march."

Harold Erkwell worked for Oscar. He had old society and money connections. More than once he'd helped us with a case. "The Leverts are just a part of it? Not the main focus?" The author had not left me with that impression.

"His proposal was broad. Heaven knows what he's actually written."

"I'm amazed the little pantywaist can write."

"Might make an interesting feature story for the newspaper," Cece said. "I'll see what I can find out. I doubt he'll put it together immediately the three of us are friends. Maybe he'll let something slip."

"Capital idea!" I pronounced. Without my friends, what would I do?

When Cece took her leave—after eliciting numerous promises to be careful—Tinkie and I got down to plotting our strategy.

"Do you think Sweetie could pick up the scent of the man in the stables?" Tinkie asked.

The obviousness of her question stunned me. We had the best tool possible in our hands, the nose of a noble hound, and I'd failed to think of it. "You are brilliant!" Before I could go any further, her cell phone rang.

I could hear a woman's voice, but I couldn't make out the conversation. Judging from Tinkie's expression, it wasn't good.

"I'll be right there," she said soothingly. "We'll figure this out, Eleanor."

She put the phone down. "We have to go."

"What's wrong?" I asked.

"The bank refused to cash the insurance check. It's in both sisters' names. They need both signatures. Eleanor is very upset."

This was going to be a rough afternoon. "Can you handle Eleanor?" Tinkie was the more diplomatic of the two of us.

"What are you going to do?"

"I want to see if I can find any riding tack at Jerome's cottage. The man in the barn was big, strong. The hands of a worker. It could be Barclay, but no one has more opportunity than Jerome. And if Monica played him false, damaged his ego, treated him as poorly as she's been known to treat her other conquests—"

"He might be tempted to soothe his ego with a large amount of ransom."

"It wouldn't be the first time."

We pushed open the restaurant door and stepped into the hot summer day. Summer in Mississippi was a physical slap. The humidity after the rain was thick as wool.

"Are you sure you're okay?" Tinkie asked. "You're looking a little owlish."

"Thanks, I think. I'm fine." I shook off the heat. "Let's get back to Briarcliff."

"How will you get Jerome out of his cottage?"

"If he thinks Sweetie and Chablis are lost, he'll help me hunt them."

Tinkie took two steps to every one of mine. "You're one clever woman."

"And you have impeccable taste in friends."

As it turned out, sending Sweetie and Chablis on a romp was easier said than done. The pups circled my legs and nipped at my heels instead of dashing for the woods. The storm was building to the south—once it got close enough, the dogs would head straight for the house. I figured I had at least an hour.

Tinkie had her hands full with a desperate Eleanor. She was near the breaking point, and Tinkie took her inside. The plan was to call Oscar to intervene with cashing the insurance check. It was Eleanor's only chance to have the ransom money.

Having a banker husband was at times very helpful in the thick of a case.

At last, with much urging on my part, Sweetie caught the scent of something and she took off, her sorrowful baying voice floating across the lawn. Chablis was right behind her, leaping and running, oblivious to the brambles and briars that snagged her expensively highlighted coat.

Just as I planned, Jerome emerged from the herb garden at the sound of the dogs.

"Help me!" I yelled, rushing toward him. "Sweetie and Chablis took off after something and I'm afraid they'll get lost in the woods."

"They're dogs, not wild creatures." His brows drew together as he assessed my intelligence. "They'll come back."

"They don't know where they are," I insisted. "Please help me find them."

"I haven't got a lick of work done all morning," he grumbled. "The dogs will return on their own. They've got a sight more sense than most people." His direct look left no doubt to whom he referred.

"If anything happens to Chablis, it'll kill Tinkie."

He threw his shovel to the ground. "The dogs will show up when they're ready. They're smart creatures. But I can't accomplish a damn thing if you stand there, yammering at me. The roses are all a'bloom and need attention. Move along with you."

If he gave the rosebushes any more attention, he'd have to read them to sleep. There wasn't a leaf out of place. "I think the flowers are fine. I need your help."

He faced me. "Monica wants fresh flowers in the house every day. Roses. That's what she likes." He stabbed his shovel into the ground. "Now let's find the buggers so I can get back to my digging. Which way did they run?"

I pointed away from his cottage. "East."

He trudged off, but when I didn't follow, he stopped. "Well? Have you grown roots?"

"What if they go to the highway?" I used all of my acting skills to appear distraught. "I'll drive around the estate to the road. If they come out there, I'll pick them up."

"A little exercise might work wonders for you. Blood flow to the upper regions, you know."

"In all the best movies, the gardener isn't a smart-ass."

Jerome let out a bark, which I realized was a laugh. "Ride your car, then. Let's round up the sinners and be done with this."

I jumped in the Caddy and wheeled around, heading for the road. When Jerome disappeared into the thicket of woods, I took the fork of the driveway to his cottage. I would have to be fast and thorough.

We'd gone through the cottage once, but that was for signs of Monica's presence. Now I needed evidence of horses . . . or Barclay Levert. The relationship between Monica and Jerome had so many levels. I remembered the bottle of fine wine, the shared cheese and crackers, how Jerome reacted when we found the scrap of Monica's gown. He cared for her. But Monica seemed incapable of reciprocating. Perhaps Eleanor was the only person she'd ever loved. Monica had abandoned her own child. And Jerome knew she'd slept with numerous men.

I pulled up to the cottage thinking of the inequity of class. America pretended there was no class structure, but a classification as rigid as the Indian caste system was well and truly in place. The haves and the have-nots. An heiress—even the heiress of a bluebeard type—didn't marry a gardener.

As Eleanor stressed, Monica once had her pick of European royalty and business entrepreneurs. These men traveled in her social strata. Why had she romanced a gardener and, for that matter, a Gypsy sponge diver? Was there cruelty in her choices? She selected men she could abandon without a qualm. Was it an aphrodisiac for her to feel superior to the men she slept with?

The more I learned about Monica, the less I liked her. She used people as though they were paper towels. Such conduct could easily earn retribution. If Barclay hatched a plan to abduct and ransom Monica, Jerome might have cooperated because he was hurt, not greedy. The man loved the grounds of Briarcliff. Had he loved Monica equally, her heartless conduct might have pushed him too far.

The cottage was small, but time worked against me. I rushed to get through it without leaving any indication I'd been there.

When I finished with the kitchen cabinets, I looked out the window. Almost hidden in scuppernong vines that Jerome had allowed to swallow a wild cherry was a small fountain. The vines, the natural trees—these were not what I'd expect in Jerome's backyard. He was a gardener, one who created and maintained the more formal Briarcliff grounds. Scuppernongs and cherry trees were "volunteer" plants. Many considered them weeds or trash.

I loved the wild grapes, and I could see the purple clusters, ready for harvest, hanging on the vine. I walked out, intending to gather a handful to eat before the storm broke. Once I got to the natural arbor, though, I realized this was a place created by design, not happenstance. Behind the curtain of vines, a hammock was strung between two small trees.

On the hammock was a wooden box. Elegantly carved, exquisite craftsmanship, and beside it, tools. Jerome not only gardened, he was gifted in woodworking and design. The boat replica in his cottage showed equal talent.

The elegance of the box drew me to it, and when I picked it up, something inside shifted about. Letters.

I opened the lid and smelled cedar. The wood grain glowed red in the summer light. At least five dozen letters were neatly organized. They'd been read and reread, and none of the envelopes bore a postmark or even a name. They'd been personally delivered.

Knowing Monica's penchant for cruelty, I was almost hesitant to read them, because I had no doubt they were love letters. And Jerome cherished them. He'd taken them to his place of respite to read again, never dreaming a snoopy private investigator would find them and invade his privacy.

Which was exactly what Eleanor was paying me to do.

I opened the first letter and began to scan it.

My dearest Jerome, the gardens are thriving under your care. You have a gift.

Such tenderness from Monica was a revelation. I checked for a date, but there was none, so I continued.

Tonight we can be alone. Meet me in the back garden. In the moonlight we can plan the future of

Briarcliff. Monica has no interest in living here. Soon she'll be off on another adventure. Then we'll have the house and grounds to ourselves.

That line stopped me cold. I checked the bottom of the letter, but there was no signature. I didn't need one to know the author. I read on.

You know there are limits. Our relationship must always remain private, just between us. I've always been honest with you about that fact. But once she's gone, we can share a life together as fully and completely as if we were wed.

With all my heart

My legs seemed rubbery as I sank onto the hammock. Of all the things I'd expected to find, evidence of a love affair between Jerome and Eleanor had not been among them.

This put a new spin on the entire investigation. Had Eleanor paid someone to abduct Monica? In my mind I heard again the splash of a nightgown-clad object hitting the water of the mighty Mississippi. It was a helluva way to get rid of a body—and one in the tradition of the Levert family.

Though Gunny had organized a river search, no body had ever been found. Since Eleanor had convinced the police all was well, there'd been no need for Gunny to continue searching.

"Holy moly," I muttered. If this was true, Eleanor was a mastermind. She'd stolen the family necklace, collected the four-million payoff, and gotten rid of the sister.

The sky rumbled and the first rain began to fall. A

bolt of lightning flashed and struck so close the blast nearly deafened me. The ground shook and sulfur filled my nostrils, making me slightly nauseated.

Now that was an odor I could easily identify with Briarcliff and the inhabitants. If I were the type to believe in curses, I wouldn't doubt that the heirs of Barthelme Levert were in the clutches of a dark blight. I didn't know if it was possible for DNA to be corrupted by evil, but I also didn't know if it was impossible.

I had to get back to Tinkie. She was alone with Eleanor.

13

Jerome stood on the front lawn in the pelting rain with Sweetie and Chablis. He'd tied a rope around their necks and glowered at me when I got out of the car.

"I waited on the road for you," he said. "Where were you?"

"I made the loop. Twice. I must have missed you." My acting skills were good, but Jerome could calculate time and distance. He'd snared my lie, and though he might suspect me, he wasn't sure of what.

"Keep the beasts on a leash, else you'll find them yourself next time." He thrust the ropes into my hand and stalked off. I didn't need my psychic friend Madame Tomeeka to tell me his thoughts were ugly and directed at me, but I had my doubts about him, too.

His long stride quickly took him down the garden

path. He disappeared in the sheets of rain that fell from the leaden sky. No doubt he was worried about the letters he'd left outside where the rain might ruin them. I'd taken care to shut the box firmly and knew no water would get inside. Such was the craftsmanship. Jerome's memories were safe, but they might not remain private for much longer.

I dashed through the downpour with the dogs and stood while they shook themselves on the stone entrance.

"Stay here." I put the word on Sweetie. She was mostly obedient and a fabulous hound. But her head could be turned by a handsome canine such as her last beau, a New York harrier named Danny. The two dogs had given me a bad turn when they'd turned Bonnie and Clyde in a shoe-thieving campaign across Sunflower County while I was out of town on a case. Poor Oscar, their designated caregiver, had nearly had a heart attack.

I cradled Sweetie's soft muzzle and lifted her soulful eyes to mine. "Don't leave," I told her.

Eleanor had offered to let Sweetie and Chablis stay at Briarcliff, but a dry dog and a wet dog were two different animals. I didn't want to presume. The rain would let up and Sweetie would shake herself dry. Chablis could be easily toweled, so I took her inside. Hunting for something with which to dry the dog would give me the perfect excuse to poke around the mansion.

I'd made a serious miscalculation when I'd asked Eleanor to search Briarcliff. I'd assumed. While it might be logical to trust that the person paying me to find her missing sister would really want the sister found, it was still a mistake. And one that could easily result in injury for me or Tinkie. If Eleanor was that diabolical—and that pissed off at Monica—she wouldn't think twice about putting her hired investigators in the way of danger.

Or possibly killing her own sister.

As I slipped into the house, I heard the murmur of voices. Tinkie and Eleanor were in the ladies' parlor. Easing upstairs, I went to Eleanor's bathroom. Instead of the linen closet, I opened the medicine cabinet. There wasn't a single prescription bottle in sight. Vitamin D, E, C, and over-the-counter antioxidants were her only "medicines."

In the wastebasket I hit pay dirt. The little amber prescription bottle was in Eleanor's name. I recognized the drug as one popular among unhappy people who suffered from anxiety. It was powerful. Used improperly in heavy doses, the medication could render a person nearly comatose. Or dead.

The prescription had been filled only the week before, yet the bottle was empty. This wasn't proof positive Eleanor drugged her sister in order to abduct her—and might be keeping her drugged if Monica was still alive—but it was certainly circumstantial.

Footsteps approached the bathroom. I grabbed a towel and began to vigorously dry Chablis. The little dustmop growled at my enthusiasm, but when the door opened and Eleanor gasped at my unexpected presence, I successfully feigned innocence.

"I hope it was okay to use a towel from this bathroom," I said. "Chablis was soaked and I didn't want her to shake in the house."

"It's fine," Eleanor said, but her face told another story. She was pale and her words came out clipped. "There are numerous bathrooms upstairs and down. This is my private bath."

"So sorry." I picked up Chablis. Another low growl warned me I was on her shit list. I'd slipped the prescription bottle into my pocket and I used the towel to cover the bulge. "Where's Tinkie?"

"Downstairs waiting for you. She said you were fetching the dogs from Jerome."

I was all concern. "Did you get the check thing resolved?"

"Oscar will help me, but it can't be done overnight. What if the kidnappers call and I can't get the ransom?" She sounded scared. No matter what role Eleanor *might* be playing in this drama, I had no proof of any wrongdoing. Like every other suspect, she had motive, means, and opportunity, but nothing yet proved her guilty.

"I'm sure Oscar will work this out." I patted her shoulder. "Do you think the abductor will call again this evening?"

She nodded. "I know he will. I feel it. And if I can't meet his demands, he'll kill Monica."

I had to give her credit. She was a damn fine actress—if this was an act. Such talent came with the bloodline. Her distant ancestor, Terrant Cassio, had been the only woman to pull the wool over Barthelme's eyes. She'd willingly married a murderer with five dead wives. And in a beautiful moment of irony, the minute he'd married her, he'd been done for. The fox had been stalked by a tiger.

That was the DNA the Levert sisters descended from. Monica abandoned her own child—if Barclay was telling the truth. She'd deliberately set out to wreck the homes of her Natchez peers. She'd slept with the significant others of her friends, and maybe even of her own sister. Why was I finding it hard to believe Eleanor would abduct and possible kill her flesh and blood? The whole family was capable of any deviant act.

"Call in the cops, Eleanor. Tell Gunny the truth."

She shook her head. "I can't risk it."

"The risk is open to interpretation. You stand to gain a lot if Monica is dead." I withdrew the empty prescription bottle from my pocket and held it out. "Care to explain this?"

Eleanor started to reach for the bottle but faltered. "I should be angry you're snooping around my house, but I'm not. In a strange way, I feel better. You're really searching for Monica."

Her reaction wasn't what I'd expected. "There should be almost thirty pills here. They're all gone."

Eleanor brushed her hair back from her forehead. "I flushed them down the toilet. When I found myself holding the prescription bottle, thinking about taking them all, wanting only the release of . . . death. I put them out of my reach." She straightened her posture. "You see, I can't go on without Monica. She is my other half, my twin, the person who completes me. Without her, I don't want to live."

"But you didn't take them."

"If Monica can be saved, I have to do it. This one time, I must be courageous. I will be the strong sister, the one who doesn't falter. I'll figure a way to pay the ransom."

"Before you risk any money, you need to be certain Monica is still alive." I deliberately made my voice cold. "We need proof of life."

My tone shocked her. She stepped back and narrowed her eyes. "She has to be alive. I've done everything the kidnapper asked."

"I don't think he—or *she*—or *they*—have to play by

any set of rules. You need to understand this up front. Criminals who abduct people have already broken a whole bunch of laws. Expecting them to play by rules, even ones *they* impose, is foolish." My cruelty surprised even me.

Eleanor blanched. "Do you really think she's dead? She can't be."

I couldn't push it any harder. She was about to faint. "I don't know," I said. "Let's wait for the kidnapper's call." Abruptly I walked past her and down the hall to the stairs. "Tinkie, I have Chablis," I called out.

I needed my partner to occupy Eleanor so I could search Briarcliff again. It would give me something to do to pass the time until the kidnapper called.

If he called.

If he'd ever called in the first place.

As it turned out, I didn't need Tinkie to distract Eleanor. My conversation with her sent her straight to her bed with a migraine.

When I reported the encounter—and my suspicions— Tinkie was a tiny bit miffed.

"We have no proof, and you all but said her sister was dead." Tinkie cuddled Chablis to her face. I'd toweled Sweetie, and she was napping on the floor beside the sofa in the ladies' parlor where Tinkie and I were having a powwow. "Don't you remember how you felt when Coleman accused you of murder on circumstantial evidence?"

Tinkie was good at applying the taser to my weak spots. Being falsely accused was unpleasant. "I told Eleanor the truth."

"The harshest truth. I saw her just before she took to her bed. I thought she'd keel over."

Tinkie had a point. Eleanor had looked sickened at the thought her sister wouldn't survive the ordeal. Her explanation of the prescription drugs was plausible. And she didn't seem overly concerned about the loss of the ransom money.

Still, the house had to be searched again, and I did so while Tinkie sat outside Eleanor's room as a guard. If she came out, Tinkie would divert her until I finished.

With the dogs helping, it didn't take long to investigate the place. I didn't find a single locked door or anyplace that looked suspicious. There was no trace of Monica; she wasn't being held in the house.

During my search the rain clouds passed and the sun burned hot. Humidity at a thousand percent. The air outside was liquid with moisture, creating the highest possible *ick* factor.

Tinkie and I were in the kitchen. She'd put a kettle on to boil to make herbal tea for Eleanor. "We should talk to Barclay. I need a full accounting of his whereabouts since he arrived in Natchez. I still can't believe Kissie let him stay in Briarcliff without permission from the sisters."

Barclay definitely had some 'splaining to do.

"Barclay could charm his way into a convent. I don't believe Kissie intentionally endangered the Leverts."

"Do you think he stole the necklace?" Tinkie asked.

The theft of the necklace had fallen so far down my priority list I'd pushed it to the back of my mind. "Why would he stay in Natchez if he had the necklace and money was his objective? He could sell it for a lot of money."

"Revenge? To make his mother acknowledge him? I'm glad Eleanor gave him the DNA. Maybe the lab will put that issue to rest."

"I'll stay with Eleanor if you want to interview Barclay." I made the offer because Tinkie had a thing for Barclay and also because I did, too. He could work me. Tinkie, who'd grown up manipulating men, wasn't as susceptible to his charms as I might be. Not that I would betray Graf, but only that I might not be at the top of my game. Barclay was crafty, and I didn't want to fall victim to his scams.

"I'd love a chance to grill him. At least we know why Marty Diamond was so aggressive toward him. Barclay put Kissie in a bad spot." Her eyebrows lifted. "A case where we have two handsome, talented men. It could be worse."

Tinkie was incorrigible. "And it probably will be."

"I'll be back here by eight, in case the kidnapper calls."

In the past, the ransom calls had come late in the evening. Tinkie would have plenty of time to find Barclay—Natchez wasn't that big a town and Barclay was hard to miss. In the meantime, though, she showed me how to turn on the telephone tape recorder. She left her laptop so I could do some research.

After it was brewed, I took the herbal tea to Eleanor. I tapped and there was no answer. Eleanor was sound asleep, as still as a corpse on top of the bedspread. She was so wan and lifeless I feared for a moment she actually might have died. On closer inspection, I deduced she was in a deep, deep sleep. She was utterly exhausted.

I returned the tea tray to the kitchen and gathered Tinkie's laptop. In the investigation, we'd learned a good bit about Monica's sordid love life, but not much regarding Eleanor's past. Other than Jerome, I had no idea who Eleanor had dated or desired. Somehow, I felt it might be useful information.

Eleanor told us to take our pick of the second-floor bedrooms, but I set up in the front parlor, where I had a good view of the main staircase and also the door to the back staircase, a small, narrow, dark passage the servants used to tend to the needs of their owners or employers, as the case might be. If Eleanor awakened, she wouldn't get by me. Perhaps I'd jumped to the wrong conclusion about her involvement in this mess, but I couldn't afford to put aside my concerns based on Tinkie's say-so. If I'd learned anything from past cases, it was not to give my trust too willingly to anyone.

The afternoon slipped away while I read online articles in the local Natchez newspaper documenting charity drives, pilgrimages, fetes, soirées, dances, balls, political organizations, garden clubs, and civic organizations. Monica had been quite active. She was often elected to boards and positions of authority, though judging from the photographs accompanying the articles, not liked. The other women stood apart from her in most of the shots.

Eleanor was mentioned in some of the reports, but often in the background. Monica was always front and center, which might be another reason Eleanor would like to do away with her. As Aunt Loulane would say, no woman enjoys the role of "always the bridesmaid, never the bride." Eleanor, at some time or other, would have wanted to shine.

Gossip gave a picture of the Leverts' role in Natchez society. What I needed, though, was a historical perspective. I dug back in the files. Luck was with me. Natchez is a town that relishes its history. Preservation societies, Daughters of the American Revolution, Daughters of the Confederacy—plenty of organizations had a Web presence, and all of them had detailed information on members and events.

I went back to the 1970s, when the Levert girls came of age. I found a write-up and photographs of Helena Banks Gorenflo's wedding. Eleanor and Monica were double maids of honor. The photos portrayed a happy grouping of young, beautiful people. So the troubled water between Helena and Monica had come later and, based on what I knew, likely involved a man.

To my utter surprise, I hit on an engagement announcement for Eleanor Levert and Gaston Gaudel, a French artist. Eleanor was only twenty. The nuptials was scheduled for May 1. She was to be given in marriage by her sister. Which made me curious where her parents were.

My Web gallivanting took me to the Mississippi archives, where I found death certificates for Middler Levert, who died of a massive heart attack in 1978, and Marcella Ardoin Levert, who—I had to read it twice—fell from the bluff of Briarcliff in 1973. The death was ruled an accident.

I called Jassine, Cece's newspaper reporter friend, and got her to dig up the obituary for Marcella Levert. The story was another example of the tragedy dogging the Levert family.

As Jassine paraphrased from the numerous newspaper clippings kept in the morgue, or newspaper library, she grew excited. "Marcella took a fall from a horse early in the day. Suffering a terrible headache, she took to her bed.

The doctor made a house call at Briarcliff and pronounced Marcella shaken up but uninjured. He gave her a sedative to relax and ordered the household to keep her as still as possible.

"During the night, Marcella got out of bed. She accidentally wandered into the yard and fell from the bluff. The family didn't discover her death until morning, when the gardener saw her floating in the river. In a freakish twist, the current didn't catch her body."

"Good lord." I regretted my earlier harshness to Eleanor. She'd had enough loss in her life—I felt bad about implying that her sister was dead.

"Okay, here's some more information," Jassine said. "The twin girls had just entered their teen years. Grief-stricken, their father took them to Europe for the next five years. They returned only for the girls' debut into Natchez society and the announcement of Eleanor's engagement to the artist Gaston Gaudel, a man she met in Paris. There's a photo of Eleanor and a very handsome man. They look ecstatic."

"I wonder what happened. Eleanor never married."

"What's your interest in Eleanor's and Monica's past?" Jassine asked. Like any good journalist, she'd caught a whiff of a story. "This can't figure into an insurance claim case, but I have to say their lives would make a fabulous movie."

I couldn't tell the truth, so I did the only other thing available—I lied. "I'm writing a movie script. About the Levert family. I thought a little background on the sisters, their lives in Natchez, participation in the community, all of that, would help me render them more vividly. I can also use parts of this in my insurance report." I was proud of my breezy ability to fabricate on the spot.

"Why didn't you ask Eleanor? Or Monica?"

I gave a tolerant laugh. "One reason Delaney Detective Agency is so highly regarded is because we do a thorough job of investigating. Asking our employer isn't exactly . . . impressive."

Jassine chuckled with me. "There're tricks in every trade, right?"

"That's right. Did you find anything on the wedding?"

"Hold on a minute." There was the sound of something heavy dropping onto a desk and pages turning. Jassine was flipping through the bound issues of the paper. She was a very good friend of Cece's to go to all this trouble for me.

Finally, she came back on the phone. "You aren't going to believe this."

I knew from her tone it was bad. "What? Was she dumped?"

"The night before her wedding, Gaston was murdered Under-the-Hill."

I felt as if a fist were pressed against my sternum. Breathing was difficult. "What were the circumstances?"

"It's a huge story. 'French Artist Stabbed in Brutal Robbery' is the headline. The bachelor party was going on, and the group of young Natchez men left the rehearsal dinner at the Eola and went Under-the-Hill. At the time, there was a club offering adult male entertainment."

It wasn't hard to imagine. Bachelor parties where the groom had one last fling at freedom were standard practice. Groomsmen did their best to insure a hangover so intense the actual wedding was a foggy memory.

"Was there a fight?"

"No, it seems Gaston went outside to get cigarettes from his vehicle. The other groomsmen finally missed him and went out to check. They found him in the parking lot. He'd bled to death. Can you believe the luck of it? Eleanor has lost everyone she ever cared about, except Monica. No wonder those two have such attitude. They act like the rest of us aren't fit to wipe their feet."

"No wonder," I repeated. Jassine didn't know Eleanor now stood to lose her sister. "Thanks, Jassine. I'll tell Cece she owes you big-time."

"Tickets to the Black and Orange Ball in New Orleans this year would be a nice compensation."

"I'll put a bug in her ear."

I'd just hung up when I heard my hound's low, serious growl. Sweetie stood at the front door, her hackles raised and her lip curled as she snarled. Easing back a curtain, I studied the front lawn. Night had fallen, a soft, misty summer night that gave the stars a magical glow. I didn't need Sweetie Pie taking off after a deer, and it was highly possible wild game hovered at the edge of the woods, so I slipped outside and gently closed the door. Behind me, I heard Chablis's frantic little paws at the door trying to dig her way out to me. The sound brought to mind old movie clips of fingernails digging at a coffin, a cheerful thought that made me want to rush back inside and slam the door locked.

Briarcliff was a house that invited visions of the macabre. Edgar Allan Poe would have been right at home.

Planting my feet on the front porch, I listened to the sounds of the night. Laughter, dim and muffled by the fog, drifted up from Under-the-Hill. Inside the house, Sweetie bayed a complaint accompanied by Chablis's ear-piercing bark. I had to get back inside before they woke Eleanor.

As I put my hand on the knob I heard the sound of horse hooves. They came toward the front of the house hard and fast. Without thinking I rushed down the steps and into the driveway. The ground trembled beneath the weight and power of the horse, but I couldn't see anything. Fog carpeted the front lawn, disguising even the familiar shapes of the trees.

"Barclay!" I called, my heart thudding. I knew it was Barclay, but at the base of my reptilian brain, a red alert sounded. Childhood fears of bogeymen and headless horsemen made me want to turn tail and run for safety. Instead, I held my position. "Barclay!"

The horse burst from the fog, a black mountain of muscle and flying mane. The massive creature slid to a halt in the gravel of the drive three feet in front of me. It reared, a wild whinny breaking free of its throat.

The horse seemed to be twelve feet tall. Front hooves pawed the air directly over my head. I couldn't move. I was paralyzed by fear.

"No!" The scream came from the front door.

Everything happened in slow motion. Eleanor was framed in the doorway. She was yelling, but I couldn't hear a sound. Sweetie and Chablis charged out of the house toward the horse.

I stood there unable to do a thing to save myself.

The rider's black cape swirled around him as he swung the horse hard to the right. The front hooves slashed down two feet from my shoulder with a thud that shook my bones.

With a snort of exertion, the huge horse leaped forward and away as Sweetie and Chablis barked at its heels. Then horse and rider were gone, consumed by the fog and the night.

"Sarah Booth, are you okay?" Eleanor came down the steps and put an arm around me and led me to the porch. "I thought you were going to be trampled. Why didn't you run?"

I didn't have an answer for her. But before we could get inside, headlights swept the driveway. Thank God. Tinkie had returned.

14

Tinkie took command of the situation. She ordered me, Eleanor, and the dogs back into the house while she took Eleanor's handgun and a flashlight and followed the hoofprints across the front lawn.

"Sit down before you fall." Eleanor eased me into a chair. "I'll get us a drink."

She returned with three glasses, ice, and a bottle of Bushmills 1608. She filled the glasses and handed me one. "Did you recognize the rider?"

Before I could answer, the front door shut with a solid thud and Tinkie stormed into the room, her cheeks burning with angry color. "Whoever it was can certainly ride."

"Did you recognize him, Eleanor?" I asked.

"I didn't get a clear look. A large man, broad shoulders. I'm sorry. You were under the rearing horse and I was so focused on you." She poured Tinkie a drink and gave it to her.

My hand had stopped shaking, so I could sip the whiskey without chipping my teeth. "It has to be Barclay. Broad shoulders, long legs. He knows the property."

"I don't think so." Tinkie sat beside me and rubbed my back. "Barclay was with me until half an hour ago. He couldn't have driven here, gone to the stables, saddled up, and ridden."

I hated to admit it, but she was correct. It would be an act of superhuman speed. "If not Barclay, then who?"

"I don't know, but I can assure you I'm going to find out. No one nearly tramples Sarah Booth and gets away with it."

Eleanor started to speak but was interrupted by the phone ringing. Tinkie switched on the recording device and signaled Eleanor to pick up. She did so, but before she could say hello, Monica's voice crackled from the speakerphone. "I'm alive, Eleanor."

The line snapped with static, and there was a strange echo, as if she was in a huge empty room. "I'm being held in a terrible place. I'm cold and scared. But I'm not harmed. He hasn't hurt me . . . yet. The kidnapper wants me to tell you that today you went to the insurance company and then the bank. I'm saying this so you know I'm alive and it's today. If you don't get the money for him, he will kill me. Don't doubt it. Do what he says. He'll call tomorrow with specific instructions. I—" The line went dead.

We sat in stunned silence. I'd never expected Monica to call. I'd honestly begun to believe she was dead.

Eleanor's relief was palpable. She vibrated with emotion. "She's alive. She's alive!"

"Thank god." Tinkie stood and gently held Eleanor's shoulders, either supporting or restraining, I couldn't tell which. "She had information that proves she is alive. A very good sign. If the kidnapper wanted to kill her, she'd be dead by now."

I'd recovered my wits enough to realize one of my best suspects, Eleanor, seemed to be in the clear. She'd been in the house all afternoon and evening, and she was with me when Monica called. As to Barclay, I'd been positive he was the marauding horseman. Now I had to rethink the knotty problem of the horseman and why he was rampaging around Briarcliff.

At most, we had twenty-four hours to come up with the money and devise a plan for the drop. I'd make another appeal for Eleanor to call in the law, but I knew it would be futile. The best Tinkie and I could do was protect her when she took the money and ransomed her sister.

"Can Oscar get the cash?" Eleanor asked Tinkie. Her mind had obviously forged ahead. "The insurance check is good. Once Monica is rescued, she'll endorse it. There won't be any liability for your husband."

"He'll do his best." Something was troubling Tinkie. I started to ask what was wrong, but she gave me a glance that told me to hold off. She went to the recorder and played back the message. Monica's voice was strong, even broken up by the static. "You're sure this is your sister?"

Fear passed across Eleanor's face. "Do you think it's an imposter?"

Tinkie tried to hide her worry. "No, I believe it's Monica and I think she's unharmed."

"Then we have to be ready." Eleanor drained her glass and put it down. "Whatever they want from me,

I'll do it. I've lost everyone in my life I ever loved. I will not lose my sister."

Tinkie re-cued the machine, but she didn't play it. "If Oscar helps with the money, Eleanor, we have to be ready for the kidnapper when he calls with the details of the drop. Could you listen to the call again?"

"Why?" Eleanor was distraught. "It makes me feel so helpless."

"Does it sound like she's calling from the same place the kidnapper called from the first two times?"

Eleanor considered for a moment. "Play it again, please."

Tinkie hit the button and Monica's voice once more filled the room.

"I can't say for certain." Eleanor went to the mantel and steadied herself. "I don't remember the static or echoey sound, but maybe I wasn't paying attention. Maybe it was there all along." She tugged a handful of her hair. "Why *can't* I remember? What's wrong with me? This is my sister's life!"

Tinkie caught her hand and stopped the tugging. "It's hard to remember details at a time like this. Relax. Let the conversations come back to you. Anything you remember could be helpful. Background noises, things we can use to pinpoint the location. Is there any place in Natchez with acoustics like that? An old, empty building?"

Eleanor's eyes closed. "There're dozens of old buildings all over Natchez. I could make you a list, and I will if you think it'll help. But Monica could be a prisoner in at least sixty different places. You'd require weeks to check them all out."

"Could you narrow the list?" Eleanor might unwittingly give us helpful information. I believed the kidnapper, singular or plural, was familiar with the Levert family. "Do you own any empty buildings?"

"We do. Our accountant keeps up with all properties, rented and empty. My brain isn't working properly. Now, of all times, I simply can't think clearly." The pressure had been relentless since Monica's abduction. Eleanor was exhausted and her body was demanding rest.

"Write a list for us. Tomorrow we can check any spaces you come up with." Daylight would serve us far better in our quest. I wasn't a coward by any means, but we could be thorough and quick with sunshine to help. And much safer.

"Tomorrow." Eleanor shifted away from the mantel and almost fell.

"Try to sleep." Tinkie offered assistance, but Eleanor righted herself and waved her away.

"Tomorrow, I'll call the accountant and he can help me write down the locations. I doubt they'll be helpful, but I'll try. Whatever it takes. Monica must be saved."

I had a question for Eleanor. "Before you go to your room, one more thing. Monica referred to the kidnapper as a 'he,' which jibes with what you told us about a man calling twice before. Was there anything about the voice you recognized?"

"He was so . . . confident. So cruel." Eleanor shuddered

"Who is this person?" I spoke aloud, though I didn't intend to.

"I don't know." Eleanor sounded as if she might cry.

"You need to eat something," Tinkie told her. "I can whip up an omelet or something—"

"No." Eleanor held up a hand as if warding off a blow. "I can't eat. My stomach churns at the thought of food. I'll go to my room. If I can catch a few hours of sleep, I'll be able to help more." Eleanor reached for the handgun Tinkie had placed on an end table, but I picked it up first. "I should keep this."

Eleanor only nodded and left the room.

True to her word, Tinkie prepared a delightful omelet. After we cleaned up the kitchen and fed the dogs, we retired to our bedrooms on the second floor. I took a moment to assess the layout of the room, which reminded me of one of the suites in the old black-and-white horror movies that featured Vincent Price as a man who brewed exotic and horrible experiments in the basement of the house.

The furnishings were lush—heavy silk draperies and bed hangings on the four-poster. Wingback chairs and a sofa in front of a fireplace, unlit because of the season. A thick Oriental rug glowed with patterns of crimson, turquoise, buff, and navy. The mantel held several family photographs, and when I picked them up I realized they were old tintypes of young women, the Levert brides. Whatever else could be said for the family, the women were a handsome lot. Especially the wives of Barthelme.

But what would possess a young woman to marry a man whose prior wife had died so shortly after the wedding? A man with a history of wives who perished. Staring at the features of the women, I saw their youth and naïveté. They looked no older than eighteen at the most, wide-eyed with innocence.

During the 1800s, marriages were often arranged. Women had no say in whom they married as long as the match was considered financially sound. But how could a father and mother barter their child, their daughter, into wedding a murderer?

I returned the pictures to the mantel and prepared for

bed. It wasn't even midnight, but we had a long day ahead of us. I'd just crawled under the covers when I heard a tapping at my door. "Come in." I knew it was either Tinkie or a raven. If it was a large black bird, I was outta there, case or no case.

"It just doesn't make sense." Tinkie shuffled into the room wearing Barney pajamas and big purple slippers. Her petite size allowed her to buy in the children's department when the whimsy struck.

"What doesn't make sense?"

She plopped on my bed. "The ride of the horseman. If it isn't Barclay trying to shake up his relatives, what's the purpose?"

I propped up beside her in the bed. "Do you think Jerome is exacting some type of revenge?" I told her about the love letters from Eleanor and my suspicions that Monica had deliberately busted them up. We hadn't had much of a chance to compare notes on our activities, and since neither of us could sleep, it was an opportunity we couldn't waste.

"He has to be involved with the horse. He's not a stupid man. He knows the animal is on the property." She wiggled her purple-encased feet. "I feel sorry for Eleanor. She's lost everyone, Sarah Booth. Her parents, her fiancé, and now her sister has been taken."

I cleared my throat. "I regret I was mean to her earlier."

"She seems sincere in her concern for Monica."

"She does."

"Tinkie, we aren't hostage negotiators, and we aren't trained to retrieve kidnap victims. She should call Gunny, but since she won't, remember, Eleanor must make the drop. Neither of us can afford to be put in such a dangerous position."

"I agree."

I was surprised. "You do?"

"Absolutely. While I think the kidnapper would have already killed Monica if that was his intent, delivering the money is too dangerous. If Eleanor won't call in the law, she needs to do it herself."

Her response was a load off my mind, but something else troubled me. "Does Oscar know he's cashing a check for ransom money?"

Tinkie studied her slippers. "No. I couldn't tell him."

"You have to, Tink. He can't risk all that money without knowing the details."

"The check is good, no matter what Eleanor does with the money. If Monica signs it later, great. If she's . . . dead, they'll reissue the check to Eleanor. It's the insurance company behind the check, not Eleanor or Monica."

Tinkie was normally the partner with the business head. She understood money far better than I do, so I couldn't believe the sentiment she now professed. "This is wrong and you know it."

"Oscar won't lose the money."

"Tinkie—"

"Eleanor said she'd make it good, no matter what. She has assets, but she isn't liquid." Her tone was defensive.

"What if she's killed making the drop? What if she and Monica both are killed? And the kidnapper steals the money. Where will that leave Oscar, cashing a check with a forged signature on it?"

At last she saw reality. One side of her mouth quirked up. "You're right. We have to handle this *and* protect Oscar." She kissed my cheek. "Thank you, Sarah Booth. I mean it. You saved me from a serious miscalculation."

Amen! "Tell him tomorrow. If he decides the risk is acceptable, then it's fine. If not—"

"Monica may die." Tinkie sounded as if she might cry. "We can't let the kidnapper hurt her."

"Whoever took Monica knows every move we make. He knew Eleanor went to the insurance company and the bank. I'm sure he knows the bank refused to cash the check, which is why the ransom demand has been delayed."

"The kidnapper has to be local. He watches us without drawing attention to himself."

I remembered the figure wearing night-vision goggles in the bushes outside Briarcliff. "Yes, and we need to figure out who it is. We've done good legwork, but we're no closer to knowing who's behind this than we were the first day we arrived."

"First light. We'll get that list of buildings from Eleanor and comb through them." Tinkie stifled a yawn. "I'll set my cell phone for five a.m."

"It's a date," I said, crawling into the sack myself. As I settled into sleep I had one last thought. Despite my best efforts, Tinkie and I were sinking deeper and deeper into the Levert quicksand.

The weight of the covers pinned my body like a straitjacket, and though I struggled, I couldn't free an arm. The air against my face was bitter cold. Someone shuffled in the dense shadows near the fireplace. A flint was struck and a spark flared. In a moment, fat lighter wood crackled as it caught fire.

I fought to sit up, but I was completely confined.

"What are you doing?" I couldn't shake the shackles of the bed or of the deep sleep into which I'd fallen. A better question arose in my brain. "Who are you?" My surroundings were unfamiliar, and panic constricted my chest as I thrashed in an effort to throw back the heavy coverlet.

"Calm yourself. There is no escape from the prison of bad choices," a soft, feminine voice said. It came from near the fireplace, and when I finally managed to fight my way into a sitting position, I saw a female form. She wore a dress with a full skirt that touched the floor. A peculiar collar circled her neck, and her hair was bound in a tight bun.

"*Who are you?*" I asked again.

"Look into your heart. You know me." She spoke in a lilting brogue as she approached the bed.

The fireplace illuminated one side of her face, and despite the red hair and voluminous dress, I recognized my haint. "Jitty?"

"Who else would come to warn you?" She was all business, in a historical kind of way. Judging by her attire, I would guess the Victorian era, but I'd never been a student of history.

"Am I in danger?" I asked.

"Are you breathin', lass?" She snorted. "Trust no one hereabouts, Sarah Booth. Each mother's son has his own agenda. Power and politics. Each puts his heart's desire above anything else. The men, the women. Never believe love comes before power in a bloodline destined to reign. Lust is a tool of those hungry to rule."

I knew who she was then. "Mary, Queen of Scots," I whispered. The resemblance was remarkable. Whoever did hair, makeup, and costuming in the Great Beyond deserved an Oscar for this getup. "Where is the danger? Is it here, in Briarcliff?"

Jitty's features filled with sadness. "There is no haven, save what you find in your own heart."

"Is it Eleanor?" I asked. "Is it Jerome? Or Barclay?"

"Deception is the card, but the question is, which hand dealt it. The answer can be found in only one place, Sarah Booth. Search for it. And guard your virtue."

"Jitty, I—" But she was gone. I looked up at the bed hangings and realized I was still beneath the spread and cotton sheets of my room in Briarcliff. It was summertime, and the fireplace was dead. The heavy tapestries of my dream room had also vanished.

"Jitty?" I couldn't be certain if she'd actually paid me a visit or if I'd dreamed her presence. It didn't matter. I'd been left with plenty of cryptic chunks to chew on. Like Anne Bolyne, another of Jitty's recent incarnations, Mary Stuart had lost her head at the order of her cousin, Elizabeth, a sister queen. Like the Leverts, the royals were a complicated, and convoluted lot.

Sweetie came to the bedside to check on me. Her presence lulled me into a sense of safety, and I fell back into slumber with her warm tongue caressing my hand. I'd been asleep for what seemed like moments when I heard her toenails clicking on the hardwood floor. She left the room and went down the hallway.

At the top of the stairs, she growled. The sound, following on the heels of Jitty's lurid warning, was as effective in waking me up as a slap. I swung my legs out of the bed as her growl deepened.

"Sweetie." Grabbing my jeans, shoes, the flashlight, and the .38 I'd taken from Eleanor, I eased out into the upstairs hallway. Sweetie started down the stairs, growling. I followed, pulling on my pants as I went.

When we got to the first floor, she went straight to the front parlor. The sheer curtains billowed on a light breeze. The window where the intruder had entered was wide open; the new lock Jerome had installed lay on the floor. The skin of my arms prickled. Sweetie bared her teeth and growled out the open window.

Before I could snare her collar, she jumped through it and took off.

15

"Sweetie!" I called after her as I leaned out the window. She'd vanished into a blanket of fog that completely covered the grounds of Briarcliff.

Torn between waking Tinkie or chasing Sweetie, I finally dashed out the window after my hound. Someone needed to stay in the house with Eleanor. If I didn't find Sweetie quickly, I'd call Tinkie on the cell phone in my jeans pocket.

The air was like a cool, damp soup, thick enough that it brushed my skin with an unpleasant sensation. "Sweetie!" I kept to the gravel path, moving around the house and into the rose garden. When I looked behind me, Briarcliff had been swallowed by fog. "Sweetie!"

The fog was so thick she could have been ten feet in front of me and I wouldn't see her. "Sweetie." I gave a low whistle. She always responded. Sweetie was loyal to the bone. "Sweet-ie." The mist swirled and drifted around me, but no hound came out of the night.

The first warning flag went up in my brain. Sweetie had to be nearby, yet she wasn't responding. I'd been around the estate grounds enough to know my way even in the thick fog. The flashlight I'd taken from Eleanor was all but useless—the light reflected back at me like a mirror.

Pausing for a moment, I listened to the whir of crickets and the cry of a night bird. *Predator*. I did my best not to let the omen creep me out. Along with the barn owl, the only noises came from the natural world, and those were softened by the fog, blurring my heightened imagination with reality.

Someone had opened the window at Briarcliff—either to enter the house or to spook the inhabitants. That was a fact. Sweetie was on the trail of someone, another fact. My hound wasn't in the habit of dashing off into the night unless there was good reason.

My heart almost stopped when I realized that while Sweetie and I were pursuing one intruder, a partner could have slipped inside the house. Even now, he or she might be skulking up the stairs to attack Eleanor or Tinkie.

"Sweetie!" I didn't want to leave her outside, but I also needed to get back to the house. I stopped to listen, but the night surrendered no secrets.

Wrapped in the dense hanging moisture and illuminated by a hidden moon, the grounds of Briarcliff had a magical quality. The sweet scent of roses, trapped in the thick atmosphere, clung to my face as I walked through the cool mist. Statues of maidens and angels loomed out of the miasma, giving me an initial jolt of fear, until I recognized them and could use them as landmarks.

I couldn't be certain, but it seemed Sweetie had taken the path to the gardener's cottage. Was Jerome the one breaking into Briarcliff? That didn't make any sense, but so little in this case did. Jerome had failed to disclose so many things, including his relationship with Eleanor, a smoldering omission—and where there was smoke, there was often a conflagration.

Up ahead, I heard a faint human voice. I glanced south, hoping to catch a glimmer of Briarcliff. I felt a compulsion to go back, to protect my partner and Eleanor.

The cry came again, weak and indistinguishable. It occurred to me I was being set up. Pulling my cell phone from my pocket, I dialed Tinkie to alert her to the possibility of danger. Maybe she could convince Eleanor to call the authorities, as she should have done long before now.

To my disgust, my cell phone was dead. I'd charged it, I was certain. But there was no denying that it was useless. Technology was not my friend.

"Please!" The cry came from the woods beyond the rose garden.

The voice was male, I could detect that much, and the person sounded hurt or in danger. Even as my fingers tightened on the gun, my brain sent panicked messages warning me of a trap.

"Help! Oh, please, help!"

I couldn't ignore the pleas. I left the rose garden behind and moved along the narrow path that cut through a wooded area. Branches damp with fog scraped my face and neck. The trees and shrubs crowded close to the path in this section. I had to move carefully or risk poking out an eye.

I thought I was headed in the direction of Jerome's

cottage, but the fog was disorienting. Though I searched the distance for a porch light or some indication of the cottage, I couldn't see a thing. The Delta's flat cropland suffered weather like this, but generally in the fall, when a warm front smacked into a cold front and created their love child—fog. This heavy curtain of non-rain blew in off the river and swirled like the swift currents that spawned it.

I'd been walking for what felt like hours and was about to turn back, realizing I'd been played, when I heard rustling in the underbrush ahead. Sweetie or an ambush? I couldn't tell. The poor visibility worked in my favor as well as theirs.

Stepping off the path I cut quietly through the gallberries and undergrowth toward the sound. A pitiful cry came from the soupy darkness and my hair literally stood on end. Briarcliff was a place that stimulated the most frightening fantasies. There was the sense that evil deeds from the past roamed at night. The cry coming from the woods made me want to run in the opposite direction.

Gripping the gun, I moved forward.

"Help me." The voice was weak. "Please. I'm bleeding."

Not twenty yards away, the mournful howl of a hound on a scent waffled through the night.

A sharp scream ripped through the woods, followed by someone crashing through the underbrush. Sweetie's howl sounded again. She was on a hot trail.

"I'm hurt! Please help me." The plea issued from the darkness only ten feet in front of me. Keenly aware that it could be a trap, I inched forward. More groaning ensued.

"Who are you?" I asked.

"John Hightower. The writer. Please, help me."

I couldn't be certain it was the eccentric writer—the upper-class British accent had slipped considerably. I inched forward, flicking on the flashlight to sweep the ground directly in front of me. At last my beam picked up what appeared to be a human form in a fetal position curled at the base of a tree. He was dressed all in black. Leather straps constricted his chest.

"Hightower?" I knelt down.

"Thank god. Help me."

"Did the horse trample you?" If so, it would be best not to move him.

"I've been beaten."

It was impossible to see much in the fog, so I relied on feel. When I touched his head, something warm, wet, and sticky coated my fingers. His wound was bleeding profusely.

"Who hurt you?" I tried to find the source of the blood. I tugged at one of the leather straps and found a camera with a telephoto lens. Another strap was connected to night-vision goggles. "What the hell?"

"I can explain. Monica said I could help her, that she needed me." He clutched my shirt. "She set me up."

He had to be delirious. "I have to get help for you." This was easier said than done, since I wasn't certain I could find my way back to him in the pea soup if I went to the house for help.

"Find Monica!" He pulled himself into a sitting position by holding on to my shirt. "She's in dire straits." The accent was restored, and Hightower appeared to be regaining his strength. The fog had suffocated the night sounds, and I had the sense that danger lurked in the misty darkness, but my ears detected no movement. The sense of urgency to get Hightower up and moving was great, though. Sweetie was bird-dogging another intruder.

"Who attacked you?"

"The fog was so thick. I saw someone. I thought it was Monica. She struck me." He slumped, and I thought he'd fainted.

Instead, his grip tightened and he drew me down so that his face was in my hair. "Listen," he whispered.

I heard it then—limbs rustling and snapping and the harsh breathing of someone running.

He grasped at my neck and shoulders, trying to gain his feet. "We have to find her. She'll do harm to herself. Like her mother. She'll throw herself off the cliff. The Levert family is unstable." His fingers dug into my shoulders.

My impulse was to push him back to the ground, but I controlled it. If I could get him to the path, I could leave him while I went for help. It was my only option.

"Work with me." I put his arm around my neck and pulled him up.

"Forget about me! Find Monica!" He lurched and I almost fell, with him on top of me. That was it. I snapped. I didn't care for the pompous man and his disappearing British accent. He was making it impossible for me to help him.

"Hightower, we're going to the path. Then I'm going for help. But you're going to do what I say, and if you push me again . . ." My threats were empty, and I knew it.

To my utter astonishment, he moaned. "I never meant for any of this to happen. Never. I've been in love with Monica since the first. I thought she loved me, too. I thought we'd have a future together. I would write and she would be my muse. I only threatened to write about her mother's tragic death because—" He broke down completely. "She threw me over."

"If you ever want to see Monica again, get up and walk!"

Sniffling and whimpering, he pulled himself together and we inched toward where I thought the path might be. He was heavy, and by the time we'd gone only a few yards, I was sweating. Off in the distance, I heard Sweetie's loud bay. She'd treed something. "Come on, Hightower. We're almost there."

"Listen!"

He didn't have to warn me. I heard it, too. Something was running toward us. It came through the underbrush fast, without regard for injury. I remembered the black horse that had nearly trampled me. I couldn't afford to let go of Hightower. If he fell, I might never get him to his feet again.

I swung the flashlight just as a buck crashed through a hock holly and leaped right at me.

"Arrrghhh!" Hightower cried as he pushed against me, gained his balance, and began to run like he'd trained for the Iron Man competition. I hooked his leather camera strap and hung on until it broke. I fell to the ground clutching the camera and rolled, mad enough to kill him. The man had sacrificed me to save his own skin. And if he was injured, he didn't show it as he hauled ass.

The deer veered north, Hightower south. I sat in the middle of the woods holding his camera and doing my best to hold my temper.

"Hightower?" I called out. "Hightower?"

Nothing. Far in the distance, I heard Sweetie Pie at work. I swung the flashlight beam and caught a beautiful piece of gossamer lace dangling from a limb. The same lace we'd discovered the night Monica disappeared.

The scrap of material could have blown about the property for the last three days. Or the person who'd assaulted Hightower—if he *was* assaulted—could have left the lace for me to find. Or Hightower could have planted it. He knew about Monica's mother's strange death. If he was masterminding the abduction, he could be setting the scene for another "suicide."

And I'd let him escape.

Using Sweetie's bay as a guide, I stumbled onto the path again. Sweetie seemed to be leading me toward the gardener's cottage. If Jerome was involved . . . if Monica was safely inside . . . I couldn't hope for a better outcome.

"Get 'im, Sweetie," I whispered under my breath.

To my utter delight, the fog was lifting at long last. From my knees down, the air was clear. Even at eye level it was beginning to thin. My joy was short-lived when I heard my dog cry out. Sweetie had been taken by surprise.

And then silence.

I stopped, the only sound my breath. I didn't want to call out to Sweetie. If someone had harmed her, he might be waiting for me.

I stood for several moments as the fog dissipated and the path cleared. I couldn't hear Sweetie or anyone else. The night seemed completely empty. I felt entirely alone.

Moving stealthily, I continued toward the cottage. No light showed inside, but I could still break in and use the telephone to get help. Tinkie could be here in a car in a matter of minutes, and I was done with shutting out the police. I wanted Gunny and a squad of officers on the scene. Monica, Sweetie, Hightower, and Jerome were MIA, and I intended that they be found and forced to give an explanation of their actions. Well, not Sweetie. Her actions were perfect, as usual.

As I neared the front porch, I saw her. My dog sprawled across the steps, unmoving.

"Sweetie!" I threw caution to the wind and ran to her. She was breathing. Her chest rose and fell in shallow gasps. Blood leaked from her mouth and down her chest.

Tied to her collar with a strip of gossamer lace was a note. I used the flashlight to read it. "Stop screwing around and get the money. Otherwise Monica is dead, and you won't be far behind."

"I'll get help," I reassured Sweetie as I readied the gun and opened the cottage door. I needed a landline, and woe be unto anyone who got in my path.

"Jerome!" I called out, but there was no answer. My fingers found the light switch. The cottage was empty. To my immense relief, the phone still worked. I called Tinkie, my fingers clumsy on the buttons. She answered groggily.

"Come to Jerome's cottage. Hurry, please."

"Sarah Booth." She was wide awake. "What happened? Why are you out on the grounds in the middle of the night?"

"Sweetie is hurt. Don't leave Eleanor alone. Bring her, but hurry."

"What—I'm on the way." Tinkie wouldn't waste time with questions since my hound was injured. "Hang on, Sarah Booth. We'll be there in three minutes."

By the time Tinkie and Eleanor arrived with the car, I'd revived Sweetie. The side of her head was cut and she was groggy, but otherwise not seriously injured. Fuming with a desire to rip the offender's throat out, I stroked Sweetie and whispered comforting nonsense to her.

Tinkie careened up to the front porch in the Caddy, unconcerned by the branches scratching her tomato red paint job.

"Is Sweetie okay?" Tinkie asked as she and Eleanor hurried toward me.

"Where's Jerome?" Eleanor's voice caught, as though emotion clogged her throat. She motioned at the open door. "He never leaves the cottage unlocked. Is he inside?"

"What, exactly, is your relationship with the gardener?" I'd had it with lies and half-truths.

"What do you mean? I haven't seen Jerome since this morning when he was mulching the roses." Eleanor's tone was stiff.

"Cut the act." I ran my hand over Sweetie's soft fur and waited for her to show me she was ready to move. "I know about your affair with Jerome."

She didn't say anything, but she closed her eyes as if shutting out memories. "He wouldn't have told you. How did you find out?"

"We're investigators. It's what we do. Now I want the truth. All of it. My dog has been injured, John Hightower is running around Briarcliff bleeding, and your sister is involved with people who may harm her."

"I don't know anything about John Hightower," Eleanor said. "He's always snooping around snapping photos. He was probably here spying. He tried to blackmail us—I told you that. He fell in love with Monica, and she treated him poorly, as she has so many others. That's all I know about him. I swear it."

"Then where's Jerome?"

"I wish I could answer."

The defeat in her voice made me believe her. "Eleanor, I don't know what games you and Monica are engineering." I thrust the note and scrap of nightgown at her. "This sounds serious. We need the police. Otherwise, Tinkie and I are out of here."

Before she could answer, another cry for help came from behind Jerome's cottage. This time it was a woman.

"Help me! I saw the car lights! Help!"

"Who the hell is that?" Tinkie asked.

Sweetie lifted her head and gave a mournful bay.

"I think that was who Sweetie was chasing. This is like a Monty Python comedy, except it's not funny and people and dogs are being hurt." I picked up a flashlight and eased out from under Sweetie's head. "Stay here, girl."

My hound was having none of it. She faltered to her feet and shook, then cocked her head.

"Help! I'm up here!"

With a brisk *arf*, Sweetie led us around the cottage to a tall magnolia tree.

"I'm up here!"

I aimed the flashlight. Tinkie and Eleanor added the strength of their beams. Caught in the light was Millicent Gentry, dressed all in black. Her pale face glowed in the illumination.

"That dog"—she pointed at Sweetie—"tried to tear my legs off. I got lucky and gave her a good lick with a magnolia pod."

"What are you doing on Briarcliff land?" Eleanor sounded imperious.

"It won't be yours forever," Millicent said haughtily.

"Why are you here?" I repeated, my aggravation showing.

"I don't have to answer your questions." She shot me the bird.

I handed Tinkie the .38. "Shoot her," I said. "She's trespassing and she tried to attack us."

"That's a damn lie—"

I cut her off. "It's our story and we're sticking to it."

"I just love it when you let me follow my urges." Tinkie cocked the gun and pointed it at Millicent. Without hesitation she pulled the trigger. A chunk of magnolia only inches from Millicent's head blasted out of the tree trunk.

"You crazy bitch!" All smugness had disappeared from Millicent's face. Eleanor had sense enough to stay quiet.

"I missed." Tinkie thumbed the hammer again and made a great pretense of aiming more carefully. "This is embarrassing. I never miss. But you won't be around to tell anyone about it, Millicent."

"I was helping John Hightower set up surveillance equipment. He said he was going to get the goods on Eleanor and Monica for insurance fraud." She tried to scrabble higher in the tree, but Tinkie fired again, this time just above her head. I had to hand it to my partner, she was a damn good shot. Close enough to put the fear of god in Millicent, but not a hair on her coiffed head was mussed. Either Tinkie was the reincarnation of Dead-Eye Pete or she'd been practicing behind my back.

"Come down out of that tree," I ordered.

"No. The dog will bite me."

"She's all yours, Tinkie. Shoot her." I started to walk away as I heard Tinkie cock the gun again.

"You're crazy," Millicent screamed, but she started down.

"I'll have you arrested," Eleanor said hotly. "You've

been told again and again to stay off this property. Now you're going to jail."

"I saw the horseman." Millicent dropped to the ground. "I hit the dog with a pod, but it didn't hurt her. The horseman whacked her with a tree limb. The dog was trying to hem him up."

I whirled around. "A horse hasn't been through here."

Millicent wiped her hands on her jeans. "Not the horse, just the rider. He was on foot. Running toward Briarcliff."

"Where was the horse?" I asked.

"How the hell should I know? I meant to follow the rider, but the dog came out of nowhere and sent me up the tree."

"Why not sell tickets and let everyone run around Briarcliff at night? Maybe it could be a reality TV show. Find the ghost rider? Hit a dog? Lose a gardener?" Tinkie was outdone. She waggled the gun at Millicent. "You first. You're going back to the house, and then we're going to hear the whole story."

"Screw you!" Millicent broke to the right, tearing through shrubs and bushes. Sweetie started after her, but I grabbed the dog's collar when she staggered.

"Let Millicent go." I gathered Sweetie into my arms. "We can find her tomorrow. And trust me, she will talk."

I sat on the floor before a roaring fire with Sweetie's head in my lap as Eleanor paced the back parlor. Sweetie had fully recovered. The wound wasn't serious. She'd scarfed down leftover steak and now snoozed in the warmth of the fire Eleanor insisted on lighting. A fire in August—just another Levert eccentricity. But the foul weather, though now dissipated, had cast an air of chill and gloom over the estate. Perhaps the crackling fire wasn't a total extravagance.

"I'm so sorry," Eleanor said for the hundredth time. "I think we should call a veterinarian to be sure Sweetie isn't injured."

Chablis, who'd been shut in Tinkie's bedroom and missed all the action, gave a tiny yap of agreement. Sweetie thumped the floor with her tail. She basked in the attention. "She's okay, Eleanor."

"Where do you suppose Jerome is?" she asked. She was worried and no longer tried to hide her feelings.

"I don't know."

Tinkie returned to the room with a tray of coffee. She gave each of us a cup. "Eleanor, we can't continue like this. John Hightower is on the grounds, maybe injured but not seriously if he can flee like a gazelle. Millicent is conspiring with him. We don't know what's happened to Jerome. You haven't been honest with us about your relationship with Jerome. If we're going to help, you have to tell us about him."

Eleanor sank into a leather sofa, one of the few modern furnishings in the house. "Jerome was born in Scotland. There's a long family tie to the Leverts. Jerome's great-great-grandfather captained the *Lillith*. He was in cahoots with Barthelme. At one point, Barthelme saved his life, and there's a bond between our families." Bitterness touched her tone. "Master and servant. Jerome came to Natchez to help my father, and we fell in love." She gazed out the window into darkness. I thought she'd slipped into a memory. When she spoke again, it was on another subject. "The kidnapper said he would kill Monica." She faced me. "I'm concerned for Jerome and Mr. Hightower. I hate what happened to your dog. But Monica is my sister, Sarah Booth. If I call the police and it results in her death . . ."

She was caught between a rock and a hard place, no doubt of that. "I believe Gunny will use discretion," I said. "We'll explain the situation. He'll make sure that if the kidnapper is watching Briarcliff, his officers won't be obvious. This is serious, but you have to keep in mind that, so far, except for Sweetie and Hightower, no one else has been hurt."

"I'm afraid." Eleanor set her untouched coffee on the low table. "For the first time in my life, I'm truly afraid that whatever action I take will result in injury to someone I care about."

"Such as Jerome?" I asked.

She sighed. "Yes. Jerome. He wouldn't just leave. Ironic, isn't it, that he's been within reach for most of my life, but I wouldn't take him. Not as my husband. Monica wouldn't hear of it. So I let class dictate my happiness, and now I have none. My sister is gone, and so is Jerome. Perhaps it's justice."

My palm traced the contours of Sweetie's warm hide. "You've put us in a bad position, Eleanor. Tinkie and I operated in good faith. You've lied and withheld vital information. Your life, and your sister's, are webs of deceit. Sons, lovers—lies at every step. I'm not even certain you and Monica didn't arrange the theft of the necklace. I feel Tinkie and I must resign from the case."

Eleanor stood abruptly. "Please. Please don't! I need you. I've come to rely on you. You're the only people I trust."

My mind was made up. Sweetie could have been killed, and for what? To protect two women who wouldn't know the truth if it bit them on the leg? "I'm sorry."

Tinkie knelt beside me. Her hand drifted over Sweetie's coat, earning a thump of my dog's tail. "Sarah Booth is right. We've both been injured helping clients, but we won't be hurt protecting liars." She stood up. "I'll pack our things, Sarah Booth. You stay with Sweetie."

"I implore you," Eleanor said. "I don't have the ransom money. I can't save Monica without your help. I'll tell you the truth about everything. It isn't what it looks like. Monica and I aren't swindlers. We've made bad decisions, but they've mostly hurt us."

"And Barclay?" I said. "What kind of mother abandons her child because he's an inconvenience?"

Eleanor had cast aside all dignity and begged. "Please. Please help me save my sister. Whatever we've done, she doesn't deserve to die alone and scared."

Tinkie crossed the room. "Sarah Booth was right in the beginning. We should have insisted the authorities handle this. You need law enforcement to hunt for Jerome and Mr. Hightower. If they're injured on the property, you need to find them, and quickly."

Pride for my partner formed a lump in my throat. Tinkie always had my back—and Sweetie's, too.

The ringing of the telephone stopped us cold.

A dozen thoughts shot through my brain, but the predominant one was that only bad news came at three in the morning. Judging from Eleanor's face, she had exactly the same thought. Instead of answering, she didn't move.

The phone rang twice more before Tinkie turned on the recording device still attached. "Answer it," she directed Eleanor.

Eleanor started to refuse, then a shaky hand reached for the phone. "Hello."

A man spoke sharply. "The drop will be at midnight.

You have twenty-one hours. I'll call with further instructions."

"Wait!" Eleanor cried. "Wait, please—"

The burr of the dead line echoed in the silent room.

16

Eleanor returned the phone to its cradle. She tottered, as if she would fall, then stiffened her spine. "Please don't quit now. See this through until he calls with the drop instructions. Please. I have no one else. Jerome is missing. Millicent hates me. I intend to call that man, Barclay. If he is a true Levert, perhaps he'll help me."

The log in the fireplace snapped. Sparks flumed up the chimney. It wasn't that Eleanor's plea didn't touch me—my heart wasn't completely made of stone. But she'd acted in bad faith from the moment she'd called us, and I couldn't afford to forget it. I owed it to Graf and Oscar to remember.

"I need a word alone with my partner," Tinkie said.

Eleanor reluctantly left the room. For a long moment,

there was only silence. I didn't look at Tinkie. I waited to hear what she'd say.

"I know we should leave," Tinkie said. "Eleanor hasn't been honest about all the personal stuff, but is that really even part of the case? I don't think Monica has been taken by a lover she dumped. Yes, she's gone all over town making trouble, but this isn't about sexual payback. You heard the kidnapper. This isn't some love-sick guy wanting to punish Monica. He was cold. I'm afraid he'll kill her if I don't help Eleanor get the money together."

The exact same thought had crossed my mind. "I'm sorry for Eleanor and Monica, but they're liars. Can we really help them, Tinkie? The FBI would have a much better chance of securing Monica's safety." I took a breath. "There's too much at stake. You're right, the person who has Monica is deadly earnest. Once again, I've risked you, Sweetie Pie, Chablis, and myself. Whoever struck Sweetie could have killed her. It could as easily have been you."

"Jerome may also be in danger. Was he taken or did he leave on his own?"

"I have no idea. Affiliation with the Leverts is obviously dangerous. And I'm sorry. I won't risk your safety or mine. We can't fix this."

Tinkie took a poker and stabbed at the fire. "We can't just tuck tail and run home."

"What do you suggest we do?" I wanted to go home. I wanted to call Graf and see if there might be a possibility to hop a flight to La-La-Land with my dog and spend a few days in the golden California sun. The darkness of Briarcliff had tainted my soul. I was ready for light and love.

"Let's help Eleanor get the money, at least. We'll review the drop instructions with her—try to prepare her. You and I both know she won't call the police. She'll try to do this by herself." Tinkie seemed to stand taller. "We aren't prepared for this, but we're a lot more prepared than she is. I can't just walk away."

When Tinkie took a stand, her head was harder than mine. "If the drop sounds too dangerous, we'll warn her. That's it. Nothing more." Like my partner, I had some guilt at the idea of just walking away. Even if it was the smartest thing to do.

"Do you think Hightower is still on the grounds? He may know something about Monica and Jerome." Tinkie inhaled deeply and stretched.

"He wasn't hurt. He's just a crybaby. He popped up like a jackrabbit and took off." I leaned down to kiss Sweetie's muzzle. "So what do we do about the open window?" I'd almost forgotten the incident that had driven me and Sweetie out into the night.

"Tomorrow Eleanor can find a hammer and nails. To hell with historic detail. I intend to make certain all of the downstairs windows are secure. The nails can be removed later."

It was too little too late, but I nodded in agreement. My brain was still knotted around the whole John Hightower incident. That Monica was a predatory lover, I didn't doubt. What I didn't believe was that she'd be attracted to a man like John Hightower. He simply didn't have the va-va-voom factor.

And Millicent. What was her true role in all of this?

"Let's get some sleep," Tinkie said. "It's after four o'clock. We can still snatch a couple of hours before daybreak."

I held no hope of sleeping, but I pretended to go to my room so Tinkie would rest. As soon as her door closed, Sweetie and I went to the front parlor. I settled on a sofa with my hand dangling onto Sweetie's satiny head. Together, we waited for the dawn.

Against her nature, Tinkie was up at first light. I heard her in the kitchen grinding coffee beans and humming an old standard. I hadn't truly slept, but I had drifted into a strange dreamy state where I knew exactly where I was and what was happening around me, but I also traveled backward through time to summer mornings when my mother hummed in the kitchen at Dahlia House. She'd loved the tunes of the 40s and often sang them around the house. And she could sing, in a clean, resonating contralto.

I knew the lyrics to Tinkie's melody. "A Dreamer's Holiday," a Perry Como classic from 1949. It was one of my mom's favorites. Sometimes, in the music room, she'd crank up the old stereo and play the 78 rpm record so she could hold me and dance.

"'Climb aboard a butterfly . . . ,'" I crooned softly, until Sweetie Pie started to howl.

Tinkie popped around the corner. "I knew you weren't asleep, but you looked so peaceful."

"Is the coffee made?"

"It's brewing. Shall I wake Eleanor?"

"I think so." We had to determine if John Hightower had left Briarcliff, and we couldn't leave Eleanor alone. She'd have to come with us.

Tinkie started up the stairs just as a heavy knock fell against the front door. I had a momentary visual of the old Vincent Price classic *The Fall of the House of Usher*.

I'd heard the story of director Roger Corman, when asked by the studio, "Where is the monster?" replied, "The house is the monster."

So it was at Briarcliff. Everything, even a knock at the door on a summer morning, seemed sinister.

The heavy rap came again as the person outside demanded entrance. Dread, my current BFF, marched in goose bumps along my skin as I walked to the door. I put my hand on the knob and opened the massive wooden doors of Briarcliff.

"Ms. Delaney." Barclay Levert looked every inch a descendant of the Levert clan. He wore a black shirt open at the throat, black slacks that suited his build, and his dark hair was clipped in a queue at the nape of his neck. "May I enter?" he asked.

"Are you a freaking vampire?" I snapped. "Do I have to invite you in?" Barclay unsettled me, and I turned abruptly and walked back to the parlor. Tinkie, on the other hand, almost skipped out of the kitchen to greet him.

"Oh, Barclay," she called merrily. She acted as if she'd slept a full ten hours. "Care for some coffee? And I found some scones Kissie baked the other day. Eleanor tells me that Kissie has a talent for baking."

"So I've heard." Barclay winked at me, which made me want to smack him upside the head. I was sure he'd sampled Kissie's baking skills as well as many others.

"What are you doing here?" I wasn't in a mood to flirt or banter.

"I have the DNA results."

"What, you have an inside track at a crime lab? No one gets results so fast."

Barclay chuckled softly and pushed a strand of my

hair out of my eyes. "You're something of a grump in the morning, aren't you, Sarah Booth?"

"When she doesn't get her seven hours sleep, she's a gorgon," Tinkie said.

"Like I ever get seven hours of sleep." I glared from one to the other. "Why are you so damn perky, Tinkie? And what are you doing here before the sun even clears the horizon, Barclay?"

"I thought I might move my things here." Barclay pushed in the foyer, drinking in the elegance of the house and the furnishings. "I grow weary of rented rooms and the kindness of strangers. I'm ready to come home, and this place is even better than I imagined."

"So the test results prove you're a Levert?" In this instance, one plus one resulted in baby Barclay Levert. He not only looked the part, he was beginning to sound like landed aristocracy.

"Monica is my mother. I have the evidence I need. A lab in Jackson performed the test. The results are indisputable. As they say on all the crime shows, DNA doesn't lie." There was almost a challenge in his attitude, as if I wouldn't believe him. Before I could respond, Eleanor's stern voice came from the stairs.

"You might have a blood test, but you don't have permission to be in Briarcliff. Monica is the only person who can offer you a place here."

Eleanor descended the stairs in an old-fashioned satin robe cinched at her slender waist. It fell around her with a swirl of shining fabric. With her dark hair tousled from sleep and in disarray, she looked as if she'd awakened from a time past. The beautiful chocolate color of the dressing gown heightened her penetrating gaze. The resemblance between Eleanor and Barclay was clear. They could as easily be mother and son as aunt and nephew.

"Where is my *loving mother*?" Barclay asked. "I would think she'd be on pins and needles to meet her boy. Our parting was so abrupt and unexpected." He turned his palms up. "Poof. Like magic. How can a boy resist a mother who performs magic?" Irony laced his tone.

Eleanor was in his face in a flash. She drew her hand back to slap him. Only Barclay's quick reflexes saved his cheek.

"I'd planned to call you here to help me, but I see my judgment was clouded. What have you done with my sister?" Eleanor said through gritted teeth.

Barclay held her wrist. Stepping close, he forced her back to arch away from him. "What, exactly, are you accusing me of, my dearest Aunt Eleanor?" He, too, spoke through his teeth.

"Stop it!" I punched Barclay's arm and he released her. Eleanor stepped back and rubbed her wrist. "Have you both lost your minds?" The Leverts provoked questions to which there was no simple answer.

"Where's Monica?" Eleanor was almost breathless with rage.

The confusion on Barclay's face seemed genuine, but I'd been duped before by a handsome face. "How should I know where Monica is? She's not in the habit of communicating her whereabouts to me. Let's see, the last she spoke to me or my father was to say she was going for a pack of cigarettes, or something to that effect. That was, what, thirty-five years ago?"

"Stop it." Eleanor's eyes flashed danger. "Stop mocking Monica."

"Defensive of *Mom*, are you? I always dreamt of having a mother I was proud to defend. Life has its disappointments, though. I get a mother who is indefensible."

Although we didn't physically move, Tinkie and I eased into the background. This was family turf, a place where we had no standing. Barclay was angry, and he had every right to be. Eleanor was protective, a role she'd obviously played since birth for Monica. The two would have to work this out, and we had no right to interfere—as long as they kept it to the verbal arena.

"You may be her son, but that doesn't automatically give you a place in this family." Eleanor had plenty of backbone when put to the challenge. Maybe she'd do better at the ransom drop than I anticipated. "If Monica wanted you to be part of her life, she would have told me about you."

"I'm not a fool, Aunt Eleanor. I have standing. Legal standing. If put to the test, I'll wring every last ounce due me out of you and Mommy dearest."

"It always comes down to money." Eleanor's fists clenched at her side. "Always money. You don't care about anything else."

"It's the altar where you worship. Monica left me behind so she wouldn't have to care for me. She never even sent a birthday card—all to protect her fortune from my father, a man who would have starved rather than take a dime."

"Too bad you don't take after him."

I thought Eleanor had taken it too far. Barclay stepped back as if he'd been slapped. The earlier blow Eleanor intended to deliver came in the form of words so cutting, even I gasped.

"Tell Monica I'm at the Eola. She can call on me if she desires. Otherwise, my lawyer will be in touch. I advise the two of you to meet me head on rather than drag this into court. I have all the time in the world, and I'll likely get a judge's order allowing me to reside here at Briarcliff while we battle it out. Think of it, Auntie. Dinner at eight in the formal dining room, just the three of us."

Barclay stalked out of the foyer and down the front steps. A moment later his black sedan tore down the driveway.

Sweetie Pie was up for an outing, so I took the dogs down the path to Jerome's cottage. Tinkie and Eleanor had to call Oscar about the ransom money. I was just as happy to be out looking for clues.

The day was beautiful—hot and sunny, as if the night had never happened. Walking toward the cottage, I remembered the sense of someone watching in the thick fog. In the bright sunshine, with a breeze off the river and birds singing and calling, it seemed improbable. Even Sweetie acted as if her injury had been part of a nightmare.

I came to a place in the dirt path where it was obvious a scuffle had occurred. John Hightower's camera had flown into the underbrush somewhere near here. I had to find it. The camera would tell me a lot about what Hightower was up to at Briarcliff.

Chablis bounced in and out of the underbrush, yapping, and I had to smile at her joy and enthusiasm. She was so puppy-like at times, but I'd seen the lioness emerge when necessary. She was, indeed, Tinkie's child.

The dustmop gave a bark of excitement, and I stepped off the path to see what she'd found. I wasn't surprised when she pawed at a camera lying under a huckleberry bush. Tinkie was the photography buff, but I could manage the basic functions. I picked it up and checked to see if there was obvious damage sustained when it was thrown into the bushes. It seemed fine, so I turned it on and went to the view function.

Hundreds of photos were cached on the memory stick. In dozens of grainy images, a horse and rider moved blurrily through the fog. Hightower had camped out in the front shrubbery near where Jerome had reported an intruder the previous night.

Hightower had a bird's-eye view of the horse and rider—had the weather cooperated, his pictures might have identified the rider.

One frame captured the horse rearing over my head. An Andalusian. A magnificent animal known for its athleticism, good temperament, courage, and handsomeness. The rider's features were lost in shadows, but he was graceful and accomplished.

The photo reminded me of the danger I'd been in as I stood beneath the front hooves, the horse pawing the air. It was a stupendous photo that would scare the socks off Graf if he ever saw it. Which meant he never would.

I clicked to the final image and nearly dropped the camera. For a moment I thought the glare of the hot summer sun had fogged the screen or that a trick of light was playing with the images.

The sun beat down on my head and back, but a cold sweat popped out along my hairline. Surely this couldn't be real. It had to be some kind of fake. I stepped into the shade for a clearer view of the screen, and the horror tripled. It wasn't a fake.

Millicent Gentry lay in the underbrush, her neck twisted

at a grotesque angle. And someone had gone to the trouble to dress her as a Shopping Barbie. She even held a Macy's bag filled with rhinestone tiaras.

The sensation of being watched made me lower the camera and look around. Sweetie gave a low, dangerous growl, as if she, too, suddenly sniffed danger. Around me birds sang, the wind whispered through the trees, and in the distance there was the mournful horn of a tug on the river. Nothing had changed—except I knew someone was watching me.

Quickly scanning the underbrush, I searched for Millicent's body. It had to be nearby. In the photo she was partially leaned against the base of a big oak. The grounds of Briarcliff contained hundreds of old oaks.

After half an hour of searching, I had to admit the body was nowhere in evidence. Whoever had taken the picture had either removed the body or returned the camera to a spot where it would easily be found by someone on the path to Jerome's cottage. The killer wanted us to know he'd taken a life. This wasn't just about ransom money now. This was about murder.

The rules of the game had taken a drastic turn for the worse.

17

With the camera in hand and Sweetie right at my side, I jogged back to Briarcliff. Stepping into the shadow of the house I felt the temperature drop ten degrees. The place cast an impressive shadow uncomfortably reminiscent of a mausoleum.

Ignoring the sensation of lingering evil, I pushed open the front door and went straight to the telephone.

Tinkie answered her cell phone on the first ring.

"Where are you?" I asked.

"At the bank. What's wrong? You sound like someone shrank your panty hose."

"Come back to Briarcliff. Now." The phone wasn't to be trusted. I couldn't be certain who might be listening— the pervasive sense of being watched had followed me from the woods into the house. Someone knew every move we made.

My first instinct had been to call Gunny, but instead I waited for Tinkie and Eleanor to return. The police had to be called. No more fooling around. To put the best face possible on an ugly situation, Eleanor should be the person to contact the police.

"What on earth is wrong with you?" Tinkie was more concerned than annoyed.

"No questions. Come quickly."

"It must be bad if you won't say. Is it Moni—"

"Don't say anything else," I interrupted, paranoia alive and gnawing at my gut. "Trust me and just get Eleanor and bring her here."

"We're on the way." She was confused by my request, but she knew me well enough to know I had good reasons for my cryptic conduct.

I collapsed into a wingback chair in the parlor and put my face in my hands. Things had escalated so fast. Millicent was dead and probably still somewhere on the grounds. The idea of a corpse left under a tree was distressing enough, but Jerome was also missing, maybe dead. Monica was a hostage. In a matter of hours, the carnage in a supposedly simple insurance investigation had climbed to a level I could never have imagined.

I was about to curl up in a fetal position and wait for Tinkie when a fist pounded on the front door. My first impulse was to run out the back and hide in the woods, but I braced myself against irrational fear.

"Nevermore!" I whispered as I got up wearily to answer the knocking.

The one person I would never have anticipated stood at the front entrance. Helena Banks Gorenflo held the tether of a small, blond-spotted, beagle-type dog with the most bizarre goatee of frizzy white hair. The dog looked completely demented, as did Helena. She glared at me. The spotted beagle hiked his leg and peed on Helena's bejeweled black flat.

"Tell Millicent she's finished in Natchez society." Helena thrust the leash toward my hand. "She will pay for this. *She will pay*."

I didn't answer and I didn't take the leash. I stood there like I'd been poleaxed. Until I started laughing, which was absolutely the wrong thing to do. Helena wasn't a woman who appreciated being the butt of humor.

"Take this spawn of Satan Millicent calls her dog before I strangle him with his leash." She pushed the tether toward me again.

I took two steps back, too stunned at Helena's unexpected appearance on top of Millicent's murder to say or do anything except giggle.

"Are you on drugs or just stupid?" she asked.

When that failed to elicit a response, she snapped her fingers in front of my face. "What the hell is wrong with you? Where is Millicent? I demand to speak to her."

My brain finally engaged and I dragged my gaze from the mesmerizing eyes of the dog. There was definitely something Rasputinish about the mutt. "What makes you think Millicent is here?"

I must have looked addled, because she sighed and spoke very slowly. "She . . . was . . . working . . . for . . . John . . . Hightower . . . last . . . night . . . and . . . left . . . her . . . car . . . at . . . his . . . apartment."

I couldn't take any more of her tedious phrasing. "Stop it. I understand you, but it doesn't make sense that you would think Millicent is here at Briarcliff. The Levert sisters don't like her. She doesn't like them. They aren't in the habit of visiting each other."

"It makes perfect sense," Helena insisted. "John said he left her here. She never retrieved her car from his place, therefore she is still here. Millicent is not the kind of woman who would walk anywhere."

So Hightower had made it home safely, but he'd abandoned his partner in snooping. He'd hauled ass through the woods and straight to his vehicle, leaving Millicent to fend for herself. Weasel. No, worse than a weasel. In my book, he might be an accessory to murder.

A terrible thought crossed my mind: What if Hightower had killed Millicent? Though he didn't physically strike me as the type to commit strangulation—even Millicent, feminine as she'd been, could have bested him in hand-to-hand combat—still, he could have whacked her on the head and disabled her before he went for her throat. Judging from the photo, she had died of a broken neck.

Helena stomped her foot, which made an unpleasant squishing sound. "Have you suffered some kind of brain injury?"

Roscoe jerked on the leash and almost pulled her over. It was enough to snap me out of my gruesome thoughts. "What did the dog do? I mean, other than pee on your foot." Roscoe personified trouble with a capital T. The dog exuded criminal activity.

"Millicent has trained this creature to dig into trash. He does it all over town, and he drags things about, leaving a perfect trail of . . . disgusting items. He has an uncanny ability to find exactly the thing you most wish—" She broke off, aware, perhaps, she was saying too much.

"So Roscoe got into *your* trash and nosed up something embarrassing. What, a list of orphans you've abused? People down on their luck you've evicted?" Since she was determined to force herself on me, I decided to have some fun.

"My life is above reproach. Roscoe discovered no such thing. But he is vile and horrible. Just like everything connected to the Leverts. Keep him off my property or the next time, I'll shoot him myself."

"What is it with you?" I asked. "You were supposed to be in Eleanor's wedding. You were once friends. What happened?"

Hatred twisted her face. "Gaston would never have gone through with the wedding. He loved me, not Eleanor. He wanted to marry me."

"He died during his bachelor party," I pointed out. "To all appearances, he meant to marry Eleanor."

"That shows what you know." The fevered gleam of memory lit her eyes. "He didn't know how to get out of it. He didn't want to hurt Eleanor, but he couldn't marry her. He didn't love her. The Levert money would allow him to continue as an artist, but he would have gained financial success without it. I helped him see that. We had plans to run away, back to France. We would have been happy."

"Your family fortune wasn't enough to entice him?" I couldn't help it. The whole situation was distasteful. If what she said was true, Gaston was nothing more than a fortune hunter who had seduced Eleanor for her wealth.

"The Banks had a good name and little else. But Gaston chose me over the money. He left the bachelor party to meet me." Her voice quivered but held. "I was late. Because of Monica. She threatened me. She told me if I didn't meet her at an old plantation where we all went parking, she'd ruin me in society. She had photographs of an . . . indiscretion. Something that happened when I was very young."

"So instead of meeting Gaston, you went to talk with Monica."

She nodded. "Gaston left the party, as planned, and went outside to the place I was to pick him up. We were going to leave for France to start a life together. He was waiting for me when he was killed by muggers."

"And you blame the Levert sisters? You were stealing her fiancé the night before her wedding and you blame them?" I didn't have to fake incredulous.

"Yes. I do. They use their money to control everyone who gets near them. It cost Gaston his life and me my happiness."

"Don't kid yourself, Helena. The only person you can blame is yourself. You put your reputation ahead of your lover."

"Reputation is obviously something you don't understand." She drew herself up, gaining control of her emotions. "Because you've never had one, except as a meddling old maid." She tossed the leash at my face, but I caught it before it struck me.

Helena executed a perfect about-face and stormed down the drive to her waiting car. A driver opened the door and within seconds she was gone. I wondered how much of the true story of Gaston's death Eleanor knew. Monica obviously knew it all, but I doubted she'd shared the knowledge of Gaston's intended betrayal. Just another bit of the past that wouldn't lie down and die.

"So you're the infamous Roscoe," I said to the dog. "What did you find that upset Helena so much?"

He didn't answer, but he grinned at me. An idiotic dog

grin that said "I pretend to be stupid but I'm not. In fact, I'm way smarter than you are."

"Roscoe?"

The stump of his tail, which looked as if someone had chopped it with a meat cleaver aiming for a more vital body part, thumped. He lifted one paw, clearly attempting to shake.

So I'm a sucker. Roscoe was Millicent's dog, and though I didn't believe she'd deliberately trained him to dig through trash, it could be a handy activity for a private investigator. More to the point, with Millicent dead, Roscoe qualified as an orphan, and one not likely to find another loving parent based on what I knew of him. In fact, his criminal record in Natchez would go against him. The future looked grim for the cunning canine. If he showed up at her place, Helena would, without hesitation, send the dog to the pound for extermination.

But why was I worried about a dog with criminal inclinations when I had a missing woman and a dead body? I led Roscoe into the house and unsnapped his lead. Sweetie would show him the ropes around Briarcliff. I just had to be sure Chablis approved of this agenda.

No worries there, the three dogs met as old friends and scooted upstairs to do whatever it is dogs do when humans aren't watching.

I put on another pot of coffee and stood at the kitchen window until Eleanor pulled under the portico. I gripped the counter as I waited for the two women to get into the house. Eleanor pushed through the door, her cheeks red with emotion.

"This had better be important. We have to get the money, Sarah Booth, but Tinkie insisted we come back here. She said it was an emergency." Eleanor was upset, and she didn't bother to hide it. "Don't you understand my sister will die if I can't manage to cash the stupid insurance check?"

"Millicent Gentry is dead." I handed the camera to Eleanor.

Her fingers fumbled for a moment, but she looked at the image. "Oh, dear god," she whispered, pushing the camera back into my hand.

Tinkie took it gently and examined the photo. "You're sure this isn't fake?"

"I'm not sure of anything." I told them about Helena bringing Roscoe here. "I think the dog probably tracked Millicent's car to John Hightower's place. Roscoe obviously thought Millicent was still there, and while he was trespassing he got into Helena's trash and discovered god knows what."

"Apparently Hightower and Millicent were working together to spy on Briarcliff. They came over last night, and Hightower simply abandoned her after he was attacked." Tinkie added up the facts quickly.

"This is an awful turn of events. Poor Millicent. I never liked her, but I didn't wish harm to her." Eleanor sank into a kitchen chair and rested her forehead on her fist. "Why was she working for the awful writer?"

Eleanor's color was awful, a grayish paste. I worried her heart might give her trouble. Or maybe I just felt a little more compassion for her knowing the secret of her engagement. "Millicent was single. Is romantic involvement a possibility?" I asked.

"John Hightower wasn't Millicent's type of man. She liked her men forceful and brawny. Cowboys or cops. Uniforms and jeans," Eleanor continued, almost reminiscing. "Hightower is too . . . wormy for her taste. So why would Millicent spy on us to get material for his dreadful book? It doesn't make sense."

"That's something Hightower is going to have to answer. Eleanor, you must call the police," I said it as gently as I could. "Millicent's body is somewhere on the grounds of Briarcliff. We have to—"

"No!" Eleanor shot out of her chair. "No police. I'm sorry about Millicent, but she is *dead*. Monica is still alive. She has a chance. But she will die if we don't do exactly as we've been told. We have fifteen hours until time to drop the ransom money. Millicent can wait until then. After Monica is home, the police can set up a substation here if they want to."

"Eleanor . . ." Tinkie was as stunned as I was by the outburst.

"Monica's blood will be on your head if you call the police." She was almost panting. "We're so close. Let's just get the money. Please." She started to cry. "Please, she's my sister. I can't let her die. I can't. Don't you see? Someone killed Millicent. He won't hesitate to do the same to Monica if we do anything to upset him."

Tinkie blew out her breath. She gave me a "What should we do?" look, and I gave her a glare. We couldn't pretend that there wasn't a dead body on the premises.

"Let's find the body," Tinkie said. "While we're searching, Eleanor can go back to the bank and arrange for the money. The initial work has been done and Eleanor can handle the rest of it by herself. Maybe this whole Millicent thing is a hoax. It looks real, but photos are pretty easy to stage. We don't want to jump the gun and call in Gunny until we're sure something actually happened to Millicent."

She was buying more time for Eleanor, and while I knew what she was doing, I couldn't help but agree. If we couldn't find Millicent's body . . . maybe the whole thing was a fake and I was overreacting. John Hightower lusted for revenge against the Leverts. He was capable of anything. I picked up the camera again and studied the photo. It looked real. Still, it could be staged. What if Gunny and his forces arrived and found nothing and the kidnappers killed Monica?

"Okay," I said. "But if we find the body, I'm calling the cops instantly."

"Thank you." Eleanor picked up her keys. "I'll hurry as quickly as I can. Mr. Richmond has helped arrange a transfer of funds so the local Natchez bank can cash the check. I hope to be back within the hour." She was out the door in a flash and headed back to town.

"Where should we start looking?" Tinkie asked.

"Hold up." I caught her elbow and told her about Helena Banks Gorenflo's revelations.

"Can this family get more tragic?" she asked. "Eleanor loved this artist guy and then Jerome, and she couldn't marry either one. It's no wonder Monica hates Helena, though. She knows what that old bitch tried to do."

"I feel like a dark cloud hangs over the Levert family," I said. "Perhaps John Hightower is right. Maybe the family is cursed by the evil of old Barthelme."

"You never struck me as the superstitious type," Tinkie said with a straight face. She knew me well enough to know I was a sucker for portents and dreams and omens. Madame Tomeeka, Zinnia's resident psychic, could scare the pants off me with one arched eyebrow.

"Let's get the dogs," I said, ignoring her lie. "If anyone

can track Millicent, it's Roscoe, the dog who shared her life."

"Speaking of dogs, what are you going to do with Roscoe if Millicent is dead?"

The question stopped me in my tracks. "I guess Eleanor will assume responsibility for the dog. Millicent was her relative."

"Guess again." Tinkie wasn't being difficult, she was facing facts that I'd managed not to look at. Eleanor wasn't the kind of person who took care of a dog.

"Maybe Barclay. Since he is a true Levert, the dog belongs to him. He wants to inherit, he can start with Roscoe."

Tinkie chuckled, and even though it was at my expense, it was nice to hear. "You may need to rethink that. Barclay doesn't strike me as a man who would cotton to owning a hound."

"Roscoe isn't a hound. He's a . . . beagle-terrier mix." That was the nicest combination I could pick.

"With a bit of chow, heeler, and Tasmanian devil thrown in." Tinkie's grin was almost smug. "He's going to get along fine with your horses. About half his breeding goes to herding, and that instinct will kick-in the minute he sees Reveler and Miss Scrapiron. Yippee, ki-yay."

"He's not going home with me." I said it with feeling.

"Helena got rid of him fast. She's smarter than she looks," was Tinkie's only reply as she pushed open the door and loosed the hounds.

18

The three dogs bounded across the front lawn like sprinters. "Maybe they've picked up Millicent's scent and she's alive," Tinkie said, and I deduced a note of hopefulness. In contrast, she pulled a ladies' .38 from the pocket of her khaki pants.

"Where did you get a gun?" I was shocked and didn't bother hiding it.

"Johnny's Gun and Pawn. Very reasonable. I got one for you, too. It's in the car trunk."

"Let's hope we don't need bullets."

"Hope for the best, prepare for the worst. That's a quote from your aunt Loulane."

Now even my friends were quoting my dead relatives. "Let's see what the dogs run to ground."

Tinkie and I trudged through the underbrush, heading back to where I'd found the camera. The dogs were at least three hundred yards ahead. They seemed to be searching for a scent, tearing in and out of the hackberries and briars without success. Surely Roscoe could track his owner. Had I been lying in the woods, Sweetie would have found me.

"The last photo taken was of Millicent's body," I said, huffing a little in the heat. "But I don't think John Hightower took it. He left Briarcliff thinking Millicent was still in the woods very much alive. "

"Are you sure he didn't kill her?" Tinkie asked.

"I'm not certain, but why would he? What would he gain?"

"I don't know." In fact, I had hundreds of questions and no answers. "Where in the hell is Jerome?"

"I don't know, but I think Eleanor does. She didn't seem too surprised that his cottage was empty."

Thinking back on it, Tinkie was correct. I'd been so worried about Sweetie, I hadn't paid much attention to Eleanor's reaction, or lack thereof.

"Jerome hasn't been truthful. Years of working for the Leverts has given him their sense of honesty. Do you think he's involved with Monica's—"

Tinkie put a hand on my wrist. "I don't think he would abduct Monica or hurt Millicent. I think he left *because* of what's going on." She applied some pressure. "We should split up. I'll see if I can get any leads on Jerome."

"And I can scour the woods for the dead body of Millicent."

"The dogs will help you." Tinkie tried to look innocent.

"Thanks a lot for nothing." Jerome's convenient

disappearance had to be investigated, and someone had to look for Millicent. "Just be careful." My agreement was less than enthusiastic.

"I'll meet you back at Briarcliff in two hours. And I'll take Chablis with me. She's prone to heat stroke." She blew me a kiss before she left to go back to the manor, hopefully to get Eleanor to talk. I was left with the yellow flies, gnats, and mosquitoes—until Roscoe burst from beneath a thick, prickly bush. Sweetie was right behind him.

"Make yourself useful and find Millicent," I told him.

He put his nose in the air and sniffed, then snuffled along the ground. Sweetie followed suit, and the two dogs took off in the underbrush. I had no choice but to run after them as fast as I could.

Four hundred acres is a lot of territory to cover on foot, especially if it's wooded. My cell phone had a compass, which might have been somewhat useful to keep me going in a general direction—had I not finally discovered that the battery was not just dead but damaged. No wonder it wouldn't hold a charge. As I trudged through the woods I thought about the Girl Scout meetings Mrs. Freeman hosted in her two-story home. She'd attempted to interest us Sunflower County girls in the arts of compass and map reading, proper table settings, honorable conduct, and home décor. Glancing at the sun and trying to aim for a westerly direction, I wished I'd been more tractable.

A soft voice, Victorian in phrasing and clear with melancholy, made me stop and turn around.

"Spirit of Earth! thy hand is chill: / I've felt its icy clasp; / And, shuddering, I remember still . . . / That stony-hearted grasp. / Thine eye bids love and joy depart: / Oh, turn its gaze from me! / It presses down my shrinking heart; / I will not walk with thee!" The young woman coming toward me wore a floor-length gown of gray flannel that must have been stifling in the summer heat.

Moving between the bright sun and the shadows, she was more vision than real. Perhaps I should have been afraid, but I wasn't. My only fear was that Sweetie and Roscoe would get so far ahead I couldn't find them.

"Who are you?" I asked, when she stopped and lingered in the shade of two leafy sycamores. It struck me that she could easily be a ghost.

"You know my sister's work far better than my own."

If not a ghost than a riddler. I had no patience. "Step forward."

She did so, and I saw she carried a book. Her hair was styled in ringlets from a center part and gathered at each ear—most unattractive. "Who is your sister? Or better yet, who the hell are you?"

"I am Anne Brontë, Emily's sister. You're drawn to the men who populate her world, especially those who forego good manners for passion. You, Sarah Booth Delaney, are addicted to passion."

"I am no such thing. Come out of the shadows." I wasn't certain who—or what—I was dealing with and it unnerved me a little, but I doubted the spirit of a Brontë sister was walking the woods. The dark halls of Briarcliff, or the dense woods, might be home to any number of lunatics with delusions of literary grandeur, but not a genteel Brontë.

"Whatever pleases you, madam." She stepped forward, and the sunlight caught her beautiful mocha skin.

"Jitty!" She'd tricked me. I should have caught on to her more quickly, and it irked me that she'd had me going. "Aren't you about to sweat to death in that getup? Even ghosts surely feel the oppressive August weather."

"Ladies glow, they don't sweat." She clung to the stiff and proper phrasing and pronunciation. "I don't believe sweat was ever a condition applied to me or my sisters."

"Okay, you don't sweat. Pardon me. But you also don't look well." She wasn't sweating, and though her skin was lovely, there was a hint of dark bruising beneath her eyes and she gave a tiny cough into a white tatted handkerchief. When she lowered it, I saw it was spotted with blood. Why she'd chosen the persona of a seriously ill young woman, I couldn't guess. "What's wrong with you?"

"The moors are not a healthy climate for me. I'm the youngest and most delicate of the living sisters. Death has haunted my family, but it's such a fine topic for poetry."

I wracked my brain trying to remember my literature classes. I'd been more of a Poe fan, but the gothic creations of Emily Brontë had remained with me. The work of Anne, the youngest of the Brontë brood, was not as familiar. She'd died young, I remembered that. "Tuberculosis." At last I put my finger on it.

"Very good." She smiled wanly.

"Why are you appearing as Anne?" I asked Jitty. She always had a reason—normally one that had to do with my inadequate womb action. Lately, though, she'd given my fertility issues a rest. My miscarriage had made her slightly more compassionate, at least in that category.

"Emily and I created a fantasy world. We escaped there whenever our real world became too oppressive. When two minds create together, reality can be breached. We made Golan. Perhaps you've heard of it?"

I had, but only a mention. As I remembered it, no one

knew much about this mental terrain of the youngest Brontë girls. "Tell me about it. Or better yet, tell me why it's important. I really don't have time to stand around discussing literature."

"From the unhappiness of reality, Emily and I escaped to Golan. We were able to create a world suited to our sensibilities." She smiled. "Emily was my anchor. She was so much stronger than I. So much hungrier. And then she created Heathcliff, a man of such dark passions the world remembers her. Her creation became bigger than her."

The sunlight had begun to penetrate her and in the distance I heard Sweetie strike another trail. "Jitty, what are you telling me?" It was wasted effort to ask. She never came right out and told her what was behind her costumes or periods. I had to figure it out for myself. It was, undoubtedly, one of the rules from the Great Beyond.

She shook her head. "Danger is never where you expect it, Sarah Booth." Her stilted Victorian speech began to lessen and her dark, hot dress grew transparent. "When the world was so treacherous, who would have thought TB would get me?" And then she was gone.

"Baaaaayoooo-eeeee!" Sweetie's excited yodel filtered through the bright green woods, bringing me back to the moment and the job at hand.

"Millicent Gentry," I said softly to myself. Had the dogs found her body? I wished for the company of my partner, but Tinkie was pursuing another thread. It was up to me to march forward and see what the dogs had sniffed out.

Jitty might have presented herself as Anne Brontë, but it was *Wuthering Heights* that infected my imagination as I stepped off the path and into the woods.

Trying to follow Sweetie's insistent bay, I was totally

unprepared for the root that caught my foot and sent me sprawling. I hit the ground hard enough to knock the wind out of me, and for a moment I thought I was seriously injured, perhaps paralyzed.

"Miss Delaney, are you okay?"

The unexpected male voice sent me turtling onto my back. Digging my heels into the ground, I pushed to escape.

"Sarah Booth!"

I looked into the dark visage of Barclay Levert. True to form he wore a black T-shirt and jeans that showed off every muscular inch of a long, lean body. He was hotter than Chinese mustard on an August day.

The image of Jitty as one of the Brontë sisters came to mind—had she conjured this man in the woods, perhaps summoned him with her supernatural mojo? How far *did* Jitty's powers extend? Was Anne just a teaser to the appearance of Emily's most thrilling Heathcliff?

Barclay knelt beside me, his strong, capable hands easing beneath my shoulder blades and lifting me up as if I were dandelion fluff. "Relax and breathe," he said, his strong fingers massaging my back. "Don't fight it. Just relax."

I tried to do what he said, but I sounded like a seal barking for attention.

"Sarah Booth, relax your diaphragm." He placed a hand below my breasts and pressed gently. "Let the oxygen in."

His touch was hot and electric and I finally drew in a gulp of air. I coughed and pushed him away. "What the hell are you doing here?" I managed.

"Looking for you and Mrs. Richmond. There was no one at the house, and I heard the frantic barking and howling of the dogs. It concerned me, so I came to the woods." He looked in the direction of the dogs' cries. "Is something wrong?" he asked.

"You could say that." I tried to ease away from him, but he took my arms and pulled me to my feet as he stood. The man had the grace of a panther. My diamond engagement ring winked in the sunlight and brought me to my senses.

"Where is everyone? What are those dogs chasing?"

From charmed I went to annoyed. Barclay asked questions as if I owed him an answer. I didn't want to tell him that I was likely on the trail of Millicent Gentry's dead body. In fact, I didn't want to tell him a damn thing. I didn't trust him as far as I could throw him. Breathing easily at last, I tried to step away from him, but my knees wobbled and he grabbed me to hold me up. "I have to get my dog," I said without a lot of conviction.

"I'll help you."

I shook my head. "I have it covered." He needed to leave so I could find Sweetie and whatever she and Roscoe had unearthed. A witness was the last thing I wanted.

His strong fingers captured my upper arms, and he held me so I couldn't avoid his gaze. Staring deep into his eyes, I saw concern, compassion, a hint of annoyance, and a large dose of impatience. My body also registered the dark edge of passion, barely contained and decidedly delicious. He was sex on a stick! Had I cast a movie of *Wuthering Heights*, Barclay would have made the perfect Heathcliff.

"Millicent was supposed to meet me for breakfast this morning," he said, his thumbs working gentle circles on my arms. "She never showed. She said she had information on the sisters that could put the estate in a trust with me overseeing it. She did everything but promise to put the deed to Briarcliff in my hands." His lips thinned. "But she wanted something. A trade. I told her I'd consider her proposal, and then she didn't show up for our meeting."

He was angry, which made me believe he didn't know she'd missed her appointment due to circumstances beyond her control, like death. "What information did she have?"

"She was supposed to tell me the details this morning. Something about the ruby necklace. She never showed at the café. She wasn't home, and I can't find a trace of her in town." His temper flared. "If she's toying with me . . ."

The dogs' barking hit high frenzy and I eased a half step away from him. "Barclay, I have to go. I'll have Eleanor call you."

"I'm not leaving." His smile was lazy now. He'd found a way to curb his natural impatience—by annoying the stew out of me.

"You have to go. Now." I pointed toward Briarcliff. "I have something to do."

He reached over and pushed a wayward curl from my cheek. His fingertips were warm, slightly roughened. His touch made my gut twist. I didn't want to react, and I had no intention of letting him know how much he worked on me, but I was only human.

"I'm not going anywhere without you," he said. "I've been shut out of the Levert matters long enough. I'm a rightful heir. You know it."

My options were limited. I could go back to Briarcliff with Barclay, or I could let him accompany me in my search.

"Sweetie!" I called, realizing too late that the minute my

hound appeared with Roscoe, Barclay would realize Millicent played a role in whatever I was doing. Sure enough, Sweetie came bounding down the trail with Roscoe biting her back legs like a heeler. Instead of snapping at him, Sweetie sat on her haunches and spun around to lick his evil little bearded face. She was obviously in love with a dog that looked like Robert De Niro portraying Louis Cyphre in *Angel Heart*.

"Isn't that Roscoe, Millicent's dog?" Barclay asked, his eyes narrowing as his gaze shifted from the butt-biting canine to me.

"Is it?" I tried for nonchalance.

"You know it is. Where's Millicent?"

I could answer that without lying. "I don't know."

Before I got any deeper along the slippery slope of avoiding a real answer, the dogs spun and lit out through the woods again. This time Barclay didn't wait for me. He jumped out ahead of me, hot on the dogs' trail. His legs, long and powerful, gave him an advantage, and I had to resort to a flat-out run to keep up.

Silently cursing Barclay, the dogs, and Millicent, I concentrated on keeping up with his broad shoulders as he jumped and wove through the foliage. When he stopped suddenly, I almost smacked into him.

"What the hell . . ." His voice faded to nothing.

I leaned around him. Dozens of rhinestone crowns were scattered around the ground, along with one silver high-heeled shoe. "Those belong to Millicent. They're part of her doll room collection. Shopping Barbie or something like that. Something has happened to her and you know what it is!"

He grew louder, and in a split second, Sweetie was at my side, her hackles raised and her teeth bared. No one threatened me when Sweetie was near. Roscoe followed her lead and also began to growl at Barclay.

I held up a hand. "I was looking for her. I found a photo . . ." I ground to a stop. "I'm afraid Millicent has been murdered." There was no way to sugarcoat this truth. "There was a photo of her body here in the woods, with those tiaras. It looked like her neck had been broken."

"Who would do such a thing? She was a little wacky, but she didn't deserve to die." Barclay reached into his pocket and brought out his cell phone.

"What are you doing?" I asked.

"Calling the authorities. Listen, Sarah Booth, I know you've gone along with Eleanor and her wishes, but it's time to get the pros in here. We need a forensic patholo-gist, some crime-scene experts. This changes everything. Someone is dead."

His reasoning paralleled my own, but I found myself making Eleanor's argument. Millicent's death did change everything. If she was killed by the person holding Mon-ica hostage, then killing Monica would be no big deal. A person couldn't be executed twice. The stakes had risen considerably now.

"Wait." I touched Barclay's hand holding the phone. "Don't." I couldn't believe what I was about to say. "We can't risk Monica."

"Monica, my eye. You say Millicent is dead. Maybe the Levert sisters killed her because she was going to tell me what I needed to know to claim my heritage."

Wasn't that just like a man? To jump to the only pos-sibility that involved him. I slapped the phone from his hand and stomped it. "Everything is about you, right? The whole world is involved in a conspiracy to keep you from your just rewards."

I thought for a moment he might strike me. His face darkened and his eyes shot forks of lightning, but he gained control of himself and took a long deep breath. He smiled, but it was bitter instead of humorous. "So Eleanor bought your soul. How much? What's the price?"

"Monica's life depends on what we do for the next"—I checked my watch—"eleven hours. I don't like it any more than you do, but I think Millicent can wait that long."

He made a sound of disgust.

"Your mother's life may depend on it. If we call in the authorities and the person holding Monica sees, he may kill your mother. Tinkie and Eleanor are trying to pull together a ransom. This should be over by midnight. Can't you—"

He pushed past me and headed back toward Briarcliff. I picked up Barclay's cell phone and shoved it in my pocket. I'd likely ruined it, but no point leaving it at a crime scene. As much as he annoyed me, I didn't want to set him up for a murder he didn't commit, and I had no sense that he was involved in Millicent's death. In fact, he'd lost something—validation of his claim.

"Hey, Barclay!" I jogged to catch up with him.

"Piss off," he said, never slowing.

"Wait a minute. What do you think Millicent was going to tell you?"

"Oh, let me consult my magic ball and see. Hummm. There it is. She was going to give me evidence that the sisters are mentally incompetent and that I am the person who should control the estate."

I tugged at his T-shirt. "Why would Millicent do that?"

He stopped, curiosity dawning on his face. "Because she hated the sisters more than she hated me?" But it was a question not a statement of fact. "It *is* odd. I never even questioned her motive."

"There had to be something in it for her. If she acknowledged that you're the rightful heir, she in essence gave up her claim to controlling the estate when the sisters died."

"Why would she do that?"

He was asking me? I had no clue why the Leverts did two thirds of what they did. "There had to be some gain to her. But what? Did she say anything at all that might give you a clue?"

"She talked about the ruby necklace. She said the whole legend that Barthelme buried a necklace with each of his brides was made up to cover the fact that—and I quote—'the old outlaw and every generation since had turned a profit on that necklace.' I took it to mean the insurance money. I asked her what she meant, and she said she wanted me to sign a document pledging half the estate to her."

I must have looked worried, because Barclay's demeanor changed. "What did she mean?"

"I don't know," I answered honestly. But something niggled in my brain.

"Will you tell me when you figure it out?"

"If you promise not to tell the police about Millicent. I'll call them as soon as Monica is safely home. And you have to tell me about the horse in the stables." I could drive a hard bargain when it suited me.

"That's easy. I don't know a thing about a horse."

Half an hour later, Tinkie's Cadillac pulled up at Briarcliff, followed shortly by Eleanor in her Mercedes. Barclay and I rose from the chairs we'd moved outside beneath a bower of Seven Sisters roses. When Eleanor saw Barclay, she frowned. She strode ahead of Tinkie, who carried Chablis and had to navigate on three-inch heels. Somewhere along the way she'd managed a wardrobe change.

"What are you doing here?" Eleanor demanded of Barclay. She glanced back at her car, and I knew she'd brought the money for the ransom. No wonder Barclay made her anxious.

"He knows about Millicent," I said. "We found evidence in the woods."

"But no body?" Tinkie, like me, found that very strange.

"It doesn't matter. There's nothing we can do for her. Eleven more hours." Eleanor spoke softly. "When Monica is safe, I'll turn over heaven and earth to find out what happened to Millicent. You have my word."

"If I'd had my way, I would have called the police," Barclay said, and there was a hint of a threat in his voice.

Eleanor's rigid posture seemed to sag in defeat. "Call them. I can't hold all of you off. I'm so sorry for Millicent. This is just too much for me." She staggered toward the house, leaving us standing in the perfumed August afternoon.

"Give him your cell phone, please," I said to Tinkie. "I broke his."

Tinkie fished hers out of her purse and was about to hand it to Barclay when I stopped her. "Before we do something we can't take back, why don't we talk to John Hightower?"

"Why should we talk to that nerd?" Barclay asked.

"His camera recorded the photograph of Millicent's body. He was attacked in the woods, but he made it out safely, abandoning Millicent to her murderer. Don't you find that a little odd?"

"More than a little," Tinkie said. "And where is Jerome? He's vanished and no one seems to care."

Barclay cleared his throat. "I saw him."

"You saw Jerome?" Tinkie spoke before I could.

"He came by the Eola on his way out of town. He said he was leaving Natchez. Forever."

"Did he say why?" I found this hard to accept. "He's deeply in love with Eleanor, and she needs him now."

Barclay gave a disdainful snort. "That's the rub, Sarah Booth. The Levert sisters don't need anyone except each other. Jerome finally understood this. Eleanor wouldn't confide in him and she wouldn't trust him. Thirty years of that kind of treatment was enough."

He had a point. "There was a lot of mischief on the estate last night. Hightower was thrashed by an unidentified assailant. Someone went through the woods like a savage. They knocked Sweetie Pie unconscious." When I said her name, Sweetie rose from her doggie nap and stood, stretching. Roscoe joined her. He stood on his hind legs and tried to sniff Chablis's cute little tail as Tinkie held the dog in her arms.

"She is out of your league," Tinkie said, turning away to block the devilish-looking dog. "If she weren't already spayed, I'd take her to the vet this instant rather than risk propagating whatever genetic code that evil dog carries."

Chablis had other thoughts. She jumped to the ground and the three dogs sprinted toward the house.

The interruption had given me time to think. "Hightower knows more than he's saying. He must have been onto the romance between Jerome and Eleanor. Maybe he intended to blackmail Eleanor."

Barclay's eyes narrowed. "What do you think Millicent knew that cost her her life?"

"Depends on who killed her," I said. "It wasn't Monica or Eleanor."

"We need to search Millicent's house and talk to Hightower," I said.

"I have dibs on Hightower," Tinkie said.

"And I'm going with you." Barclay pointed at Tinkie.

"No problem." She reached up and chunked him under the chin. "As cute as you are, you can shadow me wherever I go."

And with that, she successfully transformed the brooding lord of Briarcliff into a lap dog. I had to give it to Tinkie, she could perform magic.

19

By default, I was left with Millicent's house. I put Hightower and his antics out of my mind as I walked down the sidewalk to the pink confection of a Victorian house.

The over-the-top lawn decorations now seemed sad. When she was alive, Millicent created an energy that gave her peculiarities a certain vitality. Death had stolen that. Now I feared Millicent would be remembered for her eccentricities and nothing else. It made me wonder what my legacy would be if I died suddenly. Not exactly a thought to warm the cockles of my heart. Or my empty womb, as Jitty would be quick to point out.

If the yard décor could be ignored, Millicent's home was actually elegant and a fine example of Southern architecture. One thing about old Barthelme—he knew how to build structures that withstood the test of time. Combining history, grace, and a sense of endless summer, the house sported gingerbread trim and green shutters. Hummingbird vines with bright orange blossoms twined around the porch balustrade. Millicent had created a place that was stamped with her personality yet also included a nod at a time past when folks visited on front porches. The wide, shady gallery was an invitation to "sit a spell and talk."

Which I might have done if one of the seven dwarves holding a sledge hammer hadn't jumped to life and begun tapping the porch. The evil little gnome almost scared me to death. I snatched it up and discovered the thing was battery operated. Apparently my footsteps had jarred the on switch. Or else Millicent remained on the premises, still enjoying a practical joke. I knew plenty about prankish ghosts.

"Jitty?" It could be that Dahlia House's haint had come to keep me company. But there was no answer. "Jitty?" I moved forward carefully.

With the happy pink paint, the house was like a birthday cake. What would happen to it now? I tried, unsuccessfully, to block the photograph of Millicent's dead body from my mind as I knocked on the leaded-glass door. No one answered, of course. I twisted the knob, which wouldn't turn. It would have been so much easier if she'd merely left her house unlocked, but Millicent had never been about making life less bumpy for others.

No prying neighbors watched, so I slipped into the high shrubbery and crept to the back. It took nothing to jiggle a screen off a back window and ease the pane up. Like Briarcliff, the house was old—built in a time when home invasions were virtually nonexistent. And since the house had belonged to Barthelme, the head robber and gangster in town, he had little to fear from others. Security wasn't a priority, and Millicent hadn't felt the need for burglar systems and bars. While those living in large cities might find the lack of protection odd, I didn't. I had no security measures at Dahlia House, to speak of. Other than Sweetie, who was pretty much as effective as a team of Pinkerton agents.

As I hoisted myself into the window, I wished for the company of my hound. I'd left Sweetie and Roscoe in Eleanor's care. She remained at Briarcliff to answer the phone. The call from the kidnappers could come at any moment. Their normal routine was to wait until late in the evening, but this was the night designated for the drop. They could call at any hour.

With that thought in mind, I hurried through the library and parlor and stopped in the doll room only long enough to scan the life-sized replicas of Millicent, each one adorned in a costume that would be perfect for a porn film. She'd lived life on full-tilt boogie. My desire to tour the room was cut short by my need to hurry. If I could find a clue to what Millicent intended to relay to Barclay, I might expose the motive for her murder. Somehow, I doubted that information would be tucked in Medical Barbie's bag.

I checked behind pictures, hoping for a wall safe or something easy to identify. In the dining room, a sixteen-foot mahogany table beautifully set with fine china and crystal awaited a dinner party. No doubt Millicent had a maid to wash and dust. That concern was answered almost immediately when I found a check on the kitchen counter made out to Kissie, along with a list of chores, and a small key. So the singing housekeeper worked for the Levert sisters *and* Millicent. Now that was interesting.

The check, written for a substantial amount, bore to-day's date, which meant Kissie was likely due at any moment. Her cleaning services were apparently a standing engagement. Looking around, I realized the house was immaculate, as if Kissie had just finished. But why would she leave her check? It didn't make a lot of sense. Then again I was dealing with the Levert family.

The chores included polish silver, mop bathrooms, do laundry—the normal list. Until I got to the next-to-last item. *Pick up packet at bank and deliver to Barclay Levert.* The number 2446 was noted beside the list.

Millicent had told Barclay she knew something that would put him in control of the Levert estate. Did this mysterious packet speak to that? So many questions and no one to ask. Except Kissie. Was she climbing both sides of the family tree—spying for Millicent while pretending to be loyal to the twins? I'd discuss this with Tinkie before I approached Kissie.

The key was small, like the type used for a safety deposit box. The number 2446 could easily be a bank box. I knew which bank the Levert sisters used, and it didn't take much to figure Millicent would use a competitor. I pocketed the key and went out the front door, making sure to leave it unlocked in case I had to come back.

Eleanor and Monica were First Mississippi Bank customers, so I raced to the Bank of Natchez in Eleanor's car. Time pressed hard against me. So much had happened in only a few days, but it felt as though I'd been in Natchez for a year. Now every second was precious.

Tinkie's tutoring in the art of presentation paid off. I entered the bank with poise and an attitude that said I expected immediate service. Tinkie had taught me so much in life comes down to the persona one projects. Wearing my jeans like they were designer labels, I strolled across the cool lobby, my boot heels clicking on the marble floor.

With all the dignity I could muster I asked for access to the safety deposit boxes, showed my key, signed the register with Millicent's name, and went into the vault. The bank employee inserted her key into the lock on 2446. My key worked like a charm. The door swung open and I pulled out the flat metal container and waited for privacy.

When I was finally alone in the room, I lifted the lid to reveal a manila envelope on top of a large bundle of legal documents. I ripped open the envelope, and dozens of photographs spilled onto the table. Each shot contained Monica or Eleanor.

Most had been taken with a long lens through the windows of Briarcliff, and they bore various times and dates. So, Millicent had been on her spy mission more than once. She'd kept tabs on her cousins for the last nine months. I wondered if John Hightower had put Millicent up to this and if he had additional pictures.

I spread the pix out on a table. Nothing sensational. Nothing too personal. Just nasty little paparazzi sneak-shots of the Levert sisters in the privacy of their home. Several were of Monica on her balcony at dusk; others of Eleanor in the rose garden with Jerome. In unguarded moments their affection for each other was clear to see.

In one photo, Eleanor and Monica sat on the sofa in the front parlor. The curtains were lifted on a breeze, and the sisters were laughing. It took a moment to realize what was wrong. When I did, I felt as if a mule had whacked me in the gut.

Monica was wearing the ruby necklace. The kicker, though, was the time and date stamp on the photo. It was taken the day after the sisters had reported the necklace stolen.

"Holy crap," I whispered, suppressing all sorts of colorful curses. The Levert sisters *had* committed insurance fraud. Big-time. So big that the idea turned my knees to Jell-O. I sank into a straight back chair the bank thoughtfully provided in the room, reminding myself to calm down. This must have been the straw that finally broke Jerome's back. He couldn't support the sisters in this fraud, so he left.

My impulse was to call Tinkie, but I stopped. I had to think through my next actions very carefully. If I alerted the cops, Eleanor would be arrested, leaving Monica hanging in the breeze, a nice euphemism for facing death. Bringing Tinkie into this now would involve her in insurance fraud. What she didn't know couldn't hurt her—literally.

There was no way around it. I had to keep this information to myself until Monica was safe. To divulge it now would put her in tremendous jeopardy. No one could know what I'd found out, especially not Barclay.

And no wonder Millicent told Barclay she had the key to the kingdom. With Monica and Eleanor behind bars for insurance fraud, Barclay would take over all of the Levert holdings. His DNA gave him the claim he needed.

I now had a very good motive for someone to murder Millicent. Someone at Briarcliff. Someone who wasn't accounted for last night. While I was running around the grounds and Tinkie was helping me, no one had paid the least attention to Eleanor's whereabouts.

Briarcliff crowned the high bluffs of Natchez, a dark presence in the August sunlight. As I drove down the winding shell road toward the mansion, I had the sense that the house drank the sunlight. No matter how bright the day, Briarcliff brooded in gloom.

Or maybe it was the fact one person was dead, another attacked, my dog whacked in the head, and Monica was still missing. Not to mention the horseman and the object thrown from the cliff. All had happened on the estate, and if I told these circumstances to Sunflower County Sheriff Coleman Peters, he would insist I was tricking him with a gothic tale of murder.

The door leading from the portico opened as I parked. Sweetie and Roscoe rushed out to meet me. Eleanor, looking drawn and upset, stood in the doorway. "I'm glad you're back," she said.

"We need to talk." I sounded harsh and meant to. Now was the best opportunity because Tinkie hadn't returned yet.

She arched her eyebrows. "Is something wrong?"

"You could say that." From my back pocket I pulled out one of the photos showing Monica wearing the necklace.

She studied the photo for a moment before she slowly lowered it. "So you know."

"Yes. I do. And so did Millicent. Now Millicent is dead. Very convenient for you."

"What do you intend to do?" Her shoulders slumped in defeat.

"I'm calling the police. And the insurance company."

She steadied herself on the doorframe. "I can't fight this anymore. My sister may die today. The prospect of jail for insurance fraud doesn't even faze me, Sarah Booth. Do what you have to do."

"Insurance fraud is the least of it. Murder is what I'm talking about."

"Me? Kill Millicent? If you truly believe that of me, there's little point in continuing." She turned to go inside.

I followed her, feeling a pang of sympathy, which I rooted out and squashed. She and her sister had involved Tinkie and me in a four-million-dollar scam. Delaney Detective Agency's reputation could have been ruined. Eleanor and Monica had acted with selfishness, not to mention criminal intent. It was staggering.

"Where's the necklace?" I asked.

"In the vault in the basement. I returned it after you photographed the vault for your report." She tossed the photo on the kitchen counter. "Where did you get this picture?"

"Millicent intended to give it to Barclay."

Eleanor indicated we should go to the parlor. "I know you won't believe it, but I didn't know she had a photograph. I clearly see her plan, though. To align herself with Barclay and get rid of me and Monica. Millicent was always out for only herself. She'd do anything to get the Levert land out of our control."

"You fail to see that you've lied about a stolen necklace and committed a stunning fraud." My voice rose, though I fought to keep it under control. "Why? Why would you do such a thing? You don't need the money."

"To the contrary." She gestured toward a sofa. "Monica and I are broke. It's as simple as that."

"But . . ." I looked around. "This place is worth a fortune. You could sell Briarcliff or the necklace and move to Europe. You could enjoy the rest of your lives and you'd never have had to do an illegal act."

"Sell Briarcliff?" She laughed, and for a moment she mirrored her sister's more aggressive behavior. "Maybe you don't believe in ghosts, but I do. Barthelme would be after us like a hellhound. We *are* Briarcliff. It's part of us. Our family is buried here, and it is Monica's and my responsibility to keep it in the family."

"But you're the last. You didn't know about Barclay. What did it matter about Briarcliff or any other Levert holding?" She ducked to hide her expression, and I realized I'd swallowed yet another lie. "Did you know about Barclay? You did, didn't you?"

"The year Monica disappeared for such a long stretch, I suspected. She was always independent, but she came and went. Suddenly she was just gone. But Briarcliff isn't for Barclay."

She walked to the front windows. "I wanted Jerome to have it. Monica was opposed, but I said I wouldn't help with the insurance scam unless she promised that if we died before Jerome, he could have the estate."

She turned around slowly. She was backlit, but I could see her expression. "Jerome has worked this property his entire life. He loves it. He deserves to live here until he dies. I wanted that for him, and if we'd lost the estate for taxes, it would be taken from him. Now even he's gone, disgusted with me and what I was willing to do to save our home."

"You ripped off an insurance company for four million dollars." It was simply audacious.

"Yes, and we would have the money and the necklace, had Monica not been kidnapped. We'd planned to say we dug up one of the graves and found another of the Levert necklaces." She couldn't conceal the hint of a smile. "You have to admit, it was sheer brilliance. Monica and I staged the vandalism of the family cemetery, the holes dug, the whole ploy."

"Jerome helped you, didn't he?"

"He was opposed, but he loves me. I convinced him it was a harmless prank, something to annoy Helena Banks Gorenflo and her ilk. So he did it. When he found out the truth, he left."

She acted as if she sincerely cared whether I believed in Jerome's innocence. I didn't trust a thing she said now. The sisters practiced deception with uncanny ability. The Barthelme apple hadn't fallen far from the tree. "Give me the necklace."

She hesitated. "You'll jeopardize Monica's life if you do this."

"Really? Why should I believe that? The kidnapping could be another con."

"I have the insurance money in hand. If Monica were not a hostage, we'd simply leave town. Our plan was for her to have plastic surgery. She always wanted to be a blonde." Her attempt at humor fell flat. "We'd pay taxes on Briarcliff from Europe. Jerome could live here undisturbed. "

"It wouldn't be that easy." Living a life in exile sounded romantic, but it wasn't.

"If we can save Monica and retain the insurance money, I'll return it. You have my word." She conveyed cool, unflinching determination. She could have sold me high ground in the Florida Everglades. "Once burned, twice shy." My aunt Loulane had a saying for every situation.

"After tonight, we all go to the police."

"Agreed. On two conditions. Monica is back safe and sound. Once she's safe, I'll call the police, but not Chief

Randall. That's the second condition. I don't trust him. He was lurking around outside the bank this morning. He's been following me in town. I don't have any evidence, but what if he's involved? Call your sheriff friend in Sunflower County. Once Monica is released, I'm willing to face any punishment."

"Coleman has no jurisdiction in Adams County." It was curious she'd ask for him.

"I can surrender to any law officer. The Sunflower County sheriff will do as good as the local authorities. Just not Randall. What if he's involved in the kidnapping? He could kill Monica and dispose of her body and never be found out."

Despite myself, I felt a pang of pity. "I doubt the kidnapper will kill Monica now. He's kept her alive this long. He wants the ransom." I observed Eleanor's face carefully. "When you make the drop, be certain to see Monica before you leave the money."

"See her? I mean to have her beside me."

Once again I realized how little Eleanor knew of the type of person who would commit a kidnapping. For all her financial crimes, she was unprepared to cope with kidnappers. "You have to be smart, Eleanor. And tough. Or you and Monica both can be hurt. Or killed."

"I know, Sarah Booth. I'm terrified. My sister's life hangs in the balance. I will do whatever needs to be done. I want to be prepared. I can be as tough as I need to be to save Monica. But I need your help. Will you coach me?"

Sure, I was aggravated at the sisters, but I still had a heart. And I had the time. I just wasn't certain I had the skill to truly help her. But I was going to try.

20

I splashed straight bourbon over ice cubes in a Waterford glass. Eleanor accepted the drink with a trembling hand. "This is so much more difficult than I imagined." The regal wingback chair in the front parlor seemed to swallow her. Outside, the sun beat down on the front lawn, and the cloudless August sky promised a lazy summer day. Inside was a different story—emotions zagged around the room like lightning in a tornado.

I was gratified to see Eleanor was finally taking the idea of dropping the ransom seriously. At last she'd come to accept the exchange of the money for her sister entailed danger—and a lot of it. Her pallor worried me. With each passing day, her health declined.

"If everything goes well, this should work." I didn't want to soft-pedal the risk, but if she went into the ransom drop with no hope and only fear, it could easily be a disaster. "Remember, getting Monica away safely is the goal. If the money can be recovered after that, even better, but Monica's safety, and yours, is the top priority." A thought gave me pause. "Tinkie can talk to Oscar about getting some dye packs to put in with the cash."

"No!" Eleanor sat up so quickly the ice in her bourbon rattled. "What if the kidnapper opens the bag before Monica is free? It might provoke him to kill her."

I couldn't argue that point. "Once we know the location of the drop, Tinkie and I can find a place to observe from. We won't interfere, and we won't be seen, but maybe we can get details that will allow the police to find the kidnappers, once Monica is safe."

"She will come through this, won't she?" Eleanor asked.

"That's the goal." I gave her a big, fake smile, then changed the subject. "We must reimburse the insurance company." I had an idea, and I decided to float it by her. "Assuming this goes as planned and we get your sister and the money back, Monica could pretend she found the necklace with the kidnappers."

Eleanor's eyes filled with tears. "That's a wonderful plan, Sarah Booth. We'll return the money and not be charged with fraud. This whole scheme was ill conceived. It sounded simple, like no one would be hurt." She sat forward. "Insurance companies. They screw everyone, so why not screw them back." She smoothed her slacks. "I just want this to end."

"Tinkie has to agree," I reminded her. "Remember, you put her husband on the line with the lie about the stolen necklace. Tinkie may not be willing to let it go so easily."

"She has every right to be furious. I would never have

jeopardized her husband or his bank. I wouldn't have. But I can understand you'd have difficulty believing anything I say."

"I do. Embezzlers tend to keep a distance from the truth."

She flushed. "I deserve that."

It's hard to kick someone when she's down, so I stopped. Monica and Eleanor were crooks, but they loved each other, and I had gone a far stretch to save Dahlia House from being repossessed by the bank. I'd betrayed a friend. I wasn't in any position to cast stones.

"What should we do now?" Eleanor picked up the bottle of bourbon and topped off her drink.

"Wait." There was nothing else to do. "Maybe when Tinkie gets back she'll have new information." Speaking of my partner, I was getting a little worried. She should have been back at Briarcliff by now. Almost as if I'd conjured her, the Caddy sped down the drive. Tinkie had news. I hoped it would be the good kind.

She came in the front door, Chablis jumping at her side like a whirlwind. "You will never guess what I found out!" she exclaimed. It took her a moment to register the tension between Eleanor and me. "What's wrong?"

I explained about the necklace. Tinkie's expression went from confusion to volcano-hot fury in under ten seconds. "We've been beating ourselves silly to help you and the whole necklace theft is a rip-off? My husband offered to front you the money!" She looked at me. "Thank god for you and your common sense, Sarah Booth." She bent down and picked up Chablis. "I'm leaving. I've had enough of these . . . lowlife, conniving people."

I caught her by the hem of her blouse. "Wait a minute, Tink. Monica is still missing."

"And that's my problem how?" She was madder than I'd ever seen her. No one liked being played for a gullible fool, but Tinkie had almost put her husband in a very bad place because she'd wanted to help the sisters. Help them perpetrate a fraud! That was unforgivable in her book, and I didn't blame her.

I held on to her shirt. "Let's finish this. Eleanor has agreed to return the insurance money—if it's recovered. If she loses the ransom to the kidnappers, she'll confess to fraud and suffer the consequences."

Eleanor white-knuckled her drink. "Please don't abandon Monica. I'm so sorry, Tinkie. I can't change what we did. I can only beg your forgiveness. We're bankrupt. Monica and I will lose everything. That's why we did it. Not to be greedy, but to save Briarcliff. It's the last property we have left, our heritage. Everything else, the European holdings, the boat, all has quietly been sold off."

"You were millionaires. What happened?" Tinkie's anger gave way to curiosity.

Eleanor's half-smile was rueful. "We were scammed by an investment advisor. We managed to keep it hushed up. He's awaiting trial now, but punishing him won't help us recover what we lost. Nor does it excuse what we did with the necklace, but we thought we didn't have a choice. We just lost our way. . . ." She let the sentence fade.

So it was a case of "Do unto others as they'd done to you." Not exactly the application of the golden rule I'd been taught. In my world, people got jobs to save what they loved. The Leverts, though, suffered from entitlement syndrome. Crime was the option that sprang into their heads instead of finding work.

"Nice way to pay it forward," Tinkie said bitterly. "I

don't want anything to do with people like you Leverts. Sarah Booth, are you coming?" She started upstairs to collect her things.

"Wait a minute, Tinkie." I had to stop her. "It's wrong, but what's done is done. Monica is our focus now. Once she's safe, we'll let the law handle the insurance mess."

Eleanor checked her watch. "It's three o'clock. Please, just a few more hours. Sarah Booth has agreed to give me advice on making the drop. I need to be prepared and ready to get my sister back. Please, help me through this."

Tinkie groaned and blew out a breath. "I shouldn't. *We* shouldn't."

Eleanor slid to her knees. "For my sister's life, I'll beg."

"Get up," Tinkie motioned impatiently. "Just get up."

Eleanor resettled into her chair. The whole episode made me queasy. Desperation is ugly to watch. Eleanor on her knees brought back all of the dark emotions I'd felt while trying to save Dahlia House. I sympathized with Eleanor because I'd let my love of home cancel my integrity. I'd sacrificed everything I knew to be right to save a place I loved.

To give Eleanor a moment to collect herself, I asked Tinkie what she'd learned from Hightower.

"Barclay isn't the horseman."

"You're positive?" I asked.

"I am, and I have proof." She brought forth several photographs from her briefcase-sized designer purse. "Millicent and Hightower were busy little shutterbugs."

The pix were shot at night with a telephoto infra-red lens. Though grainy and slightly blurred, the image of the horse and rider were easily distinguishable.

Tinkie used the tip of her Summer Blush fingernail to point. "See, the rider has long legs, like Barclay, but not such a long torso. In fact, this is a rather short-waisted person." Her face softened for just a moment. "I measured Barclay to be sure." She almost drooled. "His torso is proportionate to the length of his strong, muscular legs." She paused, lost in thought, but then snapped out of it. "This person has a shorter torso ratio."

"The broad shoulders indicate it's a man, though," I said, studying the grainy and blurred image.

"If it isn't Barclay or Jerome, who is it?" The look Tinkie shot Eleanor would freeze water in hell. "Care to tell us?"

"I don't know." Eleanor tilted back her head and inhaled. "I don't. I would tell you if I could. Jerome lied to me about the horse being on the property. The animal has nothing to do with the necklace, as far as I know. Probably someone pulling a practical joke."

"What else did Hightower say?" I asked Tinkie.

"Once he started talking, it was hard to stop him. We thought Millicent was working for him, but it was the other way around. She came up with the idea of the photos. She said the sisters were up to something and she meant to find out what. She told Hightower the whole grave-robbing thing was a hoax—she never believed other necklaces existed. She'd figured out Barthelme recycled the same ruby necklace for each bride. The rumors of the buried jewels added to a legend, nothing more."

So far, Millicent had been dead on, dead being the significant word.

Tinkie continued. "Once Millicent and John Hightower agreed to work together, he promised her a portion of the book earnings. I think the two of them hoped the sisters would pay big money to halt the book's publication."

"Blackmail can be quite lucrative," I said.

"Hightower is a fool!" Eleanor snapped. "He has some faux history and a vendetta so old no one even knows the truth. No one cares about the history of his family's past. I wouldn't give him a penny, not that I have a penny to give anyone. That's the irony. Everyone thought we could be bled for cash, but Monica and I are so anemic we're on life support." She laughed, a brittle, ugly sound. "We should have told the truth and let the parasites shrivel and fall off us."

There was one very important point to cover. I asked Tinkie, "Hightower didn't mention the photos of the necklace and the fraud?"

"He doesn't know about them. I'm sure he would've said something if he did. And he has no clue Millicent is . . . was injured. He thinks she's miffed at him for abandoning her here and simply won't return his calls."

"Millicent wasn't going to cut him in on the necklace payoff." There was no honor among blackmailers.

Eleanor got up and put several ice cubes in her glass. She refilled it with bourbon. Before she could settle back into the chair, the phone rang, a loud, shrill bell that cried disaster. We all three froze.

"Answer it," I finally said, breaking the trance. "It could be the kidnapper."

Eleanor scurried to the portable as Tinkie switched on the recording equipment.

"Hello?" Eleanor's voice trembled.

"Do you have the money?" a male voice asked. In the background I detected an echo. Like an empty warehouse or building, just as Eleanor had described it.

"I do. I just want my sister."

"If you want her returned alive, you'll do everything I tell you." The voice was cold, completely without emotion.

"I will." Eleanor didn't hesitate.

"Then shut up and listen. At six o'clock, walk to the edge of the bluff at Briarcliff. Bring those two snooping friends of yours along."

Eleanor looked at us with horror. "They aren't involved in this. They came to help with the insurance claim. That's all. They're going home today."

"If you want your sister to die, keep talking."

I motioned Eleanor to silence. It was clear whoever had Monica watched everything that went on at Briarcliff. I went to the window and looked out. There was no way anyone could see inside the house. Briarcliff rode the highest bluff in Adams County. The sole vantage point was miles away across the river.

"Good," the kidnapper said. "I repeat. Be on that bluff at six o'clock this evening. Have your cell phone in your hand. I'll call with further instructions. Just have the money ready to move."

"Okay, I'll—" Eleanor staggered and held out the phone. The line was dead.

She raised the phone to her ear, unable to accept the call was over. "I didn't get to speak to Monica. What if she's dead? What if he's already killed her?"

My own heart squeezed at her plight. Patting her lightly on the shoulder, I took the phone and turned off the recorder. "We'll demand to speak with Monica at six. At least now we know when the next call will come. We can begin to make plans."

"What plans?" Eleanor was frantic. "What can we do?"

"Leave it to Tinkie and me. We'll put the money in the trunk of your car and gather up equipment." Binoculars, cameras, rope, duct tape. I hated it that the kidnapper had included us in the instructions. He knew we were with Eleanor, and he'd figure a way to keep us busy while Eleanor made the drop. The good news was he didn't consider us as enough of a threat to fear Eleanor was working with the authorities on the abduction.

Eleanor twisted her watch, revealing raw, irritated skin that looked as if she'd repeated the same action over and over again. "I can't miss a call. I have to stay here. What if he calls the house phone instead of my cell phone?"

Even Tinkie relented and lost some of her frosty attitude. "He won't call back until six, Eleanor. You have nearly three hours to ki—to use up."

Eleanor was about to jump out of her skin. "Go." I propelled her toward the kitchen. "Eat something. Rest. Everything depends on you. You have to be ready."

"What will you two do?"

"Prepare for tonight."

"How?"

"Don't worry. We'll handle it." I put her in front of the refrigerator and opened the door. "Food first. You'll need to wear some comfortable slacks and walking shoes. There's no telling what this guy is going to demand. Whatever it is, we have to be ready."

"Okay."

She was zombielike as she finally left. Taking a deep breath I turned to Tinkie. The pink tinge on her cheeks was not from flirting with a handsome man. She was highly *agitato*, as my hero Kinky Friedman would say.

"We should leave now," she said. "We've been lied to enough. We didn't agree to involve ourselves in a kidnapping, and the case we agreed to take is a fraud."

"I know."

"But you're going to stay, aren't you?"

I nodded. "Eleanor is about to implode. The sisters should be punished for what they've done. And they will. Tinkie, if we walk away and Monica dies, I won't be able to live with myself. What happens if we don't show up on the bluff at six? Will the kidnapper allow Eleanor to explain that we quit? Bottom line—we're in this like it or not."

"I don't ever want to hear you say I'm pigheaded." She tried to hide her worry behind a smile. "I don't have a good feeling about this, Sarah Booth. You've always said when a client starts lying, it's time to pull the plug. Eleanor and Monica have lied to us the entire time."

I couldn't argue against her logic, but I could make a plea to her heart. "I'd do the same to save Dahlia House. And you would for Hilltop."

"I'm not sure that's true. You got a job to save your home. Insurance fraud wasn't the first option that jumped into your brain." She lifted the coffeepot and began to rinse it out. Once it was brewing, she said, "Let's have a cup and think through what we need to do."

So we were still in the fight. "You have coffee and get our gear ready. I'm going to talk to Kissie," I said.

"Forget the coffee. I'll come with you."

We made sure the dogs had done their business before we left them to guard the house. Then we headed to the apartment of the singer-maid who seemed to turn up around every corner of this case.

Tinkie was charmed by the house where Kissie lived. We circled around to her apartment, Tinkie admiring the architectural wonders of the old gingerbread trim and cool porches. The door, standing ajar with the window air conditioner churning as hard as it could, set me on red alert. I motioned Tinkie behind me. We'd both suffered our share of hard knocks and injuries while working on cases, but my head was harder than hers. I signaled I'd enter and for her to remain outside and call help if necessary.

Tinkie's response was to put her hands on her hips and try to stare me down. It didn't work, because I didn't hang around. Ducking low, I entered the apartment as quietly as I could. I didn't need to go farther than three steps to realize something was very wrong.

The sign in the kitchen window said it all. For Rent.

When I peeped in through the back door window, I saw the cabinets were open, all dishes and staples gone. Even the curtains had been removed. Kissie had cut and run.

"Excuse me, ladies, may I help you?"

I turned to find an older man standing at the bottom of the steps.

"I'm looking for Kissie McClain," I said.

He slid a hammer into a tool belt. "You're about ten hours too late. She pulled out of here this morning."

"She moved?"

"To Nashville." He gave a wide grin. "That little girl is taking her talent to the city where dreams become reality. Before long, you'll hear her tunes on the radio, mark my words."

"Did she give you notice?" Tinkie asked.

"Wasn't necessary. She was one of the best renters I've ever had. She got a golden opportunity and she had to take it. No hard feelings from me."

This was more than coincidence. Kissie didn't just skip off to Nashville. She'd been opposed to gambling everything on Music City for a second time, and she also had no money. "Did she say what kind of opportunity?"

"No, she didn't. But it must have been a good one. She took most of her furnishings to Goodwill and packed her clothes in her car. She barely had room for her guitar."

"Did her boyfriend go with her?" Tinkie asked.

He pursed his lips. "With young people today, who knows? Now did you want to see the apartment?"

We did, but after a quick look around, we accepted there was nothing to be learned. Kissie and her convenient opportunity were gone and there was nothing left to tell us the story of her circumstances.

21

Backing out of the driveway, Tinkie seemed lost in thought. We headed west, toward downtown and the river. I didn't ask where she was taking me, because I had no idea what to do next.

"Where did Kissie get the money to move to Nashville?" she asked.

"Moving is expensive. She left a paying gig here, for what?" I had my own set of questions.

"Do you think she and Jerome are together?"

It was strange the Leverts' housekeeper and gardener, both with access to the Levert estate and the sisters' secrets, had decamped. Briarcliff was experiencing a domestic crisis, on top of all the others.

"Do you think Kissie really went to Nashville? And Jerome? Did he just vanish?"

I could tell Tinkie was worried something unfortunate might have happened to the housekeeper and possibly the gardener. "We can check on Kissie in Nashville, but it will take too long. I don't even know where to begin with Jerome."

"He isn't missing. Eleanor knew he'd left." Tinkie clenched the steering wheel.

"You still think he's the horseman?"

"I honestly don't know what to think. I just know once Monica is returned, I want them both arrested."

I couldn't disagree.

Tinkie cruised by the insurance company and the bank, but nothing looked amiss. My mind kept worrying the matter of Jerome and Kissie, both gone.

"Hello, darlink!"

I looked around me at the shady Natchez street flying past.

There was the sound of snapping fingers, and I saw the most beautiful blond woman perched on the hood of Tinkie's car as we drove along Franklin Street. She wore a flowing gown with layers and layers of beautiful teal material that came together in a drop-dead V, centered with a bodacious diamond brooch. The neckline plunged to an inch above her navel. Full breasts peaked dangerously at the edge of the material, swaying as if they meant to spring free at any moment.

I couldn't say anything. Tinkie drove as if the woman weren't there. And she wasn't—except in my head. I was on the receiving end of another visitation for my haint.

"I'm a wonderful housekeeper, Sarah Booth," the blonde said. *"Every time I divorce, I keep the house."* Her laughter tinkled inside the car like little drops of joy. Jitty

was on another rampage. The woman she emulated was iconic and familiar, but I couldn't quite put my finger on her.

"*Who are you today?*" I didn't have to speak aloud. In fact, if I talked with Jitty, Tinkie would think I'd lost my mind.

"*You know me from your childhood. You and your parents watched reruns of my sister's very popular TV show. Don't ever go to television, Sarah Booth. You're meant for the big screen. I kept telling Eva that, but she wouldn't listen. She played a farmer's wife.*" She laughed. "*My sister, on a farm. Now think about* that *ludicrous image, darlink.*"

"*But the show was a success.*" I remembered *Green Acres*. Eva Gabor on a tractor in rubber boots. Hysterical comedy in the 1960s.

"*Eva never stopped pointing out what a success her show was.*" Jitty flipped a fur boa around her neck. The wind caught it, sending it streaming behind her. "*She never tired of telling everyone she was the successful sister, the star, the one who brought home the bacon—even if it meant sharing billing on a stupid television show with a pig.*"

The sibling rivalry of the Gabor sisters had begun to bore me. "*Why are you riding on the hood of Tinkie's Cadillac?*" I asked.

"*Look closer, Sarah Booth.*"

I leaned toward the front windshield. Tinkie stuck out an arm and pushed me back into the seat. "What the hell is wrong with you, Sarah Booth?"

"Nothing," I managed to mumble.

Jitty laughed. She tapped on the window. "*I like you.*

You can call me Zsa Zsa. All of my friends do. It's just my sisters I have to watch out for. Beautiful women are always the most dangerous. Keep that in mind."

"*What do you want?*" She was straining my brain.

"*In order? Number one on my list is a baby for the Delaney womb to carry. Number two is a husband for the last Delaney, a—*"

"Oh, for heaven's sake. Give it a rest, Jitty. I'm doing everything I can."

"Who the hell is Jitty?" Tinkie asked.

My head swiveled from Jitty on the hood to Tinkie and back to Jitty, who had begun to fade! "Damn it, get back here! This is no time for your pranks!" I said, obviously aloud, because Tinkie looked shocked.

"Sarah Booth! Sarah Booth!" Tinkie jabbed me in the ribs. "What in the world is the matter with you? You're talking crazy, about to drool on yourself, and you're acting like you want to climb through the front window of my car."

I'd been so deep in my imagined conversation with Jitty / Zsa Zsa I'd lost sight of the real world. We were still on Franklin Street, the river to our west. This was one of my favorite parts of Natchez, with historic homes and elegant trees—Barthelme should have been hanged from one, along with the other thieves and rascals of the nineteenth century. I'd lost my place in present-day time. "Where are we going?" I asked.

"Where *should* we go?" Tinkie countered.

"Let's get a burger." My watch showed 4:40. Time moved too slowly while we waited for the kidnapper.

"A hamburger?" Tinkie's tone said it all.

"I'm only human. I have to eat. What else should we do for an hour and forty minutes? We're hamstrung until the call comes in. I eat when I'm nervous." Cranky wasn't pretty when I wore it, but waiting was never my best activity.

"Kissie and Jerome have taken a runner. And you're slipping in and out of reality and worried about a hamburger. You are making me a crazy woman." Tinkie slowed the Caddy and pulled off the street in front of Turning Pages Books. I could see the shop owner stocking a shelf. The instant her back was turned, a beautiful Westie jumped on the books and tumbled them to the floor. Ah, everyone is a critic. I slumped down in the seat.

"We should go back to Briarcliff and wait with Eleanor."

Tinkie put words to action and sped down the tree-lined Natchez streets.

"Wait!"

Tink startled so badly she slammed on brakes with enough pressure to send me into my seat belt. My right breast was permanently crushed.

"Don't do that!" she said with some heat.

"Sorry. We need to find Barclay."

Tinkie looked at her Rolex. "It's four forty-five. We have to meet Eleanor."

"Call her. Be sure she's at Briarcliff. Tell her we're on the way and we're bringing Barclay with us."

"I'm sure she'll be thrilled with that." Tinkie searched her briefcase-purse for her cell phone.

A car behind us honked, and Tinkie eased into a parking spot down the street as she talked. When I looked in the rearview mirror, I felt a jolt of dread. Gunny, his badge shining in the late afternoon sun, walked toward us.

"Why Chief Randall, you do look handsome in that uniform." Tinkie oozed pleasure at the unexpected arrival of the very buff policeman. His dark uniform pants were tailored to a fare-thee-well, and his shirt stretched across well-developed pecs. He lifted dark glasses to reveal irises a deep forest green. None of this did a single thing to make me feel less threatened.

"Ladies." Gunny eyed me like I carried a disease. I had the sense his presence wasn't an accident. The man had tracked us down like rabid dogs. And he meant to make us bark.

"We're on our way to help Eleanor with a chore," Tinkie said. "Why don't you come out with us and have a big ol' bourbon? Eleanor keeps the best liquor."

"I don't drink on duty. What's going on at Briarcliff?"

"Whatever do you mean?" Tinkie was all blue-eyed innocence.

"Cut the crap. Eleanor's been dodging me for two days." Gunny was nobody's fool. "Why are you two still in town? The insurance company paid out. Eleanor cashed the check this morning. I figured you'd be done with the Levert sisters and back in Zinnia."

"We're tying up some loose ends." He made me uncomfortable, and it didn't help that I couldn't see his eyes because of the dark sunglasses he'd put back on.

"Four million is a lot of money for two middle-aged women to have lying around a big ol' haunted house." His grin was disparaging. "Why did Eleanor cash the check and walk out of the bank with the money?"

The way he said it made my skin twitch. He knew way too much about the Leverts' business. I gave Gunny another visual once-over. He was a handsome man in a wrapped-too-tight kind of way. His torso short, his legs . . .

"I believe the sisters know how to handle their money," I said easily. "Gunny, how long have you been in Natchez?"

"Five years." He frowned at the change in topic. "What's the sudden interest in my career?"

Tinkie gave him a slow smile. "Allow a girl her indulgences. Sarah Booth and I have a bet. She says you worked in Memphis, but I say you spent some time in the North." Tinkie was quick on the uptake.

"Then you'd win the bet. I put in five years at the Cincinnati PD before I took this job." He tapped the car door. "Eleanor should put her money somewhere safe, and I don't mean the vault in Briarcliff. She's a sitting duck for a robber . . . or worse."

He sauntered to his car and drove past us.

"What was that all about?" Tinkie asked.

I didn't answer. I borrowed her phone and dialed Cece. When her voice mail prompted, I said, "Check the Cincinnati PD for an Albert Randall. I specifically need to know if they have a mounted unit and, if so, was he a member. Thanks!"

"Saint Francis in a flock of vultures." Tinkie had followed me straight to my conclusion. "Gunny could be our midnight cowboy. His body type fits the photos."

We hadn't gone two blocks when the phone rang. I answered.

"Sergeant Albert 'Gunny' Randall was not only on the mounted unit, he was one of the trainers," Cece said. "He was highly respected as a law officer and an equestrian."

We had our answer. "Thanks, Cece. You're the best." I hung up and relayed the info to Tinkie.

"Why would Gunny pretend to be the ghost of Barthelme Levert?"

"I don't have a definitive answer."

"Shall we pick up Barclay or not?" Tinkie asked.

Barclay would serve a purpose. "Let's find him. If we have him with us, he can't make trouble. Besides, if we're standing on the bluff with Eleanor, it might be good insurance to have a compatriot in the house. A fallback. A witness to whatever transpires."

"You're smarter than the average bear, Sarah Booth." Tinkie flipped down her visor as she angled toward the golden flow of the Mississippi River. Again I was struck by the water's placid appearance, but I knew beneath the surface, the currents were treacherous.

Barclay was surprisingly complacent. We found him at the Eola, and he got in the Cadillac without a complaint or even a question.

"Are you okay?" Tinkie asked him.

I rode in the backseat so I could watch him. His brow looked like a thundercloud. Heathcliff, in the flesh.

"The whole thing with Millicent is unreal. She was going to help me, and now I'll never know how. She was my cousin." He seemed bemused by the blood tie. "We have to find her body. We can't just leave her out there for the bugs to eat."

Tinkie drove and talked. "Eleanor has agreed to call the police as soon as Monica is returned. She'll admit to insurance fraud. Chances are, you'll end up in the catbird seat, Barclay. For right now, the only thing we can do is get through this ransom exchange."

"That night in Bennator's, you and Marty Diamond almost tied up. Why?" I was curious if Kissie was the source of their animosity.

Barclay twisted so he could see me. "He hates me. He refuses to believe Kissie and I are friends. Nothing more. She put me up when I first got to town because I didn't have money for a hotel. I told her I was a Levert, and she believed me. Even though she's fond of the sisters, she said I deserved my inheritance. I had to clear out of her place or Marty threatened to make a scene, so she let me into Briarcliff for a couple of weeks."

"If you didn't have money when you came to town, care to explain how you can afford to stay at the Eola?"

Barclay straightened in the front seat. "I'd rather not, but I know you won't let it drop." He paused. "I'm not proud of my actions."

He was hedging, and I caught a whiff of important information. "I think you'd better tell us."

"My clever mother has never walked hand in hand with the truth."

"Meaning?" I wanted to thump him the back of his head, but I refrained.

"Monica pulled a double cross on a rich man before she ended up in the Tampa area. The boat she arrived in wasn't hers. She'd . . . essentially, she stole it. Took it by deception. The elderly man came out from under the spell she'd woven and realized he'd been fleeced. So he called the law and said she'd stolen his boat, a fifty-foot schooner."

"She had a bit of her ancestor in her, didn't she? Barthelme was a river pirate." A week ago this tale might have shocked me, but not now. The Levert sisters were capable of any degree of theft.

"What happened?" Tinkie asked. "Was she arrested?"

"My father intervened. He knew the sheriff and convinced him not to arrest Monica. He said Monica was a confused young woman who thought the boat had been loaned to her. He made it out to be a misunderstanding."

"And then she stayed with your father."

"For almost a year." Barclay's fingers dug into the back of Tinkie's seat. "And what she stole from him was far more valuable than a boat. She took his future. She broke his heart."

"How does this relate to earning money?" I asked.

"John Hightower paid me for this insight into Monica's character. Handsomely. The story of my conception brought in enough money for me to rent a room at the Eola and dress for success."

He spoke with such bitterness I felt sorry for him. "Monica was very young then. She was, what, eighteen?"

"She's a user. And she hasn't changed."

"She was just a kid," Tinkie said. "That doesn't make it right, but she—"

"Anyway, now you know how I got the money." Barclay was done with the subject. "So why are you taking me to Briarcliff?"

"We need your help." I wasn't certain he would go along with my plan.

"To save Monica?"

"Yes."

"Why should I?" he asked.

"Because she's your mother, because Eleanor loves her, because if she dies you'll have to carry the guilt the rest of your life."

When he didn't say anything else, Tinkie pressed the pedal to the floorboard and we zoomed toward Briarcliff and a date with a kidnapper.

22

By the time six o'clock arrived, Eleanor was in a state of total anxiety. I wasn't far behind her. Tinkie and I decided not to mention our suspicions about Gunny. But when it came time to call the law, we would contact the sheriff we knew to be honorable—Coleman Peters.

At five minutes before the appointed hour, I walked out the front door with my partner and Eleanor. Barclay remained in the house, watching us from a second-floor window. Hidden by the draperies, he used Tinkie's telephoto lens on her camera and binoculars to try and pinpoint a vantage spot from which our kidnapper was spying us. We speculated the abductor to be on the Louisiana side of the river.

As we approached the bluff, all in a line, I noticed the bridge. The highest bridge in Mississippi. I knew instantly how the kidnapper had kept tabs on us. He'd rigged a camera with an extreme telephoto lens to a high beam on the ironwork—he'd have a clear view of Briarcliff and all that went on. I nudged Tinkie and whispered my thoughts.

"It's impossible to spot the camera from here, but I think you've solved part of the mystery," she said. Eleanor was too focused to heed our conversation. She held her cell phone so tightly I thought she'd crack the plastic. Very gently I touched her arm and took the phone from her. At first I thought she'd resist, but she yielded with a strangled gasp.

"Why doesn't he call?" she asked.

"It's only five fifty-eight. Two minutes to go." I prayed the kidnapper was time conscious. The anguish of waiting for someone who couldn't meet a deadline would be too much. The darkest of thoughts surfaced at such times.

Eleanor faced the river and an expression of nostalgia settled over her features. "When we were children, I loved Briarcliff. My parents came here every winter after they tired of Aspen or Geneva or Rome. This was where we were truly a family. We played croquet on the front lawn. Mother had tea parties or holiday fêtes with lanterns and torches. Everyone laughed. That's what I remember the most, the sound of laughter mingling with a breeze in the oak trees. I thought this was the most beautiful place in the world."

She sounded so lost—I wanted to comfort her, but I didn't know how. "You have to believe Monica is alive. Don't lose your faith in your sister."

"You know my mother died here." She extended her toe to the cliff's edge. "She plunged to her death. The talk in town was that my father pushed her."

I could only imagine the difficulty of living with such

cruel gossip. The curse of murder came with wealth for the sisters.

"They said it was the Levert family legacy, our tradition, for the Levert heir to kill his wife." Eleanor's voice had grown short and choppy, and I was worried she would have a stroke. The hot August light was full on her as the fierce sun slipped toward the horizon across the river. "After Mother's death, Monica and I vowed never to marry. Never to have children to carry on the horror of this family blight. We both broke that oath, and we have suffered greatly because of it."

I knew Eleanor referred to the artist who was murdered by muggers the night before their wedding. And Jerome, the loyal gardener, who could never be good enough. Those were the burdens she carried. For Monica, it was Barclay, who safeguarded us even as we waited for the call that would determine her life. She'd never allowed herself the joy of motherhood.

"I'm sorry, Eleanor."

"Don't be," she said with scalding bitterness. "Sorrow never yields any crop except grief."

Before I could respond, her cell phone rang. It startled me so badly I almost dropped it over the cliff. Tinkie steadied me as I handed the phone to Eleanor. It was six o'clock on the dot.

"This is Eleanor Levert." She spoke with admirable dignity and strength. "I'm going to put the phone on speaker so Sarah Booth and Tinkie can hear you. We want to be sure to follow your directions to the letter."

"Good thinking," the male voice said. A hint of amusement infuriated me. I tried to focus on the qualities of the voice, any sounds in the background. The kidnapper was smart. He'd realized we were likely recording him on the house phone, so he'd designated a place where we couldn't.

"I want to speak to my sister." Eleanor sounded forceful. That was good.

"You're in no position to demand anything," the caller said harshly. His voice had a strange, echoey tone. Once again I thought of warehouses and abandoned places. Tinkie and I had never checked Eleanor's list—she'd never given it to us. Once this was over, it would be a good lead to hand to the authorities.

"We have the money," Eleanor said. "You'll never see a dime unless we know Monica is alive and unharmed."

"Oh, she's alive." He laughed. "Unharmed? You might be stretching a fine point. I can promise she'll hurt a lot more if you try to fuck with me."

Eleanor couldn't control the sob that shook her frame. Tinkie put an arm around her and shored her up.

Stepping into the breach, I said, "I want Monica to recite the Pledge of Allegiance." It was the only thing I could think of and earned me a questioning look from Tinkie.

"Your patriotism is fascinating," the kidnapper said, "but I understand. You want proof of life. If she recites for you, then you'll know she's alive. For the moment."

The phone clattered onto something hard, rattled around, and then a breathless Monica came on, her voice thready and weak. "I pledge allegiance to the flag of the United States of America and to the Republic for which it stands—" She broke off with a whimper and a cry of pain.

"She's alive. Now listen up. Have the money in the red Cadillac you're so fond of riding in. Take it to Natchez Under-the-Hill and park in the lot beside Bennator's. Be there at nine tonight. Wait for me to contact you. When I'm certain no one is following, I'll call this cell phone and give further directions."

"All right," Eleanor said, her voice quivering. "Don't hurt Monica."

"Don't try to boss me," he said. "Do what you're told and your sister will be returned. Screw this up, and she's a dead woman."

"I'll be there." Eleanor said.

"You'll all three be there. I'm not stupid. You can't leave the two private investigators behind. I want to know where all of you are at all times."

There was no time to argue. He hung up.

"Shit," Tinkie said, clearly unhappy with the last turn of events. "We shouldn't be involved in the drop. I don't like this at all."

"Neither do I." We'd told Eleanor all along we weren't part of the drop. But she clearly wasn't at fault. She had no control over what the kidnapper ordered.

Eleanor's thin fingers clutched at my shirt. "You'll ride with me? Won't you? If you don't, he'll kill Monica." She was beside herself.

"Let's go in the house and discuss this. Maybe Barclay saw something." I wasn't counting on it, but I had the distinct impression I needed to get Eleanor away from the edge of the cliff. The Leverts had a habit of falling—or jumping—to their deaths. The state Eleanor was in, she might be the next candidate for a plunge into eternity.

"He isn't surveilling from anywhere I could detect," Barclay said as he accepted the drink Tinkie mixed.

Barclay reclined on an overstuffed sofa looking every

inch the Levert in charge. He seemed to have no regard for Monica's safety—or a worry in the world. I didn't really blame him. He had no memory of her as any part of his life other than a thorn pricking his father every hour of every day.

Tinkie relayed my theory of a camera on the bridge.

"Very good!" he said, as if I'd given the answer to a game show. "I think you hit on it. It's the only logical solution if the observer is on the west side of the river."

"What good does it do us?" Eleanor demanded. She slammed her drink onto a side table. "None of this helps us get Monica back. Barclay should leave. He's no help."

"And no hindrance," he said.

"He might be of help," I said. "We need him here, at Briarcliff, when we go to Under-the-Hill."

"What do you think is here for you?" Eleanor addressed Barclay. "Everything is gone. We lost it all. There's no inheritance. Briarcliff is all that's left, and now we're going to lose it."

Barclay shrugged. "Easy come, easy go."

His attitude infuriated Eleanor, and I stepped in front of her as she strode toward him. "Stop it. We're all on edge."

"Shouldn't we go to Bennator's and wait?" Eleanor was beside herself with anxiety. "We should leave. I want to be there early."

Early was good, but two hours ahead of schedule was a bit excessive. "Are you okay?" Her behavior worried me.

"I'm worried. I need to move."

That I could understand. "Why don't you and Tinkie go on to Bennator's? Have a bite to eat. I want to check out something." I wasn't being deliberately vague, but I didn't want to discuss my plans. Call me paranoid, but it had occurred to me the kidnapper could easily have bugged Briarcliff. He was monitoring our movements—we had proof. In the numerous times the house had been broken into, perhaps it was to plant bugs rather than steal something.

Both Tinkie and Barclay picked up on my cautious mood. Eleanor remained oblivious, trapped in her own anxiety. "Both of you come with me. Please. I'd prefer both of you. That way, we'll be there when he calls. It makes me anxious to separate. I think all three of us should go. Barclay can stay here, if he must."

"Your generosity astounds me, Aunt Eleanor."

Barclay was more amused than he had any right to be. His attitude annoyed me, but I had to stop all talk of importance. "Tinkie, y'all head down to town. I'll be behind you in twenty minutes." I leaned to whisper, "No more than an hour. This place may be bugged."

She nodded her agreement, and in quick dispatch she loaded Eleanor and the money in the Cadillac and they took off down the drive.

Barclay was at first reluctant to help me hunt for a bug, but he got into the spirit of the search. To my frustration, we found nothing. "The kidnapper knows everything we do. How?" I glanced around to be sure we hadn't forgotten some place.

"I'll take a drive over the bridge to see if I can spot anything, but a camera could be tiny."

"Thank you, Barclay."

"Don't thank me. I'm only safeguarding what little may be left of my inheritance." His brow furrowed. "Why should I care what happens to Monica? She never cared for me."

"I don't know. Why do you?" I could only wait for his answer, which came more quickly than I'd anticipated.

"I want her to know me, to see what she left behind like I was so much trash."

No matter how old a man got, his mother could still wound him. Barclay carried a lot of scars from Monica's callous behavior. "Can you ever forgive her?"

His answer was unexpected. "I want to. Since my father died, I don't have anyone. Monica and Eleanor are my family." He gave an uneasy laugh. "I guess blood *is* thicker than water."

Upstairs, Sweetie, Roscoe, and Chablis were roused from a nap by an approaching vehicle. "Oh, shit," I whispered. Coming up the drive was a patrol car, with Gunny at the wheel. If the kidnappers saw this, it could mean curtains for Monica.

"Go!" Barclay pushed me toward Monica's car. "He'll follow you. Get him out of here before Monica pays the price."

He was right, I had to lure Gunny away from Briarcliff. Every moment he stayed on the property put Monica at risk.

I jumped in Monica's car, tore through the portico, and headed around the house. The Porsche handled like a dream, even when I cut so hard in the grass that it slewed before straightening. The tires caught traction, and I pulled out just as Gunny was opening his door. I went by at such a high speed his hat was almost unsettled. He hit the siren, once, to get my attention. Just to be sure he followed me, I gave him the one-finger salute. It proved to be all the provocation necessary. The chase was on!

The Porsche was built for high speeds, and I tore down the road toward the national forest where I'd found

Marty Diamond's cabin. The roads were winding—and out of the city jurisdiction. While hot pursuit would give Gunny leave to chase me, he might also decide to drop back and wait for a chance to catch me without endangering the lives of Adams County residents.

If I could get far enough ahead of him.

And that was a big if. He was nobody's fool behind the wheel of the patrol car, and he drove like a man who knew his business. Still, the Porsche out-horsepowered him. At last, after what seemed an eternity of curves coming too fast and hairpin turns, I lost him.

And I'd lost valuable time. I had to get back to Natchez and the rendezvous at Bennator's. In the national forest, I had no cell phone reception at all.

Dark fell quickly as I made my way back toward town, hoping that Gunny had better things to do than set up a roadblock. Instead of trying to reason with him, I'd run. He wouldn't appreciate such behavior. Not in the least. If he caught me now, he wouldn't listen to anything I had to say.

As soon as I got within range of a tower, I called Tinkie to tell her what had happened. God bless Barclay, he'd already delivered the news, which had calmed Eleanor somewhat. Instead of bouncing off the walls, she was merely climbing them.

"Can you pick me up?" I couldn't risk driving into Natchez proper in Monica's car. Gunny might not have roadblocks up, but he sure as hell had alerted his officers to be on the lookout for me.

"Eleanor isn't going to like it." Tinkie spoke cautiously, so I knew our client was listening.

"It's either that or manage without me. Tell her."

In a moment Tinkie came back on the line. "Eleanor

will wait here at Bennator's. I'll pick you up in fifteen minutes."

With some reluctance, I parked the Porsche behind a Laundromat and started walking to a quick-serve station about a mile away. The night was dark, the moon hidden by low clouds.

The road was completely empty, a creepy feeling. At Dahlia House, I enjoyed the solitude and sense of isolation. Natchez wasn't home, though. Here I felt cut off from everyone, and there was a nagging sense that I'd missed something important.

My leather boots crunching the gravel on the shoulder of the road as I walked, I listened to the song of the crickets in the tall grass that covered the ditches.

Summer in the South—a combination of beauty and brutality. This was not a climate for the faint of heart or those who couldn't confront harsh elements. Even though the sun was gone, the night was sticky and close. Sweat slipped down my cleavage and back, soaking my shirt and jeans.

Graf loved the hot summer nights. During his most recent visit to Dahlia House, we'd gone for a ride on Reveler and Miss Scrapiron, cantering around the cotton fields as dusk fell.

"This land holds magic." Those had been Graf's words. Sitting on the beautiful bay mare Miss Scrapiron, he'd breathed in the smell of dirt and growing things. "I love this place, Sarah Booth. I'd never take you from here. Not permanently."

I didn't tell him that he couldn't. No one could. But he could steal me away for long weeks of California sunshine and the glitzy life of a film actor. I could share his life as he shared mine.

Without warning, I missed Graf with a physical pain. The urge to call him was great, but I couldn't. Not when my intention included helping Eleanor drop $4 million in ransom money—likely a very dangerous ransom exchange where a woman's life teetered in the balance.

No, now wasn't the time to call Graf. I would only make him worry.

I'd walked so long in the darkness and silence I stopped when I saw headlights approaching me. My first inclination was to get in the ditch and hide, like a refugee or criminal.

The car approached slowly, and I knew it was too late to do anything except keep walking. If it was a cop, I was done for.

At last the car drew abreast of me and the window came down. I couldn't see into the dark interior, and my heart beat fast and furious. Poised to run, I waited.

"Need a lift, young lady?"

"Barclay!" I could have brained him.

"Tinkie sent me to fetch you. How about we get the Porsche and trade cars. I think I can stay ahead of the Natchez Police Department."

It was the most sensible plan I'd heard all week.

23

When I stepped through the doors of Bennator's, I listened to the blues singer wail the words to Walter Spriggs's "I'm Not Your Fool Anymore." The horn section was terrific— but loud. Eleanor appeared ready to explode. When she saw me, she rose from her chair, knocking the table so hard her drink and Tinkie's crashed to the floor.

Before we could stop her, she went to the bar for another round. Wisdom prevailed and instead of alcohol, she brought three coffees. Good for me and Tinkie, but I wasn't certain Eleanor needed the caffeine jolt.

"Thanks." I took the hot mug she offered.

We finished our coffee and went outside. The night was still partially overcast. Shifting clouds gave moonlight one moment and darkness the next. Far away, thunder rumbled, and I thought of Thor, the Norse god with a hammer, pounding the sky.

The river, only a few dozen yards away, sucked noisily at the shore, as the Mighty Mississippi flowed south toward Sin City. When this mess was over, maybe Tinkie and Cece and I could take a vacation on one of the old paddleboats that catered to tourists. We needed a week of idle luxury. I was ready for some time off, and if Graf was busy filming in La-La-Land, my female buddies were good company.

"What time is it?" Eleanor asked.

I wanted to say, "Twenty seconds from the last time you asked" but I didn't. "It's eight fifty-two."

"Do you think he'll call?" Eleanor fidgeted like a caged animal. "Maybe we should check the money in the trunk. Let's move the car away from the streetlight. Should we wait in front of the bar so he can see us?"

I held her shoulders firmly. "Calm down. You're going to have to pull yourself together to make this happen, Eleanor."

I thought she might cry, but she lifted her chin. This week had aged her. I could see the fine lines and the slight sag of skin along her jaw. When I'd first met the sisters, none of this had been evident. Stress had worked its hardship on her. This night would exact a toll on all of us.

To placate Eleanor's nerves, Tinkie opened the trunk. The money, in two separate and heavy gym bags, lay exactly where we'd put it.

"We should put in the ink packs I bought," Tinkie said. She knew as well as I did that once the kidnapper had the money, there was no guarantee he would release

Monica. If the ink packs went off, it might motivate him to kill her—or run for his life. There was no way to tell.

"We'll do nothing to jeopardize Monica," Eleanor said. "Let him have the money. I just want my sister." She spun on Tinkie. "You didn't tell your husband about the kidnapping, did you?"

"We haven't told anyone." I didn't care for her aggression toward my partner. Our involvement in this was only to help her save Monica, and she had no right to snarl at Tinkie.

"I'm sorry. Just do whatever he says. I need your word."

"We're here to help you," Tinkie assured her.

Eleanor's cell phone rang. She answered with grim determination. "You're early," she said. She put her phone on speaker so we could all hear.

"I'm early. You're early. Perhaps we're all a bit too eager." He laughed. "Have a nice meal? I've been told Bennator's has excellent barbecue."

"You are a monster!" Eleanor was so wired I was afraid she'd blow the drop before it began. "Where's my sister?"

"Here. Say hello, Monica."

There was a moment of confusion, again the echoey sound of a large empty space. When Monica spoke, she was agitated. "Did you bring the money, Eleanor? They know everything you do. Be careful—"

"Enough!" the kidnapper said. "So here's the plan: Eleanor, you and Ms. Richmond will go to the Eola bar and remain there until I call you. Ms. Delaney will take the Cadillac and the money and drive toward the Mississippi River Bridge. I'll call her and give further directions."

"Sarah Booth is not making the drop!" Tinkie spoke

in a very peculiar way. Her words slurred and jammed into one another. She looked at me like a helpless creature who'd been tricked. "Sarah Booth—" She slumped to the pavement, her knees taking the full impact of her fall. She didn't even utter a groan.

I caught her and held her against my thighs. Disbelief was quickly turning to fury. "What did you do?" I demanded of Eleanor.

"I had to do it," Eleanor said. "He called and said I had to drug her. He said he would kill Monica. Please, Sarah Booth. I had no choice."

The bad feeling I'd experienced all evening swelled. "I'm not making the drop." I wasn't doing it. I had everything to lose, and Eleanor had lied to me all evening long. There was nothing I hated more than a liar.

My partner leaned against me. Eleanor reached out, but I ignored her and tried to drag Tinkie to the Cadillac. If I could get her inside, I'd toss the money to the parking lot and drive to the hospital. While Tinkie was petite, unconscious she was as heavy as a load of wet cement.

"Are you still there?" The kidnapper almost chuckled.

"We're here." Eleanor was crying. "Sarah Booth won't make the drop."

"Then Monica dies."

"No, please!" Eleanor sobbed, but she made no attempt to stop me from opening the back door of the Caddy. I tried to shove Tinkie's upper body in. She was so limp I couldn't get leverage.

"He hung up!" Eleanor howled. "He didn't even give me a chance. He'll kill her and it's your fault!!" She hurled herself at me with such force I almost dropped Tinkie. My first impulse was to slap the snot out of her, but I held back, using my final reserve of strength to lift Tinkie into the backseat.

"What did you give her?" I asked Eleanor. "If she's hurt, I'll kill you."

"She's fine. It was a prescription. He has the antidote. As long as she gets it in the proper time, there won't be any damage."

I remembered the empty pill bottle in the bathroom. How long had she been planning to drug one of us? "You and your sister are total liars. I'm not involved in this any longer." I wanted to say a lot more, about how they were cheats and thieves with no moral compass or compassion. But Tinkie was my priority. I had to get medical help. I wished fervently I was closer to the Zinnia hospital where Doc Sawyer worked. He'd saved Tinkie—and me—more than once.

Eleanor's cell phone rang again. She answered immediately, then gingerly handed the phone to me. "He wants to talk to you."

"No." I arranged Tinkie in the most comfortable position I could manage. Her lips smacked as if tasting nectar and a look of pleasure settled on her features. Whatever Eleanor had given her, it had an upside.

"Sarah Booth?" The male voice came over the speakerphone.

"Screw you." I wasn't in a mood to play nice.

"Listen to me. Monica's life hangs on your decision."

"I'm not part of this and you can't force me to be." I tried not to listen, but I couldn't stop myself.

"Bring the ransom to the road under the bridge. Park there. You'll find a rowboat. Put the money in it and wait for my call."

"Eleanor is making the drop. I'm taking my partner to the hospital."

Eleanor started to say something, but I slashed my hand through the air in the universal sign for silence so emphatically that she stepped back.

"If you drive away, Monica dies." The man was cold. "Perhaps of more significance to you, so will Mrs. Richmond."

I looked at the hint of a smile that touched Tinkie's face. Was it a smile of pleasure or a grimace? Was she in pain and unable to express it? "What did you give her?"

"The drug is safe if administered properly. An antidote will clear it from her system very quickly, but I wouldn't rely on the hospital to have it. She'll be fine, Sarah Booth, if you do what I say."

Eleanor whispered, "He'll give us the antidote when he releases Monica. He promised. I had to get Tinkie out of the way. I had to. He made me."

I wanted to kill her with my bare hands. She'd trusted my partner's life to a kidnapper and a liar.

"Miss Delaney, will you bring the money or not?" The kidnapper was growing impatient.

"How do I know you have an antidote or that you'll administer it?"

"That's a risk you'll have to take."

He was so damn smug I wanted to smack him. "Not true. I don't have to take any risks. I'm taking my partner to the hospital."

"Good luck with that, Ms. Delaney. And when Mrs. Richmond dies, you can spend the rest of your life blaming yourself. To be effective, the antidote must be administered within two hours. You have, what? An hour and twenty-five minutes? Good night, ladies. I'll be sure and tell Monica you sent your good-byes."

"Wait!" I couldn't risk Tinkie's life—and I couldn't let him kill Monica. "If I take the money to the bridge, you'll give me the antidote? Where will Monica be? I won't leave the money unless she's free and able to walk away."

"She'll be there, waiting. With the antidote in her possession. The exchange will be . . . civilized."

"I'll do it," I said, knowing it was a mistake. This man had kidnapped Monica and likely killed Millicent. I had no reason to believe him. But I also had no choice. "Eleanor, you take my partner to the hospital."

She backed slowly away. "I have to do what he says. Just take the money and get Monica and the antidote. It's the safest thing for all of us. Maybe to be on the safe side we should call your sheriff friend in Sunflower County. Tell him what's happening here. He needs to know you're making a ransom drop."

"No." Coleman would be compelled to contact Gunny—I didn't have time to convince him the local lawman might be dirty. I simply couldn't risk it. There was no one to help Tinkie but me. If I didn't cooperate, Tinkie might die or be permanently injured. I didn't have a choice.

The clouds that had played a frisky game of tag with the moon had thickened to a roiling mass energized with thunder. The night was pitch black, except when lightning bloomed behind the clouds giving an eerie effect. I parked as close to the river's edge as I could and got out. Hauling first one bag and then the other, I loaded them in a small aluminum boat conveniently beached under the bridge.

The shoreline was muddy. My feet caught in places, held in the viselike grip of thick goo. Above me, traffic echoed as it crossed the span.

The boat hadn't been on the bank for long—otherwise kids or vagrants would have taken it. It was a nondescript, flat-bottomed fishing two-seater with one paddle.

Eleanor's cell phone rang on cue. The kidnapper had the best surveillance around. He knew my every move.

"Paddle out to the third piling. There are two hooks above the waterline. Hang the bags on them. Then paddle back to shore."

"Where is Monica?" I wasn't about to leave the money without getting the sister and the antidote.

"When you reach the piling, look up. You'll see her. She'll be right there, ready for rescue. Row back to shore, and call 9-1-1. The fire department EMTs can get her. She has the antidote. "

The kidnapper was smart. This arrangement allowed him ample time to escape. Either I could do what he said or leave without the antidote or Monica—which meant I would do what he said.

As I clambered into the boat, I remembered how much I hated boats of all sizes. The river current was treacherous, and I was inexperienced to say the least. I was also nearly blind. The night was so dark the pilings that supported the bridge were barely visible. Upriver, where the casino boat was docked, there was light and laughter. Down here, nothing but fear and worry.

I pushed off from the shore, and the current caught me. I was swept thirty yards downriver with the boat spinning like a carnival ride. When I finally got it controlled, my phone rang.

"Quit wasting time." The kidnapper was no longer amused. He was pissed.

"You should have asked for a boater to make the drop," I said through gritted teeth.

I took care to lay the cell phone on the second boat seat. All I needed was to drop it overboard and have the kidnapper think I was being uncooperative.

It took all my strength and concentration to paddle the boat nearer shore, where the current wasn't as strong. Fighting as hard as I could, I finally managed to pass the first two pilings and move to the third.

Vehicles crossing the river echoed, and sounds I couldn't identify seemed to come from the water itself and the dead space among the pilings. My heart pounded. I had to focus on saving Tinkie. This was almost over.

I saw a hook on the third piling bored into the heavy cement. I made for it and grasped it with one hand.

My cell phone rang. "Very good. Now look up."

I did, and in the glow of lightning behind the clouds, I saw a vision in white. A woman in a peignoir seemed to hang suspended from a brace above me.

"Monica?"

She didn't answer. She was possibly gagged. I couldn't see that clearly.

"Leave the money or she'll die." The voice came from the phone.

"Where's the antidote?" I wouldn't budge without it.

"Monica has it with her."

The current snatched at the boat, almost pulling me away from the piling. I had little time to make up my mind. It was leave the money and trust that Monica would bring what Tinkie needed or be swept out into the main current of the river. From there, I would never be able to paddle back upstream.

I hung both bags. "There's your money." I cast free of the piling and paddled like crazy for the shore. My shoulders burned with the effort.

"And here's Monica!"

To my utter horror, she plummeted from the brace and went straight into the water only a few yards from my boat.

In an instant she vanished below the surface.

"Shit!" I wrenched in my seat, searching for her. The black surface of the river was undisturbed.

"You bastard!" I cried out as I tried to maneuver the boat to find Monica. The current tugged at me, pulling me away from the shore. I fought against it while trying to stay in the place where Monica went under.

I saw her then, only a dozen feet away from me. She came to the surface slowly, floating facedown, the peignoir I recognized as the one she'd worn when she disappeared floating around her like a lace shroud.

There wasn't a doubt in my mind she was dead. The bastard killed her before he threw her in the river.

Try as I might, I couldn't snag the body. The current teased the peignoir, then slowly caught the body. As I struggled to make shore, Monica's corpse moved into the main current of the river and started the long journey down to New Orleans.

And with it went the antidote for Tinkie.

Before I could do anything else, a shot rang out from the bridge. I heard a *ping* and a jet of water shot up by my foot. River water rushed into the bottom of the boat. The smell of mud and fish rose around me. I was sinking. Fast.

I've always been a strong swimmer—not pretty, but powerful. The Mississippi River, though, wasn't the placid Tallahatchie or Yazoo. This was "the Father of Waters," as the Indian name went. The treacherous currents claimed numerous lives each year.

As the boat foundered, I divested myself of my favorite boots and struggled out of my jeans. I couldn't afford the extra weight of the clothes.

The night was pitch black, which worked for and against me as another shot rang out. A bullet plunged into the water only six inches from the sinking boat. The kidnapper continued to shoot.

Monica's body was now twenty yards downriver. I didn't believe anything the kidnapper said, but the possibility that Tinkie's antidote was on the body forced me to take action.

I stripped off the rest of my clothes and plunged into the cold water. I entered a world of black. When I resurfaced several yards away from the boat, I had trouble distinguishing the water from the horizon. My sense of direction was totally screwed. At last I sighted in on the traffic on the bridge and reoriented myself. The delay had been costly. Monica was now fifty yards away.

As I struck out for her, I felt the tug of the eddies that made the Mississippi so formidable. I'd grown up on stories of searches for lost swimmers and boaters in the Mississippi—the long hours of probing the banks and dragging for bodies snagged by trees or other debris that lodged along the bottom and created small whirlpools that sucked a person, or a corpse, to the bottom and held it in a close embrace for days.

When I was ten I found an old photograph of a body search for my great-uncle Crabtree's son, Rayford, who'd fallen from a boat while fishing along a bend in the river. The photo had haunted me for a long time. Family members stood on the riverbank, weeping, while men in boats tossed ropes with grappling hooks into the water. Their hope was to catch the body and pull it up before the fish and water did too much damage.

I forced those thoughts from my head as I stroked toward the place I remembered seeing Monica's body. I had to get the antidote. If there was a chance Monica was stunned and not dead, I had to recover her. I couldn't let her drown because she was unconscious.

Using the bridge as a reference point, I swam blindly. Lightning flashed behind the thick cloud cover, and for one brief moment the entire river was illuminated. I was another thirty yards from shore—much closer to the center of the river than I'd intended. I should have known. The current sucked at my legs with an iron will. The river meant to have me. That thought was terrifying.

I searched for Monica before the illumination failed, but I couldn't find her. I felt a sob building in my chest. She was gone. She'd either sunk or been swept away, unresisting, by the current.

I faced a terrible choice. I could abandon Monica and Tinkie's antidote and try to save myself, or I could continue to search for Monica and possibly drown. My body screamed exhaustion, and my arms felt as if they were being pulled from the shoulders. I wasn't even certain I had the strength to get back to shore.

For a long moment I treaded water.

There are two things always associated with a Delaney. Love of land and hardheadedness. I struck out for the center of the river.

The clouds bloomed with lightning again, a pulse of wicked illumination that made the entire sky bright enough to see. I couldn't find Monica.

Another shot rang out and the bullet bit into my upper arm. The pain made me gasp. Water rushed into my lungs.

My right bicep was on fire with pain. I rolled in the water, kicking and stroking weakly for the shore. I no longer had a choice. I doubted I could save myself, much less find Monica's floating body in the vast black river. I couldn't see the shore, and that was good, because if I knew how far I had to swim, I might give up.

The water turned icy cold, and my legs wanted to stop kicking. Sinking wouldn't be so bad. I wouldn't have to face Oscar and tell him I'd lost the antidote to save Tinkie. I wouldn't have to confess to Graf that I'd betrayed him by doing something so dangerous I put his heart at risk. Letting go might be for the best.

"Sarah Booth!"

Shaking free of the lethargy that held me, I squinted at the shore. I'd swum farther than I thought. But maybe this wasn't the bank of the big river. Maybe this was something else. Maybe this was the river Jordan, and the person calling my name, a deep, masculine voice, was . . . Was it my daddy?

"Sarah Booth, hold on!"

I could see him, a lanky man who disdained the traditional planter garb for khakis and a crisply ironed blue oxford. Sunlight touched his chestnut hair and sparkled in his hazel eyes. "Sarah Booth!" But he seemed to be waving me back, as if I shouldn't go to him.

"Daddy!" My arms and legs felt weighted by cement. Water swirled around me, but I couldn't understand why. It was black and cold and I pushed harder to get to the sunlight and my father.

"Sarah Booth!"

Another voice called to me, a male, demanding, authoritative, angry. I ignored him and fought a bit closer to my father. But Daddy was distressed. He kept pushing me back, forcing me away from him and toward the darkness of the water.

"Sarah Booth, damn it! Fight!"

Something large and warm brushed against me. Strong arms circled me and pulled me into an embrace. Suddenly I was in a rocking chair, moving gently forward and back, forward and back, cruising through the water like a sea dragon.

And then my sea dragon gained firm land and we surged out of the river onto the bank. My body struck the mud, and in a moment someone was beside me, turning my head and pushing firmly on my abdomen.

"Breathe, damn it. If you quit now, I'll kill you."

I couldn't think who was fussing at me. All I wanted to do was go to my father, who stood pacing on the edge of the water in a shaft of the most perfect light.

"Sarah Booth, you have to fight." The annoying man shook me. "Fight!"

But I didn't want to. I only wanted to slip into the sunlight and walk down a shady lane with my father. The familiar sycamore trees swayed in a light breeze, and in the distance I could see Dahlia House. Daddy strode toward home. If I hurried, I could catch him.

24

Pain woke me. I fought against consciousness, wanting only to get to the sunshine and my daddy's side. Even as I struggled, Daddy began to fade. He smiled at me and nodded, as if he approved of something, and then I felt harsh pressure on my rib cage. Fingers pinched my nose shut and lips covered my mouth as someone forced air into my lungs.

Water surged up my throat and I gagged. I pushed at the man who was trying to suffocate me, causing a red-hot blaze to zing through my right arm.

"Thank God." Barclay Levert rocked back on his heels and gave me some room to flail and struggle. I tried to swat him in the face, but my arms refused to obey my commands.

Beside my head a horse's hoof stomped, and I wondered if I had truly come awake. The creature shook and droplets of waters sprayed over me. When lightning illuminated the sky, I could see the Andalusian standing over me, his long mane tossing in a wind building to gale force out of the west. Any minute the sky would crack open and I figured a band of angels would swing down in a chariot.

"Can you sit up?" Barclay gave me an assist.

I could and did, though I cried out in pain. My arm blazed. Blood dripped from a bullet wound. I'd been shot. The whole nightmare on the river came back to me.

"Monica!" I tried to rise, but Barclay pushed me back to the mud, which made a sucking sound around my near-naked bottom. I wore only panties and a bra. My clothes had been swallowed by the river.

"Take it easy. You're hurt."

"He threw Monica in the river. I think she was already dead." I had to get it all out. "The antidote for Tinkie is gone. So is the money."

I thought for a moment he was daft as he pulled off his black T-shirt and tore it into strips.

"Did you hear what I said?" And then another thought struck me. How the hell did Barclay and the black devil horse from Briarcliff get down to the river to rescue me?

"Listen to me, Sarah Booth." He forced me to focus my thoughts and hear him. "After we traded cars, I went back to Briarcliff. I started through some of the old family history books in the library. I found a map of underground tunnels that link Briarcliff to the river. I'm sure Eleanor knew about those tunnels. Old Barthelme used the cliff tunnels to rob boats docked at Natchez and make good his escape. For generations the family must have kept this secret."

What was it with this case? All roads led back to a man long dead, Barthelme Levert. He'd branded his legacy of deceit, lies, and murder on his family in a way that was inescapable.

Barclay caught my chin, forcing me to look at him. "I took the maps and began searching, thinking maybe Monica was being held hostage in one of the tunnels. That's when Tinkie texted me, 'Sarah Booth in trouble at bridge. Help.' I assumed this bridge and I got here as quickly as I could. One of the tunnels connects with the stables, so I saddled Lucifer and came down through the tunnel thinking you might need help. I saw you in the boat. I saw you get shot, and you were drowning. Lucky for you Lucifer is a strong swimmer. He was able to get to you and then struggle back to the bank."

So it was Barclay who'd swum the horse into the river and rescued me. I owed him and the black hell-horse. But my worries centered on one person. "Where's Tinkie?"

"I don't know."

"We have to find her."

Lighting flared across the sky revealing Barclay's stomach, rippling with muscle. "Someone meant to kill you out in the river. The whole plan was for the money to disappear, and you to die. Monica is dead. Millicent is dead. If I'm discounted as a true Levert, that leaves one person to inherit everything. We have to call your friend, the lawman, and tell him all of this."

"Eleanor is behind it all." My pulse accelerated. "She killed her own sister and she has Tinkie. Jerome must be helping her."

Barclay's features were grim in the next flash of lightning. "She means to kill you and Tinkie and me. She has the insurance money, the necklace, and she can't afford loose ends." He bound the strips of T-shirt around the wound, which almost made me scream, but I bit it back. We had to move. He pushed a cell phone into my hand. "Call your friend in Sunflower County."

"Tinkie first." I pushed it away. Coleman couldn't help me. There wasn't enough time for him to get here. "We have to find Tinkie."

"We need backup. Call him. Tell him Monica has been killed. Nothing more. We need him to be on his way here."

I used the phone he offered. When Coleman answered, I almost lost my composure. "I'm in Natchez. Tinkie may be dead," I said. "Monica Levert was kidnapped and murdered. She's floating down the Mississippi. I need your help."

"I'm on the way, Sarah Booth."

Barclay took the phone, snapped it shut, and hauled me to my feet. "We have to hurry. We'll ride the horse back through the tunnels."

"Screw the tunnels. I'm going to look for Tinkie." I had a perfectly good car not forty feet away.

Barclay's sardonic grin was as intimate as a touch. "I suggest you find some clothes first, Sarah Booth. I appreciate the view, but Natchez is still a bit . . . provincial."

"You are lower than a snake's belly," I ranted, and then realized he'd provoked me with cause. Getting my fighting Irish up energized me to battle for my partner's life.

"Let's ride," he said.

"I'll take the car." But then I realized I couldn't. The car keys were at the bottom of the Mississippi River in my jeans pocket.

Barclay mounted the big stallion, who danced, eager to run. The dinner-plate-sized hooves moved up and down like pistons keeping a beat. When Barclay reached for my hand, I let him pull me up behind him. Lady Godiva might have been a sex symbol riding nude, but sitting astride the rump of a big horse in mud-caked panties was not my idea of erotic.

My arm throbbed with every beat of my heart. A visit to the emergency room was in order, but first Tinkie. And then Eleanor. She'd murdered the last vestige of her family for money. And she'd tried to kill me.

Eleanor and her conspirator were about to confront the wrath of Sarah Booth Delaney. It was going to get bloody.

The ride up the darkened tunnel on Lucifer took at least five years off my life. I clung to blind trust in the horse's superior sight and Barclay's balance. My good arm wrapped tightly around Barclay's lean and muscled torso, I put all of my concentration into not sliding off. Lucifer surged up the steep incline into blackness so dense I shut my eyes to keep from getting a headache.

Amazingly, we arrived at the manse within minutes. Barclay dropped me at the front door, then he cantered to the stables to tend to Lucifer.

I took three minutes to wash the mud off so I could examine the bullet wound.

A groove sliced through the muscle of my right arm. I'd been grazed, not hit directly. I applied a tube of antibiotic salve I found in the medicine cabinet and clumsily wrapped gauze around my arm. The injury was painful, but not anywhere near life threatening. Then I got dressed and picked up the phone. The desk clerk at the Eola knew Tinkie by sight, and he hadn't seen her or Eleanor Levert.

My fingers hovered over the touch pad, but I didn't

dial Gunny. Something held me back. The police chief would be furious, no doubt about that. But it wasn't his wrath I feared. I still didn't trust the Natchez lawman.

"Who are you calling?" Barclay asked as he came in the back door, panting from his sprint.

"We should call the local law officers."

"No."

"You don't trust Gunny." I understood Barclay's reluctance because I shared it. There had been that moment when the chief had stopped me and Tinkie downtown. He'd made reference to the insurance money. It had struck me wrong, but Barclay obviously sensed something, too. "Why not?"

"I went to see the police chief when I first got to town. I wanted to be upfront, to let him know who I was and that I intended to claim my legacy."

"How did he react?"

"As if I'd personally insulted him. He warned me off and told me if he got one complaint from the sisters, he'd bury me in the Natchez jail so deep no one would ever find me. He wasn't interested in justice; he was protecting the sisters. Or one of them. I think he's neck-deep in this mess."

Thirty years ago, small-town police chiefs and county sheriffs had nearly total power. People without family or friends to inquire after them did disappear. The lawman's interpretation of the law was often based on personal interests—their cronies were protected and their enemies suffered.

Gunny's allegiance to the sisters could mean a number of things, but first and foremost was that he stood to gain from the association. Four million could buy a lot of goodwill from a man with a badge.

"Let's go," I said.

"Where?"

"Back to the tunnels. Do you still have the maps?"

"I do." He leaned down beside a sofa and brought them forth from beneath a cushion. "I didn't want to leave them lying around. I haven't had a chance to really study where all the tunnels lead."

I carried the maps to the kitchen counter. It was nearly eleven o'clock. Tinkie had been drugged for more than two hours. Was she still alive? "Let's see if there's a place Tinkie might be stashed close to Briarcliff. Eleanor had to put her somewhere no one would find her."

"What about the money?" Barclay asked.

It was a logical question from a Levert heir, but I was over worrying about anything except my partner. "Talk to your aunt Eleanor about it once we round her up."

"You think she really killed Monica?"

I was about to answer in the affirmative when footsteps sounded in the parlor headed our way.

"The answer is no."

We both whirled. Eleanor Levert stood in front of us, gun leveled. She looked capable of using the weapon, too. Gone was any shred of the Southern belle who'd paced and wrung her hands. This version of Eleanor was cool and contained. "Barclay, move away from her."

Barclay, too, remained calm. "Of course, Moth—"

I saw it then. Before he finished the sentence. "You're Monica, not Eleanor."

"Bada bing!" She was very pleased with herself. Her posture shifted and assumed a demeanor I recognized as Eleanor's. "I'm just worried sick about my sister." She laughed out loud. The woman was a total chameleon. "I've been in Briarcliff the entire time and you never suspected."

"Where's Tinkie? If you've hurt her—" All my threats were empty. I had no weapon, no phone, and no hope of anyone coming to my rescue.

"As you guessed, Sarah Booth, Mrs. Richmond is in the tunnels, where you'll join her. For eternity."

"Give me the antidote for Tinkie."

"There isn't one. She was never in danger from a drug. I gave her Rohypnol, the date rape drug. It's worn off by now. Of course that won't help her since she's securely tied. Surely you've come to conclude I can't let you go. You and Tinkie have served your purpose marvelously, Sarah Booth. I couldn't have planned this better if I'd gotten old Barthelme to climb from the grave and help me."

"You killed your own sister." The idea still astounded me.

"You're always jumping to the wrong conclusion, Sarah Booth." Monica swept the maps Barclay had gathered into a pile. "Can't have these lying around. The tunnels will make a convenient tomb. I must say, Barclay, you did a superb job riding Lucifer up from the river. He's a real handful. I applaud your skills."

"You're the horseman!" Why hadn't I seen it sooner? The shorter torso, longer legs. And the old football pads in the stables. Monica wore them to lend the illusion of being a man.

"Nice deduction, just a trifle late in the game." Monica smirked.

I heard a scuttling on the hardwood floor beyond the kitchen. Monica heard it, too. She checked over her shoulder. "I have a delicious surprise for you both." She was almost giggling.

But I had a surprise, too. "I can hardly wait." Just beyond the parlor, Chablis darted past a doorway, her little nails skittering on the wood.

"Ah, the dogs." Monica didn't bother looking. "I may keep the little one. The big hound will join you in the tunnels."

The idea that she would kill Sweetie without a qualm—and steal Chablis!—anger surged in my chest.

"You won't get away with this." It was such a clichéd line I almost groaned.

"Yes, yes, I know." She waved the gun. "Justice prevails and all of that."

In the brief moment when she allowed her vigilance to slip, Sweetie rounded the corner and catapulted herself directly into Monica's back. Seventy pounds of hound rammed her at thirty miles an hour.

Monica flew forward. The gun discharged wildly as she smashed onto her face. Her chin hit the tile floor of the kitchen with such force that she cracked a tile and shattered several teeth.

I kicked the gun free of her hand and knelt in the center of her back with all of my weight.

"Good job, Sweetie!" I had nothing but praise for my heroic red tic. "Barclay, get some kind of rope or cord."

Monica moaned beneath my knee, and it gave me great pleasure to grind my kneecap harder into her. "Where is Tinkie?" I demanded as Barclay went to the parlor and ripped a cord from a lamp.

Monica spat blood and tooth fragments, acting as though she were suffocating. I had no problem with that.

"Get . . . off—"

I leaned down. "Screw you, Monica. Where's my partner?" Sweetie Pie licked my face. A new notch would be cut in Sweetie's leash—she'd brought down another criminal.

Barclay bent beside me to tie Monica's hands. "What a pleasure this is, Mommy, dearest."

The first warning of anything wrong was Sweetie's long, low growl.

"What is it, girl?" I started to stand but froze when I felt the cold metal of a gun muzzle against my head. Very slowly I turned to face . . . Monica. No, Eleanor.

"You aren't dead, either."

"Far from it. Now get off my sister." Her shove sent me into Barclay.

Monica flopped and moaned. "My teeth! My teeth! She broke my teeth out."

"Four million can buy a lot of dental work, Monica," Barclay said. Beside him, Sweetie growled fiercely.

"Just add it to the plastic surgery list," Eleanor said.

"You'll pay for this." Monica scooted away from us and used the kitchen counter to pull herself upright. "Shoot the dog, Eleanor. Then shoot them."

"I don't want to carry them to the tunnels. They can walk." Eleanor's hand was level as she held a gun on us. The one Monica had used was against the kitchen counter about ten feet away. Neither Barclay nor I could reach it in time.

Sweetie bared her fangs and snarled.

"Shut that freaking dog up!" Monica slurred through bloody lips. "Or give me the gun and I'll do it." Eleanor swung the weapon out of her grasp.

I don't know where Roscoe came from, or how he knew to intervene, but he sailed through the air and his jaws clamped down hard on Eleanor's gun arm. Chablis streaked around the corner and leaped high in the air—a truly Michael Jordan vault. She caught Monica's blood-ied lip with her little underbit teeth and clamped down with a *snap* I heard clear across the kitchen.

Monica and Eleanor, a dog hanging off each one, slammed together in a screaming frenzy. Eleanor still held the gun, but Roscoe controlled her wrist. When the mutt finally gained his feet and began to shake his head back and forth, Eleanor screamed and released the weapon.

In a moment I had scooped it up. Barclay went for Monica's gun, just as Chablis lost her lip grip. Undaunted, the Yorkie leaped at Monica's face, narrowly missing her nose. Cupping her mangled lip with one hand, Monica lashed blindly at the little attack canine.

"Call off the dogs, Sarah Booth," Barclay said.

I hated to, but I did.

"Monica, Eleanor, up against the wall."

"You both think you're so smart." Eleanor was furi-ous. "You won't inherit a thing, Barclay. Harm us, and you'll never get Briarcliff."

Inheritance was the last thing on my mind. Tinkie was the only thing I cared about. While Barclay held them at gunpoint, I gathered the things I'd need to go for Tinkie.

The cavalry was on the way.

25

Even if Coleman flew on the wings of Mercury, I couldn't wait for him. I helped Barclay tie up the twins before I gathered the three dogs, a gun, the maps, and a flashlight. Tinkie was underground—and I couldn't stand the thought of my partner and my friend alone in a dark, dank place.

"I should go after Tinkie, Sarah Booth. You guard the sisters," Barclay said.

"No." I couldn't trust this job to anyone else.

"Then be careful. Remember, another person is almost certainly involved in this," Barclay reminded me. "He could be down there, waiting."

"Make Monica and Eleanor give more details of where Tinkie is?" Briarcliff's underground maze could have me wandering about for hours. "If you find out anything, call me." I picked up Monica's cell phone. Where she was going, she wouldn't need a phone.

"How hard should I try to force information from them?" Barclay had a hard glint in his eye.

"They're your relatives."

"After years of dreaming about confronting my mother, this is what I get." He gave a snort of disgust.

"It would help if I knew which tunnel they left Tinkie in." According to the maps, the tunnels led directly to the river, but branches forked off and led to numerous cul-de-sacs where Barthelme had undoubtedly stored his stolen goods, including slaves. The old river pirate had constructed an amazingly complex grid of underground routes. Tinkie could be anywhere.

I left Barclay checking the bonds on the sisters. At the front door of Briarcliff, I realized that while we'd been inside, the fury of the weather gods had been unleashed. The threatening storm had broken, and the wind howled up from the cliffs. Rain fell in sheets while lightning popped all around, as if Briarcliff were a rod. The place was evil, down to the bedrock.

I jogged to the rose garden, where the trapdoor to the tunnels could be found beneath a mulch bed. Jerome had known about the tunnels all along. And he'd known that Monica was the horsewoman. He'd pretended ignorance, but a fourteen-hundred-pound horse living on the estate could not have escaped him. How much else had he known?

Jerome was the Leverts' confederate. It had to be him. Maybe I could bargain with him for Tinkie's whereabouts. I took shelter in an old gardening shed filled with tools and pots and the tender shoots of new plants. Jerome's number was in Monica's cell phone. I dialed and waited. To my surprise he answered, but then Monica's number would have shown up on his caller ID.

"Is Eleanor okay?" were his first words. Which meant he was in on the whole kidnapping scam. And how much else? The murder of Millicent? The attack on John Hightower? The Levert girls had woven quite a web of deceit, and Jerome was trapped in the center of it.

"Depends on what you consider okay," I said evenly. "Eleanor is alive and unharmed, but she's going to jail, Jerome. And you might be, too."

A curse came out on a whisper. "I told the sisters this wouldn't work."

"What wouldn't work?" I wanted him to say it.

"The insurance scam. The fake kidnapping. I knew it would backfire. I tried to stop them."

So he wasn't a willing participant, as he told it, but he'd known what the sisters were up to. "They've taken Tinkie hostage and are holding her in the underground tunnels. Where is she?"

"There's no good to come from a twisted deed." His voice sounded thin and tired. "Try the main tunnel until you come to a right-hand turn. It leads to an opening about a hundred yards upriver. There's a room Barthelme used as a holding area for the slaves he stole. It's safe enough, unless there's a big storm. The only danger is the river rising."

Around me it sounded as if the battle for the future of the universe were being waged. Water poured from the roof in a gusher. "What happens in a bad storm?"

"The water comes in from a flaw in the Natchez drainage system. The storage room will fill up with water. I told

Monica the tunnel structure had been weakened, but she wouldn't listen to me. It could be very dangerous down there."

I felt like a fist had slammed into my gut. "Who else was involved with the sisters' plan?" I had to know who I might come up against.

"That's beyond my ken. I swear it. I told Eleanor I wanted no details, nothing to do with her schemes. Monica needed my help with the horse—the feeding and the care. I couldn't let the poor beastie go without food and water and she had no interest in him except for her midnight rides. I knew she was up to no good, but I didn't really understand until . . . it was too late to stop them."

Thunder cracked overhead so loudly I almost dropped the phone. With each moment, Tinkie's prison could be filling with water. I didn't have time to drag information from Jerome.

"Pray my partner is unharmed," I told him, "because if anything happens to Tinkie, I'll make sure Eleanor and Monica get the gas chamber."

I closed the phone and put it in my pocket. The deluge had washed the mulch off the handles of the trapdoor to the tunnels. No wonder Jerome was always puttering around this part of the rose garden. He had to keep the trapdoor concealed.

I pulled it open and stepped down a ladder. Rain pelted me until I pulled the trap shut and plunged into total darkness. Turning on the flashlight, I found myself in a narrow passage that went straight down for ten feet, then opened into a tunnel high enough for me to walk upright.

Lined with handmade bricks, the tunnel had likely been made by slaves. How many lives had been lost in the endeavor to give Barthelme Levert easy access to the river and his nefarious deeds?

When I hit level ground, I jogged. Moisture seeped along the walls and my footsteps echoed. The place was creepy, and I could only imagine Tinkie alone and thinking she would die of starvation. Or drown. Her suffering was unbearable.

Moving through the tunnels I lost all sense of time and direction, except that I was heading down, sometimes steeply. The river couldn't be too far away, but I'd lost all sensory connection to the outside world. If the storm continued above me, I had no way of knowing.

I moved as quickly as I could, finally coming to the Y in the tunnels that Jerome had spoken of. I followed his directions while my mind pondered the question I had to answer. Who was the Leverts' partner?

I thought back over the phone calls. The caller had been male with a nicely modulated voice and clear diction. The speaker was Southern. It could have been anyone in Natchez or the surrounding area. There was absolutely nothing distinctive about the caller, which in itself should have been a clue.

In the distance a noise I couldn't identify made me hesitate. It was best described as a sloshing sound. When it registered what it could be, I gave up jogging and hit a flat-out sprint.

"Tinkie!" The echo in the tunnel mocked me. "Tinkie!"

The sound of a large fish flopping in the shallows drifted from the darkness.

Cursing silently, I ran forward into water that covered my feet and then my calves. The flashlight illuminated a scene from my worst nightmare. Water covered the bottom of the tunnel and lapped hungrily at the walls. What seemed to be an opening gaped to the right, and I slogged toward it and the sound of something big struggling in the rising water.

When I made it to the opening, I saw Tinkie. She was tied to a chair, which had fallen over. She struggled to keep her head out of the water, but she kept going under.

I dove for her and hauled the chair to an upright position. She was gagged, and I removed the nasty bandanna that had been tied around her mouth.

After a bit of coughing and hacking, she finally said, "It's Eleanor. She's the one."

"I know." I worked furiously at the knots that bound her, aware that the water in the room had risen at least two inches in the few moments I'd been there. The rope was swollen and refused to give.

"The water is getting higher." Tinkie spoke calmly, but the quiver in her voice told me of her fear. "Can we get out?"

"We will." My thumbnail tore back to the bed as I tried to work the knots.

"Leave me," she said. The water was up to her waist.

"When pigs fly." I had to find something sharp, and then I remembered Monica's cell phone. Screw it. I pulled it from my pocket and used the wall to crush it. From the twisted remains, I found a sharp edge and sawed at Tinkie's bonds. Precious seconds slipped away, but the rope gave. We both had to hold our breath as we bent to free her legs. Luckily the knots on her right leg gave and I shredded the rope holding her left.

"Let's get out of here." She held on to me in the darkness.

Which way led to safety? To the right was the river.

To the left the passage I'd come down. I couldn't be certain how high the river might be—the whole entrance to the tunnel could be underwater. But to head back up the tunnel meant we could be trapped in a cave-in if the structure collapsed.

"Which way?" she asked, trusting me to know the answer to our fate.

"Left," I said. At least I knew high ground was in that direction.

Holding hands and casting the wavering flashlight beam ahead of us, we waded in water up to my waist and her chest. Any moment now, the batteries were going to give out.

Behind us something large splashed. All I could think of was an alligator. "Can you run?" I asked Tinkie.

"Try and stop me."

Still holding hands we charged through the water. All around us was the sound of sloshing, splashing, the creepy echo of water in a confined space. Even though I tried to ignore it, someone, or something, was pursuing us from the direction of the river. If not some river creatures, then it had to be Monica and Eleanor's partner, the man who'd worked with them.

"Run faster!" I tugged Tinkie along behind me. It wasn't that she couldn't run, but her legs were a foot shorter and the water was now up to her neck. We both panted from exertion as the water hobbled us.

Ahead I caught a dark shadow in the flashlight beam. I slammed to a halt until the beam picked out the features of Barclay Levert. His sculpted chest—the only part of him not underwater—glistened, and he smiled when he saw us.

"You found her," he said.

"Someone is after us." I waved for him to help Tinkie. "We have to run."

He took Tinkie's hand and pulled her to him. There was a *click*, and I swung the light to discover he held the barrel of a gun to Tinkie's head.

"Barclay?" I sounded like a complete fool, and felt even stupider. Tink and I were dead. Monica and Eleanor's partner held my partner at gunpoint. "You bastard." I flung the words at him.

"A mild understatement, Sarah Booth. I admire your eloquence." His arm shifted around Tinkie's neck and chest as he almost cradled her against him.

"You were working with the sisters all along." I couldn't believe it—didn't want to believe it. "But it wasn't your voice on the ransom calls."

"Monica had a voice synthesizer," Tinkie said. For a woman with a gun barrel pressed against her temple, she was amazingly calm. "That way we never suspected Barclay. It was a very clever setup, and they meant to use us from the very beginning."

"This is going to work out so much better," Barclay said. "Both of you will drown here in the tunnels. Eleanor can tell Gunny and your friends from Zinnia that you came down here searching for . . . whatever. And never came back up. You've already called your sheriff friend and told him exactly what we needed him to know. You saw Monica fall and drown, only it was a mannequin, but they'll never know. Her body will be lost in the river."

"And you'll take the insurance money and the necklace and all of the Levert holdings and divide the spoils between the three of you." How could I have been so stupid as to believe Barclay's story of abandonment. He was a sprout from the Barthelme root. The whole mess of them were crooks, scoundrels, and accomplished actors. "But why the whole kidnapping ruse? Langley Insurance paid out. You had the four million and the necklace. There wasn't a need—" Oh, but there was. I saw it then. A double scam. "How much is Monica insured for?"

Barclay laughed aloud with delight. "I wanted to see your expression when you finally caught hold of the breadth of our plan."

"How much?"

"Another four million. Double that if she dies of violent means."

"And you needed Tinkie and me to set up the kidnapping and make it real."

"Several of your conversations have been recorded. As the grieving son, I'll turn them over to the police. Aunt Eleanor will verify that you three decided to handle the abduction on your own, and that it went awry. The kidnapper threw Monica's body in the river, took the insurance money, and left. Monica is dead. Both of you are dead." He waved the gun to indicate I should move down the tunnel into deeper water. "The loose ends are all tied up."

"You're worse than the sisters."

"Not hardly."

"When Coleman gets here, he'll figure it out. He isn't gullible or dumb. You'll never get away with this."

"A risk we're willing to take. Too bad you won't be around to see if we get away with it." He pushed Tinkie toward me so hard that we both splashed backward into the water. "Start swimming. I doubt you'll be able to get out of the tunnel now, but you can try."

"You're crazy. We aren't going to make it easy for you."

"I can always knock you out and hold you under." He waved the gun down the dark corridor. "At least swimming you have a chance."

The batteries in my flashlight had been steadily weakening. Darkness would work better for us than him. I threw the light at Barclay's head as hard as I could. Score one for me! It hit with a dull *thunk* and he cried out in pain. I grasped Tinkie's hand. "Dive!" I whispered, and we both arced below the cold water as he pumped bullets into the water around us.

When we surfaced, we were treading water. I could feel the top of the passageway. The whole place was filling with water. And I couldn't see a damn thing.

We had to swim back to the place where Barclay waited or we would drown. We couldn't risk trying to swim out to the river. I tapped Tinkie's shoulder. We had to stay close so as not to lose each other in the darkness. "Let's go."

"Wait." She whispered. "Look."

I couldn't tell where she indicated, but I spun in the water, praying I didn't lose my sense of direction. I saw it then. A light. It bobbed slightly, moving along the wall. And it came from the direction of the river.

Tinkie and I pressed ourselves against the cold, clammy bricks of the passage. The baked clay was slick beneath my hands and I wondered how much longer the tunnel could withstand the ravages of time and water.

Very slowly the light drew closer.

"William Wallace, if you've ever helped an old Scot, show me where those lasses are," the voice grumbled into the darkness.

"Jerome!" Tinkie started forward as if she meant to swim toward him.

I stopped her. "We can't trust him."

"Then we'll take his boat." She shook me off and struck out for the light. I was only two seconds behind her.

When we came up beside the small skiff, Jerome caught us in the beam of his light. "Get in. Hurry!" he said. "The water's rising faster than I've ever seen. If we're to escape the way I came in, we only have moments."

I helped boost Tinkie into the bottom of the small boat and I managed to haul myself in after. Jerome applied muscle to the paddle and we shot toward the river.

"Stay low," he said. "It's going to be a tight squeeze to get out of here."

"Why did you come to save us?" I asked.

"I couldn't let you girls come to harm. Monica is a bad person, and she's corrupted Eleanor. Stealing money was bad enough. Murder? Well, I couldn't just let it happen. When I realized how bad the storm was, I knew you'd be in danger. So I came."

"You left Briarcliff. Where have you been?"

"Here and there, trying to decide what to do. I meant to go back to Skye. I should have gone years ago. But I couldn't stand back and see anyone else get hurt."

I heard the pain in his voice and realized he still loved Eleanor. Despite all she'd done and what she'd become, he loved her.

"Can we get out this way?" Tinkie asked.

"Pray," Jerome said.

And I did as he plunged the paddle into the river. Luckily the water in the passage had no current and he was able to move the boat rapidly toward what sounded like thunder. It was the storm! I could hear it. I found a second paddle in the bottom of the boat and with every ounce of muscle I had in my back and arms, I applied the wood. When the boat shot out of the tunnel with only a foot of clearance, I wanted to shout with joy. Even the pouring rain was wonderful as it struck my face.

"My truck is upriver," Jerome said.

I knew we couldn't paddle the boat against the current, but we could beach it and walk. I put my last reserve into pumping the boat to the shore. "We have to get to Briarcliff."

I had the terrible sense that Coleman might be walking into a trap.

26

Briarcliff, lit by flashes of lighting, could not have looked more like something from Baron von Frankenstein's story. Jerome idled the truck at the base of the driveway while we considered our options. Jerome was determined to see this through. And protect Eleanor as best he could. He would put his life on the line for her, even knowing who and what she was.

The three of us sat in the cab of the truck looking up at that mansion, a place built on human suffering. Jerome spoke softly, the brogue of his native Scotland clear. "It's hard to believe, but Eleanor was once a tender girl. The badness is in the blood—she wasn't strong enough to fight it. Once, she was sweet and innocent, like a fragile rose, but the Levert heritage was stronger than her nature.

Even knowing that a gentle creature has turned evil, I still love her. I canna help myself anymore than she can."

I put a hand on his shoulder. "I'm sorry."

He only nodded. "You should call the law. If your friends are up there, they could be in real danger."

And he was right about that. Except we had no cell phone, and I wasn't about to waste time driving to town to make a report. Besides, I still wasn't positive Gunny wasn't playing for the wrong side. Just because we'd learned Barclay was a deceiving bastard through and through didn't mean there weren't others on Team Levert.

"What are we going to do?" Tinkie asked.

"They have our dogs in there." I should never have left the pups, but I knew the tunnels would be danger-ous. I hadn't counted on Barclay betraying me.

"Chablis!" Tinkie opened the truck door as if she meant to run to the house. Jerome grabbed her before I had a chance.

"Let me drive up there. They won't suspect me." His tone was urgent. "You get in the back of the truck. I'll park and once I'm inside, you can check out the house."

It was the only feasible plan. "Be careful, Jerome. Don't think because Eleanor cares for you, or once cared for you, she won't kill you."

"I know the truth about her. I watched the family curse take her. Monica killed that French artist and with that single act she changed Eleanor's heart. Monica couldn't stand the thought Eleanor would marry away from her, so she killed him. I think Eleanor just gave up and became what Monica wanted her to be."

"I won't feel sympathy for either of them," Tinkie said. "They meant to kill me and Sarah Booth. They lured us here with the intention of using us and then killing us."

Tinkie was wounded by the betrayal in a way I wasn't. I was just plain pissed off. "Let's get in the back of the truck."

The rain had finally stopped, but the sky still roiled with lightning and thunder. The front was passing, moving toward Jackson and the center of the state. Meteorology-wise, the worst was over. For Tinkie and I, the darkest hour had begun. We had to defang three very dangerous snakes and hold them until help arrived.

Jerome stopped at the front door while Tinkie and I hid in the bed of the truck. A quick look around told me Coleman was already inside. His forest green pickup was parked down the driveway.

When Jerome knocked at the door, Eleanor gave him a halfhearted welcome. To his credit, Jerome pushed past her and went into the house. He'd entered the vipers' den.

As soon as the door closed, Tinkie and I ran toward the front windows the sisters had used to such advantage with false reports of breaking and entering. Looking through the glass, we had a good view into the parlor. From the scene within, it was clear that the Leverts had no clue Tinkie and I had survived the river.

Coleman—and Cece—brandished drinks while Eleanor and Barclay paced in high drama, arms waving here and there. Eleanor even squeezed out a few tears. No doubt she was telling Coleman how Tinkie and I had bravely tried to rescue Monica—and all had perished. This was the finishing touch. By pulling Coleman, a sheriff in a nearby county, and Cece, a journalist, into the web, Eleanor and Barclay were perfecting their scam. In their plan, Coleman and Cece, grief stricken, would search for our bodies, which would conveniently reveal we'd drowned in the tunnels. The end result: Coleman would ultimately accept our deaths. My verbal report in the phone call I'd made from the riverbank at Barkley's prompting gave credence to the claim that Monica had been killed by the kidnapper. The insurance company would have no recourse except to pay off—double indemnity—a kidnapping gone wrong.

The fly in the ointment centered around the fact we were very much alive and about to blow their world apart.

I'd almost turned away when Millicent Gentry entered the room with a tray of snacks. I couldn't believe it! She wasn't dead. Hell, no. She was playing hostess for her cousins! She'd whipped out some cream cheese roll ups, a basket of hot bread and herbed butter, and those damn cheese straws that appeared at every Southern gathering, even a murder scene.

"She's in on it, too," Tinkie whispered.

"Why are we surprised? She's a Levert. Obviously, John Hightower was supposed to find his camera with the photo of her dead corpse. I think they meant to frighten him off the book."

"And to think, I felt bad for her, dressed up like a stupid Shopping Barbie and left in the woods for the flies." Tinkie was boiling.

"I'll bet it was one of her dolls they threw off the bridge to make me think it was Monica. And the first evening, when that object went over the cliff. They did it because we'd mentioned the ghost tour. They planned this very carefully." Born to it or simply talented, the Leverts were master criminals.

I signaled my partner to the back of the house. If we could slip into the kitchen, we might find a gun. Or two. Eleanor wasn't holding one and the Leverts owned weapons, I knew that for a fact. Coleman was off duty, so he might not have a weapon on him.

We had to use caution, though. We might also find Monica, who had to stay out of sight for obvious reasons. There was no doubt, though, she was somewhere in Briarcliff.

Moving stealthily, we pushed at the door under the portico, which swung open without a sound. Tinkie and I were in the house. From far upstairs I heard the bay of my hound. Sweetie was alive. Chablis's high-pitched complaint rang out, along with Roscoe's deep grumble. The dog had a personality like W. C. Fields.

To my delight, a loaded handgun lay on the counter beside a flour canister. Because I'd seen her in action, I gave it to Tinkie. I grasped a flashlight and a butcher knife. Bludgeon and slice. Whatever it took.

Together we crept toward the parlor door. I wished for a way to alert Coleman and Cece. I could hear them talking. Coleman was tense. He kept asking Eleanor questions about what had happened to Tinkie and me.

"They were so brave," Eleanor said, her voice clotted with crocodile tears. "They went to deliver the ransom and save Monica. I tried to stop them. I begged them to let me call the local police chief, but they wouldn't."

Damn, she was good!

"They were afraid the kidnapper would kill Monica if the police became involved." Regret and sorrow weighted Barclay's baritone. "They put Monica's life ahead of their own. Now they're all three gone."

"We have to recover the bodies," Coleman said. "There's no closure without a body. Oscar will be comforted to have Chablis home. It's all he has left of Tinkie.

He'll need that little dog to help him put his grief behind him."

I had the urge to smack him upside the head. Closure? Like seeing my corpse would put an end to all we'd shared? What was wrong with him? And Oscar? As if seeing Tinkie dead—and Chablis alive—would give him license to find a new wife and just get on with living. For a man who'd once claimed to love me, Coleman sure wasn't taking my death very hard.

"We all knew this would happen to Sarah Booth and Tinkie eventually," Cece said. "We tried to talk them out of this P.I. business, but those girls, heads as hard as coconuts."

Tinkie and I exchanged a look. Oh, Cece was so going to hear about this later. There we were, dead and obviously floating down the river, and all she had to say was how stubborn we were!

That was the blast of adrenaline we needed. Tinkie and I lunged into the room with weapons at the ready. "Monica is alive! It's a scam!" I screamed.

Then all hell broke loose.

A figure in black firing a handgun appeared on the stairs. Bullets exploded in walls and the floor. Barclay bolted over the sofa, heading for me and Tinkie, but before he could make it halfway, Coleman shot him in the leg.

He just whipped his gun out, aimed, and fired without a second's hesitation. Millicent threw the tray of food at him, but Coleman ducked, and Cece karate-chopped the undead wench in the throat with a blow that dropped her to her knees, choking and gagging.

Acting on instinct and with a speed I never knew I possessed, I hurled myself across the open space toward

Monica. She'd come out of her hidey-hole in the mansion, but I was ready for her. I brought the flashlight down across her gun arm with such force I thought I heard bone snap. And then I used the heel of my palm against her chin. Watching Jackie Chan movies was not a waste of time. She went down hard, and I kicked the gun out of her unresisting fingers.

Jerome threw Eleanor to the floor, then covered her with his body. Even knowing what she was, he protected her.

Tinkie and I were left panting side by side.

"Quick reaction," I said to Coleman. I was still smarting at his easy dismissal of my death. "I see grief didn't slow you down at all."

His easy smile broke across his face. "Why, Sarah Booth, I see that reports of your death are greatly exaggerated." He pulled me hard against his chest and held me, and I could feel his heart pounding.

"I'm not hurt," I whispered.

His answer was to grip my hair and hold me tighter for a long moment until he released me. "Of course you aren't," he said.

"You knew I wasn't dead?" I looked at Cece, who was also smiling.

"Dahling, you are too mean to die. That one, too." She pointed at Tinkie.

"You knew they were up to something. How?" I demanded.

"Barclay." Cece gave him a long look of regret. "Such a pity. He could have made a fortune as a gigolo." She turned to me. "I was obsessed with him. So handsome. So charming. Such a liar. The whole story of his birth and abandonment was just a crock of shit, if you'll pardon my bluntness, dahling. Once I really started looking, I realized a con was in progress."

"How did you know it was the sisters?" I asked. With my wet boot—the second pair I'd ruined in this case—I prodded Monica, who was out like a sack of stones. Her teeth were a total mess, and I wondered if the Mississippi state prison at Parchman had a dental plan.

"We didn't," Coleman said. "But we were prepared for a double cross. The minute you rushed into the room, we knew. We were primed to react."

"Get an ambulance!" Barclay demanded. "I'm bleeding."

"Blood will tell," I told him.

"But it often tells too much," Cece concluded. "I learned that from Don Marquis, who created an intelligent cockroach. This is the perfect ending for a man who came to town as one literary figure and will go to jail with his kith and kin."

Coleman helped Jerome off Eleanor, but she remained prone since he had a gun pointed at her. "It's time to call the local police," Coleman said. "I spoke with Gunny on the way over here. He's on standby. He's suspected the Leverts for a long, long time, and he's been watching them. Now he can charge them with a long list of crimes."

"You call Gunny," I told him. "I'm going to free the dogs."

The sun rose as yellow as the yoke of a yard egg. I sipped a cup of coffee on the front porch of Dahlia House while Sweetie snored at my feet. Roscoe, incorrigible as ever, was right beside her. Later today, Harold was coming for

an adoptive parent meeting with the evil—but charming—
pooch. In his devious heart, I think Harold was hoping
Roscoe would continue with his Dumpster-diving ways in
Zinnia and stir up the local gossip. The dog had a reputation throughout the entire Delta, and while Harold emulated "proper," there was a deep vein of mischief in his
soul. Since there were no unjailed Leverts to care for the
dog, Harold had agreed to take him on.

On the other hand, it seemed that Lucifer, the Andalusian, would remain at Dahlia House and had a date with
destiny in the form of Dr. Patrick Cleveland. He would
have to be gelded.

Jerome continued at Briarcliff. For the moment he was
out on bond, pending a deal with the prosecutor. Whatever happened, he didn't want the responsibility of the
horse. Monica had confessed to beating John Hightower
and she, Eleanor, and Barclay would be in jail for a long,
long time. Millicent's involvement was yet to be determined, but there was no doubt she'd serve some time.
Gunny was still sorting through the tangle of lies and
falsehoods the Levert family had generated.

Speaking of falsehoods . . . I pulled my cell phone
from my pocket and put it on the wicker table beside my
chair. I owed Graf a call. I'd wrangled Cece into calling
him to say that I was fine and would call today. He'd
been curious, but not suspicious. And that troubled me.

Tinkie and I had almost been killed. Again. And I'd
promised Graf I would protect his heart. Yet even with
the best of intentions, I'd ended up facing danger. Tinkie
had, too. Oscar, once he got over the joy of having her
safely home and began asking for details of the case, would
be angry with us.

And our men had every right to be upset. But Tinkie

and I also had a right to our careers. Where was the middle ground in this impasse?

Sweetie's tail thumped a tango beat and Roscoe growled and grumbled in his sleep.

"Pull on your big-girl panties and give that man a call."

I closed my eyes for a moment before I opened them to find Joan Collins, one hand on her hip, posed on the steps of Dahlia House. Her dark hair was messy perfection and her leopard-print jumpsuit, tight in all the right places, was perfectly accented with patent-leather stilettos made of tiny crisscrossing straps. Those were some sexy shoes! The giveaway was the beautiful mocha complexion. Jitty had come to call.

"I'll call him," I told her.

"Then do it." She mounted the steps with her hips wagging in a way that would make a grown man quiver. Impersonating the *Dynasty* television icon, Jitty had some deadly moves.

"It's not even daybreak in Hollywood," I reminded her.

"If you run your love life like an efficient train depot, you're gonna kill all feelin'. Who cares what time it is? You nearly drowned, and you slugged it out with an evil vixen. Call that man and let him know you're glad to be alive." She grinned. "Make him glad to be alive. A little randy talk long distance can be a good thing."

I frowned. "If I wake up a man whose job is to look rested and compelling for the camera, what kind of fiancée am I?"

"The kind that puts a smile on a man's face." She walked toward me and I thought of the big cat whose fake spots she wore. She was beautiful and dangerous.

"So why Joan instead of Jackie? Both are beautiful, talented women. Why did you pick the actress?"

Jitty didn't hesitate. "Joan lived life. Jackie wrote about it. Which would you rather be, a doer or a documenter?"

"That's not fair."

She shrugged. "One thing about being dead—I don't worry about fair no more. But I do worry about you, Sarah Booth. You don't use the skills god gave you. Call that man. Make him long for you. Whisper those words that make him groan with desire. Then gloss over this whole mess and move on to some steamy phone sex." She arched one eyebrow, and her lips, so red with lipstick, curved into a smile. "You think Tinkie is drinkin' coffee, worryin' about things?"

She had me there. Tinkie was far smarter than I was when it came to the opposite sex. "I don't want to trick or manipulate Graf."

"Oh, dear lord. You are dumber than a sack of rocks!" She threw up her hands.

"Hey!" Jitty was always bossy, but seldom belittling.

"Call that man. Make him feel how much you love him and want him and miss him. That's not manipulation, that's reality. Give him a taste of yours, Sarah Booth. You're sittin' out here in the dawn thinkin' of him, wantin' him to love you despite your hardheaded ways. Don't lie to him about the sisters and don't linger on the facts. Keep the focus on how you feel about him."

Even as I resisted, I heard the wisdom in her words. "Will he forgive me?" I realized then how much I dreaded Graf's reaction. What if he decided he couldn't risk his heart? What if he felt I'd broken his trust?

Jitty did a brisk about face and strutted to the door of Dahlia House. "If my man were in Hollywood, I'd be on the first flight out there. I'd give my explanations with my hands moving over his wonderful, virile body."

I stood up abruptly. Jitty—or Joan—was dead on. Tinkie would take care of the dogs and Lee would mind the horses if I took a weeklong trip to see my man. Once things were solid with Graf, I could focus on the rest of my life.

And my next case.